MW01154664

SAVAGE

Written by Tiana Laveen
Edited by Natalie Owens
Cover Layout by Travis
Pennington

BLURB

Maximus Savage is no ordinary man. His distinctive and dysfunctional upbringing was the catalyst to a wild life, one lived by his own rules. When his natural talent as a brilliant marksman and skilled fighter is discovered in the seedy underworld of Sin City, Maximus quickly makes his mark on the world, slash by bloody slash…

Dr. Zaire Ellington is a psychologist who runs a successful vlog and podcast from Los Angeles, California. A workaholic, she spends long hours doling out expert relationship advice to those in need of soothing and direction in their lives. Stressed and needing a weekend away, she and her girlfriends take a trip to the Las Vegas strip for fun and relaxation. The last thing she is looking for is a one-night stand, but when she spots Maximus rolling the dice, all bets are off…

The unlikely duo cross paths and become quickly entangled in each other's lives, unravelling secrets, unlocking passions, and dangling the keys to survival and love…

Can a heartless top hitman with a penchant for violence find a way to emotionally accept and embrace the woman who has captivated him from the moment he laid eyes on her? And can an educated, classy lady look deeper into the black abyss known as Savage, and see the fervent, beating heart he's tried to deny since the moment he drew his first breath?

Read, "Savage", to find out!

COPYRIGHT

Did you buy this book? If not…

Where are you going with my booty?!

Copyright © 2019 by Tiana Laveen
Print Edition
All rights reserved.

Warning: The unauthorized reproduction or distribution of this copyrighted work is illegal. Criminal copyright infringement, including infringement without monetary gain, is investigated by the FBI and is punishable by up to 5 (five) years in federal prison and a fine of $250,000.

Names, characters and incidents depicted in this book are products of the author's imagination or are used fictitiously. Any resemblance to actual events, locales, organizations, or persons, living or dead, is entirely coincidental and beyond the intent of the author or the publisher.

No part of this book may be reproduced or transmitted in any form or by any means, electronic or mechanical, including photocopying, recording, or by any information storage and retrieval system, without permission in writing from the publisher. PIRACY IS AGAINST THE LAW.

IN OTHER WORDS: If you do any of the above, the karma bus is waiting for you. If you steal this author's work and illegally loan and/or share it, request illegal/free copies online and/or in printed version, you are no better than a burglar that breaks into someone's house while you think they are away. You are a criminal. A thief. A cheat. You don't work for free, so why should authors?!

WE WORK HARD. SHOW SOME APPRECIATION.

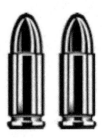

DEDICATION

"Savage" is dedicated to my amazing readers who love a damn good bad boy! The kind that isn't beyond redemption, but is true to his core – f**kless, as they say. "Savage" is a book that has been on my mind for a minute, twirling around within my imagination, and now, it is finally here.

Thank you so much to my dedicated and beautiful fans, especially the ones who've ridden with me from day one, and '1-click' my novels without a second thought because you know I work hard to bring you the best from me. I put my all into each and every one of my books and grow a little every time, in part due to your incredible support.

Enjoy!

This one is for YOU!

TABLE OF CONTENTS

Before we officially begin this tale, I have an announcement to make: A BIT OF INCORRECT COUNTRY GRAMMAR

ALERT: I said this in my previous two books, "Le Roi Du Sang" and "Gumbo" and I am now also saying it here. I know that the correct swear term is 'Goddamn.' I have always hated writing that word, although I have done so many times in the past, in order to keep things grammatically correct. However, going forward, please allow me to spell this wrong, for my own comfort. I am now using, 'Gotdamn.' I will repeat this statement in future books for the benefit of new readers, so no one reads it and thinks, 'Well, that isn't right!' Reader, I know ... but I am using creative license. We all have our triggers and pet peeves. I am not religious, but I am a spiritual being with important beliefs and this word has always rubbed me the wrong way. Therefore, it doesn't sit well with me to keep writing it.

Thank you for understanding!

Tiana Laveen

"I was born to be a fucking killer. It's in my soul, ensnared within my DNA from the core. I will die with the never-ending, all-consuming desire to hunt mankind—not the weak among us, but the feral fuckers, the rancid, no-good bastards on my soulless level who wouldn't piss on you if you were on fire. I'm the king of the Sin City jungle, the sharp, spiky top of the food chain, doing what I do best: Demolish the malevolent of our society.

You can't be angry at a fox for being sly...

A wolf for leading a pack...

A lion for ripping an antelope to shreds...

It's in their nature, and I don't fight what I am.

I embrace it.

My mother always told me, 'Maximus, be the best at whatever you do. If that's being a janitor, then you mop those floors until they're spotless. If it's the CEO of a company, then you run that empire as if your life depends upon it.'

My mother was right.

I answer to my last name: Savage...

Because that's what I am.

My father handed this name down to me, and he was just as deserving as me to have it.

From the moment I came out of a whore's pussy, I knew who and what I was... and I was never apologetic or ashamed. I claimed it.

And now I've been unleashed upon the world like a plague with no cure.

No one I've sought to annihilate has escaped from my grasp and I guarantee you, no one ever will. My targets? By the time they see me, it's too late.

I am their judge. Their jury. Their demons. Their karma. Their reaper.

I am the man who doesn't give one single fuck about their pitiful pleas or pretentious prayers...

I am your wet dream and your worst nightmare.

I am Savage.

CHAPTER ONE

Guns and Girls

"MONEY" BY PINK Floyd blasted through the sur-
round-sound speakers of the large house, situated in
a cul-de-sac on Robin Drive in L.A.. Savage wrapped one
ringed hand around the front of the graceful, slender neck
attached to some hot babe. The beautiful specimen, a woman
with long dark brown hair, sported a detailed tattoo of a
winding, bright red snake from her nape to the top of her
plump, pale ass. She was bent over before him, serving wet,
fat pussy lips around his groin as he thrust his cock inside her
canal.

With each plunge into her addictive valley, his red and
black striped satin robe flew open like bat wings, exposing
his sweaty naked body covered in black tribal art he'd

acquired from some of the best artists in the country over a ten-year span.

"Ahhh!" the woman groaned as she gripped a fistful of burgundy and black silky sheets. She cooed then bit hard into the fabric, screaming at the top of her lungs from each powerful, unforgiving dive. He went balls deep, and her loud moans and whimpers blended in with the beat of his favorite song, being an avid Pink Floyd fan. Even the people moving about outside seemed to go with the rhythm of the music.

Savage sped up his pace, fucking the woman all the harder as he continued to people watch through his tinted bedroom window. The creatures of the night, dressed in their sexiest swimsuits, and the men sporting jewelry and flashing keys to their cars, paraded around his pool enjoying themselves, many of them holding expensive mixed drinks served by his stable of bartenders. A few were passing joints amongst each other, as well as other drugs in pill form to take their partying to the next level. He glanced lazily at the various cameras hanging along a nearby wall, giving him a full view of the rest of the house and his surrounding property. Suddenly, a red light pulsed and glowed in the upper corner of his bedroom. It went bright then dull, bright then dull, repeating like a beacon.

Shit.

Someone had rung the bat signal.

He continued to thrust and pound within the beautiful creature before him as his eyes narrowed on the people who enjoyed the pool party on his dime. In quick fire succession, he assessed his surroundings—nothing looked out of place, but of course, there had to be something wrong. In a matter of seconds, the poor bastards began to scatter like ants dashing away from an oversized magnifying glass while Pink Floyd bellowed, '…Root of all evil…'

Pressing his chest into her back, he reached for his cigar that rested in a nearby ashtray and took a deep inhale. He fucked her faster, sweat trailing down his face and hairy chest, flowing over his tattoos like the lines on a map. Swirls of white smoke billowed out his lips and filled the air, drifting upward then disappearing into the atmosphere like hazy memories long forgotten.

"SAVAGE!!!" one of his property guards yelled into a speaker, his tone frantic. "There's a break-in! We've got— FUCK!" The staticky message went abruptly dead, cut off like a decapitated head with a sharp machete.

Unfazed, he kept drawing on his cigar and ramming the woman before him as if jerking a pinball machine, trying to get that high score. He coolly glanced out at the pool area, now empty with the exception of one dead security guard floating on the top of the pool surrounded by crimson waters. The other dead man was a gun dealer lying on the concrete, the spinning disco lights reflecting on his face in swirling rainbow colors that changed with the beat of the song. An unfortunate causality, one that Savage would make the culprits regret.

"What's going on?" the woman asked breathlessly, eyeing him from over her shoulder. Her glassy blue eyes sheened over, wrought with fear.

He ignored her, then regarded the cameras through narrowed eyes. With a grunt, he flooded the condom with quick-fire blasts of cum, and pushed the woman away, forcing her to fall headfirst on the bed. He couldn't recall her name, so he bypassed addressing her altogether.

Snapping his fingers, he caught her attention. "Slide in here. Don't make a sound until I come get you." He pointed to a small room within the master suite where she quickly raced to, then locked her inside. Discarding the silk robe, letting it fall to the ground in a heap, he put on a pair of jeans he grabbed from a dresser drawer and pushed a white button. A door that looked like the entrance to a closet slid open to reveal his precious motherload. The display revolved, showcasing a host of assorted artillery, his heart's desire.

While removing several firearms from their resting place, his adrenaline soared. Out of the corner of his eye he spotted several strange men making their way throughout his home via the cameras, crawling about like insects, invading his privacy and personal space. He gritted his teeth when he saw two more dead guards, one of whom he'd taken a bit of a liking to. With the sound of gunshots ringing out like 4th of July fireworks, he marched towards the front door of his bedroom. The moment he swung it open, two men approached at full speed, their guns blazing like lights from a million candles.

His bare feet smacked against the glossy wooden floors as he returned fire, shooting at rapid speed in their direction. He spit his cigar out on the floor as he popped one dead center in the middle of his head. The bastard fell over the railing, crashing down to the first floor. In swift succession, he shot another in the chest, over and over, and at last, he dropped to his knees and slumped over. He rushed to the

4

guy and confiscated all of his weapons before moving in stealth mode along the wall and climbed down the stairs to meet the rest of his unwanted guests. Once he got to the first floor, he stooped low and checked out his surroundings.

Gunfire continued to ring out in all directions, accompanied by grunts, groans, and curses. Standing straight, he took several steps.

"Savage!" an unknown voice called out. "Don't try anything stupid! Give up! You're outnumbered!" A man dressed in army camouflage came into view holding an AK-15, aimed right in his direction. Savage glanced quickly at the ceiling, shot twice at a beam, then dropped to his knees when the man shot at him multiple times, crouched down, and cocked two of his weapons, one in each hand. Pieces of ceiling rained down in heavy chunks, cracking against the floor and hitting everyone in their path. A cloud of white and misty gray smoke wafted up as he shot the guns in every direction. Footsteps echoed and deafening screams ensued. His muscles burned with the effort, but he kept firing round after round, as long as he heard even the slightest whisper coming through. After a while, everything went quiet.

When the dust cleared, eight dead men surrounded him, all buried in a grave of ash, splattered blood and debris, their bodies riddled with bullets from his AK-47 and Desert Eagle. One had a knife sticking out the side of his neck. Savage stood and assessed his surroundings, the soles of his feet crunching on the jagged fragments of the house he cherished. He bent down over one of the bodies, pulled his knife out of the bastard's throat, and made his way to Ivan, his favorite guard who stared lifelessly up at the ceiling, blood pooling from the sides of his gaping mouth. The guy had tried to call him when the chaos commenced. Going on one knee, he gently closed the fella's eyes and shook his head.

"Damn it, Ivan," he muttered, then climbed up the steps towards his bedroom. He could hear the whimpers of the woman he'd just fucked, still safe behind the locked door. After pressing in the code to make the door open, she screamed in horror, then relaxed when their eyes met. She shivered and held herself before running into his arms and holding him tight.

"What was all of that noise? What happened?!"

"Get your clothes on. It's time for you to leave." Several minutes later, he had her placed inside the back of a black Lincoln, her face streaked with mascara and her hair in disarray. She slumped forward, gazing listlessly down at the floor. After offering her a stiff drink and telling her a cockamamy story about a Hollywood movie being filmed in his domicile, he gave instructions to his driver to take her home. He went back inside and dialed a number as he leisurely stepped over several dead bodies.

"Austin, we had some party crashers. I need your guys to get over here and clean this shit up."

"Damn it. How many arrived with cakes and wine for the merrymaking?"

"A dozen fuckin' donuts, jelly filled and spilled just in time for the office party. Yup, twelve... Looks like my guards got rid of a few before I had even joined the festivities. These bastards took out Ivan, too. So, I'll have to make sure to give their handler a very fine thank you gift."

"Fuck!" Ivan had been one of their best lookouts, a rare

breed indeed. "Any survivors?"

"I've got one ready for a debrief. He's a sitting duck. I put three slugs in him. One in the leg, two slugs in his chest, both of them framed around his heart, one on each side. Twins." He chuckled as he negotiated around the wreckage to ensure the coast was clear.

"Sounds painful and drawn out. You're an amazing sadist. That's why I love ya!" The guy chuckled. "Anyway, I'll send a crew over to clean up the afterparty. Longhorn must've arranged this shit. Son of uh bitch!" Savage shrugged as he went back upstairs and saw the bastard he'd shot in the chest a mere two centimeters from his heart, lying there panting hard like some dog in need of water. His eyes were glossed over and his lips twisted in pain. They looked at one another and the sheer terror in the fucker's eyes almost made his dick hard. "This is payback no doubt. He's still looking for me, Savage... and he wants you, too. That's to get back at me, of course."

"He's always working, as are we." He stifled a yawn. "If he went through all of this, that means he's up to something... wants me out of the way. Anyway, I need to get the fuck outta here before the tardy for the party squad arrives with after-dinner refreshments once they realize half of their crew is growing stiff like boards. I'll call you back when the smoke clears." Savage ended the call, his chest heaving as he glared down at the piece of shit before him. "I'm going to ask you two questions and I want clear, concise answers. Number one: Where's Longhorn? Number two: What's he got planned?"

The guy grunted and rolled his eyes, blood oozing out of

his wound, saturating the fabric of his taupe colored shirt.

"Fuck you…"

Savage dropped to his knees, placed his hand around the bastard's neck and squeezed, released, then squeezed again, this time so hard, his arm shook as he sucked air, relishing in the agony he inflicted. The man's legs flailed, dragging against the wooden floor. The oxygen to his lungs came to an abrupt stop and the evident pain he now endured as his windpipe took a bruising was certain to cause the fucker irreparable medical consequences once he let go.

Savage slowly lessened his grip for a fourth time, squeezed, then again, and relaxed his grip. He grinned as the fucker's back arched, his face turning blue. The man coughed violently and gasped for air.

"I can break your spinal cord in three seconds, shoot you in the throat and let you lie here and die, bleed the fuck out. Final time. Where's Longhorn?" he asked once more.

"Savage… You asshole! YOU FUCKIN' ASSHOLE!" The guy coughed up blood, which spluttered against his lips and chin.

"Yes, my name is Savage and yes, I am an asshole, but I didn't ask you to identify me. I asked you to tell me where your puppet master is and the reason he sent you."

"I'm… I'm not telling you shit!" the man spat.

Savage slid over the prick's body like a blanket for the newly deceased, pressing his weight against him as he pried his lips apart with a jerk of his hand. His prey made the oddest noises as he toyed with his face, taking steps to ensure that things ended one way or another.

"Well then." Savage smiled down at him as he turned into

an impromptu dentist. "Since you're not telling me shit," he sneered, "as you've so nicely stated, I'll make certain that you not tell *any*one shit ever again... okay?"

Taking the dagger still stained with another fucker's blood, he reached into his mouth, grasped his tongue and sliced it off in one fell swoop. The man's body writhed and rocked beneath him as he groaned in pain, his mouth now looking as if someone had poured a pitcher of Bloody Mary inside it. The man's eyes bucked and rolled as Savage leisurely got to his feet, leaving him there to bleed to death.

"In about ten minutes," Savage glanced casually at his watch, "several men you love to hate will be here, and they're going to collect your dead friends that are lyin' around here, getting ready to stink up the joint. Then, they're going to grab you too, the new mute, and bury you alive with them ... Damn. Maybe I was too hasty?" He shrugged. "I bet you were going to eventually tell me where Longhorn was, huh?" He chuckled. "I bet the answer was on the tip of your tongue." He tossed the loose pink muscle onto the ground. "But as they say, silence is golden. Shine bright like glitter, motherfucker. It's showtime..."

...Several days later

"THIS IS DR. Zaire Ellington with 'Confessions of A Better You.' I want to welcome everyone back to the show this evening.

Sitting in her radio studio built into her home with her engineer and producer close by, Zaire leaned into the microphone. Her long, dusky gray shrug slid down one shoulder, exposing her black bra strap, and a cool breeze from the air-conditioning vents above tickled her flesh.

"Just a little housekeeping before we begin. I am a licensed psychologist in the state of Nevada specializing in marriage and family dynamics." She clasped her hands together and took a deep breath. "I graduated from Yale University, receiving my PhD in Clinical Psychology, then worked for many years in several local hospitals in the mental health and well-being units. Soon thereafter, I entered the private sector. Now, I run my own show where I talk to you, my wonderful listening audience, addressing your marital, familial and relationship issues.

"Last week, we were speaking with Karen from Las Vegas who was explaining that her husband of three years, had recently joined various online dating services. After months of suspicion that her husband was cheating, she figured out his password and lo and behold, stumbled upon a treasure trove of sites aimed at setting up intimate hookups between consenting married adults. Karen is back on the line with us this evening." She pushed a button and crossed her ankles. "Hello, Karen, welcome back..."

"Hi... hi, Dr. Ellington." The woman sniffed, as if she'd been crying.

"I'm so glad we managed to speak again, Karen. I didn't feel as if we discussed the issue enough before we'd run out of time, and I certainly didn't want to leave you so abruptly. You know, Karen, what you've discovered is not uncommon, unfortunately. You're not alone. In this virtual age, it is rather easy for people to have discreet sexual liaisons, thus breaking the trust between committed partners. These phone apps create a virtual playground right at our fingertips, a fast food sexual service, if you will, which removed the need to sneak around whispering on a phone, or meeting up for drinks in secret to break the ice. Eliminating all of that saves time and reduces the risk of being discovered. It also aids in the spinning of a false narrative, where people can pretend to be what they are not."

"He is definitely not the person I thought he was." The woman laughed dismally.

"Perhaps, but what may be more true, Karen, is that he is not the man you wanted him to be. Now, back to the online thing, particularly these apps... I need to address this because I've been getting a lot of calls and emails about this very issue. I believe in the saying that the eyes are the windows to the soul. There are no eyes to look upon when these interactions begin, only photoshopped or filtered photos and whatever notions pop into our head, ones to fill a void and cater to a fantasy. That aside, there is a clear intent—no need to grab coffee before the grand event, right? It's a meeting of the genitals, not the minds. Your fingers simply do the typing to arrange such a thing. Now, in the interest of privacy, we'll call your husband 'Ken'." Zaire leaned forward, took a sip of her hot green tea, and continued. "Please let's pick up where we left off. You were in the midst of telling us what occurred, Karen, when you confronted Ken regarding your recent findings about his infidelity."

11

"Well, needless to say, I uh, I was devastated! I cried… I still do, everyday… So, after I got myself together, I took several screenshots and sent them to myself as backup, knowing he'd try to get rid of the evidence once I brought it to his attention—make me seem like I'm crazy or misread something. When he got out of the shower, I confronted him. At first he tried to say they were old profiles." Zaire nodded as the woman relayed the painful details. "Then he told me I had no right to mess with his phone, invade his privacy. He became irate and tried to turn it around."

"Those are all typical responses when one is caught in such situations… especially if they wish to maintain their marriage, for whatever reasons. In this case, it's more than likely financial incentives for him to stay in it. Where do you and Ken stand now, Karen?"

"We're not speaking and he is calling me a nut… saying the accounts are old, when I could clearly see that they weren't."

"Playing Devil's Advocate here… are you certain?"

"Yes I am because several of the photos he posted were of him inside our new house and we've only lived here a little over six months."

"Did you check the websites to see if he still had active profiles?" Zaire jotted down a few notes.

"Yes. I created a fake account for each service and sure enough, his were all gone. I'm sure he has more that I don't know about though."

"Okay, so you're at a stage where Ken is still feigning no knowledge of the incidents and blaming you when *he* was the one engaging in, at the very least, inappropriate conversation that delved into a sexual nature with women other than his wife. Correct?"

"Yes. All of that is accurate."

"The first thing you need to do, Karen, is not wait for confirmation from him or expect an apology at this point. There are three typical reactions to such a situation: 1. Admission followed by an apology and request for assistance towards a reconciliation and healing. 2. Denial and blame-gaming... often used by narcissists, sociopaths, or simply people who are unable to deal with their inadequacies and wrongdoing in a mature manner. 3. Admission, but then accusing the significant other of being the prime reason for the infidelity. What you have, Karen, is number two, and boy is it a piping hot pile of dung. So, let's put Ken aside and focus on you for a change."

"Okay."

"Because your wellbeing, with or without Ken's help, is what's important here. He has made his choices; now it's time for you to make yours. I want you to tell Ken that he's demonstrated absence of devotion, is missing moral charac-ter, and has insulted your intelligence. He has shown, with his actions, a lack of respect for you and he believes he is entitled to do as he wishes. But as for you... if you care one iota about yourself, you will be forming a new life that doesn't consist of acceptance of this level of disrespect."

"Are you... are you suggesting I divorce him?"

"A marriage, in my opinion, can survive one instance of infidelity, Karen. What it cannot survive is repeated emotion-al abuse and manipulation, gaslighting, frequent lying, then more of the same. Karen, I'm going to send you my book,

'In My Own Arms', as well as 'Enough is Enough', which is my bestselling self-help book. Both discuss self-love and appreciation, and the steps one needs to take in order to navigate what you're currently enduring. Remember, the reasons why one considers cheating are not always the cheater's fault. The act of cheating, however, *is*."

"Thank you, Dr. Ellington," Karen said around a nose full of sniffles. "This has been incredibly painful."

"I understand that you are upset and hurting. The fact of the matter is, however, you do not have children with this man, so you can make a clean break. I tend to avoid telling callers and my clients to divorce. This should always be a last resort and ultimately their own decision, but what you're experiencing is one of many instances over the course of three years where you've been disparaged and treated lesser than by this man. In our first conversation, you stated that in the first year of marriage he cheated with a co-worker."

"That's true... it's been awful. I love him so much though."

"Do you see how you just glossed over that and went back to how much you love him? Love doesn't have anything to do with this! Love is nowhere to be found in this equation, not even self-love or you would not keep subjecting yourself to this person who has proven time and again that you mean nothing to him. A one-time affair doesn't mean that person doesn't love you—that's bad enough—but repeating the abuse is a huge issue! Ken does not love you, okay? He does not care. He does not want you, Karen. Do you hear me?! Our actions speak louder than our words."

"I think he may have a problem."

Zaire rolled her eyes, fell back in her seat and sighed. She didn't know if she could go another minute with this call, but she was determined to fight through it.

"After that first indiscretion, Ken didn't stop there, did he?" She grabbed a pen and twirled it between her fingers like a tiny baton.

"No, he didn't."

"Right, because you told us that the second year, after he swore to leave her alone, the co-worker, there was a pregnancy scare in which he had to submit DNA testing and was ruled not to be the father. But the stress that brought upon you and your marriage was traumatic. He then lost his job, or quit I should say, since he felt that position was beneath him; and he allowed you to carry the financial burden all by your damn self while he ran off into the streets with his friends and played video games. That's of course when he wasn't passed out drunk."

I hate this motherfucker and I don't even know him…

Zaire rolled her eyes as memories of her own ex-boyfriend burst through her mind. A brilliant man who'd turned into a jerk when he drank too much. After three years and two months of that, hoping, wishing and praying, she left him and never looked back.

"Now here we are, Karen, three years in, and he is back at it again. He's a consistent bastard, that's for sure! Worse yet, as in most cases such as this, I am certain you don't even know the half of it." Zaire tapped her black stiletto shaped fingernail against the work desk. "This is only about what you caught him doing red-handed so trust me, the rabbit hole is deeper, *much* deeper."

"I understand! It's a mess!" The woman sniveled. "How can I get my marriage back on track? I don't want to divorce, Dr. Ellington. I have too much invested in it. We understand each other."

"I need everyone to hear me on this next part. If you pay attention to nothing else I say today, listening audience, at least listen to this." She leaned in closer to the mic, placing one hand on her hip and pointing her finger in the air as she made her point. "What some women seem to not understand is that emotional cruelty, habitual cheating, and mental anguish due to dishonesty and lack of accountability in a relationship, disregard for how one's actions affect one's mate are *all* forms of abuse. Karen here is in denial. She doesn't see this for what it is. There is no saving a pig from mud—that's where it wants to be! Just because a man is not slapping you around doesn't mean this is any less serious. If you are being lied to, cheated on, or made to feel inferior on a continuous basis, I must break it to you: you're a battered woman. You're mentally and emotionally tormented. Your bruises and scars are on the inside, not the outside, but they are very much there, just as real and just as important."

"Dr. Ellington, please! I get what you're saying, but you're not in our home. It's not how you think it is. We have good times, too."

"So did many serial killers and their victims on occasion. What's your point?"

"I have faith that he can change. He just needs help!"

"Karen, when will you have enough love and faith in yourself to pull the plug on this entire operation? That's my question. When will you help your own self? You're going to do like so many others… call in to shows like this, badger psychics on those 1-800 numbers, bother your friends and family and complain, then go right back to the source of your pain, a glutton for abuse! We're tired of people like you, okay? People who really don't want support and assistance. You want a magician to wave a wand and change this piece of man! Because that's what he is! Real men don't do this to their wives!

"Then, you'll be in this same spot, ten years later, after he's emotionally beaten you to nothing, drained you dry, saddled you with children that he isn't there for emotionally or financially either, and you'll be singing the same old sad song. Only this time, you'll be bitter. Your best years would've been wasted and you'll use the children as an excuse to stay, though you hate his guts and daydream of slitting his throat in his sleep. At that point, it isn't his fault. It's yours for not taking your truth serum like a woman, swallowing it down and getting better, because baby, you're sick! I am not going to pussyfoot around with you. You are playing with fire to even *consider* staying with someone like this and I am no longer interested in trying to change your mind—because you're not ready, honey, I get it, but some-one out there who's listening is prepared to make a change! So, *this* message is for you out there that care about yourself enough, love yourself enough, cherish yourself enough to say, just like my book, 'ENOUGH IS ENOUGH!'"

The woman was sobbing now, falling apart.

"Karen, I come from a place of love! I am not trying to hurt you, but baby, you better wake the hell up. He talks to you like trash because you keep putting yourself out on the curb! Will he have to produce children outside of the marriage, like so many others, for you to finally rid yourself of this addiction known as Ken?!" The woman sobbed loudly on the other end of the phone. "I understand that you're in pain, but if you wish to begin healing, you must start from within… And now, we are moving on to other callers… I wish you well."

Zaire went on with her show, each caller announcing their issues with a loved one, going into detail about how their lives have been turned upside down due to a wayward teenager running amuck, or a mate who found love outside of the home in the arms of a dear family friend.

After the two-hour segment was complete, she lay back in her chair and smiled as her producer, Emanuel, gave her a thumbs up. She looked up at the ceiling then closed her eyes, her mind spinning around and around, falling into a daydream. Some days, the calls were so emotionally draining that it felt like a vigorous gym workout. At times, she too, witnessed bits and pieces of her former self in these people who called in, declaring their heartbreak caused by someone who didn't live up to their expectations.

"Great show, Zaire," her engineer, Robert, stated as he slid his white jacket on, the keys to his truck dangling from his fingertips.

"Thank you! Any plans tonight?" she asked, half listening to the music playing, something she always did at the end of each show. Right now, Taylor Swift's 'Everything has Changed' featuring Ed Sheeran weaved its musical magic spell through the speakers.

"Tiger and I are probably headed out to Hyde for the

weekend." He reached down and grabbed his satchel.

"Hyde Bellagio? You're going to Vegas today?"

"Yeah. I love the Bellagio. Hyde is amazing. You should go if you've never been. It's nice and upscale, great Italian food. I figured Tiger would want to get away for a bit, visit her sister."

She and Robert waved goodbye to Emanuel as he slipped out the back door.

"Well that's a coincidence because I was thinking of having a Vegas weekend with a couple of my girlfriends. I told them earlier in the week we would go tonight, but I haven't confirmed. I'm known to change my mind at the last minute." She grinned, though she wasn't particularly proud of that. "After the week I've had, I really could use it." She laughed dismally and shook her head, finishing off her drink.

"Yeah, it's been rough. Must be a full moon this week," he teased. "You told me a few weeks ago you hadn't been to Vegas in a while. How long has it been?"

"Geesh." She tapped her chin and thought it over. "I've been to Vegas a few times for conventions over the past twelve months but for a pleasure trip?" She grabbed a bottle of water, twisted the top off and took a hard chug. "Over a year. I called Kim and Allison, and they said they're up to it. I just need to confirm like I said. Yeah... I'm going. I will call them for sure."

"Well." He slung his bag over his shoulder. "I hope you do! Maybe we'll bump into each other! Have a great weekend, Zaire." He winked at her and waved, and she responded in kind.

"You too, and tell Tiger I said hi!" Grabbing her cellphone, she dialed her good friend, Kim, an amazing real estate agent she'd met eight years ago while house hunting. They'd been practically inseparable ever since.

"Hey you!" The lady's smile poured over her words like thick, sticky syrup. "I was just thinking about cha. So, are we going or not?"

"First things first… How did the closing go today?"

"Oh, it went great! I have another one next week. Things have really picked up. So, are we going to get sloshed this weekend in Vegas or what? Tired of waiting! I could use the break, Zaire. Braxton is driving me crazy! Never get you a guy in their twenties. Learn from me, please!"

Zaire laughed, envisioning Kim rolling her eyes.

"Well, what do you expect from a guy who is almost fifteen years your junior and you've turned him out? You and all of that hot, Latina fire you bring! You showed that guy shit he's never seen in his whole entire damn life! He never had it so good."

"I tell you what, if he wasn't such a staunch Republican, we could probably make this work for at least a few months longer. Well, at least for scheduled booty calls on the regular. I just don't know if it's worth the aggravation."

"What do you mean, staunch Republican? You have plenty of Republican friends! Hell, I've voted for a few Republican candidates too in the past. If you ask me, most of them are full of shit across the board, regardless of party affiliation."

"True, but he's in deep, baby, like a cult! Ugh! I mean, honestly, what did I expect? He was a political science major, former Mormon from Utah… Zaire, he's no choir boy in the sack though. Whew! That bastard can fuck! He's in my top three now… hung like a horse, too!"

"Maybe that's why he's so good in bed… because his urges were suppressed and pent up for so long? Didn't you say he only had sex with two other women before you?"

"Yeah, and one of them ended up in the hospital after he hung her upside down and drilled 'er like he was looking for oil."

They both burst out laughing.

"He seems nice enough though. Just young and a bit naïve. You said yourself he's a bridge, a friend to get over troubled waters with until you meet Mr. Right." Zaire shrugged as she got to her feet and began to contemplate what she'd throw into her small travel bag for their vacation.

"If I left him, he'd go right out there and find another woman at least ten years older than him. He *loves* him some older ladies, Zaire, hmmm mmmm! Says we're more mature, know what we want. Get this though, he is still arguing with me about that whole Jussie Smollett debacle. That happened eons ago, like, let it go already!"

"Well, there's still backlash from it. That was a strange situation, regardless of what anyone believes. I think it'll always be a case of interest because of just how bizarre it was. Anyway, I take it your boy toy wanted him prosecuted to the full extent of the law?"

"Yup. I'm sure he'll want to screw before I head out for our weekend adventure, too. I guess I can throw him a bone." Kim sighed on the other end, as if the thought of tossing the guy some pussy was exhausting within itself. She stifled a laugh. "Before I leave, I could turn him on by grabbing his dick like a Subway sandwich, Jussie Smollett style and saying, 'This is cougar country!'"

Zaire burst out laughing at her friend's antics. "You are insane! A proud cougar you are, that's true! Wear it like a badge of honor, girl. Anyway, I'll give Allison a call and we can meet up I guess at your house later on tonight and head out. It's a seven-hour drive so we can split it up like we did last time."

"Sounds good. Stop by around, say, seven-ish tonight. Let me wrap up some things for the open house I have planned, get packed, and you two can swing by. Can't wait to see ya, babe! I've missed you so much!"

"Same here. You and Allison are my peace and serenity, girl. Okay, see you in a short while." Zaire ended the call and looked around her basement radio studio to ensure she had everything sorted out before turning off the light. She headed upstairs to the first floor, her satin lime green slides slipping against the slick wooden floors of her home.

Making her way to her modern sky blue and silver kitchen, she pulled out a chilled bottle of diet cola from the stainless steel refrigerator with echo-speaker capabilities, then headed up to her bedroom on the second floor. Going to her huge walk-in closet, she called out, "Alexa, play, 'Girls Just Wanna Have Fun' by Cyndi Lauper."

She danced to the catchy tune as she selected a couple of silky shirts, then snatched a few pairs of lace and satin panties and bras from the chest of drawers. After a few minutes, she was halfway packed, her fingers snapping and her mood elevated. Grabbing her phone, she stood in front of her vanity and tussled her long, curly black hair over one shoulder as she looked herself over, admiring the small gold earrings she'd purchased from BVW Jewelers.

I look exhausted. Yeah, I definitely need to get the hell out of here and recharge.

"I was wondering when you were gonna call!" Allison yelled. "I've got my suitcase out. Just hung up with Kim!"

"Girl, I can't wait! Yes, we're going. Let's do this. Been a long time since we fucked Vegas up." She chortled.

"They aren't ready for us, Zaire! Fuck it up! Fuck it up! Fuck it, fuck it, fuck it up!" Allison's antics always got Zaire in a good mood. The woman stood almost six feet tall. Slender with huge breasts and a tiny waist, she was gorgeous. Thick black hair hung past her shoulders, so beautiful against her rich mahogany skin. They'd met at one of the conventions she'd attended a few years back. Allison was a part time dance teacher and social worker, eager to add diverse skills to her resume. "I heard you going off on the air today." Zaire's cheeks warmed. "I love it when you tell these ladies what's up! That's the shit she needed to hear Zaire. Sorry not sorry. You're eager to help, but you ain't no buttercup! Now, how much money are we wasting on slot machines this weekend? I want to splurge! How many drinks are needed to ensure that we embalm our damn livers, pickle them up and set them in jars for Ripley's 'Believe it or Not!' and how many mothafuckas are we dick riding because I am the rhinestone cowgirl honey!"

"You're married. You can't ride no dicks."

"What happens in Vegas *stays* in Vegas, and the fuck I can't! That piece of shit has got a whole family out there now! I told you he wasn't shit. This old ass bastard got her pregnant too. Thinks I don't know about it."

Zaire shook her head. "He has another woman and children? Color me surprised," she teased. "I already told you about this man…"

"I was just arm candy to him, I know, and I told you, I already saw a divorce attorney. I'm done, Zaire. I mean it this time. I'm not the one."

Zaire paused and glanced at a pretty necklace on her dresser, trying to decide whether to take it with her or not.

"You and Kim ask me for guidance then ignore me and I've about had it. I'm an advice radio therapist, accredited I might add, and my best friends never take my suggestions! Y'all are making me look bad, Allison."

"Making you look bad? Girl, nobody gives a damn that we're cool. I'm grown. I can screw up my life in peace. I own all of my choices. Hell, you told me not to marry him, but honey, I needed a sugar daddy… Working for that nonprofit foundation wasn't cutting it; I should have never gone into social work. Anyway, sugar daddy my ass! I found out too late wasn't nothin' sweet about him! Wanting me to lick his crusty ass toes and shove a ten-inch glass dildo up his ass! That's too freaky, even for *me*! He has so many strange fetishes it's not even funny. He didn't say any of that when we were dating. The truth came out after the vows! He knew what he was doing. I should've listened to his fourth ex-wife. The bitch tried to warn me."

"And so did I!" Zaire protested. "But my opinion is chopped liver to you and Kim. You both are going to learn one day, hopefully before it's too late."

"I happen to like chopped liver. Okay, let's roll out! See

you over at Kim's tonight and don't be late, Zaire. I'm hot to trot, back flat on a cot, call me a thot!"

"I wish I could forget you not... Hang up this damn phone and let's go!"

"I got some bomb ass weed, too! Yaasssss! See you in a bit, baby! We're Vegas bound for an adventure of a lifetime!"

CHAPTER TWO

No Dice

THE DICE ROLLED in an adjoining room, but this space required a good deck of cards, chips, and a fickle bitch named Lady Luck. He was playing the game he loved most: Blackjack. It was a private area—accessible by invitation only, exclusive to the ballers and shot callers, equipped with skilled dealers, free drinks and appetizers, primo pussy, luxurious furnishings and peace and quiet. The Bellagio was one of Savage's favorite hotels in all of Vegas, and they catered to his every need like a motherfucker.

Due to his affiliations with the right people, he was one of the few allowed to enter the place with his gun, and the damn thing was always fully loaded. As soon as he walked into the front door and made his way to the lobby, he often got a room on the 21st floor. This time, however, due to the situation at hand, he switched it up, just in case that little tidbit leaked to the wrong damn person.

Snitches were a dime a dozen and all it took was one bastard living pay check to pay check being offered a Scooby snack to drop the 411 on his whereabouts for a mere measly one hundred bucks. Besides that, he was fairly comfortable here. They certainly made sure of it.

He was typically presented with free show passes, a host of exotic twerking dancers flapping their enhanced ass cheeks in hopes of him making it rain, meal comps, free plays on the slot machine games he seldom partook in as they were more rigged than a pair of tits in a cone bra, and top notch, high priced gorgeous whores with doll faces and goddess' bodies. The ladies of the night would all be lined up to do his most depraved, pleasure-seeking bidding, and grant his nasty little black heart's desires. Those nights often ended with him fucking until he passed out of sheer exhaustion, and he'd sleep like a baby. Savage's relationship with the Bellagio was definitely not one-sided...

He always dropped loads of money in the casino when he came around and the staff and management had gotten accustomed to it. He was a celebrity of sorts, but he kept them all at arm's length. After all, one lesson his prostitute mother had taught him was, 'Trust no one except family'— and that one stuck. Funny though, people often trusted him. Perhaps too much.

He, on the other hand, made certain he knew every damn thing there was to know about this place and the regulars within it. He knew all of the security team by their first and last names. Some of them were retired police officers, so it was important to keep track of such things.

He began to tap his foot to a catchy beat. Muted music

thumped from The Bank Nightclub, about 110 feet away. Yup. He kept the coordinates on his surroundings; this was essential too, especially when he needed to dash and get away. Although usually he wasn't the one doing the running...

Time ticked by, the music grew louder, the crowd thinned then grew, and the drinks poured.

He sat there sipping on his Whiskey Sour, mixed to perfection by the bartender. The room erupted in a loud ruckus—the slapping of hands, curses and the like. A small, elite crowd of lucky bastards surrounded the table along with the obscenely rich, all huddled together. He smiled with pure, smooth satisfaction as many waved their arms about, their faces twisting in angst. Savage sat in the plush white seat, his brain swimming in alcohol, his finger clutched around a freshly lit cigar and his vision slightly blurry as he watched his stacked chips turn into money right before his eyes. A woman with platinum blonde wavy hair, ruby red lips, and a white fur coat covering a sheer white negligee underneath approached him between breaks when the tension had died down.

He'd seen her around; she had quite the reputation. Allegedly, she could suck the paint off a fucking wall, slurp cocks while doing a handstand. As she leaned to whisper in his ear, her large, artificial breasts swayed forward.

"When you're ready, big boy, let's go back to your room so I can show you a real fucking good time." She toyed with the white collar of his shirt, her long, red painted nails glistening under the lights. Soon, her hand meandered along his chest. She took advantage of the shirt being only partially buttoned, exposing his black chest hair and thin chain, and took the liberty of running her fingers over his skin, giving him a good feel.

He smirked as he reached into his glass of water that had sat there practically untouched all evening and rolled several ice cubes in his hands like dice, keeping his eye on the game, never pausing to look her directly in the eye.

"You're workin' late tonight, huh?" He grinned. "Sin City keeps the legs open and busy."

"Always."

"I'm not certain I'm in the mood tonight."

"I'll get you in the mood baby… Don't you worry your handsome head about that," she quipped, smelling of strong perfume and cinnamon gum.

"What makes you so much better than the rest? I can have my pick." He shrugged, more interested in hearing her response than the validity of the pending answer. "Peddle yourself to me. Not just your body, but your salesmanship."

"Is this a job interview big daddy?" She grinned wide as she took his gold chain between her fingers and rubbed it as if needing luck.

"I'm accepting a shit load of resumes tonight. You whores just keep comin' out the woodwork, but tonight?" His brow arched. "With the week I've had… Hell, I am only in the mood for *primo*…"

"Screw those other bitches." She let her finger creep up the back of his neck and ran her heavily jeweled hand over his short dark hair. "Nice hair, *Papi*…"

"I'm not Hispanic."

"Hmmm, well, you sure are sexy… whatever the fuck you

are." He offered a weak laugh as he watched the dealer. "What are you playboy?"

"A man."

"Oh, I know that one hundred percent! All man, baby! Let me guess… Mixed?"

"Yeah, I'm mixed, but not as you're thinking. My mother is Armenian, my father is Italian and Irish."

"Armenian like the Kardashians?!" He nodded. "Wow… I love them! Hey, let me ask you something—are they White?"

He snickered at her question.

"It depends on who you ask, Blondie. Some think they're Middle Eastern, some say White, some say Asian." He shrugged. "I don't give a shit. I'm just here. My parents fucked one day; Dad busted a nut and didn't pull the fuck out. Bada boom, bada bitchin' bing. Here the fuck I am, in the living flesh." He tossed up his hands. "End of story. Now, enough about me. Tell me what you have that others don't? What makes you stand out?" He blew smoke out the corner of his mouth as he eyed her up and down. His dick saluted her once he zoomed in on her luscious lips.

"Oh honey, you're one lucky, fine man tonight."

"Am I, huh?"

"I have a pussy that can grip your cock like a vise, or stretch out so wide you could drive a damn tractor trailer up inside me, parallel park and go in reverse."

He laughed casually as he shook the ice in his palm some more, then jammed them in his mouth before they'd completely melted. Wiping his wet hand along his slacks, he sat up a bit straighter, moved some of his chips around, and rested his elbow on the table.

"And if rumors are true, Mr. Lucky, that stretching out part will do some good..." She flicked her tongue along his earlobe, then gave a gentle tug and suck. "I didn't call you big boy for shits and giggles..." She slid her hand across his thigh then against his cock and gave it a few good, hearty strokes. "Ohhhh, baby... is all that hard concrete for little ol' me?" she cooed, sounding like a sex kitten. He placed his cigar down in a black ashtray, leaned forward, and clasped his hands together, his mind back on the game. "Mmm, yes... hurt me, Daddy. You're nine inches easily, fat as a bitch with an addiction to birthday cake trapped in a bakery... Oh my, what a nice curve you have! Your nickname must be dips and valleys, sugar. Off to the right... Mmmm! My favorite. That's your anaconda, yes? I'm ready to be bitten. I will suck you dry; all fifty gallons of cum, baby, and beg you for more..."

He tossed her a glance and smirked, shaking his head.

"Nice sales pitch, Blondie... Rule number one, know your customer. You did well. Played up to the male ego. Even if I'd had a small cock, you still would've said it was big and been convincing. Bravo. You shoved your best assets in my face. Good job. Stand over there in the corner and wait," he snapped, wanting to be rid of her until he was ready to take her off the shelf and play. The woman turned away but not before he spotted a proud grin on her face, her blonde hair swinging behind her as she did exactly as instructed like a dutiful pet. Moments later, a man next to him hurled curses while the dealer announced him as the winner for the third time in a row.

Savage's eyes narrowed, growing a bit heavy as he continued to drink… and play… drink and play… After another twenty or so minutes, he'd had enough.

I need a break. Maybe another game and then that's it.

Getting to his feet, he waved his hand towards the dealer, signaling he'd be back after a while. With his gun strapped against his leg, he shook his limbs, awakening his senses, getting the sensation back and the blood flowing. He twisted then cracked his neck, then looked out the glass box he dwelled within. He could see the vast casino floor. People sitting at slot machines or surrounding various game tables, bright letters and lights, piercing electricity that fueled one's dopamine to pour out in droves. Individuals were moving past as they had been all evening, but at that moment, one person in particular caught his eye…

Who the hell is that?

Walking slowly past were three women, all of them attractive, but the one in the middle caught his eye and wouldn't let go…

Two Black chicks and a Latina. Hmm, they're not workers here. They're guests, patrons… If I were to guess, it's some sort of girls' night out… One looks clearly inebriated, but is still functioning. Another one looks bored… and the one in the middle is enjoying herself. I bet she's usually uptight. Look how fucking perfect her hair is… She needs me to come and mess it up. Pull on it while I fuck her from behind…

The one he had his eye on, a Black woman with a medium brown, smooth complexion that stood about five-foot-eight, was wearing a sleeveless white turtleneck and tight black pants that hugged her ample hips in just the right way. Her long black curly hair bounced with each step she took. Though he couldn't hear her due to the glass separating them, he could see her laughing, having a damn good time. From her body movements and gestures, the other two ladies were her friends, people she was quite familiar with. They leaned against one another, paused, laughed, and walked a few steps before stopping once again to point and laugh, reacting to their surroundings. Without a moment's hesitation, Savage walked briskly towards the exit.

"Hey! Hold on. Where are you going, honey?" Blondie hollered.

"If it goes my way, to my hotel room with your replacement…"

ZAIRE STOPPED IN her tracks and leaned against Allison, trying to catch her breath. She could barely breathe. Her friends served as two bookends, she being the shortest of the triple threat, as she tried in vain to reel herself in, to stop the childishness fueled by alcohol and a deep need for a damn good time. Her face was flushed with heat from laughing so hard at Kim's antics. The woman had a knack for spotting the strangest people in the throes of doing the oddest of things.

"And look at that guy! How can anyone come out of the damn house like that?! His hair looks like a dead cat… rigor mortis has set in, too. Mr. Stiffy used his ninth life, then somehow managed to climb about that fool's head."

"You're killing me! Don't point to anyone else, you hear

me?" They all burst out laughing again, and the joy amongst them felt amazing.

Zaire's head and stomach hurt from the constant hilarity hurled her way, but she couldn't control herself. They'd arrived right in the nick of time to check in, put down their luggage in their respective rooms, got a couple of cute drinks in the Bellagio Hotel, and made their preliminary rounds in the casino, exploding into fits of garish giggles from all the people watching. Las Vegas, Nevada certainly had some livewires.

It was a playground for the twenty-one and older crowd—a place to become entangled in a blitz of blinding color, magical pizzazz, fantasy, and dark hedonism with a splash of faux class and sophistication. As they began to move again, Zaire screamed, this time in fright, nearly startled to death.

To the left of her, a glass door swung open so quickly, it was a miracle the damn thing didn't break into pieces. Standing in the frame was a tall man, at least six foot five, with such intensity in his bright, piercing hazel eyes. She clutched her purse hoping it offered a bit of comfort, though she felt foolish doing so. His shoulders were broad, as if they needed their own damn zip code and his facial structure was so chiseled it seemed he was constructed out of granite. He sported short cropped black hair in a Caesar cut, stubble on his face, succulent lips, and tanned skin.

Is he Hispanic? On second glance, I don't think so...

He wore black slacks and a loose fitting white shirt that hung open to the middle of his chest, showing a display of chest hair and a variety of tattoos.

"Oh, I'm so sorry," A crooked smile creased the face of the beautiful beast that now stood before them. "I was in a hurry. Looks like I scared you ladies."

Kim snorted. Placing her hand across her mouth, she said, "FAF alert!" That stood for 'fine as fuck.'

Zaire turned away, swallowing a smirk as Allison burst out laughing once again. The man chuckled, his voice low, hoarse and sexy, as if he were in on their inside joke, though she highly doubted it. Zaire swallowed... He flexed his long legs and clasped his hands as if he'd been expecting them.

"You, in the middle." He waved his long finger in her direction. "You're fucking stunning, ya know that? What's your name, baby?" Zaire looked at Allison, who only offered a shrug. She looked at Kim then, who was now giggling so much, she'd become a mere nuisance.

"My name is Zaire. Thank you for the compliment." The man slicked a cigar and lighter out of his pocket and quickly lit it.

"You're welcome. I mean that though." He lifted his chin high as he blew out thick ringlets of smoke. "You've got that sexy, classy shit goin' on for yourself... I like that."

Kim and Allison were really rolling now.

"I see you're in the high rollers room." Zaire smiled as she put on her professional voice and took a peek at the small space with rich furnishings... a space no one could enter unless they were prepared to spend, and spend big.

"Yeah."

"Are you a professional gambler?"

"No, this is just for fun... a hobby. Did you wanna come inside? I can bring you in, and your friends, too." He hitched his thumb in the direction of the door behind him.

"No, thank you. I was just merely making an observation. Well, let me move out of your path." She skirted to the side, gripping Allison's elbow like a lifeline. "Me and my friends will be on our way. It was nice meeting you."

"First of all, you're not in my way. I came out here especially for you." She swallowed. "Secondly, I was taking a break so I've got a little time. Zaire, huh?" He ran the tip of his tongue along his lower lip, like some animal who'd caught a fresh kill. "Like the place in Central Africa, now known as The Democratic Republic of the Congo."

"Yes. That would be it."

Well, he definitely gets points for that. Most people think it's just some made-up name to sound cool.

"That's an unusual name for someone. I like it though. You look more like a, hmmm, I don't know." He shrugged. "A Lisa, Evelyn, Angela, Monique… maybe a Michelle…"

"You were pretty close! Her name is really—"

"Don't you dare!" Zaire hissed at Kim who was now looking at her like some puppy who'd gotten yelled at for soiling the new rug. "It's actually my middle name, but that's what I go by."

"She's a celebrity." Kim offered. "Ouch!" Zaire elbowed the lady. When she looked back to her right, Allison had floated away like some damn cloud.

"Allison… Allison!" Zaire hollered, but the woman kept on walking until she'd disappeared from view.

I can't believe this! Oh… so this is how these two are going to do me tonight, huh?! I knew I should've told Kim to wait to smoke that weed, with her silly ass, and now Allison has nothing but sex on the brain!

"My name is Savage," the man offered, snatching her out of her thoughts.

"Ohhhh, fuck!" Kim chortled, shaking her head as she leaned against the glass of the high stakes room. "Savage?! Your name is Savage? This night can't get any better." Just then, a bartender from the private room walked by to enter the enclosure. Savage grabbed two of the drinks from the tray and offered one to Zaire and one to Kim. Kim happily took hers and indulged in a big gulp without a second to lose. The damn thing could have been vanishing potion; the woman apparently didn't care.

"No, thank you." Zaire refused hers. The man now known as Savage nodded and took a sip from the glass filled with vibrant green liquor, then another. "Savage? I take it that is some sort of nickname, right?" Zaire stood straight, hoping to wrap this little convo up and be on her merry way. She saw no reason to be rude, but the man gave off a vibe that perplexed her. Something about him screamed trouble. The kind of trouble that once someone got in, they could never get out.

"Nope. It's my last name but like you, it's what I use." She nodded in understanding. "So, Zaire, since that's what you prefer to be called, can I interest you in some dick?" He blew more smoke out from between his lips, his expression serious.

Green liquor spewed out of Kim's mouth like a damn fire hose, or perhaps more like the possessed child from the Exorcist movie. The alcohol splattered all along her arms and part of her face, including the dangerous, ballsy, and appar-

37

ently mentally challenged creature before them. Zaire fought the urge to laugh at the specks of liquid landing all along his jaw. His shirt now had a green polka dot pattern.

Can I interest you in a dry cleaner? Nasty bastard. That's what you get.

"Oh, God! I am so, so sorry Mr. Savage!" Kim offered as she removed a ratty old napkin from her purse and began to pat his chest and face, making it all the worse. Instead of pitching a fit, the man burst out laughing.

"It's okay, baby." He gently took the napkin from Kim's grasp, dabbed his face a bit more, then slid it into his pants pocket just as cool as he pleased. Rocking back on his heels, he threw Zaire a hedonistic stare, the kind double dipped in illegal kinks and forbidden seduction. "Well, what do you say? Are you ready to head off?"

He started right back up from where he'd stopped! One track mind...

"Mr. Savage, the answer is definitely no. Now I am certain that you—"

"What? Are you married? You don't come off as married..."

"I'm not certain what coming off as married exactly is," she rolled her eyes, "but I was going to say, it is apparent that you are well off, since you are playing in the private club room and all, but—"

"My money isn't the topic of discussion. It has nothing to do with this." He shrugged, as if annoyed. "And married women tend to act a certain way. I know what to look for, regardless of whether they have a ring on their finger or not."

"Well, I certainly wish everyone had that discernment.

Regardless, that's no way to speak to a lady. Now, that may work with many, but not with me. I'm not like most women but even if I were, that's still no way to behave towards me." She crossed her arms over her chest.

"I'm sorry if my honesty upset you." She grimaced at his choice of words. "I just see no reason to be pretentious or fake about it." He shrugged. "It doesn't have shit to do with me not seeing you as a lady, as someone to respect. A lot of women have this crazy idea that if we respect you, we won't try to fuck you right away. That's just not true." He chuckled. "I just I call it like I see it."

"You approached me as if I were some prostitute, which I'm not, and for the record," she stated calmly, "I'm not upset. To be upset would mean I would have had expectations from you and you'd somehow let me down. I don't appreciate what you said. It's just not how I roll. Now, if you'll excuse me, I—"

"Wait, hold up." He took a hard toke from his cigar then quickly extinguished it by tossing it in a tall ember receptacle. "I wouldn't ask a prostitute if she wanted some dick, Zaire. A prostitute fucks all day for a living. Now *that* conversation would have a reason for money to be brought up. I made a proposal, asked a simple question. A 'yes' or 'no' would've sufficed."

"Oh, so you think I'll screw for free?" She chuckled and shook her head, hating that she was enjoying toying with the bastard. What a piece of work!

"Are you now saying that you charge?" She swallowed her response for it was filled with four letter words… all of them as colorful as the strip. "I didn't care either way, but

I'm not a john. I just knew that I wanted you." His eyes narrowed on her. "I fuck working girls, blue collar girls, white collar girls, and the girl next door. Sex is sex, baby." He shrugged. "There's no shame in paying for pussy. A guy's gotta do what a guy's gotta do, though I don't do that. Whether it was a whore or a virgin, I never had to shell out a dime for some snatch—my mere company was enough. In fact, women approach me far more than I do them nowadays. I rarely get the chance."

"Awww, you poor thing! Guess I am one of the lucky few!" She placed her hand over her heart, sending Kim into a tizzy of laughter.

"Yeah, you are fortunate, actually. I'm an amazing fucking person... a rare fucking breed. You're not in a situation where you have to find out why. Lucky you..." The man's eyes grew dark. A hidden rage seemed to brew within him, cloaked by his crooked smile, swag and confidence. "Anyway, no hard feelings. Can't fault me for trying. You have a good night."

He winked at her, waved lazily, and went back inside the glass enclosure as if not a damn thing had happened. It all transpired so quickly, the way he dismounted his imaginary horse and walked off, she didn't know what had quite hit her. Zaire stood there watching as he pulled out a white seat at one of the few blackjack tables in the fancy set up. Within seconds, a blonde drew close to him, practically landing on top of him like a fly on shit. The woman was donning a thick fur coat, her face nothing but a smile. A second woman came over then; she looked Asian. She was soon hanging on him like a second skin, too. A third woman approached after that, scantily clad, her dark eyes gleaming like some snake out for the kill.

"Girl, he was an entire hot mess." Kim chortled as they began to walk away. "Did you smell him though?" The woman's lips twisted.

"Smell him?" They continued their jaunt in search of Allison. "What do you mean?"

"He smelled really good. You know I have a thing for cologne. If I were a betting woman... Well, I am in Vegas so I guess I am a betting woman tonight," she cackled at her own joke, "I'd say he was wearing Stefano Ricci Royal Eagle."

"Ahhh, expensive, huh?"

"Definitely. Oh, there's Allison!" Kim pointed up ahead. "Allison! All-lis-sooon!"

The woman's face was practically glued to a tall, handsome guy sporting a mint green tie and navy blue blazer. Their friend glanced over at them, disinterested. Giving them a curt wave, she turned right back around, continuing her conversation with Mr. Preppy.

"Well, that was a total blow off."

They both chuckled.

"She did say she had a bucket list to fulfill this weekend while here. One, get drunk. Two, get high. Three, eat as if she didn't care about the calories and carbs. Four go to at least one show, and five, ride some decadent dick. Looks like number five on the list is being worked out as we speak." They both watched the woman work the guy over for a while.

"As she explained on the drive here, her soon-to-be ex

was a real piece of work, Zaire. I knew he was giving her a hard time but had no idea it had gotten that bad! How could she stand being with him for so long?!"

"I tried to—"

"We know, we know! You tried to tell her, Mama Goose. Hey, Zaire, look! "O" by Cirque du Soleil is being performed here! Let's see if we can get tickets." Just then, out of the corner of her eye, she spotted Mr. F-A-F walking past with an entourage of women escorting him—all of them beautiful, and most definitely trashy to the tenth degree. He didn't pay her any mind as he navigated his way through the crowd. The man took heavy, leisurely steps, a twisted smirk on his face. Donning a leather jacket over his shirt, he looked good enough to eat. His eyes practically glowed like a viper under the glowing lights. Just when she thought the show was over, he casually looked over his shoulder, blew her a kiss, and kept moving…

What an arrogant son of a bitch. I swear, some guys get a little money and think they can buy anything. I'm not on the menu. He's quite attractive, too, so that makes the situation so much worse. Definitely a potential narcissist. He seemed completely oblivious as to why I'd be offended by being spoken to that way. He didn't know who he was dealing with. I'm not one of these silly hoes. My next book should be titled, 'Want Some Dick? And other low-lying fruit scavenger lines to avoid.'

"So, do you want to see it or not?" Kim's ultra-feminine, slightly high-pitched voice shook her out of her deliberations.

"Uh, yeah…" Her friend's lips curled in a satisfied grin as she dug inside her purse, scooting over a plastic baggie with a few pre-rolled joints. Kim grabbed her phone and swiped the screen, likely looking up the show information, or perhaps to view her Instagram feed. Who the hell knew? Minutes later, they were headed back up to their hotel rooms, laughing, easygoing, free.

"Did Allison text you back?"

"Actually, she's texting me right now." Kim paused in front of her door and glanced at her phone.

"Okay, let's freshen up and change clothes, and meet downstairs in twenty minutes."

"That sounds good. Allison said she'd be there too…"

"Oh, good! Or is it?" Zaire suddenly had second thoughts about Allison joining them. Perhaps something had gone askew.

"Oh, my goodness, check this out, Zaire." Kim cradled her phone in her palm as she looked down at it. "She texted back again… Said ol' boy is married but tried to play it off." They both sucked their teeth at the same damn time. "She checked him out on Facebook on the low while he was trying to sweet talk her. These motherfuckers are so stupid. Don't they know we can find out that sort of thing in five seconds nowadays?" Kim rolled her eyes, clearly disgusted as she jammed her phone back into her purse, removed her hotel room door key, swiped the slot and when the light turned green, she pushed the handle, taking a step inside. "She'll meet us downstairs. She's on her way back up."

"Okay, see you in a minute." The woman nodded and the door slammed behind her. Zaire turned around and walked up the hall, the journey taking far too long. She daydreamed, thought about work, feeling a bit like a fish out of water. It was difficult to just leave all her duties behind, to act silly and unwind. Allison and Kim helped her take a load off though. Those two had a knack for allowing her to decompress and simply be herself. There was no denying it, sometimes her life was like a juggling act, plain stressful. She'd get the occasional looney toon; one guy had even called her relentlessly from various numbers on her 1-800 number for months on end. Sometimes it was just the nature of the job. She'd put so much time and energy into her podcast and books, it wasn't uncommon for her to get only a few hours of sleep.

'I kind of wish I could go in this room and just fall out. Kim would never let me hear the end of it though. She'd say I could've stayed home if all I was going to do was sleep...

She sighed when she was a few feet away from her door. *What's that?*

When Zaire arrived in front of her room on the twenty-first floor, her heart practically boomed out of her chest...

There, on the carpet, lay at least fifty red rose petals. She tried to navigate them, prevent from stepping on the damn things, but it proved impossible. She walked inside her room, the cool air blasting so hard, she felt like she'd stepped foot inside a glacier. When she hit the light, she squelched a scream by covering her mouth with both hands... eyes wide... blood pumping.

There, on the bed, sat a large bouquet of dark red roses wrapped with a black satin sash. Attached was a white note with a black lace border. She picked it up and read it:

Zaire, I think you're beautiful. You have the type of eyes a man could drown in and be happy to be dead, as long as you were the last person he saw before taking his final breath.

You said you're not like the women I'm used to. I'm not like the men you're used to. We're even.

I won't apologize for what I said, only for how it made you feel. If I apologize for actually saying it and vow to not say it again, then that's a lie.

To me, lying is starting out on the wrong foot. What I *will* do is ask you to accept this peace offering and allow me the opportunity to push the 'DO OVER' button.

Let me take you out. Let's have lunch tomorrow.

I will pick you up at 12:30 P.M.

— Savage

Zaire's chest damn near burst as she re-read the note. Placing it back on the bed, she lifted the bouquet to her nose and sniffed. The scent was simply divine. The sweetness was amazing. They were so aromatic and perfect, as if freshly plucked from a garden right there on the premises. The fragrance filled the entire room.

How in the hell did he find my hotel room?! So much for customer privacy...

Though her annoyance was woven around her curiosity like a finely knitted sweater, she couldn't help but smile. Savage was an interesting man to say the least.

He's intriguing... Maybe I will go out to lunch with him, maybe I won't... Let me sleep on it. One thing is for sure, no matter what I do, I won't plan to see him again after I leave this place.

What happens in Vegas, stays in Vegas...

CHAPTER THREE

Allies and Artillery

HEAD LEANED TO the side, eyes focused, Savage meticulously dug the last bit of soot, greasy oil, and dirt from under his nails with the edge of a razor blade. When he was satisfied, he wrapped the razor in a thick wad of toilet paper and tossed it into the hotel bathroom trashcan. After checking himself out in the mirror, he walked into the bedroom, adjusting the white towel wrapped around his waist along the way. When he neared the bed, he looked at his nails once again. They'd become a bit of a nuisance to him lately. Just the other day, there was so much blood caked under them, he wasn't certain he'd ever get it completely out by soaking his fingertips in a hydrogen peroxide bath, which he did on occasion—a long, boring process he hated.

Yeah, I think I got all the dirt out...

For a few hours that day, he'd worked on one of his motorcycles that was stored in the casino garage. He enjoyed his alone time, just him dancing with his thoughts. Anything was welcome to help him decompress after the three women that had trounced to his room the previous evening. He grinned as he reminisced over the whole sordid encounter…

After an evening of drinking and non-stop fucking, his adrenaline rush was coming down, mundane like the fried eggs, toast, and oatmeal he'd had for breakfast. The memories of two of the women locking glossy lips and bumping their pussies against one another spun inside of his head like a flicked coin on a table. He then paused… recalling how at one point he wanted to tell them to get the fuck out of his room…

That feeling had come over him suddenly. A wave of heated rage… absurd and bizarre in mid-dick stroke…

He was a bit peeved, preoccupied. The image of someone else swam inside of his thoughts, had him caught up in a strange rapture. Disappointment settled in like creases and wrinkles on an elephant hide. Savage stared into space, pondering the moment he'd almost lost his Zen last night.

He'd envisioned his night differently. Simply put, he'd wanted to taste Zaire's pussy, give her the fucking of her life. Her rejection of his frank advances had left a bad taste in his mouth, like the rancid coffee he'd had at the gas station a few days ago. Her arrogant responses, however, had impacted him in some way. He walked to the window and pulled the curtains open. He blinked as blinding sunlight filtered into the room.

I'm going to swing by and get her at lunch, do exactly what I said I was going to do. Yeah, last night was definitely not exactly what I wanted… I always get what I want because I can… She was fucking gorgeous. She talked like she was educated, a little snooty thing, wasn't she? Not like the chicks last night… All their fake giggling and carryin' on just to get some cash. I'm sick of bimbos. Why can't I have a chick with brains, beauty, boobs and butt too?

When he'd arrived at a different room within the hotel that he'd be using only for his raucous romps, he stepped out into the hall right before the festivities had begun. He was half naked, but needed a bit of privacy and quiet; between the music and the three women making such noise with their high-pitched laughter, he didn't waste a second to dial the hotel florist immediately and to place an order. He then alerted the hotel manager on duty that he wanted the bouquet placed in the lady's room ASAP. He only had the name she'd given, but recalled it wasn't her first name, as her friend had let slip.

With a bit of quick thinking on his part, he suggested hotel security look at the footage of where he stated he'd encountered her and have staff follow his wishes. They promised to take care of it, and he only wished he could have seen the expression on her face when she saw the rose petals scattered in the hall along the threshold of her door, the bouquet on the bed, and the decadent European chocolates hidden beneath a towel in her bathroom…

He shook the imagery away and focused on the tasks at hand. Grandson's, 'Bury Me Face Down' played on his phone as he devised ways to pass the time. Keeping his music low and the television on mute, he made his way to the king sized bed where his clothing was neatly placed. A black shirt, black leather vest, silver buckled belt, motorcycle boots, and black denim jeans lay across the shimmery gold and black tiger striped sheets, tacky as they were.

They know I hate these fucking animal prints. I asked for white fucking sheets. How hard can it be?! What do I look like? Tarzan? 'Oh! We've upgraded your room to an even nicer suite, Mr. Savage! You'll love it!' Looks like the fucking Lion King threw up in here…

"I was first in line until the little hairball was born!" He chuckled at himself quoting the movie. He'd never seen the Broadway production. Just then, his cellphone buzzed. He snatched it off the nightstand, immediately cutting the music short.

"Yeah, it's about time, motherfucker."

"Fuck you." His friend chortled. "So damn impatient…"

Savage sat on the edge of the bed and tossed the thick towel that had been wrapped around his waist across the room.

"All I know is that you better be callin' me with some info. I'm tired of this shit…"

"From what I've heard, you're having a ball. Women every night, winning at your favorite games, drinking your liver into oblivion, smoking Cuban cigars, stuffing your big fat mouth with prime rib and shrimp and watching all the shows your heart desires. You need to calm the fuck down. Don't shoot the messenger, Savage."

"I will if they pay me enough," he teased. "Hell, with the way you've been acting lately, I'd do it for a melted ice cream cone and a rusty nickel. Anyway, any new information, soldier?"

Harlem, a longtime friend of his, army Vet, retired NYPD cop, and member of the organization could be heard taking a long drag on a cigarette.

"Yeah… Stay ten toes down."

"Always, motherfucker. What else? Am I still trapped

here like some animal in a cage or what? I'd like to get on with it."

"You might as well treat yourself like a big time freakshow and start sellin' tickets, man, 'cause you're the main attraction."

"What do you mean?"

"Longhorn has got guys crawlin' around your houses like fuckin' rats in a butcher shop, man." The man snickered, his voice deep and husky with New York swag dripping all over each syllable. "Got your place in Vegas locked down too, just in case you had any bright ideas."

"I'm not surprised. That's exactly why I came to the hotel instead of going home. I could always go to the bunker, but receiving information there is sketchy. Shitty reception." Besides, the bunker was more for raids, city shut-downs, things of that nature. No one knew where the hell it was except for him—that made it the ideal hideout, but he needed contact with the outside world right now, so fast communication was key.

I'd really love to just go home and get wasted...

Savage loved his house in California where the whole sordid ordeal had begun. It was his favorite property of all, but he was rarely there. With all the latest bullshit, there was no way he could even get within two hundred feet of the place without being involved in a gun war. The estate was being digitally monitored, but his physical presence would start a second bloodbath, and he definitely didn't plan to be among the casualties. Although he didn't give a split fraction of a fuck and could hold his own, he had to think smart.

Only fools rush in. He'd survived so long in his profession thanks to his natural discretion. His ability to wipe a motherfucker out in the blink of an eye and keep the noise level low as a whisper from a ghost was part of his claim to fame.

"You fucked them dudes up, Savage. Took out at least two of his commanders. Longhorn is pissed."

"Commanders my left hairy ball." He rolled his eyes in disbelief. "He shouldn't have sent his ballerinas to a massacre ball. I don't give a constipated shit if the King of England was there. You come bustin' up my spot and you get sprayed. Period."

The last update he'd received several hours prior from Austin was that his little extermination festival had not been well received, not only from Longhorn, but from many of his own allies. Allegedly, he'd gone overboard, made a terrible scene. But what the fuck did anyone expect? A warm welcome with homemade soft batch sugar cookies and milk? Longhorn had stepped over the line. He got what the fuck he got, and as far as Savage was concerned, he should be happy Savage didn't go against protocol and track his ass down too—put a bullet right in the middle of his gotdamn forehead then stomp his spirit to death when it departed from his lifeless body.

"Can I leave soon? I feel like a five-year-old asking permission to take a piss."

"Stay put."

"How long before I can bust outta here and get on with the next assignment? Did Austin tell you? I asked him this morning, but we got cut off. He had to hang up before I'd gotten an answer. I bet I won't hear from him for another day or two."

"I spoke to him last night about it. He doesn't have an exact timetable right now… too many balls are in the air. He needs to get you outta there in one piece, so everyone is keeping watch, lying low, hiding the fact we can see their every move. Just chill, man."

"I don't feel like chillin', Harlem. I'm getting sick of this shit already but more importantly, something doesn't feel right about this, ya know? This ambush doesn't make sense."

"What do you mean?"

"Look, Longhorn has known about me for years. He hates me, but respects me. He has his guys, Austin has his. Everyone knows he wants Austin dead. They've got too much bad blood. I do gigs now and again for Austin because I respect him and how he runs his operation. He tried to hire me full on, as you know, but I enjoy my independence. I told him I can't work for anyone but myself, but I have no issues with helpin' out every now and again. He was fine with that, but hopes to eventually change my mind one day. So, with that said, why wouldn't Longhorn go about this differently? This is a beef between *them*, not me."

"Well, yeah, that's already been established, but I'm still not following you."

"I feel like I don't have all the pieces. That hit was for me, yeah, but why, Harlem? Why would he send that many damn people, to my home of all places, during a fucking party?"

"Who in their right mind would only send one or two guys to do you in, Savage?! An idiot! That's who!" He couldn't help but laugh at this. "You're the poster child for,

'You'll need an army to take me out.' And if you think about it, a party atmosphere was perfect. Your defenses wouldn't be as heightened. You'd be distracted and there would be people around. You'd have to try and protect them and fight at the same time. It was perfect planning, if you ask *me*."

"Yeah, my defenses were a little down, but I'm always alert, Harlem, even in the middle of chaos. He knows this. I haven't had a good night's sleep since I was a baby… always got one eye open."

"But everyone has a weak spot…"

Savage drew quiet for a spell. Of course everyone had a weak spot. He'd just never told anyone what his was. He was fully aware of his weaknesses, the things that made him tick and the tunnels that needed travelled in order to manipulate him, make him do another person's bidding. No one had found those buttons yet; they were protected by a steel vault, a cage wrapped in chains and a flesh-eating monster with an axe to grind.

"I think you're reading too much into this," Harlem added.

"Nah, it's gotta be more than that."

"Like what? Seems pretty cut and dry to me, Savage. If Longhorn can't get Austin on a slab with a toe-tag, you're the next best thing. He'd cripple his entire operation with you being gone. Everyone knows you and Austin are tight."

"This could all be over and done with if I could just blow Longhorn the fuck off this planet. Give me ten minutes, maybe fifteen… but noooo! Austin wants to be square about it. Meanwhile, my kitchen is painted red and this bad ass broad I was fucking during Longhorn's ballsack riders' break-in probably is tied up somewhere and confessing to where the guns are. You told me to never trust these hoes…" he grumbled, causing Harlem to burst out laughing. "Anyway, in all seriousness, yeah, all of that shit you said is true. I dunno though… I just don't know."

Savage ran his hand across his jaw, feeling the stubbly hairs of his beard. The nagging feeling that many of the puzzle pieces were not fitting together still perplexed him. Made him wonder.

Some of this shit just isn't right. I hope I'm being paranoid, but I doubt it.

Harlem started talking about some other things, mundane details that needed to be addressed. Savage half listened as he reached into a small black satin satchel inside the nightstand drawer and pulled out a hand-rolled cigar. He lit the damn thing and dared someone to phone him about smoking in his room.

He'd already removed the smoke detectors as soon as he'd stepped foot inside, didn't want to cause a scene and have those ridiculous sprinklers going off, wetting up everything. As he lay back smoking, ankles crossed, nodding his head and speaking every now and again in response to Harlem's laundry list of things he needed to do, he glanced lazily towards the window.

The city was waking up now; it was finally 7:00 A.M. He could hear a bit of honking, the traffic moving along. He'd only slept for an hour, but his adrenaline was soaring. He imagined that would be an ongoing condition until he got to the bottom of all of this.

I need to get up and do something before lunch. I'm going to lose my fucking mind if I don't get some blood pumping.

"Harlem, I hate to cut you off, but I got the gist of it. It'll be taken care of. I need to blow off some steam, get my work out in."

"All right. So are we straight weapon wise? You have everything you need until you can push 'GO' again?"

"Yeah, for now anyway."

"Let me hear it before you hang up, so I can be certain."

"Let's see, in the hotel storage I've got some pretty little ladies." He sighed as he got to his feet. Shutting his eyes, he rubbed the skin between his brows and concentrated. "I've got two pump action rocket guns, a flamethrower, .357 Sig Glock, two 9 mms with .40 S&Ws, three .44 Magnums and a host of blades."

"Sounds good. That should hold you for a bit. What do you have on you right now, on your person?"

Savage yawned, took another toke of his cigar and smashed it in a black glass ashtray. He stretched his arms and went through the files in his mind once again.

"Fully loaded with backup, Smith and Wesson and an AK-47. I've got two blades and can get more if need be from across the way. Yeah, you know what? On second thought, send me a couple extras so I can get started on the next project. I know I can't physically move into position yet, but I want to be ready. I refuse to keep playing this hide and go seek game, though. Time is money and it's the only thing that, when it runs out, I can't replace. Let Austin know he needs to call me ASAP."

"Will do. He'll have a new phone line for you by tomorrow. The other one he ditched."

"Good." Savage disconnected the call, grabbed a pair of black jogging pants from the dresser drawer and slid them on. He dropped down on the floor and did 200 pushups, his nose practically touching the carpet fibers. His arms burned once he reached the 170 mark, but he was determined to get this work out in for it always made him feel better. After a short while, he followed it up with 100 jumping jacks then pulled himself up and down over the room door ledge. He took a second shower, perused some of the local shops, made a few calls, walked the hotel grounds, then let the excitement take over...

...It was time for lunch...

"MS. ELLINGTON, THERE is a gentleman here in the lobby to see you."

Before Zaire could deliver her well-rehearsed response of one word, 'NOPE,' the phone clicked and a deeper voice came on the line.

"Hello, baby. Are you ready for lunch?" A raspy, rich voice had taken over, one that sent tingles down her spine and worked its way to her ears, leaving her heart beating a tad bit faster. Now, hearing the crass maniac's voice without alcohol roaming in her system like some thief stalking about in the night hit her in a different way...

Damn, he sounds sexy...

"Is this Mr. Savage?" She was determined to keep her

tone even as she wound the hotel room phone cord tightly around her fingers and pulled. If she did it a little harder, the entire contraption would come out of the wall.

"You know damn well who this is."

Her eyes bucked at his response, and she grimaced. It was sobering indeed. The spell he'd suddenly put her under was cast aside, the veil lifted.

"I don't know who the hell you think you are, but I don't wish to go out with you. Goodbye." She disconnected the call and immediately dialed Allison. "Bitch! He called!"

Her friend burst out laughing, but for the life of Zaire, she couldn't see what was so damn funny!

"I told you he would…"

"I was hoping all of that hoopla last night was just from his drunken antics, you know? That after an evening of sobering up he'd give this up, if he even remembered me at all!"

"Nah, even though I wasn't with you the entire time, I could tell he meant business. Besides, Kim said he didn't seem drunk though."

"Now, how in the hell would Kim know?! She was high as a fucking kite on a mission to Mars, kept licking the wall by the buffet and calling it a tall sexy stranger, then yelled that the man she was seducing had dry lips! I told her several times that it was a partition, but she wouldn't listen." Allison broke out in a fit of laughter that made her ears ring. "She also began to sing 'Amish Paradise' by Weird Al Yankovic when she saw that old lady sitting at the bar wearing a doily! Now why would she think that woman was Amish? She was in a casino at a bar for goodness' sake and even if she was, how rude!"

At this, Allison laughed even harder, working her nerves all the worse.

"Kim is so fun when she's drunk, isn't she? We had a blast!"

"Yeah." Zaire rolled her eyes. "She's a shining star, a real bundle of joy!"

The previous night had been practically a damn blur.

Allison had been no angel, either. She'd slipped away again before their evening had come to a close. The woman had found some rebound replacement peen around four that morning and according to her chipper report, rode it hard and long. After kicking the young man out of her room with nothing more than a half chewed apple Danish and a 'Fuck you very much,' she was already looking for another contender. Apparently, the guy was some exotic dancer who barely spoke a word of English, but according to Allison, when it came to sex, only three words mattered: 'Yes, right there.'

"Zaire, you need to loosen up. Come on, don't be a buzzkill this weekend."

"I'm truly not trying to be, Allison, but we have to use common sense, even on a girl's trip. I have never seen Kim throw caution to the wind to this extreme, and you've also gotten out of hand!"

"Out of hand? Okay, I had no idea I was enrolled in preschool again."

"Say what you will, but it's like I'm hanging out with two strangers, yet your faces are quite familiar."

"Maybe it's because we are using this getaway like medicine. Did you ever consider that? I get tired of having to be the bigger person all the damn time, Zaire! Of being professional and reliable every hour of every day. I know you care, but sometimes you're just so judgmental and harsh! I'm sick of it! You do that for your job, I get it; it brings in ratings. But we're not your clients, honey. We're your friends. And I know the *real* you... you're much more vulnerable than you let on."

Zaire closed her eyes and nodded. Perhaps she had been acting more like their mother than their friend? It was how she showed love.

"I just... I've been through so much this year. I just wanna be free..." She could hear the hurt in her friend's words, and it brought her down a notch or two.

"I'm sorry if I came off the wrong way, Allison." Zaire sighed. "That was not my intention. I just think there is a right and a wrong way to go about things is all, even in the midst of our pain. I'm not perfect, far from it, but I want to help and have people learn from my experiences so they won't make the same mistakes, but you're right; I'm not your mother, and there's a time and place for advice and guidance, too. You don't want that right now—duly noted. I do understand what you're saying, even though I want to dispute it. You're not my child and I get that the way I articulate things, at times, can sound—"

"Bossy, controlling, domineering."

"Uh... not exactly what I was going to say, but all right." She smiled tightly. "I'll try to be more careful about the words I use when I am showing concern, okay?"

"Better yet, unless I'm about to get hit by a bus, don't

show concern for me at all during this trip, okay? I got this." Allison's words stung, but the last thing she wanted was to fight with her dear friend.

"All right, I agree to that."

"Thank you. That's all I ask. Hey, I think you should—" But before Allison could finish her thought, the hotel phone rang once again.

"Hold on, the front desk is calling. It's probably that son of a bitch again." She stared at it for a good while—her cell phone in one hand, that damn red hotel phone buzzer blaring like a beacon.

"Answer it," Allison stated over the speaker.

Snatching it up, she cleared her throat.

"Hello?"

"Ms. Ellison, there's a gentleman who wishes to see you."

Zaire hissed, rolled her eyes, and stomped her gold sandals on the floor.

He just doesn't let up!

"As I stated to him, and now I will to you, I do not wish to see *him*. Now please relay the message that I—" She nearly jumped in her skin when she heard a commanding knock at her door. It had power... the kind of knock that had double doses of testosterone and smelled of danger, determination, and damnation.

"Ohhh, girl... Savage is in the building. I guess you have company."

"This isn't funny, Allison. Please help me! Come out into the hallway and greet him. Maybe that'll deter him."

"I'll be right there!" Allison disconnected the line, but all Zaire could do was stand there with her damn heart beating almost clear out of her chest. Allison's room was only a few doors down; it shouldn't take her long to provide the perfect distraction. Kim would definitely be of no assistance in this new venture to shoo away a vulture. The woman was zonked out in her room, recovering from what she'd described earlier that morning as a three-ring circus in her head—clowns included, the mother of all hangovers.

BOOM BOOM BOOM!

Came the knocking again… followed by muted voices.

Oh good… Allison is talking to him.

Zaire slowly crept towards the door to get a better listen. Her cream and baby blue sheer shrug with a soft floral design dragged on the floor as her little gold sandals floated towards the banter. She rose on her tippy toes and peered out the peep hole.

My Lord…

There on the other side stood the golden colored man with a well tapered beard and mustache, sporting dark shades that shielded his eyes. His short, black hair was shaped perfectly. His clothes, however, gave her pause. Black leather and biker attire, as though he were some renegade thug. The shiny silver buckle of his belt practically glowed. A slender silver band gleamed on his pinky finger and now that his arms were exposed, she could see they were muscular as hell, and littered with dark tribal-like tattoos.

"Yes! Uh huh, I totally get it!" she heard Allison say, excitement and mirth in her voice.

The deep, masculine response soon followed. "So, you know, if you want to come along, that's fine. I sent her flowers to apologize for making her uncomfortable last night, but I meant what I had said. I'm just a truthful person."

"Well, honesty is definitely at a premium these days!" Allison grinned. She had on a black jumper, her lovely hair tousled and gathered over one shoulder. "People lie so much nowadays, it's a wonder the truth is even understood or recognized. Seems like a foreign concept to most if you ask me."

"Yeah, true… So, uh, what are you lovely ladies doing here? Girls' trip?"

"Yes! Zaire works so hard on her broadcast, Savage. I mean, she's a real beast."

"She does advice, right? Write self-help books 'nd shit?"

"Yeah, and her focus is on women making better choices and living their truth. Due to her rarely taking a break, especially lately, she needed a fun time away from home. I've had a lot of stuff going on vocationally and in my personal life and so has our friend, Kim, so we just decided to drive on down here from California, regroup and indulge in some fun self-care, ya know?"

"Yeah, I totally get it," the man stated. Just then, she noticed he held a bouquet in his hand.

"You smell great by the way, Savage! What cologne is that?"

Are you kidding me? Allison is no damn help at all! She was supposed to help shoo him away! Now she's complimenting him and rolling out the red carpet!

Zaire could not believe her ears! She placed said ear against the door and listened closer… The two were having a good ol' powwow, yucking it up! Seconds turned to minutes, and they were chuckling like old friends, as if they'd forgotten why they were in the hallway in front of her door in the first damn place.

"Zaire!" Allison called out, tapping on the door and startling her. Zaire took a step back and gripped the chiffon material of her long shrug in the palm of her hand. She held on tight to it, the soft material balled up in her fist as if someone had deeply insulted her, asked her for personal information, things that were none of their business.

"Zaire, I know you're standing there. I can see you've blocked some of the light beneath the door," the man said. She took another step back, remaining quiet. He sighed loudly, as if exhausted. "You just moved again... probably about ten to twelve inches back. You're not Houdini and even though this is Vegas, you have no magic shows here. We know you didn't just disappear. Now open the door." She looked down at the floor and wanted to scream. The bastard was right! She had moved about that distance away.

"Allison, tell him that I don't want to go to lunch with him."

"Why do we have to play telephone, Zaire? He can hear you. Tell him yourself."

I'm going to choke the shit outta her when I get her alone! On second thought, maybe I shouldn't. She'd probably like that.

"Please leave me alone!"

"Zaire, you're being silly! Open the door, sis! He looks so nice! You do, you know... very nice getup."

"Thank you, thank you very much..." the man stated in a silly Elvis-esque voice.

Zaire swallowed, anger now boiling within her as she snatched open the damn door, ready to end this once and for all.

I apparently have Ren and Stimpy for friends...

There the two stood like rotten peas in a spoiled pod. Bastards.

"You look amazing, baby... wow." Savage stood there with his bouquet of flowers. These were long stemmed golden calla lilies, and they instantly perfumed the air. "I was just, uh, telling your nice friend Allison here that she could be our chaperone if you felt, you know, skittish... afraid of me." He winked at her as he cocked his head to the side.

She wanted to smack that smug smile clean off his face. White teeth sparkled in his mouth like snow caps, and his eyes glimmered with manic mischief. Allison nodded in agreement, as if she'd somehow taken a great weight off her shoulders by offering babysitting services.

"I am certain you think that your persistence will win me over, Mr. Savage. Well, I suggest you think again. You apparently do not take rejection well. Now, this can end one of two ways. You walk away peacefully, or I call the police and you are dragged away in the most embarrassing of ways."

Savage grinned, casually removed his phone from his pocket and shook it at her.

"Here, call them. If Officer Steve Frank answers, tell him Savage said hi."

She gritted her teeth. Out of the corner of her eyes, she took notice of Allison shrugging.

"I mean it. I will call the police," she stated sternly, though she was losing her nerve. Was his insinuation true? Was he a cop himself? What in the Rin Tin Tin, Huckleberry fucking Finn was going on here?!

"And I said feel free to call them. I know all of them very well."

"Oh. So you have a record." She smirked, poking at the bear.

"Nope. They're just fully aware of my existence."

"What do you do for a living, Mr. Savage?" She was honestly intrigued now, but calling his bluff.

"Come out to eat with me and I'll tell you."

"Nope. Not taking the bait."

"Come on, Zaire. It'll be fun. Did you know he can get us into almost anything here—even the sold-out shows? Besides, I'll be there with you! Look, you two go out, and I'll sit a few tables over. Deal?"

She was making it so much worse! Why in the hell was Allison pushing this so hard?! Zaire now regretted telling the woman about the entire ordeal, and admitting that she found him panty-soaking sexy.

"Look, Zaire, I know you think I'm some prick."

"That's quite insightful of you. Yes, I do." She crossed her arms and held her chin high.

"And that's fair, but you're not going to be here long. You don't have anything planned right now according to Allison, so I will treat you and her to a wonderful meal on my dime and if I were someone that can't be trusted, there's cameras all around this place." He motioned to a few hanging in the hallway. "And as you know, the staff here know me well. If I did anything to you, I could never get away with it because my face is all over the video footage and it is well known now that I've been trying to get your attention. The initial meeting in the casino, the flowers sent last night, the calls from the lobby, all of this..." He shrugged. "I'd be stupid to try and pull some shit if that was my plan."

She mulled his words over for a spell, chewing on her French manicured fingertip as she darted her gaze between her Benedict Arnold pal and this gorgeous motherfucker who refused to take no for an answer. He had a point.

"Oh, all right!" The man grinned impossibly wider and Allison clasped her hands together as if she'd just won a prize. "But I am not staying long."

"And it won't take long... unless you want it to." He winked as he handed her the bouquet. "I've got multiple speeds, and I don't need batteries. The duration is totally up to you, beautiful..."

CHAPTER FOUR

Psychopath

THE HOST, A middle-aged man with a refined face, opened the door to the Michael Mina Restaurant in the Bellagio, allowing the group of three inside. The guy was dressed in a white tuxedo jacket and black slacks, and from the expression on his face and demeanor, he knew exactly what to do. He led them to a private, simply decorated table by a window.

"Thank you," Zaire whispered to the man as she looked at the table covered in white linen and a single pink rose sitting in a vase in the center of it.

Savage took the reins. He first pulled out Zaire's seat, then Allison's. He scooted them both in so fast, hoisting the chairs off the floor a little, then setting them down gently, he drew a laugh from her friend. He walked to his seat and paused when he noted the beautiful sun shining through the window, reflecting on Zaire's face in the most amazing way. Her dark hair fell in thick, textured spirals, flowing down her back while the rays zigzagged along her deep bronzed face, illuminating half of it while the other half remained shrouded in shadows...

He sensed the same could be said about her personality. A duality of sorts that clung to her. She was the type of lady who presented the world with one version of herself, but kept the other part hidden from the world. A real life Dr. Jekyll and Mr. Hyde.

That, in all honesty, made her even more alluring—a dark gift he wanted to unwrap. He wished to see what pushed her buttons, made her shine, and made her cry and scream, too. Savage was determined to not waste one second in getting to know her. He already relished this time with her, and they'd just begun, despite the third wheel who'd tagged along. Allison seemed nice enough, but for him to truly work his magic on a woman like Zaire, he'd need alone time.

Doesn't matter. I'll have to manage. I'll find a way to improvise.

"It's nice in here." Allison bit on her glossy pink lip, evidently impressed as she looked about the place. She brought her wine glass filled with water to her mouth.

"This is your first time at this restaurant, I take it?" he asked, sliding his cellphone out of his pocket and carefully placing it on the table.

"Mmm hmm, been to this casino a few times, but never came in here before. I've walked past... Fancy."

"What about you, Zaire?"

"Same." The woman seemed to have developed a keen interest in her gold thumb ring. She toyed with it, rotating it from left to right along her well-manicured digit. He took a moment to case the place before sitting down, making mental notes of the exit locations, lingering patrons along the perimeter, anyone appearing strange or out of place. The Michael Mina Restaurant in the Bellagio was known for delectable, freshly flown-in seafood, and high-priced, one of a kind seaside fare. It was completely empty.

As if noticing the lack of patrons and staff, Zaire appeared confused as she looked about while spreading her white linen napkin across her lap.

"Are they even open?" she inquired.

He finally took his seat at the table with Zaire to his left, and Allison to his right.

"Nope. They aren't ever open for lunch, only dinner. I think that starts at 5:00 P.M."

"It's only about 12:45," She glanced briefly at her cellphone. "So how did you get in here then?"

"I'm used to getting into tight, closed spaces. It's one of my specialties." He grinned at her, but was met with bunched brows that dipped low and lips that were now pursed so hard, they wrinkled like the veins of a succulent orange wedge. Minutes later, they all ordered their meals and then, Allison kept him entertained with her tales of a wayward husband with odd sexual proclivities.

"And so, you know, as a man yourself, maybe you can explain it, Savage? It was ridiculous!"

"Well, uh, honestly, Allison, I don't think I can help you much there. I really can't explain to you why gummy bears would turn a guy on."

Gummy bears?!

"He wanted me to put them all over his body and eat them off, and sometimes he'd just hold some in his hand,

and look at them with lust in his eyes… like they were porno stars!" *Little mini squishy sweet porno stars… I wonder if this crazy bastard named these motherfuckers? Here's Gummy Glenda, Sticky Sharon, Watermelon Wanda…* "What a fucking weirdo!" Her voice escalated, making Zaire's eyes buck and breaking him free from his strange, wandering thoughts.

Zaire is polite. Too polite. Mannerly. But that's all an act. She speaks her mind freely… What an uptight woman. I listened to one of her podcasts before going to her hotel room. What a fucking brute. She's ruthless. Not usually my speed, but I'm still attracted to her. She's a ball buster. She's got an inner freak wanting to come out to play with me… I never read people wrong.

"Zaire, ya know, is a psychologist." He nodded, but truly didn't give a fuck. "She told me as long as the sexual fetishes don't emotionally, physically, or mentally harm anyone, they are deemed acceptable and not exactly a psychological issue, but I beg to differ."

Zaire turned away in warp speed, as if the stacked tables and chairs around her had suddenly become interesting as hell.

Yup. I knew it. She's a freak. He chuckled to himself.

"I guess, uh, everyone, has their kinks." He shrugged, barely able to keep a straight face. "Remember when edible underwear was all the craze? Maybe it's like that?"

"He didn't want the Gummy Bears eaten if they were lined up along the bed rail. He once screamed at me for several hours about eating one. I could only eat them off his body… like some sacrifice."

He swallowed, needing a moment to compose himself. The laughter bubbling within him almost couldn't be contained. His face flushed with heat as he counted to five in his head, finally regaining his composure.

"Well, it sounds like your husband has some sort of comfort with the Gummy Bears. Would you like something else to drink?"

Maybe a Gummy Bear martini…

"Ex-husband… the wheels are already in motion." She sucked her teeth. "No, I'm fine. Okay, what about this, Savage? And I know we don't know each other and you might think this is crazy or out of line, but he made me get rid of all of my male friends when we got married. Jealous bastard! So I can't bounce this shit off anyone else. I'm sorry for talking about this sort of thing and you don't even know me." The woman looked suddenly regretful, and her eyes sheened. "I know it sounds crazy!"

"It's okay." He shrugged before reaching for his water and taking a taste. "Obviously, you need to get this all off your chest. Go right ahead."

The woman wasted not one second before she lit up with a cheery smile and began again. This was met with a clearing of the throat from Zaire. Now, the lady with the fancy academic degrees and dark steel in her eyes was sitting with her chin high in the air, her legs crossed, and an irked expression on her pretty face as she peered at her friend… her judgment dripping all over the place like melting wax.

She's a snobby little hypercritical, pretentious thing, isn't she? Her friend is obviously much more open, yet upset, and this is how she acts? I find a lot of highly educated women are like this… full of themselves. It's an interesting dynamic…

"So, there's an age difference, right? I thought older men

were more mature. Wrong!" Allison rolled her eyes and huffed. "He's the biggest baby I know. Cryin' and complaining all the time. You'd think he'd require an afternoon nap, a diaper change, and the television tuned to cartoons on Nick Jr. The only thing truly baby-like about him though is that shriveled up little dick of his!"

Savage dropped his gaze for a spell and stared at his shoes. He placed his forehead in his palm and he was certain his shoulders were shaking from trying to control himself once again. He was trying so hard not to blow this shit by laughing in this woman's face. A smile forced itself across his face, threatening to betray him. He secretly sighed with relief when he managed to shake it loose right before looking back up and meeting eyes with Zaire.

They quickly turned away from one another, both listening intently to Allison tell them about the struggles and sacrifices she'd made for her marriage, how she'd lost herself in the process. Unfortunately, those declarations were also sprinkled with bizarre tales, stories of a deeply disturbed man who likely should've never been allowed to make it to the age of thirty if natural selection had done its due diligence.

"...And that's when he decided to have a séance to see if Cookie Monster on Sesame Street was possessed by the Devil."

At that point, he'd noticed several times how Zaire was practically cringing, sliding down low in her seat, softening like a pat of butter right there on the spot. The woman practically disappeared like a dollop of chocolate out in the sun, growing smaller and smaller by the second. Her shoulders slumped and her cheeks rounded, turning a deep ruddy hue. Oblivious, Allison continued her tirade, citing even more examples of a man who was clearly in need of mental evaluation.

"And after I found out about the baby he had on the side, that's when he had the nerve to tell me he could have gotten someone better than me, but he was tryna help me out... like I was the bottom of the barrel for him, and this was an act of mercy, our marriage... like I was some charity case. This motherfucker must've thought I was some idiot! He lied about everything, Savage, but I really did love him. As Tina Turner said though, 'What's love got to do with it?!'" She sucked her teeth and shook her head as if disgusted.

Savage leaned forward and took a deep breath. After a few moments of quiet, he signaled the host over with a wave of his hand and a snap of his fingers.

"Hey man, can you, uh, change the music in here? It's dry like three-day-old turkey. You ladies like Jill Scott?" He tossed a look at both of them, not missing how Allison's eyes lit up. "I'll take that as a yes." Sliding some cash out of his pocket, he placed it into the host's hand. "Play some Jill Scott... 'The Way', and whatever else you have."

"Certainly, sir." The host nodded and walked away, but not before Allison burst into raucous laughter.

"What in the hell do you know about Jill Scott?!"

"I like all kinds of music." He flopped back in his chair, his eyes hooded. "Anything that gets me right here, I like." He tapped his chest.

Allison's nose wrinkled as she smiled, as cute as she was. "I dunno, you just don't look like the type who'd be into that. I took you as more of a Rock 'n Roll type of guy."

"You can't judge a book by its cover."

"It seems you're right."

"So, you think because we're Black, we'd like Jill Scott?" Zaire asked tersely, breaking up the synergy and good vibes like a wrecking ball in gold sandals. "Because I really hate stereotypes like that."

"Zaire, damn! He's just tryna—"

"Allison, stay out of this." Zaire pointed in her friend's face, the tension mounting. "You don't want me in your business right now during this trip, which you've made abundantly clear, so please enter this zone at your own risk. Now, as I was saying." She snapped her neck back in his direction. "I can see you think you're real smooth... renting out a restaurant that's closed—better known as flexing, bringing my grieving, emotionally spent friend along because I insisted, giving that man money so he can do your bidding, pretend to be a DJ to now play 'Black people' music." She put her fingers in air quotes as Jill Scott's voice began to flow through mounted speakers around the place. "But let me tell you something, Mr. Savage. I write about men like you." Her eyes narrowed on him.

"Ohhhhh noooooo!" He laughed and shook his hands. "Whatever the fuck shall I do? First I was afraid, I was petrified!" Allison giggled and hid her face in her hands. "You write about men like me! LIKE *ME*?!!! Oh me, oh my! That's the ultimate shot to the heart!" He burst out laughing. "Fuck a bullet. She writes about guys like me, everyone! Deadly Zaire, I do-de-fucking-clare!"

She ignored him and carried on, as if he were some tyrant unworthy of her acknowledgement. "I warn my listeners and readers about men like you, Savage, because you cost too much for our peace of mind. Yes, I speak about men like you at conferences... and I've saved thousands upon thousands of women potential heartache."

"I just saved a bunch of fuckin' money on my car insurance by switching to Geico."

"You're predators."

"Like 'Predators vs. Aliens'? That was a terrible sequel, by the way. The first one was the best."

Allison was now laughing so hard, her face was flushed in shades of deep red.

"Guys who use their charisma and distractions such as humor, much like you're doing now, as well as their money and prestige, manipulative powers and when applicable, physical attractiveness to lure women and then discard them like trash are a dime a dozen."

He smirked and took a sip of his water. "I'd like to think I was worthy of at least a dollar, okay? But I'll even settle for fifty cents. Go shaaawty, it's ya birthday!" He began to bob his head and snap his fingers to the classic, 'In the Club' tune by 50 Cents. "You can find me in tha club! Bottle full of bub! I'm into having sex, I ain't into making love!"

Allison shook her head, then dropped it. Her shoulders jockeyed up and down. Zaire shot the woman a death glare, but he doubted she noticed.

"I just want to make sure we're clear, Mr. Savage. I can see that you think you're pretty funny and amazing, but I won't be another notch on your belt."

"What does that saying mean, anyway? Who is putting notches on their belt every time they have sex with someone?

Oh! Just had sex! Better put another notch on the belt! What kinda silly shit is that?"

"I won't entertain your foolishness."

"Admit it... you're amused." He picked up his glass and swayed it in her direction, as if to give a toast. "To Savage! I'm funny as hell! Cheers!"

"Now, if your mission is just to have a nice lunch, that's perfectly fine, but whatever else you're expecting, like a dessert that is not on the menu, you can forget it."

"Sometimes the desserts aren't written on the menu; they're on a chalkboard or are only listed and described verbally by the waiter. Does that count?" She rolled her eyes and looked away. "What if I ask for a sharpie and wrote your name on the menu myself, then? Zaire, a chocolatey, sweet and sassy mallasy, scrumptious treat served just right! Be careful, she could be frozen in the middle! $7.99 ... coupons accepted."

Just then, their food arrived.

Medium rare steaks, blackened grilled shrimp, bacon-wrapped scallions, buttered asparagus, wedge salads and more—all expertly prepared and placed before them. A carafe of ice water arrived soon thereafter, along with bottles of red and white wine. The conversation was rather bland from that point forward, but it was organic. Nothing seemed forced, though Zaire kept sporting a rather stern expression, even while eating her medium-sized shrimp which, for some odd reason, she cut with a fork and knife. When Savage had gotten half way through his meal, he tossed his napkin on the table, leaned back, and clasped his hands. His eyes landed on Allison who, at times, still appeared lost in her head, drowning in her thoughts.

"Allison?"

"Yes?" the woman answered while chewing on some lettuce.

"You want some advice about your husband? Some *real* advice, from a man's perspective?" He shot Zaire a glance and grimaced.

"Yes, I do."

Zaire scooted about in her seat, clearly agitated at her friend's response.

Too damn bad. Step aside and let the real expert go to work...

"It's simple, really. Look, baby, you've got a guy who saw a sweet, pretty, young thing like you. He had a little money but exaggerated the amount. He figured that would be the way to lure you, not thinkin' you'd actually wanna be bothered with him otherwise. So, he wined and dined you. It's too late for the shoulda, woulda, coulda, sweetheart—but a background check woulda let you know he'd already been married four times, not twice, like he told you. When someone has that type of track record, it means one of three things." He raised a finger.

"One. They're an asshole women run from once the real them is exposed. Sometimes they show ya who they really are on purpose because they've gotten bored and want you to leave. Either way, no one can keep up a charade for too long. Our true self manages to come out sooner or later. Two." He held up two fingers. "They just don't take marriage seriously, and it's a numbers game to them, like gambling. Or three, they've got some sorta shit goin' on in their head, like true blue loony toons. They're stone cold crazy. He told you that you were different from the others, didn't he?"

"Yes!"

"He told ya he'd give ya the world, and all he needed was your love and support."

"Yes! Yes, he did!"

"Then he started doing strange shit. It was passive aggressive, sometimes to get rid of ya, but then..." He shrugged. "He probably had a change of heart. Called your bluff and got pissy when you seemed fine with moving forward. He wanted you to stay only if you needed him. If you no longer needed him, he hated you, treated you bad, started saying things he knew would get you angry and out the door."

"Oh, my God! How did you know?! It's like you were there watching our lives!"

Zaire rolled her eyes and huffed. The green-eyed monster was in full effect.

"He's not a psychic, ya know? He just put two and two together and I pretty much told you the same thing!"

"No, you didn't, Zaire. You said that due to his age, he was stuck in his ways and that—"

"It doesn't matter now." Zaire waved her off. "You're leaving him, thank God."

Anything you can do, I can do better. I can do anything better than you. No, you can't. Yes, I can... BRAVOOO!

"Nah, I'm not psychic, and like Zaire said, yeah, I put two and two together, but only a man truly understands another man's mind." He narrowed his eyes and fixed them on Zaire. "You can study us, read about us, write all the fucking books you want about us, do your little podcast shows about us, screw us, beg for our confessions and go to fancy schools that teach you about us. But you'll *never* fully understand us, because you're *not* us. We're wired differently. End of story."

If looks could kill, he'd be six feet under.

"Savage, you did an excellent job dissecting my friend's marriage. So, let's dissect you, too."

"Do you want to use your knife or mine? Yours has bits of shrimp on it though." He grimaced. "Who the hell cuts up shrimp with a fork and a knife?"

"I'm not going to do this with you, this silliness you're apparently prone to. Now stay on topic. I sense a resentment towards women in you." Zaire sat a bit straighter, picking at and prodding her asparagus while everyone waited for her to complete her thought. "I'm not trying to pick a fight, I promise." She smirked as she waved her fork to and fro before popping the green, lanky vegetable into her mouth.

"Here's some advice. Don't eat that. Your urine is going to smell funny later, but more importantly, what did I say to make you believe that I resent women?" He leaned slightly forward and poured a glass of wine for Zaire and Allison.

"It's just your demeanor, the way you speak. Oh, and not everyone reacts that way to asparagus, but thank you for the tip. It's almost as if you resent me for being educated and doing well." She grinned proudly, then swallowed. "I don't pick up a racist inclination in you, though I believe most people do have some racist ideologies. This is more gender related. Isn't it, Mr. Savage?"

"You're the expert, right?" He handed Zaire and Allison a glass of wine, then poured one for himself. "You tell me."

"I bet your relationship with your mother was tumultuous. Your father was either weak minded or not in the picture at all. Perhaps he was a drug addict? You come across as very rah! Aggressive!" She laughed... but he knew she wasn't amused.

This chick has serious anger issues. She definitely needs some dick. Should've taken me up on my offer last night...

He clicked his tongue against his inner cheek, then shrugged before tasting his beverage. It was smooth; a little fruity. Quite unusual for a white wine.

"Go on. I like it when people tell me about me." He grinned, showing all of his teeth.

"Sure. I'd love to give you a full psychological workup, but we simply don't have the time. You're a textbook case, though I must admit, you do respond well under pressure. I haven't seen you flare up; your tone has remained steady during this lunch date. You're quite witty, engaging in silly repartee and humor to try and defuse an intimidating situation, one you're being evaluated on so it can be shown what you truly are. In all honesty, I believe you may even have a personality disorder."

"Oh, really? What kind? Psychopath?" He smirked.

"It would be unwise for me to diagnose you with so little information, but—"

"No, I was asking you what kind of personality disorder, but calling *you* a psychopath." He chuckled as he took another sip of his wine.

"You do show some telltale signs of narcissism. Your behavior right now is indicative of it."

"Here's the funny thing about narcissism, Zaire. From

my understanding," He took another swallow of his wine then leaned back in his chair. "It's not something you can get rid of. You're either a narcissist or you're not, and it's triggered due to trauma. Rarely is someone born this way, right?"

"That's debatable... the whole nature versus nurture. Regardless, yes, that's been argued. Have you had trauma, Savage?"

"Haven't we all?" She looked at him. He looked back. Out of the corner of his eye, he noted Allison crossing her arms and watching them as if she were sitting in front row seats at a Grand Slam tennis match. "Yeah, let's talk about trauma, baby..." He ran his hand along his jaw and narrowed his eyes on her. "Isn't it trauma that causes a woman to not only crusade for other women as ruthlessly as you do, but create a hostile environment, for even a lunch date, due to her very fucked up attitude, and then become annoyed when the man—who is her test subject—doesn't jump through her hoops? Feminism was born out of trauma. World wars were born out of trauma. Anything that is reactionary or radical in nature was born out of trauma. So, isn't there a psychological diagnosis for people like you, too? The in-denial-savior complex? Some shit like that? Or did they skip that chapter in school?"

"Ooooooh, girl! Whew! Now that was a read!" Allison giggled, clearly taking delight in her know-it-all friend being served what she cooked for others, shoving it down their throats one grotesque spoonful at a time.

Zaire cocked her head to the side and clasped her hands together, resting them on the table.

"I've had no trauma that led me to crusade, as you say, for women. I do it out of the love and concern in my heart. It's my calling. I saw a need, and I fulfilled it. You're trying to twist and turn this around, warp the truth."

"I don't have to warp the truth. The lies you've told yourself are warped enough for the both of us." He tossed his hand in the air and snapped his fingers. The host came over in record speed.

"Yes, Mr. Savage?"

"Please bring out that dessert tray. My friend Allison here deserves it. She's had a hard time lately." He grinned at her, and she smiled back.

"Of course." The host disappeared.

"Mr. Savage, you've apparently—"

"Not to cut you off, but I wasn't finished. Let me explain something to you, Zaire. First of all, as I told Allison here, looks are deceiving. I *love* cerebral conversations. Betcha didn't even think I knew what that word meant, did you?" He tapped the side of his head. "You don't know shit about me. What you do know is based on textbooks—books written by people who've never met me. I'm a different breed. There's no one else like me on this planet."

"Thank goodness..." Zaire grimaced.

"Yes, thank goodness because this entire world would be burned to the ground if there was." Their eyes locked. "I love watching NASCAR; I race cars for fun myself. I ride my motorcycles. I speak English, Armenian, Spanish and Russian fluently. I could probably drink most guys under the table. As you know, I enjoy gambling too, particularly Blackjack, and I'm damn good at it. My I.Q. is through the fuckin' roof, and yeah, I've been tested. I am very fuckin' smart. Nope. I have no degrees." He shrugged. "I went to no fancy schools like you. I have a high school diploma, and barely got that. It wasn't because I couldn't handle the curriculum, but because I had other priorities, pressing matters to take care of. Regardless, I'm not ashamed of my past. I'm comfortable in my present and I'm lookin' forward to my future. I *do* have mommy issues, Zaire. In that respect, I am a classic case, as you say." He paused and scratched the side of his nose. "My mother was a prostitute, a paid whore, a cum dumpster for my entire childhood."

Zaire's eyes widened ever so slightly.

"She'd been an orphan, had a really hard life. She was an immigrant. She used to trick in Armenia, and then, she moved to America, specifically, California, where she met my father while working at one of the strip clubs. My father saved my mother's life. She'd been living with a man who was kicking her ass, but she had nowhere else to go. My father got her away from him, but there was a catch. My old man is a card-carrying member of the Vagos Motorcycle Club, a biker gang." Allison gasped. "Unlike your theory, yes, he was and *still* is in my life. I see him often. My parents were never officially married, but everyone knew they were together. They loved one another. He is one of the smartest, funniest and scariest motherfuckers I've ever known.

"He is not someone you want to cross. So, I learned from a wicked yet honorable master." He shrugged. "Now, contrary to any stereotype you may have floating in your head, since you think my suggesting Jill Scott was strictly because you're Black, my mother didn't fuck her johns in front of me, all right? She had more sense and class than that. I didn't become somehow scarred by that and end up on the next undiscovered serial killer database due to a mother sellin' her pussy right beside me as I watched cartoons and ate my fucking Fruit Loops. In fact, I wouldn't have even known she was whoring had she not been honest and told me when I asked her where was she goin' late at night when she left me with the babysitter.

"My mother is a complicated woman. She's sneaky... devious... because she had to be in order to survive. She's at times a cold woman. She's a paranoid woman, but she's a fighter, and she did the best she could with what she had. I also know she wanted me. My mother had never gotten pregnant until she was with my father. She told me she wanted to give him a son. He already had a daughter, my older sister, with another woman. Her wish came true. Despite all the crazy shit in my childhood due to having what many would call unconventional parents, I know that she loves me, in spite of everything. Love isn't determined by one's occupation. It's determined by how a person treats you. I was never hungry. I was never left unclothed. I was never ignored when I truly needed either one of them. I was hugged and kissed, even by my father, Mr. Tough Guy. I was told I was special. Didn't matter that a pretty high-priced foreign whore and a brutal bike gang leader were tellin' me that—all that mattered was that they said it. And they meant it."

An uneasy sort of quiet reigned when he finished talking. Zaire looked down into her lap and fidgeted with her napkin.

"Hey, uh, I'm going to take a little walk. I'll be back in a few minutes." Allison stood from her seat, a sad smile on her face. When she walked past Zaire, she stroked the woman's shoulder. It was time for a one-on-one meeting…

CHAPTER FIVE

Did You Save Room for Dessert?

THE SILENCE CONTINUED for a few more minutes before Zaire broke it, yet her voice was now softer than before.

"Savage, I want to… thank you for being so open." He nodded. "I'd like to have a genuine conversation with you now. Get to know you better."

"Why?"

"I find you intriguing. You're right, there is definitely no one else like you. My curiosity is piqued, without a doubt."

"Okay, what do you wanna know?"

"Well, for starters, where were you raised? Are you from Vegas?"

"Yeah, I grew up in North Las Vegas though we often visited California, too, 'specially during the summers. That is where my father is from." She nodded. "While in Cali during the summers, I stayed in Willow Brook, Los Angeles with my parents at my father's rental house. See, in North Las Vegas and Willow Brook, they're real diverse – a true reflection of the world. I was around all sorts of people. Whites, Latinos, Blacks, Asians… Later in life, I really appreciated that. It helped me truly judge a man by his character, not by the color of his skin, the way he spoke, the way he dressed. In fact, I think it's stupid to judge someone for their gender, too. But you seem to do it without blinking an eye." He tossed up his hands and grimaced, not exactly frustrated, but perhaps mildly annoyed.

"Okay, we can talk about me in a moment, but that leads to my next question. Don't you think you're being dishonest? In fact, don't you see women in an unflattering light, Savage? I know I'm not wrong about your resentment toward us. I can just feel it. No degree required."

"Resenting women and not trusting you all are two different things…" Their gazes hooked. "I have no skeletons in my closet. Not because I don't have secrets, but because I never leave a crumb trail to be questioned about them in the first place."

"You seem to have a lot of influence, power, money… What is your profession?"

"Assassin."

The woman's jaw dropped before she burst out laughing.

"Come on, we were having a good conversation. Don't do this. Don't be silly. Now seriously, what do you do?"

"I told you. I kill people, usually very bad people. I'm not a serial killer or mass shooter, let's just be clear. Those people are fucking nuts."

"Okay, I'll play your little game. Shouldn't I be calling the police right now then?"

"That's the second time you've threatened to call the

police on me. Not exactly ideal for a first date." He chortled, drawing the same reaction from her, too. "Anyway, what do you think of Gummy Bears?"

"I see I'm not going to get a straight answer." She shook her head, still laughing. "You really do have a morbid sense of humor at times. Geesh."

He shrugged, but kept quiet.

"So, why don't you trust women?"

"Because you all are too emotional to realize you have all the power, hold all the cards."

"What do you mean?"

"Anyone who can't see they are in control of the whole fucking world because they're too busy crying, being hormonal, attention seeking, and trying to manipulate others, I can't deal with. You own us, and you're clueless!"

Her lips curled in a smile. Not the reaction he was expecting.

"Are you implying women are stupid?"

"Not at all! You're emotional thinkers by nature. That's not stupidity, but it is at times poor judgment and acts to your disadvantage. Let me explain somethin' to you." He shook his finger in her direction. "Women could stop over half the shit going on in the world right now, you know, the bad shit, by simply believing they *can*. But since so many chicks don't see their worth and power, they let it rot, and that gift's totally unutilized. Women think their tits and asses control us. Bullshit. All of that hasn't changed anything, has it? A man will fuck you and still treat you like shit. We can use our hands and cum. That's not what this is about. Your bodies attract us; they don't hook us. Why? Because that's only part of it."

"What's the other part, in your opinion?"

"Don't you see? It's the love you give… a special type of love. It's soft, fluffy, heavenly shit. It's the shit we can't get enough of. You all *own* that, baby. No one smells like a woman, except a woman." He watched her complexion deepen. "No one can touch and caress like a female. Your kiss, your words, your softness, your femininity. It's the medicine, the elixir for the entire world. You have it on lockdown. We can't extract it from you; you have to give it willingly. We can overpower you and take your body, your money, all that shit… but we can't *make* you love us, no matter how hard we try. We can't grow it. We can't hunt it. We can't go inside some lab and create it. It belongs to you, and we *need* it. If we don't have it, we feel lost. It's not just the pussy, it's the passion. That 'XX' chromosome breaks men down."

"Are you in a relationship right now, Savage?"

"No. If I were, I wouldn't have asked you out."

"Hey, men in committed relationships ask women out all the time who have obligations." She tapped her nails against the table.

"I'm not like most men…"

"Fair enough. However, if you don't have a woman, that means I can safely imply you're not being loved, at least not in the sense you described. So, do you feel lost without it?"

The corners of his mouth lifted.

"Well played, Zaire…"

She burst out laughing. "I'm just asking for a friend." At this, they both broke into laughter. "Okay, let's move on past that question and try this one instead. Do you believe you know a lot about women?"

"I don't believe I know a lot about women, I *know* that I do. I don't understand everything regarding women though, because I'm not you. I'm not inside your head. I can only go so far."

Soon, the desserts arrived.

"Where is Allison? She is going to miss all the fun!" Zaire smiled from ear to ear as she studied the golden tray laden with freshly baked fruit pies with thick crusts, moist red velvet cakes, buttery French pastries, and small bowls of vanilla bean and raspberry gelato.

"Shit, call her…" He selected an apple pie and vanilla gelato. Zaire nodded and grabbed her phone. "Thank her for letting us have some time alone, too." He winked at Zaire who in turn blinked several times as a smile formed across her face.

"You're a bit rough around the edges, but I have to give credit where credit is due, Savage. You're an interesting conversationalist and you have a fascinating background, too. I'll admit it. I didn't think I would, but I've enjoyed myself. I wouldn't mind speaking with you further." They smiled at each other, their glances lingering. "You've also given me a little food for thought, and that says a lot."

"Regarding?"

"Many of the things you've stated this afternoon, but mainly, regarding the love of a woman and the power it has over not only mankind, but the world." She regarded him in a dreamy sort of way as she reached for a piece of berry cobbler. He liked that.

She's attracted to me physically. I could tell right off the bat… but she's more of a mental attraction type of lady. She's the type of woman who has to find you mentally stimulating as they say… I can hang with the big brain boys. Now that she sees I can have a decent conversation and didn't let her little mindfuck games upset me, maybe she'll give it up if I can get her alone for a bit longer. I gotta admit though, I kinda like the talk we just had…

"Can we talk about *you* now?" He dug his spoon into his ice cream.

"What would you like to know?"

"Why aren't you married or seeing anyone?" he asked.

"Who said I wasn't seeing anyone?" She winked. He winked back.

"You're not, at least not seriously. You would've never agreed to have lunch with me, regardless of Allison being here or not."

"I could be a two-timer."

"You could, but you're too judgmental for that."

"Some of the most judgmental people in the world do the very acts they profess to abhor."

"Why do you speak that way all the time?"

"What way?" Her brow arched as she took a bite of her dessert.

"So proper… Just say, 'Some people do crazy shit and then, on Sunday, they're standing behind a pulpit giving a sermon.' Or, 'Sometimes people's actions don't match what they say.'"

"Does it bother you? This is just how I speak and I'm definitely not going to apologize for it."

"It's not that I'm against proper English, Zaire, but this is supposed to be your weekend getaway, and you're acting like you're still at work, writing a book or some shit. I want to get to know *you*, Zaire. The real you." She paused, looking at him closely. "That voice you use, that tone, all of it is a way to protect yourself. To keep what you consider riffraff away. I presented the real me to you." He pointed to himself. "What you see is what you fucking get. I am rough around the edges, just like you said. Rough as fucking sandpaper. I am a street kid by choice. My father was a badass, in every sense of the word, and I saw a lot of shit going down between him and his buddies. I knew how to shoot a gun by age eight. I was tossing knives and getting it square in the bullseye by age twelve. I can shoot a bottle of liquor from over one hundred feet away with pristine accuracy."

"Are you glamorizing your father's life of crime? Well, at least in your mind? He seems like your hero. Believe it or not, that is not a judgment call. I am genuinely curious."

"He *is* my hero, but no." He shook his head. "I'm not glamorizing it one bit. He told me to not follow in his footsteps, but I couldn't help it, it's in my blood... My parents were merciless with everyone except each other and me." After they stared at one another long and hard, he said, "Anyway, I gotta go soon, but before I do, can I tell you about you? Want me to take a stab at it?"

"As long as you don't mean literally. After this discussion of guns and knives, I think I need to make that clear."

He chuckled. "Of course not. All right, here we go... You have a thing for bad boys. Had two parents. One or both probably had some sort of problem that made you wrestle with your self-esteem. Maybe one was too strict, worked too much, maybe it was serious, like a drug problem or illness. Was raised in a good part of town, probably with a sister or brother, maybe both… Along the way, you found out life wasn't so perfect. You realized your love couldn't change the bad boy you liked. He had to do it for himself but the one who took your heart and twisted it up, the one who hurt you the worst, that shit probably happened right before your career zoomed off.

"You were heartbroken, torn to pieces after he fucked you a few times then dumped you. After a while, you got control over yourself, dusted yourself off, and decided to use your hatred for broken men to help repair broken women. It's noble. It's courageous, but it's a flawed plan. You're trying to heal yourself through others. That never works." She visibly swallowed. "It's flawed, Zaire, because you still love bad boys, but they have to be bad boys with a brain…"

"Go on…"

"We practically noticed one another at the exact same time. You zoom in on men like me, and it scares the shit out of you. You'll probably fall in love with another bad boy because it's your nature, even though your mind tells you no. It's your weakness… one of the few you have. You want a fairytale romance, so that contradicts your love for men like me. So, though you feel you can't fully save yourself, you want to save other women. You don't believe you're strong enough to resist, but you hope you can encourage others to avoid the pitfalls. That's why your outlook is faulty, baby. And let me tell you something else: Not all bad boys are bad to their women."

"Oh, really?" She smirked as she took another bite of her

cobbler.

"A true bad boy knows to keep his shit away from the place he lays his head and the woman who owns his heart. We don't bring that home to you. That's a fucking no-no." He got to his feet. "Thank you for having lunch with me, beautiful. Too bad Allison missed dessert. Make sure you take some back to the room to give to her later."

"I will. I already thought of that. I will get her one of everything, especially since it's on your dime." They both laughed at that. "Honestly, I never texted her, Savage. I changed my mind. I started it, then stopped. I wanted to keep talking to you, alone... just like you wanted."

He stood there and simply stared at her, loving her beauty, her honesty in that moment. The dark shadow along half of her face was gone... faded like watercolors in the sun.

"Zaire." He walked around the table and leaned down so close to her face, he could move an inch or two and kiss her. He almost did, but decided to wait... "I'd like to see you later on tonight. It might be my last evening here."

"Leaving so soon?" Her brow arched as she crossed her arms.

"Maybe. I have some business to attend to. So, before I go, answer a question for me. Is my little rundown about you right? Or a better question is, will you be honest enough to admit that it is? Nothing is sexier than the truth, baby."

The woman took a while to respond. She didn't appear flustered or disturbed, but her breathing had accelerated. He observed the rise and fall of her chest, the way her collarbones dipped then rose... dipped then rose again.

"I'd say you were about eighty-seven percent accurate."

"Well… that's pretty damn good considering you've been rather tightlipped about your own business, but rummaged through mine like it was a clothing rack during a twenty-four-hour sale at Macy's. Tonight at seven." He made his way towards the exit, leaving her behind. "Meet me in the lobby this evening. Alone. Don't be late…"

CHAPTER SIX

Rude Awakening

C AUTION HAD BEEN tossed to the wind and she never saw where the bitch landed…

Zaire ran her hand along her arm, the hairs standing on end as a light breeze caused her carefully coiffed hair to blow out of place. Tucking one side behind her left ear, she fought the urge to grin and lost. Her lips curled in appreciation as the god in human flesh approached.

Nice.

Wearing multiple layers of swag and confidence, as well as a black blazer and matching pants and shirt, he stepped close and wrapped his arms around her, pulling her into an embrace. A thick gold chain hung from his neck and he smelled like heaven and seduction, lust, and temptation. She shuddered when she felt the softness of his plush lips caress the side of her neck, then land a light peck there. Taken aback, she blinked, her balance compromised as she rocked on her heels. He quickly steadied her by stepping back and pulling her to him with a tug of her wrist, his golden eyes gleaming from the strobing lights right outside the hotel doors.

"You were two minutes early. Perfect. However," He took a quick glance at his diamonds-on-overload watch, "you didn't really follow my directions." He slicked a cigar out of his pocket and quickly lit it. "I asked you to wait in the lobby." He took a toke and blew out thick swirls of smoke from the corner of his mouth.

"I wanted some fresh air. Besides, you're not the boss of me." She grinned. He smiled back, standing tall like some mountain.

"A boss never has to tell you they're a boss. Their actions speak for themselves." He took her by the hand and led her down a few steps, to the sidewalk. Suddenly, as if timed to perfection, a shiny black limousine pulled up. A wide man sporting a black chauffeur hat and suit jacket promptly got out of the long luxury vehicle and opened the back door. Without a hitch, Savage led her inside the limo and quickly closed the door behind them. Soft music played—something with a bit of an Indian feel—and the air was cool and sweet. As they pulled away from the curb, she looked around, checking out her surroundings.

A shimmering silver bucket sat before her holding a bottle of red wine and two flutes, surrounded by chunks of ice. To her left was a small silver tray laden with caramel and dark chocolate covered strawberries. The thing was placed on top of a deep red cloth, looking picture perfect. Some were coated in nuts, others with coconut or drizzled with white chocolate.

"Where are we going?" she asked as they approached a light. A crowd of people began to pour onto the street to get from one side to the other.

"We're going to tour the city, then head over to the Mojave Desert." He inhaled, then exhaled, the smoke filling the cabin. He cracked the window ever so slightly, allowing beams of vibrant light and street noise to creep inside the private sanctuary.

"The Mojave Desert?" She grabbed a strawberry that was skewed on a stick and examined it. "That's an odd dating location choice, and it's over two hours away. Perhaps this would be a good time to call the police. Like, for real."

"Are you implying that the Mojave Desert, which is a top tourist attraction I might add, is a good place to hide a body?"

"I most certainly am." She smirked as she teasingly unlocked her cellphone.

"It's not a good spot… too many people."

Savage leaned so close to her, she thought he was going to rest his head on her shoulder. And he did.

"I see you have a picture of you and your friends as your screensaver. That's nice." He pointed to her phone depicting the three girlfriends, arm and arm in front of one of Kim's favorite watering holes. She looked down at him, resting on her as if she were some comfortable pillow. He returned her gaze. His eyes went wide and glossed over, jagged bits of hopes and crystalized dreams in their depths, reminding her of a kid wishing upon a star. She could even make out a hint of innocence—something she hadn't expected to see.

"You have the most amazing shade of eyes… Hazel? Golden chestnut?"

"My mother says they're topaz." He chuckled. "Hers are the same color. My father's are light blue. What's your first name?"

"Why would you ask that… out of the blue? Like your father's blue eyes." She laughed at her involuntary play on words, shaking her head.

"It's been on my mind." He reached over to extinguish his cigar in a gold ashtray then leaned back on her shoulder. "Actually, to tell you the truth, I already know it. I just want to hear you say it."

"I'm not surprised." She sighed. "You seem like the type to go digging around. And so am I… I know your first name, too…" Their gazes hooked as she ran the pointy end of the succulent red fruit against her lower lip, then popped it into her mouth. The chocolatey sweet flavors and juiciness merged together, exploding in her mouth as she chewed it slow and easy, then swallowed.

"What's my name?" His deep, husky voice vibrated through her as he now sat up a bit, his mouth close to her ear.

"It's Maximus." She picked up another strawberry, this one coated in white and dark chocolate. "There wasn't a whole lot about you online, but according to Google, you're a professional gambler, Blackjack being your specialty."

"Mmm hmmm, what else did you find out?" He crossed his arms.

"Just like you explained to Allison and me, you were born and raised in Vegas but spent a great deal of your time also in

California. You're known for your over-the-top motorcycle collection, some of them quite rare. You seem to own many properties in various states… a bit of a house collector, but overall, you keep a low profile." He straightened on his seat and ran his hand along his leg, then chuckled. He shook his head, in a pitying sort of way.

"You can't believe everything you read, Eva." It was so rare that people referred to her by her first name. Not anymore. "Eva is a pretty name. It suits you." He rubbed his hands together, and then she noticed how truly huge they were. The left one had a scar that extended from the thumb to the middle finger knuckle.

"Thank you. Zaire sounds edgy though. A better stage name, if you will. That's why I use it."

He nodded in understanding. Her breath hitched as he rested his heavy hand across her leg.

"Would you like some wine?" He pulled the bottle of Caymus Napa Valley Cabernet Sauvignon out of the bucket.

"No, I'm fine. I do enjoy a good sauvignon though. Maybe later."

The man poured himself a small glass as they passed through the bright and bustling Las Vegas strip. In less than fifteen minutes with him on that ride, her face was flushed with heat and her stomach constricted with laughter. Maximus Savage was a comedian at his core.

"And then the idiot pissed his name all along the sidewalk, right? He turned towards me, his dick still in his hand, going full blast."

"No!" She lost it, succumbing to pure delirium.

"So now I'm haulin' his ass home with his fuckin' piss all

over the front of my pants, which means we *both* look drunk and I look like I peed on myself!"

She slumped over in her seat, her eyes glossing over with tears of mirth.

"I know you wanted to jump on him after that." She took a few breaths, trying to gain her composure.

"Yeah." He smiled, showing nice teeth. "But that was a long time ago… right here on the strip. John was my buddy for over twenty years; he lives in Canada now. Those were good times."

"See? It's hard when you go out and have a friend who drinks too much. It can ruin the whole day. You can't become violent with them though—that's your friend. But at the same time, they make things so challenging."

"Are you speaking from personal experience?"

"Well, yes." She sighed, feeling comfortable… a bit too comfortable. Perhaps the strawberries were laced? She pushed the thought out of her mind. "Kim has just recently started drinking too much, at least in my opinion. I'm not too certain what's driving that. She's been rather tightlipped lately but in all fairness, when she's in distress, she rarely shares the details anyway. She keeps a lot bottled in."

"No pun intended." They both chuckled at that. "Maybe she's talking to people, just not to you."

A pang rang out within her. She tried to keep a straight face, but hell, his blunt words kind of hurt. Especially since she'd already considered it.

"Why'd you think that?"

"Because I think that you intimidate them… You come across as havin' it all together and even if you're reserving judgment, sometimes that makes people uncomfortable. You're a bit of a control freak, a know-it-all. I'm not sayin' you're not lovable, but that can be intimidating to someone struggling, not so sure of themselves. Some people wanna talk to people just like them… people who have walked through the fire but survived. You come across like you've never even lit a match…"

"I don't know what to make of you."

"You've been on fire too though, and it's all right to show that with your friends."

"How do you know I don't?"

"'Cause you get a kick oughta feelin' superior. You wanna be smarter than everyone else. You don't have to be the most beautiful of your friends, the richest, but you definitely want to be the smartest. What is bein' smart though, ya know? It's beyond intelligence. Being smart is also caring about people who give a shit about ya. Fuck everyone else. You're lucky to have them."

"I *am* lucky to have them, as they're lucky to have me, too."

"You have to be honest with yourself. You love them, but you like feeling better than them. That's not cool. You need to stop that shit. That's how you lose people who care about you."

"Okay, pause. Hold the hell up Mr. After School Special!" She sighed and put up her hand. "You don't know me. I've let you sit here and tear my character apart."

"I was just getting started." He smirked. "That was just a taste."

She rolled her eyes. "You're sitting here making judgments and you don't know shit about me."

"Don't you do that practically every day on your pod-cast?" He cocked his head to the side. "What's the difference? Oh, I know… You're a woman and I'm a guy, so you somehow think you have the right to be bitchy towards people."

"That was rude."

"But was it true? That's all the fuck I care about: is it true? I wasn't born to pamper. I'm not the coddling type, and I'm not fake, either. I bet if you relaxed for just one day, your entire life would change for the better."

They glared at one another then she turned away, mulling over his words.

"Why are you with me on a date if you think so lowly of me?"

"Who said I thought lowly of you? Everyone is fucked up, Zaire, some just more so than others. I am really good at reading people, feeling their vibe and energy. None of this is real. You act stuck up, but you're really not. You're the woman who would be just fine getting a buy one, get one free pizza and guzzling soda in front of an old T.V., and making love on a ratty, matted twenty-year-old rug. The problem is, that girl got hidden, the one that was down for her man, the one that loved out loud all because you got hurt. It's a story lived by billions of women all over the world. What makes you different is that you really are tryna help people, turn your pain into profit and pleasure, but it's still a struggle for you. You're with me right now because you figure what happens in Vegas, stays in Vegas, and after this weekend, you can just walk back into your 'real life', and forget all of this ever happened. But I don't want to make it so easy for you, Zaire. I want you to think about me long after tonight. I want you to imagine me being that mother-fucker you can fuck on that old rug, tell your secrets to and just relax with. The one to help you get the stick out of your tight ass."

She sighed again and shook her head.

In her time being alive on Planet Earth, she'd never been so enraged by someone, yet so captivated with them, too. Zaire didn't get angry easily, and yet right now, she was seething…

But why am I mad? Is it because some of what he is saying is true? It's possible. These are not things you say on a first date. This is just wrong on so many levels! I should demand to be taken back to the hotel. But do I really truly want to leave? This man is blowing my mind… He's crazy. He's a mystery, too. Where in the hell did he come from? It's like he fell out of the sky and landed right on my ass….

"Did I hurt your feelings?" he asked, his brow slightly raised.

"If I said yes, would you care?"

He shrugged. "I'd care, but I wouldn't apologize. The rare times I've said sorry to someone, I meant it. An apology holds power to me. It has weight. I've done nothing but tell you the truth. Anyway, this was initially about your friend Kim, her drinking… You know, we all self-medicate, Zaire, some just more so than others."

"Self-medicate? You're a doctor or a therapist now, too?" she teased. "Wow! But I'm the know-it-all. Okay then."

The man looked out the half-rolled-down window.

"Nah, not anything like that. I just know a lot about people is all. I don't know everything though, never tried to pretend that I did. If I actually did know everything, I wouldn't have my own shit to sort through. The bottom line is, we all have our demons."

"I hear that a lot, Savage, but I don't think everyone has demons. Now sure, there are temptations and bad decisions that come along in life. No one is perfect, but we have a choice. We can either do the right thing or not. The choice is ultimately ours."

"Who or what determines what the right thing is though?"

"It's connected to our moral compass."

"Not all of us have the same standards and ethics. Not all of us have a moral compass, period." His eyes grew dark.

"Do you have one?" He turned away, looking straight ahead, and took a sip of his wine. "Yes, but I doubt it's like everyone else's. My idea of right and wrong might be different from yours."

"Hmm, interesting."

"And who determines what that moral compass should be anyway? The government? Religion?" He raised his hands. "Who's in charge of what I should and should not be thinking and doing?" He pointed to himself. "No one can govern that but me."

"But when you cross the line between what you perceive as your rights and my safety," She shrugged. "It's no longer about who is in charge of what you should do and think. It's now about the justice and protection of my existence and wellbeing that you've violated."

"That's good." He shook his finger at her as if she'd

SAVAGE

passed some sort of test. Polishing off his wine, he set the empty glass down in the bucket. "That's the starting point of what you'll accept and won't accept. It opens the lines of communication… just never stop asking, 'Why?' Always question the rules and the people who make them."

They sat there for a bit, taking in the sights.

"I like talking to you." She cleared her throat and glanced at him out the corner of her eye. "You're an interesting person, Savage. Believe it or not, this is how I envision a vacation. Looking at the sights, eating delicious food, and engaging in insightful conversation. I don't agree with everything you've shared, but I enjoy the discourse nonetheless. You're rudimentary, and you look as if you'd be unsophisticated, but you're also logical and thoughtful… different from how I thought you'd be."

He intertwined their fingers. Staring at her hand, he slowly brought it to his lips for a kiss.

"And how did you think I'd be?"

"Honestly? Dumb as a rock." He chuckled and shook his head. "But you're not… you come across as rather bright and I like that."

Moments later, they had passed the main area of the Vegas nightlife. The road was dark, the limousine was zipping past white posts and street signs, and the starlit sky was the only illumination to be seen.

"Where are we going?"

"I told you… the Mojave Desert."

"I thought you were kidding!"

The man had the gall to look at her and laugh, a full head toss and all.

"But it's late at night, Savage. No one goes to a desert in the middle of the night. That's dangerous!"

"You're in no danger." He rolled his eyes as if she were being dramatic. "I know how to handle this. Exploring this area in the evening is beautiful, like nothing you've ever seen."

Her eyes widened in disbelief as she saw twinkling lights in the distance, then three small white aircrafts on a runway in the middle of nowhere. The limousine pulled into a small lot and parked.

"Are we... are we flying on that?" She pointed to one of the planes, the only one that was lit up with the propeller spinning.

Please say no, please say no, please say no!

"Yeah," was all he offered before the driver got out of the vehicle and opened her door. The man took her hand and helped her out the car, and she practically jumped out of her skin when Savage came to stand next to her. How the hell had he gotten to her so fast and without being heard or seen?! Shaking that thought out of her mind, she let him take her by the arm and lead her to the aircraft. Her stomach fluttered...

I hate these small Tonka toy sized planes! How'd I get into this mess? I shoulda known he wasn't going to drive almost three hours away for no damn date!

Less than ten minutes later, they were sitting side by side inside the small space, knees practically rubbing against one another. The bastard had the nerve to start cracking jokes with the pilot, smiling and carrying on.

"Just so you know, Kim and Allison both know my

whereabouts should you try anything strange or I disappear into thin air."

"Good. I don't give uh shit." He grinned. "Call your mom, the FBI, and the Pope, too." He shrugged.

"Smartass."

"I'm serious. I would encourage any chick in this day and age to do that, ya know, to tell people where she is going. You have no idea some of the fucked up people in this world, baby... no idea." His eyes turned to practical slits as his voice drifted. "Funny, the innocent lookin' guys are the ones doing the most dirt. Ted Bundy, for example, looked like a clean-cut politician. Don't be afraid of the guys with the shifty eyes; be cautious of the ones in the nice suits that have the gift of the gab."

He suddenly reached over and squeezed her left breast, then released it with the swiftness only known to Speedy Gonzales. It was almost as if she were losing her mind...*Did that just really happen?!*

She looked down at her shirt and could see where some of the fabric was creased from his touch. The fucker was now talking to the pilot again, yucking it up, as if nothing had transpired. Meanwhile, her body filled with the heat of a thousand infernos!

"Ow!" He laughed as he rubbed his arm where she'd landed a mighty blow.

"How dare you! Don't do that again."

"Huh?" He threw up his hands. "Do *what?*"

"You know what you did!" She hissed and turned away.

"Nice tit. You need better cup support though." He reached into a bowl of peanuts and crammed a bunch into his mouth like some greedy ogre. She hoped he'd choke. "I don't mind. The jigglier the better." He chewed noisily with his mouth flapping open. "But I could feel the underwire kinda cuttin' into your skin and the slight bulge at the top means it's not the best fit. Go up a size."

She huffed and shook her head.

He could feel all of that in a one-second squeeze?

"You're full of shit. You're a tits and bra expert now, huh? What a motherfucker you are and worst of all, you know it and don't care. Where are the checks and balances inside of that skull of yours? I should slap the shit outta you."

At this, he burst out laughing.

"I like being slapped, especially when fucking." She swallowed. "You're right. I am a motherfucker, baby. That's true… You really do have nice tits though. Nice ass, too… but like I said, tits and ass attract, they don't hook. I'm into some *other* shit. I like that you're open minded but pretend not to be. That's different, but it's cool. I dig that shit. Let your guard down for me tonight. Have some fun. You've earned it, right?"

"All right… I'm going to, but only for one night." She crossed her legs and talked herself into releasing *some* of her inhibitions. Besides, he was right; after this weekend, she'd never speak to or see him again. She could be naughty and no one would be the wiser.

"You're sexy, you know that, Zaire? I don't mean just physically, either. I like your voice… and the way you move your head when you talk. I like your hair, your scent, and the curve of your back. Let's have a good time and fuck each

SAVAGE

other's brains out. Nothin' like a good romp in the cerebral hay. This should be right up your alley. You're a sapiosexual, right?"

"Yup."

"Good. So am I."

"I highly doubt that." She grimaced.

"Who I fuck for fun or out of boredom, and who I fuck for more than that are two different categories of women. You think you are figuring me out? Nah..." He lit a cigar as the plane began to taxi. "Baby, you haven't even scratched the fucking surface."

Her lips curled in a grin as she stared out the window into blackness. Her breath hitched when the plane took off, juddering and shifting from side to side as it soared higher and higher into the air. Anxiety wrapped its hand around her neck and squeezed. She braced herself when she felt his weight against her arm, his palm glide around her waist in an embrace, his mouth close to her face...

Smoke-laced breath with traces of mint and wine filled her space, giving a strange sense of comfort and peace.

"You're good, baby. We're going to be fine. Savage won't let shit happen to you, all right? Relax. You're in good hands."

She hated herself for feeling excited with this son of a bitch.

She despised herself for finding him so damn attractive, for the fact her panties were practically soaked.

He reeked of arrogance and audacity, a playfulness she wanted to explore, and a brain that was fit for deep study.

When she turned and looked at him, he held his cigar in

one hand, and her in the other. His eyes stared deeply into hers, while his broad chest rose and fell slow and easy. Without a second to lose, he pulled her closer and gave her a firm, sensual kiss. His full, soft lips gave her new life. It wasn't long before his tongue was gliding against hers. He gripped the back of her head, drawing her into his lust... Eyes shut, breathing hard, his touch drifted low, massaging the base of her back as he delivered the best lip lock known to mankind.

He kissed like he was making love to her, ruthlessly fucking her emotions... screwing her mind with powerful analytical thrusts.

He released her at last, and she hated him for it. Placing her hand to her mouth, she enjoyed the tingle that resonated all throughout her body, finding its way to her spine. She was electric like a lit-up Christmas tree, her body and mind in harmony.

"We'll be there in about thirty-five minutes." he said, and then, the lights in the cabin went out. All she could see was the orange glow of the cigar embers and the shadow his massive silhouette. Her soul shouted out the truth, and she knew it as such...

She was sitting next to a soulless monster pretending to be a man. Or perhaps, all men were monsters, but some simply accepted their true natures and did their best with the cards they were dealt?

Maybe I'm a monster, too, because he was right about what he'd said in the restaurant. I have an unhealthy attraction to men who are bad for my heart...

He's a one-weekend kind of guy. Yeah... I'm fine with that. Men like Savage you can't be with for too long. It always ends in disaster.

They hate commitments. Just let this kind of guy give you an experience, one you shall never forget, and then pass on by—go on with your life. Hell, it'll be fun, right? That has to be the plan, because if you try to care about them, try to love them too hard, they will explode right there in your hands, taking you out right along with them... They will break you in two and laugh as they do it.

Savage is single for a reason.

He wants to be alone.

He's too hard to hold, too cold to care, and too loathsome to love...

CHAPTER SEVEN

Sidewinding Conversation

H E COULD SEE she was in awe...

The way Zaire stood on her tippy toes, holding tight to the binoculars as she stood on top of a rock in the Kelso Dunes of the Mojave Desert was a sight to behold. They'd just taken a thirty minute walk and now they stood here admiring the sights. He pointed at various types of vegetation, and they laughed and joked. Some of her layers melted away right in front of his eyes. She was relaxed, though he was certain he wasn't near her center, the heated core, just yet. That would take some work, some digging, but he'd come here with a shovel and a whole lot of determination...

Getting a woman like Zaire to lay her burdens down and give her body had to be the crème de le crème of conquests. In his mind, this sort of beast of a woman was always a succulent sweet, a rare treat to devour. A prize. He could practically smell her superiority complex, and he had to break her down. It was fun. Just like a sport. The kind of hunt that would be for the record books.

"Do you see this? Wow!" she said. "I'm in complete awe!"

With his hands around her waist, he steadied her as she studied the miraculous night sky.

"It's real nice, isn't it? I did say you'd love it."

"This is incredible, Savage." Seconds turned to minutes. She was in deep. The cosmos had a way of hypnotizing women like Zaire, reminding them how very small they were in the scheme of things... "It's like an entirely different universe." She finally spoke after a long silence.

He slowly let go of her, reached into the large pocket inside his jacket, and removed her satiny black shoes she'd worn for their outing. Helping her down from the rock, he had her sit upon it as he slid on one slipper, then the other. It was rather dark out, but he'd lit a campfire and a couple of strategically placed flares for her stargazing, allotting them room to see their immediate surroundings in clear view.

"How'd you know about this area, anyway?" She handed him the binoculars and adjusted her jacket. "It's out in the middle of nowhere."

"My father used to bring me here every once in a while." He glanced at the jeep he'd driven them in after they'd landed and gotten off the plane. "I come alone sometimes now, just to clear my head and get some fresh air." She nodded in understanding. "It can get really dark out here, like the darkest room you've ever been in times one hundred."

"Oh wow, I bet that's scary." She tugged at the zipper on her jacket, allowing it to flap open. It was a bit balmy out.

I think it's beautiful actually... the pitch black. There's power in darkness."

She tilted her head to the side, gaze on him, seeming to debate on whether to ask him about what he'd just said. But she let it be…

"I'm going to have to come out here again." She looked around in amazement. "I'm not an outdoorsy type of girl, Savage, but this right here is magical."

"There's a great book about the Mojave Desert and in it—" BAM!

"Oh shit!" she screamed, her voice ringing out into the night as she flinched and flailed her arms, bringing her hands to her ears. His smoking gun by his side, he stared at the light tan and stone colored sidewinder he'd split in two with one bullet to the head. Visibly shaken, the woman's eyes had nearly leapt out of her skull. She finally rested her eyes upon the unlucky guy to receive a visit from a steely .410 shell out of the mouth of his Taurus Judge pistol, letting her hands fall to her sides. "It's huge."

"That's what she said…" The woman rolled her eyes, causing him to chuckle. "Nah, it's a damn sidewinder."

She turned back towards it, then recoiled as if the damn thing would somehow come back, revived, and seek revenge from the afterlife. Her teeth bared, she sucked in air, regarding it with repulsion.

"Is it poisonous?"

"Yup. Some call it a horned rattlesnake but whatever you call it, make sure to know that it's venomous, fast, and will fuck you up. Funny… they usually don't like being around fire, but sometimes you'll get a brazen one like this." He slid a cigar out of his jacket and lit it. "He was probably after somethin' that ran past. A pack rat, rabbit, or lizard…

somethin' like that." He blew out some smoke and let it dissipate in the air. "They don't like smoke. Their respiratory systems are sensitive. It slows them down, makes them pause for a bit."

"Good Lord. How'd you even see it?"

He blew out a few rings of smoke, taking his time to respond. When he was done, he tossed the cigar in the sand then glanced up at the gorgeous sky.

"I didn't. I heard it."

The woman swallowed, shook her head, and stood to her feet.

"I don't like snakes." She grimaced in disgust. "Gross."

"Eh." He shrugged. "They're actually amazing creatures and some make good pets. They get a bad rap. You just have to use common sense when out here. We're in their territory, gotta watch them—they're hunting right now and the scorpions around here are not something you wanna mess with, either, especially since it's so hot right now."

"Well, despite the snake massacre I witnessed, realizing that you're carrying a damn loaded gun and lovely discussion of scorpions," they both chuckled, "tonight was beautiful, Savage. I like how knowledgeable you are on the area, too. When I think of places like this, I admit that all I imagine are extreme heat, drought and sand."

"Isn't nature something?"

"It is. Thanks for bringing me." They stood by the fire, side by side, the embers flickering and sparking like tiny fireworks in the night. "Does it bother you that I ask personal things? It's just how my mind works," she said with a smile, out of the blue.

"Nah, not really. You must want to ask me something else."

"I do."

"I get to ask you something personal too then. You have to answer honestly. Deal?"

She looked at him for a spell, swaying a bit from side to side.

"Deal. I want to ask you this, Savage, but I hope you don't find it too heavy or personal. You're just so damn interesting! I can't help myself."

"Nice touch… smearing on the compliments and charm to try 'nd butter me up before the kill."

Her lips curled. "It's that obvious, huh?"

"Definitely. Try me anyway." He unzipped his jacket.

"Okay, have you ever been married?"

"Nope."

"Considered it?"

"Nope times two."

"Why not?" she said in disbelief.

He faced her, taking her all in. The fire burned bright, casting its sweltering orange, lemon, and cinnamon essence in a frenzy upward motion. The reflection of the heated dance sparkled, the image of the flames glowing in her dark eyes like an untimely death and a brand new beginning all at the same time.

Damn, she is so fucking pretty…

"Zaire, marriage, to me, is not what it means to a lot of people so I can't sign up for some shit like that, at least, not with the way people are nowadays."

"I don't understand. Are you against it? I'm just asking because I'm curious. Not anything related to you and me." She laughed nervously.

"See, when you offer up too much information, you tell on yourself. If you're trying to cover your tracks, keep it short and sweet."

"You honestly think I'm interested in marrying you and trying to cover it up? Boy, bye!" He laughed at her words. "I don't even know you."

"You don't have to know someone long to understand you have an attraction to them on a deeper level." He grinned as she pursed her lips. The little birdie was caught with a cricket in her mouth. "Every question we ask is related to you or me right now." He shrugged. "It's a game of chess. It ties into our passions, our love, our hatred, our desires... even if it's unconscious. But it's cool. It's fine." He sucked his teeth as she kept her eye on him. Walking back and forth, he began to pace around the fire. It was hypnotic; he almost felt watched by the flames.

"You make me uncomfortable."

He paused and looked at her. "Why? Because I'm pacing?"

"No, your tone of voice dropped. You've become quite serious."

"You asked a serious question. What do you expect?" He threw up his hands then began to pace once again. "If I'm making you uncomfortable, then I'm doing my job. You make people uncomfortable every damn day you're on that podcast. I only had to listen to a couple episodes online to figure that out. You're damn good at what you do." He ran his hand along his jawbone.

"Thank you."

"You have to press people, push their buttons. That also gets the ratings, but you have to do it for yourself too, in order to be heard. No one respects the weak... the door-mats... the fuckers that just keep taking it, and taking it, and taking it. Now, back to the original question." He took a deep breath, released, and rubbed his hands together as he stared into the fire. "I'm not against marriage at all. I just think if you're gonna do it, it needs to be a forever sorta thing." He didn't miss the quick flash of a smile across her face. "I don't want to get married and be divorced six months later. When and if I get married, Zaire, that woman and I are not splittin' up unless it's due to death. Period." He turned and spit in the distance, then returned to facing the fire. "I think if when people got married they were told they had to lose a toe or finger for each divorce, they'd take it far more seriously. People are out here playing with it, like it's funny, some game. It's not a toy. That's a pact you make with your soulmate."

"You believe in soulmates? Now excuse me, but I'm truly surprised!" She grinned.

"Yeah, I do. I told you that you don't know shit about me. I open up when I feel like it, and that's not often." Her smile slowly faded. "Anyway, if we were radical with the consequences, it would stop people from jumping into it with such lack of concern."

"Are you serious? That's archaic and primitive. What

about spousal abuse or adultery? The victim loses a toe, too?"

"No. If someone is a habitual cheater or kickin' someone's ass, they are the ones who'll lose a finger or toe and the survivor gets to remarry—no questions asked."

"Okay, you are, uh, thankfully not a judge ruling the land," she quipped. "But sometimes…"

"Wait." He raised his hand. "You're really getting your rocks off right now, aren't you? You love having discussions like this! This is supposed to be a date, and you've got me out here talking about this." He shook his head.

"Yes! I love it! You have no idea, Savage, how many guys aren't able to just dialogue like this. I realized you're a pretty good conversationalist when you were speaking with Allison. This is so relaxing and fantastic to me." She blinked in a flirtatious sort of way. "Thank you for humoring me."

"I don't get to talk like this too often… I didn't think I'd want to. I guess, uh, you proved me wrong." He quickly looked away from her.

"Okay, what about this? People get married and they find out the person is nothing like who they thought they were. That happens all the time."

"See, I think you know better than that, Eva… I wanna call you Eva tonight. Is that okay?"

"Yeah… I suppose." She shrugged.

"All right. I think it's rare because women pick up things all the time, stuff you know doesn't make sense."

"Here we go with the battle of the sexes again!"

"Nah, I'm serious. Hear me out. Look, you all like to

ignore shit just so you don't have to grow some balls and kick the guy to the curb." The woman gave him the side-eye. "You don't wanna lose him. You don't wanna be alone, so you ignore the fact that he turns his phone off all the time, that you can only see him two days outta the week but he blames it on work. You sweep under the rug that he smells like perfume that isn't yours, that he's starting arguments with you then disappearing for a day or two, saying he's over at his friend's house to cool his head when your instinct tells you he's gettin' his dick wet... and not inside of *you*. He is playing you. He knows it. You know it. Stevie Wonder knows it.

"But then, one day, he's given an ultimatum. You threaten to leave, bags packed. He then proposes and apologizes, says all the right shit to make sure his security blanket doesn't walk off. You take him back and before the ink is even dry on the marriage license, he's fucking his ex-girlfriend so much it's like his life depends on it. Then, to get revenge, you're fuckin' your first husband, the one you had your daughter with, or the dude you told him not to worry about... or the guy down at the gym, or the one that works at that car stereo shop or whatever. It's always some bullshit. People don't take marriage seriously at all, and that's why I'm not hellbent on doing it."

"Could there be more to this? Could you be less inclined to want to marry because of your parents' marriage, or lack thereof?"

"Nah, that's not it at all. Everyone always thinks when someone is against marriage, the parents did it!" He laughed.

"It's the family's fault! This is exactly why head shrinks are definitely overpaid. It's not always about that." He grinned, though she didn't smile back. "Even though my parents weren't married, they showed more loyalty to one another than most."

"But… your mother was sleeping with other men for profit. Now sure, that wasn't technically cheating if your father knew and he was fine with it, but she was doing it nevertheless."

"Nah, you got it all wrong." He waved his hand about. "My father didn't want her doing it. That was no secret. My mother didn't want them to struggle though."

"Financially struggle?"

"Yes. My dad's income was sporadic. He had a long criminal record so workin' a regular nine to five was out of the question. My mother felt like he had no room to talk about what she was doing though because his means of making ends meet were illegal. She was allowed to do what she was doing, ya see?"

"So, the rabbit hole gets deeper." She sighed. "Tell me to mind my own business if you want, but now I want to know what your father was doing. Selling drugs?"

"Nah. My father dealt with arms dealership. He sold weapons, almost anything you wanted, on the black market. I don't want to get too much into that."

"I understand."

"Just want to make it clear he wasn't a drug dealer, nothin' like that. Some of his friends were into the heavy stuff, you can only imagine, but he didn't deal with that. He was too afraid it could put my mom and me in danger. He didn't keep his stash in the house, for instance, but I'll leave it at that. He stuck with what he could better control. On the flip side, he also taught boxing and archery at the community center on occasion. He was so good, Eva. He taught me practically everything I know."

He smiled sadly as he stretched his hands out towards the flames when a chill caught him. It was rather strange, considering the high humidity in the air.

"I take it your mother is no longer in the life, right? She's much older now."

"You're askin' a lot of questions. A lot of personal shit. Shit that I don't want to really get into right now."

"Well then, we can stop." She tossed up her hands. He could've sworn she smirked, as if she'd won something, a prize for making him sweat.

"Nah, it's too late now. Pandora's box is already opened. I'm no pussy. You walked in, so we'll go the distance together."

"You have nothing to prove. If you want to pull out, that's fine. Obviously this is too painful for you."

"It's not that I don't wanna talk about it because it's too painful. It's because it belongs to me, Eva. This is *my* life." He pointed to himself. "It's like having some boxes in a room, with lids on them. You point to one box and say to me, 'Savage, what's in there?' I then walk over to it, lift the lid, and you see it's a bunch of dirty laundry or something. But you don't stop there. You point to another box, then another. These boxes are mine, and you're invading. You're doing it because you're nosy. Because I intrigue you, and because you're interested in me as more than just a one night stand."

"Bull!" She laughed. "It's just that—"

"Stop it." He lifted his palm and glared at her. "Just stop lying. I can't stand that."

"I'm not lying."

"You are. You just don't know you are." Silence webbed between them. "It's all right to be interested in someone, even if you don't know 'em all that well. You've got all these silly ass, fucked up rules in your head for how this should go. For how relationships should go, period."

"Excuse me? Let me tell you something. I graduated top of my class and—"

"So fucking what?" He shrugged. "I never questioned your ability to memorize facts and figures from other people and take them as truth and then walk across a stage in your cap and gown with nothin' to show for it!"

"I have an award-winning podcast. I have been featured in countless periodicals and have received a myriad of awards. You're intimidated by intelligent women!"

"Ahhh, for fuck's sake! Not this shit again! Your ol' standby… I must hate women. I must resent women. I'm intimidated by women. Next, it'll be, I wanna secretly cut off my balls and sew the remaining space into a fuckin' vagina! Maybe then, and only then, will I truly be at peace, right?" He slapped his forehead. "Cheeseburger in fuckin' paradise. You're nuts, lady!"

"You don't respect higher education, all because you didn't have the patience, stamina, and wherewithal to do it yourself."

"Wrong again, Professor Smitty. I do respect higher education, as long as the person earnin' it understands they don't have some sorta impenetrable Superman cape just because they've got it. It's like this, Eva. Let me break it down for you since you're not getting it. You're not more intelligent because you and a bunch of other sheep went into a few buildings on a daily basis for four plus years, paid thousands of fucking dollars to get into debt before the age of twenty-five, only to come out and regurgitate other people's ideas. Then, the cherry on top is, most of the time all you poor saps can't find a damn job in your profession and have stress comin' out of your ass like smoke because you owe Uncle Sam your first-born child. Just because you've bought into this scam."

"I have no idea how we got on this topic, I forget, but it's not a scam. It's a stepping stone."

"The American dream of 'work hard, go to school and everything will be all right!' is a scam, a scam, a scammy scam scam. Do you know how many fuckers with PhDs are homeless on the street or workin' for minimum wage just to keep food on the table? Do you know how many high school drop outs, that I personally know, have more intelligence in their baby finger than some of them? See, you've bought into the hype. You look at simple shit and make it complicated, baby."

The woman's lips pursed. She had the kind of stare as though she thought him scum on the bottom of her shoe... but he knew she was getting a kick out of this. Debates made her feel good all over, from her head to her toes. She wanted to not only dig into his business, get him talking, but to see how he expressed himself.

I can go hood to boardroom in a nano second. You're fucking with the wrong man. You don't want to see how badly this can end...

CHAPTER EIGHT

Star-Crossed Lovers

"**F**UCK IT. I can see you're getting upset. Let's talk about the Gummy Bear fetish. That's more your speed," she snapped.

"I'll do ya one better. Let's have a séance and instead of tryna find out about Cookie Monster being an implant for the Devil, let's summon the ghost of common sense because you need to be possessed by it like the fucking plague. No 'fuck it' here. You opened this door, so we're going in. Like I said, we're going the distance now with these questions you've asked. I'm not a quitter. You should know that by now." He shook his finger in her direction.

"I don't know what you are, Savage."

"I don't know you, you don't know me, but each second that passes, we know each other a little bit more, right?"

"Yes, I suppose you could conclude that."

"We have an attraction, it's mutual, and believe it or not, a healthy respect for one another is forming. I knew this would happen before this weekend was over. I just didn't know when."

"You knew *what* would happen?"

"That you'd test me one final time… See if I could go toe-to-toe, if I'd fit, be worth the aggravation." Her cheeks deepened with color. "When it's my turn, I'm going to pull your entire soul out of you," he said, fixing her with his piercing gaze. "And I'm going to enjoy every agonizing second of it." Her eyes widened. "So, back to what you asked," he stated cheerfully, shoving his hands into his pockets. "My mother stopped selling herself once she got sick." He dropped his head and took a few deep breaths.

Are you really doing this? Yeah… I've got nothing to lose.

"Oh… I didn't know she was ill."

"Nah, she's fine now and doing well."

"What was going on?"

…Another box being opened.

"She was passing out, having big migraines and dizziness. She went through a lot at that time. She calls it her wake-up call. Anyway, she retired for good after that and my father was happy about it. The way she explained it, it's not that she wanted to prostitute herself, per se. She just wanted to make sure we had what we needed. She didn't want us to struggle. My mother grew up having nothing, Eva. Eating only a few times a week, dirty, cold. Her biological parents—she never knew them. When she came here to America, she wanted a new life. She realized she could make a lot of money, that men would pay her for her beauty, her body, little bits and pieces of her soul." He bent down, picked up a pebble, and tossed it into the fire. "That's the only reason why my parents argued according to her—it was over her being a whore."

"Why do you call her that?"

"Because that's what she was. Doesn't make her any less human, any less lovable… any less my mother."

"I'm speechless." Zaire exhaled loudly. "I find your background so fascinating… how challenging that must've been. Let me ask you something else." *She must take me for a joke. I'm going to break her in two.* "It's something we touched on earlier regarding morals… ethics."

"Yeah?"

"Was there… what's the word?" She tapped her chin thoughtfully. "Like rules your parents had about her prostituting, for lack of a better word? I mean, I know it's legal in Las Vegas, but I'm talking about their relationship. Their partnership."

"Yeah, there were some rules actually. I'm sure I didn't know all of them, only a few. At the end of the day, it was none of my business. But sometimes I overheard stuff which gave me some understanding, I guess you could say. For example, when she was tricking, there were guidelines they'd agreed upon soon after getting together, before I was even born."

"Do you remember them?"

She's planning to talk about this on her podcast, write it in a book or some shit… Hilarious.

"Yes. Number one, she couldn't fuck any of his friends or relatives, no one he knew. Ever. Secondly, she couldn't tongue kiss. That was reserved for my father. Third, she had to use protection at all times or the deal was off, no matter how much money the guy offered. Fourth, my father or one of his guys had to be with her or at least nearby, so she didn't get hurt by some lunatic. Fifth, no gangbangs. She got sick right after she was considering getting out of the life anyway, so it worked itself out. Funny though, I guess my mother being seen as some exotic type due to her naturally tanned skin, height, long jet black hair and accent, she didn't have to try very hard to get the ballers. She only had a certain clientele. She charged very expensive fees, so only a specific type of guy could afford her."

"Millionaires?"

"Yeah, usually the millionaires, billionaires, and Arab guys from wealthy families… most of them married."

"Doesn't the mind get warped when you think about your mother's sex life, especially with strangers?"

…Another box. She's opening everything. Not a single fuck given. This feels like an consultation. I suppose first dates usually are. I don't usually take women out though. Maybe this is the norm nowadays.

"What do you mean? Obviously my mother isn't a virgin. No one's mother is or they wouldn't be their mothers in the first place."

"You know what I mean…"

This woman just didn't let up. "It doesn't sound normal. I know what you're driving at. I already said that earlier though."

"This… this doesn't sound normal, Savage, because it's not." The woman's tone was full of sorrow, and so were her eyes. In that moment though, he didn't feel judged; he felt as if she were genuinely concerned about him, fearing for his mental well-being. He burst out laughing before turning back to the flames. "What's so funny?" she asked softly.

"Nothin'. It's just that anything that's wrong with me because of any of this, well, it's too late to worry about that now, ain't it?" He shrugged. "What's done is done. I don't hate my mother. I love 'er, and I mean that. We just don't have a conventional relationship is all. I don't have to have experienced a conventional childhood, a normal one, as you say, to feel okay. I'm all right being just how I am."

"Fair enough."

He lit a fresh cigar and puffed on it a while as silence stretched between them. He inched closer to her until they were both sitting on that boulder, side by side.

"Your turn," she offered.

"Indeed it is. So, uh, what about you?" He released smoke from between his lips, then passed her the cigar. "What was it like being in your household as a kid?"

The woman took a toke, her eyes turning to slits as tiny ringlets of smoke came out her mouth. She was pretty damn good, especially for someone who showed no signs of being a smoker. She'd watched him smoking though, with the kind of gaze one has when they miss an old habit. Seconds grew into minutes, and he knew she was stalling, maybe reminding herself of his warning regarding lying... opening up, digging deep. It seemed like a simple question, but he knew instinctively it was one that she didn't want asked. Yet there it was, lying at her feet...

"Well." She took a deep sigh, staring briefly at the sky. "I'm the youngest of three. I have an older brother and sister. My parents are still together, still married." She took another taste of the cigar then handed it back to him. Spirals of smoke eddied from her luscious lips.

Yeah, yeah, yeah... Here comes the Lie Patrol. Black Brady Bunch bullshit...

All of them had hair with ringlets, just like their mother. The youngest one had a Jheri curl...

Get on with it! I'm ready to fuck... Should I tell 'er? Naaah, I'll wait. She's still talking. Besides, I've got 'er on the hook now. It'll be fun to see her swing from it.

He placed the cigar to his lips.

"My mother was a former beauty queen and later sales clerk for a fancy boutique in Beverly Hills. My father was a firefighter. We were obviously far from rich, but we were comfortable." *Ah ha... Now we're on to something. A good ol' crack in the perfect foundation. Lower middle class, but if you're living in California with jobs like that, it could get rough...* "My mother wanted all of us to go to college—didn't want us to struggle with money the way she and my father did on occasion." *Confirmation initiated. She'll confess some crazy shit in a minute... some shit she's been keeping in. My honesty and openness made her feel more at ease. Just watch...* "My mother had big dreams... wanted to be a model and actress but..." Zaire lowered her head, a sad smile on her face as she rubbed her thumb against her palm. *10, 9, 8, 7, 6, 5, 4, 3, 2, 1...*

"She got pregnant with my brother."

DING! DING! DING! Told ya! A little fornication and an out of wedlock baby. Ohhhh, tha fuckin' horror!

"So I take it she got pressured to get married by your grandparents?" He took another inhale.

"Yup." She sighed. "So that's what they did. My mother tends to be a chameleon."

"What do you mean?"

Here we go, boys and girls. It's showtime! Will it be door number 3, 2, or 1?

Door 3: The mother is a bored wife and does zany shit to get attention. 2. The mother is a fuckin' nut job, suffering from a mental issue out of this damn world that has now fucked up her daughter, too. Or 1, she's just strange, kinda like her youngest kid, but not certifiable…

"She changes her mind a lot. One minute, she was ultra-religious like her mother—my grandmother. The next, she is free-spirited and wanting to purchase an RV and tour the land. When she was pregnant with my brother, apparently she was Ms. Traditional. Very domestic, motherly, soft-spoken." Zaire stood to her feet, as if needing a bit of space to collect her thoughts. "When she was pregnant with my sister, she went through her free spirit phase. When she was pregnant with me, she went through her Afrocentric stage; thus, my middle name. My father hated it, so they compromised and she agreed to have my first name be Eva."

She's avoiding the elephant in the room… She is skating around this. Her mother is batshit crazy… It's gotta be door number 2. I've been mind-fucking for too long. I know how people move, mentally and physically. I can smell weakness, insecurity, lies. I'm too good at this shit to mess this one up. This is easy…

"She stayed Afrocentric for many, many years… then one day, just like that, all of that was gone. The posters, the books, the albums, all of it. She was just… Iris. That's when the depression kicked in." Zaire took several steps back and returned to sit on the rock. Actually, she dropped herself on it, as if she were thrust from the sky on top of it. Slumping to one side, she glared at the fire, as if daring it, inviting it to a fight. "My mother is crazy."

She laughed loud, a choppy, harsh sound. It didn't feel as good as he imagined. Her confession was too raw; it broke her down. In fact, much to his dismay, he wasn't enjoying her reaction one bit. That beating thing he was supposed to have in his chest, a heart, actually panged on her behalf.

"I've never... told anyone this... not even my closest friends. I told them she has early onset dementia. I lied to them."

Now it all makes sense.

"Maybe I'm ashamed... I don't know. It's probably a number of reasons."

"What's her actual diagnosis?"

"Bipolar and paranoid schizophrenia. Growing up with a sick parent, a mentally ill one, is Hell on Earth." With her brows bunched and her mouth twisted, he watched a woman with a hard outer shell melt away right in front of him. Her gorgeous, almond-shaped dark eyes gleamed with unspent tears that threatened to fall. Tossing the cigar in the sand, he took her hand in his. Her gaze averted, she hesitated, and eventually, the tears fell silently. Naturally.

"Why don't you uh, get it all out? You can talk to me. It's safe. Because you know I know none of the same people you do, and after tonight we probably won't see each other again."

She was quiet for a spell, then began to do just that—talk, spill the beans.

"I tried to be the good daughter. I figured, if I worked hard enough in school, I wouldn't get yelled at for something I hadn't done for a change. I thought, well, maybe I'm not pretty enough." She shrugged. "My sister was gorgeous, just like our mother. Her hair was not as thick and a bit less kinky. She had smoother skin... longer legs."

"You thought straighter hair was prettier?"

"Well, not now, but as a child, yes. It's all a part of many Black women, especially young girls, falling prey to European standards of beauty. I thought back then that maybe if I got a makeover, Mama would get better. Well, that didn't work, either. My father took her from doctor to doctor until finally, while I was in college, she got a diagnosis. We were all devastated. But, things got better."

She swiped at her cheek, wiping the tears away. Reaching for her face, he gripped her chin then caressed her cheek with the side of his thumb, collecting some of the moisture. "She was prescribed medicine and attended therapy, and slowly but surely, Iris, my beautiful mother, received some peace. Things are still hard though, quit challenging. You never know how she is going to respond or what she is going to do on a day-to-day basis."

This is the domino effect now... Confess what happened, the consequences...

"It was too late for my brother though. Timothy is incarcerated for life. Drugs... robbed and killed an elderly couple with his druggie friends. He was so strung out that he doesn't even remember that night and I believe him. He's a minister now, said he gave his life to God. But then he sent me a letter cursing me out two weeks ago because I wouldn't give him any more money. I suspect he is still taking drugs in prison. My sister, Star, is doing well though. She's married with a son, but like me, she's got her own demons. There's that word again. Demons." She chuckled dismally. "We're going to church right now, huh? So, I better fess up." She sniffed.

"This isn't church. You tell me what you want to tell me. Whatever you don't want to, I won't bother you about it."

"Well, I want to tell you. First off, I lied. I know we all have demons, just like you said, Savage."

"I'm glad you told the truth. Seems like you needed to."

"Well, you can hate me now. To my core because apparently, I lie a lot." The tears flowed once again as she shook her head. "I lie to myself all the damn time, like the main reason I went into psychology. I did it to help my mother! To get answers. The broken women weren't just the ones with broken hearts. They were the ones with a broken spirit, a broken brain that played tricks on them! How could someone so beautiful, worthy, and loving turn into that?! She had no control over it, and it messed all of our lives up. My father had a stroke because of it. Thank God he recovered, but every time he turned around, my mother had to be taken to the damn hospital because of one of her many episodes!

"The demons came. They came because I was a liar! To my fans, to my readers, to my friends!" she yelled. "So, I did what my mother did. I transformed when things got too damn hot. I became truth in the flesh. By giving women tough love, then I've proven my point, right? I do it because… because… the truth is just so damn cruel! Since I'm Zaire, 'The Truth Sayer' on my podcast, then that means *I'm* cruel, too."

"You're not cruel. You're guarded, hypocritical. What you want is not what you got. This is why I told you that you were lying to yourself. See, when you want to get something off your chest, and someone offers the platform and you feel safe with them, you'll come clean. You came clean because I made you feel comfortable, baby." He caressed the side of her arm. "You wanted to stop running and lying. You wanted it *all* to just stop."

"How'd you know?! How'd you know I was lying?"

"Your eyes… The truth is always in the eyes."

"But I blink, and I turn away, and I hide myself."

"Yet you blink too slow, you don't turn away fast enough, and no matter where you hide, I can still find you."

"And I'm so glad you did."

Taking her in his arms, he brought his lips to hers. Their need for one another poured into that kiss, and fell upon it like the darkness transforms into day. She clawed at his body, long nails dragging along his forearms. The wetness of her face rested against his while they caressed one another, administering comfort during a date that was nothing like he'd planned… Before another moment could pass, he picked her up and carried her to the Jeep. Flicking on the radio, he turned on the lights and made his way back towards civilization where the plane sat parked. She never uttered another word, though she appeared fine. But he knew better.

Things had taken a turn. She trusted him. A big step for her…

As soon as they climbed aboard, the woman was sliding off her shoes, tearing at her clothing as tears swam in her eyes, streaking her flesh with mascara.

Following her lead, he removed his shirt.

"Savage…" was all she uttered, her voice trembling.

"You want me to make you feel better, baby? You know

I can. All I have to do is pull this curtain back and give you some good. Hard. Medicine. I may not have a PhD like you, baby, but I *do* have one in Pussyology." He slicked his tongue across his lower lip in anticipation as his dick got hard at the sight of her bra, now exposed for his pleasure. His mouth salivated, and he was so eager to taste her. All of her.

"I want you so badly..." The woman was on her knees on the damn floor, intense lust floating in her eyes.

His pants dropped to the floor, pooling around his ankles, and he was now completely naked. Her eyes drifted to his rigid cock and he didn't miss the way she swallowed, her lips parted and her breathing accelerated from the sight of his *own* sidewinder. "I'm going to take you out of your misery, baby. Suck and fuck you until you can't even breathe. And do you know when I'm going to do it?" He grabbed his throbbing dick with one hand, and the back of her head with the other. "Right fucking now..."

CHAPTER NINE

Fly By Night

S HE STRUGGLED SO hard with herself when the stark-naked man stood before her.

Don't do this...

But it was too late. The body wants what the body wants...

Zaire had promised herself no more secret one night stands and flings. That's right—she'd been secretly running through men like an athlete barreling for the finish line. It had been rather easy as of late, a mere game... and she didn't see them as anything more than a sexual release. She'd trained herself to not become attached and had become so good at it, she even had herself fooled.

In fact, it had been happening for years, but this took her by surprise. Savage had done the unthinkable. Made her give a damn, and so fast, too.

On the flipside, it didn't matter what she thought about the issue. The choice was made for her. No way was anything more than a 'fuck and go' with a man like Savage. He wasn't the serious type, not one to settle down; and speaking of serious, he turned grave matters into obscene jokes and quite frankly, he wasn't her type, anyway.

Now sure, physically, he *definitely* was. The man was drop dead fucking gorgeous. In fact, he was borderline pretty, but had enough ruggedness in the form of a couple scars, dense facial hair, a strong, deep voice and whatnot to crush the pretty pill from totally taking him asunder. Besides, the last thing she was going to do was compete with a man for mirror time. More importantly, he wasn't her type because there would be no putting down roots with this man. One day she imagined she'd want to do just that and he wasn't even in the running, let alone a candidate. Another con was the damn man gambled for a living.

That meant his income could be here today, gone tomorrow, and she wasn't too keen on the profession as a whole anyway, regardless of how damn good he was. Easy come, easy go—that was the extent of it. He lived hard and fast, ruling his roost like a tyrant, and seemed to be a nomad of epic proportions. Yes, he was intelligent, and a great conversationalist, too. Sure, he had charisma falling out of his ass but he was also one of the sketchiest, foulest individuals she'd ever encountered... and yet, all of this didn't dull her attraction for him, although it did keep her grounded in the reality that she was just going to screw this son of a bitch and be on her way...

I told myself I would stop this! But here I am doing it again...Here I am with all of my clothes off, without a care in the world. Look how he's looking at my titties... Good God. Okay, cut me some slack... I was vulnerable... He MADE me vulnerable! He set me up... He somehow turned the tables on me! What a weasel! How'd he know I'd love looking at the stars so much anyway? He is duplicitous! Just like he found out my hotel room… Ugh! The stars though… that's too much. I never told him that I go outside and do that at least a few times a week at home. I get my binoculars and look up at the sky. Worst of all, how'd he know that I'd break down and tell him, this damn stranger, my private business?! Who the hell is he?!

Why'd I feel so comfortable? Why does it feel like he and I have known each other for months, not just a couple days?

She swallowed as her mouth pooled with saliva in anticipation of wrapping her lips around the huge, thick dick that bobbed a mere few inches from her face. The large member was a couple shades deeper than the rest of his form, and yes, it was massive… the kind of dick she dreamed about… the kind of dick she searched for when trying to get her rocks off with her vibrator and free online porn. It was a thing of beauty… the kind of cock that would rock and knock your walls out, just how she fucking liked it.

This is your last chance Zaire, before it's too late! GET. DRESSED. NOW!

What would her audience think if they knew she was going against the very advice she doled out day after day, week after week, and month after month? Her pussy throbbed with need and her nipples hardened as she ran her fingers along them.

I am a hypocrite, just like Kim accused me of being a few months ago when she got drunk and angry with me over at Beth's party. Maybe this can be the last time I'm a hypocrite? Yes, just one more time for talking out both sides of my mouth… No… come on, Zaire. He's a player! You can reform yourself right now!

But at the sight of this man's bronze body, covered in black tattoos, muscular arms that surely must be able to wrap around and uproot an oak tree, and thighs that looked as if they could crack walnuts, all she could do was salivate, like a kitten presented with a seafood meal, and turn into a damn puddle right before his eyes. The big bastard stood there with a slick, seedy smirk on his tanned face… finishing her off, she was certain, at least in his mind…

He conquers. That's all he does. And that's all he wants to do to me, too.

He hops from woman to woman to woman like Frogger. I saw this motherfucker leave with prostitutes last night! He had three fucking prostitutes with him! Now sure, they were at least pretty, but who cares?! He does not give a shit!

He stroked his lengthy, fat dick with one hand, and casually puffed on a cigar with the other, then crushed the thing in an ashtray as the plane began to taxi. His dick swung back and forth with the movement and she became mesmerized with it, as if it was damn near hypnotizing her…

"Ahhh!" she screamed when he suddenly wrapped his hand around the back of her head and tugged on her hair, bringing her to her feet. "What are you doing?!" Her back slammed down hard onto the row of plush red seats. Placing his big hands between her legs, he opened her thighs wide, then dropped to his knees before her. His eyes glowing like fiery lanterns, he opened his mouth, and out curled two ringlets of smoke he'd trapped from his cigar. She watched them float in the air in amazement before he slid his long, fat tongue slowly up and down her slippery pussy.

"Shit!" The plane flew up into the air. Her ears popped

then cleared as she glared at the aircraft ceiling, her mind in a daze, her body giving salutations and praise.

She cooed and begged, arms stretched, holding onto a backseat tray handle with one hand and the pillow rest of another seat with the other. She pleaded and cursed as she ran deft fingers along his short black hair, slightly longer than a buzz cut with the strands both soft and prickly, pushing his face further into her sopping wet nature. His mouth made the loudest slurping noises, and he ate her like the big, bad wolf that he was...

"I've been wanting to get a taste of you since the moment I saw you, sexy. The pussy's been marinating for me, all damn day. Juicy, like a peach!" he said between licks, while devouring her whole. She shuddered when he flicked his tongue fast and ferociously against her bud, which quickly swelled and rose to the occasion. "Look who's come out to play..."

He gripped her waist and she arched her back, screaming, while he consumed her like he would a savory five-course meal. Her body flooded with euphoria. There was no denying it; the man could eat some pussy like nobody's business. He groaned as he slowly lifted away from her, then winked.

"Why'd you stop?" she practically cried, falling to pieces.

His lips and chin gleamed with her juices.

"I'm not finished."

Popping two fingers into his mouth, he gave them a hard suck before slipping them inside her.

"I... I don't like being fingered. Don't." She reached between her legs to stop him. He scooted a bit closer, swatted her away, his eyes narrowed.

"That's because you've never had Savage finger you be-fore..." He bit on his lower lip, his gaze piercing through her. Drifting his fingers in and out of her, he started a slow rhythm, but too soon, things escalated. Her body nearly jumped out of her skin when she felt the strangest sensa-tion... Gliding and moving his fingertips inside her at an even pace, he pushed upward, rubbing against her G-spot in a come hither motion.

"What are you doing? Shit!" She lunged forward and clutched his shoulder as her eyes welled and her legs shook.

"Bring that orgasm to me, baby. Come here, come here, pussy cat... Yeah, that's right... bring it on home..."

In a matter of seconds, a gush of juice flowed from her pussy like a dam ripped from the bank of a river. Trembling and calling his name, she lost control of herself as her body seized then fell apart. She collapsed into the seats, the multiple orgasms tearing her apart, each one more intense than the last.

"Oh, God!" Before she could form another thought, he slipped his tongue along the length of her dripping pussy, all the while romancing her G-spot. Then, he shifted attention to her clit, sucking it hard, then releasing... teasing her so.

Hugging her to him, he crisscrossed his strong arms around her back, bringing her flush against him. The plane ride began to get bumpy, but he somehow kept his footing and her steady, placing her against the curved wall with a small window, where they could peek into the clouds at night. The pilot could not be seen through the thick curtain he'd drawn to ensure their privacy.

"Hey, do you have enough gas for another hour?"

"Yes!" the pilot called out. "Are you requesting more time on the craft?"

"Yeah. Loop around if you can and slow down."

"Got it!"

Loop around? I'm not even supposed to be here! What the hell am I doing with my life? Is this for real? Am I for real? I am fucking this man on a little ass plane? I hate these types of planes! He shot a fucking snake in the damn head and now he's eating my pussy and giving me G-Spot orgasms and riding me around in limos with expensive wine and strawberries 'nd shit and... fuck!!!

She pressed her eyes closed as he yanked her hand and placed it around his cock...

She could feel the damn thing throbbing against her palm, as though it were a monster with its own mind and desires. The heat of his nature warmed her hand, its thickness and heaviness overwhelmingly beautiful. Running her fingertips against the satiny, veined flesh, she travelled up and down the length, pausing to stroke his soft, thick black pubic hair. Their gazes locked. The intensity in his eyes threatened to make her faint...

His body flush against hers, he kept her steady as he gently stroked her hair.

"You know I'm going to fuck the shit outta you, right?" His words made her rethink her choices, her purpose, her entire existence. He slowly let her down from the wall, then, with his finger in her face and his expression hard, he said, "You keep your sexy ass against that fucking window, ya hear me? Don't move."

Taking several steps back, he reached into a small black

bag on another row of chairs across the short aisle. Unzipping the sack, he removed a black and gold box of condoms and a bottle of lube, tossing them onto the next seat before zipping the pouch back closed. All the sounds in the place seemed to be amplified, in stereo—the sound of the zipper opening and closing, the vibration of his deep breaths. Everything radiated inside her.

She panted, listening to her exhales and inhales as she watched the big, bullish man tear one of the condom wrappers open with his teeth and sheath himself. Her breath hitched when he marched back to her and wrapped his hand around her neck. He lifted her higher, and much to her surprise, it didn't hurt.

When he released her throat, she exhaled, slow and easy.

"I like how you sound, how fast your heart is beating. That's all for me, and I love it…"

He jammed his body against hers and knocked her legs apart with a sway of his knee. She glanced down, taking note of his legs covered in hair, his chiseled chest and abs marked with copious ink detailing serpents, a large spider with glowing eyes, Greek Gods, sinister skulls, old time gangsters with machine guns, lewd naked women, tribal art and the like. When they met eyes once again, his lips were ever so slightly curled.

"You played me…" she uttered, sick of herself.

"You're a violin. You *wanted* to be played. Time to pluck 'nd fuck that first chord…"

"Shit!" She hissed when he drove his cock inside her.

"Mmmm…" His voice was so low and guttural, it vibrated through her as if he, the base in his tone, and his dick made up a freight train. "So fucking warm, baby... so tight."

Slow thumping echoed throughout the cabin as her body jeered up and down the slick, cold window, her ass exposed to the nightly clouds. Wrapping her arms around his neck to steady herself, she rocked into his demanding plunges. His dick was like a thick intruder, and it felt so good as it violated her walls...

Barely able to breathe, to talk herself into not loving the painful pleasure of his brutish delivery, she sighed when he yanked her hair and dispensed the sweetest, softest kisses to her collarbones. He trailed his lips lower and she cooed when the warmth of his mouth surrounded her right nipple, supplying heated affection and feeding her desires and needs.

"I was right. You're a fucking closet freak..." He switched breasts, licking and sucking her tender flesh just right. "You like bein' talked down to behind closed doors, verbally roughed up... then adored, wined and dined, given flowers, expensive gifts... and finally, fucked out of your gotdamn mind. I know all about your sickness, baby... the weird shit you hide from others so you can appear normal. You ain't normal. You're fucked up! Just like me!" She hissed when he slammed into her over and over, moving faster. Rougher. Her pussy cried hard onto his thrusting cock, making a wet mess of them both. Backbones pressed into the wall, bearing down, his weight nearly stealing her breath. Thoughts flashed in her head. What a strange world she'd entered.

It was *his* world. A dark, depraved and corrupt world. And she wasn't certain what to expect... which made it all the more tempting to enter if she dared.

He dragged her to face level so they were eye to eye.

"Admit it. You're hiding, baby... but the truth has been uncovered. You like mind-bending, hanging-from-the-fucking-chandelier sex. You like to whip women into shape on that damn podcast while you get pussy whipped from my big dick behind closed doors, don't you, Eva?" Her eyes narrowed upon him as she held on tighter, legs wrapped around him and her resolve threatened. "You want me to hit ya in the face with my dick, baby?" He smiled wickedly. "Pull your fucking hair, smack your ass until it's red and swollen? Play with your juicy pussy all night... and believe me, baby, I could definitely eat that fat pussy of yours all night. You want me to lick up and down the crack of your ass and make you take a pounding you'll never forget... don't you, baby?"

"Fuck. You." She smirked, refusing to give him the pleasure of an admission...

"Let me tell you what *I* want." He cocked his head to the side and slammed into her, making her scream and claw at his chest. Her eyes rolled back as he fucked her silly, slamming into her ruthlessly while rivulets of sweat dripped down his face. "I want you to ride my fuckin' face before the night is through. Let all that fuckin' pussy juice just cover me from my forehead to my chin like a damn face mask at the spa. I want to eat your fucking ass. I want to watch you choke and gag on my dick, spit running down it and balls, and your fucking mascara smeared all over! I want to fuck you until you go blind, then fuck you again so you can have 20 fuckin' 20 vision! I want every hole in your body filled with my cum, and I want you to thank me for that shit and beg for more! I'm not afraid to admit who the hell I am."

"Ahhh!" She came hard against him, but he didn't let up. Didn't slow down.

"Tell the truth, you beautiful coward! YOU WANT IT ALL AND THEN SOME!"

She beamed at his taunting words. The nasty grin on his devastatingly handsome face said it all…

A beautiful whore from Armenia and a fucking criminally minded motorcycle gang member, a legend in his own right, had created this crazy creature that stood before her, tearing her apart and enjoying every horrendous minute of it.

"You're fucking insane!" she yelled.

He laughed harshly before sliding his teeth against the side of her neck, threatening to bite. She winced when she felt the pinch of his incisors teasing her sensitive flesh.

"I *am* insane. But I know how to control it, baby…"

"And I am a bonified, incurable freak… but you can only have me for one night. You're the notch on *my* belt, not the other way around…"

He pulled away, seemingly amused, perhaps even turned on. That pissed her off. This was her last chance to make things right—to even the playing field. She could not corral him; he was completely untamable. Moving like the speed of light, he zoomed away with her and stood in the aisle, bouncing her up and down on his slick shaft, forcing every thick inch inside of her. Her head whirled. The sloshing noise of her pussy being pushed up and down his rod made her cream all the harder. She could hear everything so clearly again. The plane… their voices… their heartbeats…

"Anybody ever tell you that you kinda look like Robinee Lee?"

"I don't know who that is."

He studied her. Gripping her chin, he tugged it down, then up, his brows bunched.

"She's an actress." He released her. "Yeah... you two favor. Could easily pass for sisters. Similar bone structure, same complexion, eye shape... I've had a crush on her for a while now. I just realized the resemblance. You'll do as a fantasy come true." He winked at her then sped up his thrusts. Her jaw dropped when he went impossibly deeper with slow, long, threatening dick strokes. Reaching between their bodies, she ran her hand over her stomach, practically feeling him rearranging her guts. Like a professional thief, he stole a kiss out of nowhere... Landed it perfectly, sensually, and she melted at his touch. So soft, so erotic.

He claimed her lips in a kiss filled with need and in time with his thrusts. Swoon-worthy. Hands down, Savage was the best kisser she'd ever had. There was simply no competition. He was clearly born to do it. He kissed like he was in love, like she was the last woman in the world... no, the *only* woman in the world that he desired. Jerking her out of the sweetness of the moment, he set her down on her feet and quickly pulled out from her. She felt strangely empty. Hollow.

"Turn around, baby." Without waiting for her to comply, he gripped her shoulder and spun her in the direction of the pulled curtain. She could hear him breathing behind her, and then she realized their inhales and exhales were in sync. "Get on the floor." She threw him a glance over her shoulder and swallowed down both her hatred and lust for the fiend. Before she sorted herself out he pushed her down and lowered himself behind her, roughly shoving her arms and legs out, preparing her for his vicious cravings.

"Stop it! You're being too rough."

"You wanted a good screw, remember? No emotion. I'm a notch on your fucking belt. That's what you said, right? I am giving you what the fuck you want."

She snapped. A certain rage came over her, as if she'd been transformed into a panther out for the kill. The world was spinning as she extended her fingers to scratch and slap the shit out of him, but her entire body froze, throbbing with pain.

"Ouuuch! Ahhh!"

He'd caught her wrist hard, with the type of grip that would destroy you. His strength was like nothing she'd ever felt before—so painful, she was rendered speechless. He quickly released her and rubbed on her wrist, as if trying to massage the pain away.

"I didn't mean to hurt you. I was trying to block your blow." Annoyance flashed on his face. "STOP. FIGHTING. THIS." His tone was stern, yet even, as if he were not the least bit upset—just wanted to make himself clear.

She twisted and reached between them, grabbing his condom-covered cock. It was wet with her juices and still hard as a rock. Desire taking over, she guided him inside her engorged walls, watching as half of his shaft disappeared inside her. She closed her eyes, feeling him as he began to slowly thrust until he was once again balls deep. After a while, he increased his pace. She relished the pressure of his weight as he pressed his broad chest into her back, flattening her on the plane floor. He spread her thighs apart and just then, when he bumped his groin into her ass, making a slapping noise against her wet body, an orgasm took her by surprise. The whacking sound of his big balls hitting her swollen pussy lips overwhelmed her, and now she could hear him panting loud like a beast as he pivoted his hips, ramming her over and over, giving it to her as if she were a mere pinball machine.

His thrusts were harsh and driven as he forced her body to slide up and down the carpet.

"I'm so horny for you, baby! Shit! You drive me crazy. I can't get a fuckin' 'nough of you, Eva."

The tremor of the plane's engine went through her like an electric current. He reached in front of her and his diamond watch glistened, catching the sparse light. Interlocking their hands, he squeezed her fingers, rested his forehead against her back, and delivered the most deliciously nasty dick plunges she'd ever felt. He twisted and turned, leaned at an angle, and hit deep inside of her in just the right way, as if he knew her body inside and out.

"It feels so fucking good, baby!" she cooed, her mouth forsaking her, just as Allison and Kim had done when they'd practically thrown her at this savage wolf.

"I know it feels good to you, baby… I'm tearin' this pussy up!" She shuddered as her body went limp. He felt too good to be true. "Your pussy is drenched, all in my name. You love how I touch you, eat you, lick you, kiss you, fuck you…"

"I do!"

"Your body is too beautiful for me not to worship. Your mind too enchanting for me not to fuck. You keep cumming on my cock and guess what? I'm going to make you cum some *more*. I'm determined to make you feel like no other man has ever made you feel."

"You're so deep inside of me, baby... so deep." She shuddered as she anticipated his next thrust. He didn't seem to grow tired; he just kept going and going, placing soft, petal kisses along the curve of her spine, awakening her, ushering her into a carnal zone.

He fucks hard like a maniac... Kisses like a dream come true...

She had no idea how much time had passed but the man had the stamina of a lifetime. He was definitely holding out. That was, dare she say it, considerate of him.

Maybe he cares about how I feel? Maybe he truly does want to make this about me?

The thought hit her like a lightning bolt. Maybe she had Savage all wrong.

It wouldn't be the first time she'd misjudged someone. Perhaps it was time for a new strategy...

CHAPTER TEN

A Change of Heart

...One minute later

"SAVAGE..."

"Yeah, baby..."

She liked how he called her 'baby'.

"I want you to cum."

"I'll do whatever the fuck your body wants me to do. Wherever your pussy and ass go, I'll follow. If you want to feel me explode deep inside you, then I will do exactly that." She turned her head to look at him and he leaned over to press his lips to hers. He gently tugged at her lower one before releasing. "Turn over on your back. I want to look into your eyes when I do it. When I cum in you."

She stayed still as stone as he slid out of her. Seconds later, she was lying on her back with the beautiful beast on top of her while the plane rocked and vibrated beneath their bodies. While gliding himself within her with one hand, he smiled down at her so thoughtfully. It wasn't a cocky smile, but one that gave the impression he truly cared about her pleasure, and even her pain.

She shook the thought out her mind when he raised her arms above her head and administered slow thrusts, grinding from left to right, working himself deeper and deeper. Rising onto his palms, he monitored his movements, bumping against her clitoris in slow circular motions. She shuddered and trembled when a hard, treacherous climax took her under. His lips glided softly against hers as he waited patiently for her orgasm to plateau, then pass. She'd lost complete control. He stroked the side of her face, kissed her cheek, and nestled his head in the crook of her neck. Holding tight to him, she could barely believe what she was feeling...

He moved like he was making love. Slow, then fast... deep then shallow... perfectly delivered thrusts as if they were the last two people in the world to slow dance.

"Savage... I mean, Maximus, can I admit something to you?"

"Yeah..."

"I don't want tonight to end." She blinked back the emotions. "I like you..." She felt so weak admitting it, but she had to say it. She had to get it out.

"I like you too, baby. Eva, I like the hell outta you..." A grunt escaped his lips and his muscles locked up as he paused mid-stroke. He grasped her chin and glided the tip of his nose against hers, then kissed her with the passion of a thousand lovers. She relaxed beneath him. This felt so right, as if she was supposed to be there.

They melted together like cubes of ice and merged like

rivers and streams. Rocking her hips into his short, quickfire thrusts, the man came undone, exploding into a million savage stars—just like he said he would. He jerked against her, the warmth of his cum filling the condom as he pulsed inside her. They lay quiet for a moment, both breathing hard and heavy. After a while, he mumbled something she couldn't quite understand. He gently glided out of her and rested back on his haunches, panting, glaring down at her. He seemed to have something on his mind, but in an untypical fashion, he quickly looked away when she stared back.

He helped her to her feet, keeping oddly quiet as he tossed the condom in a small plastic sack. He then pointed to a small door behind which were a toilet and sink. Grabbing her purse and clothing, she made her way inside and closed the door behind her to freshen up a bit. She looked herself in the mirror and shook her head.

You look exactly like what happened... Like you've been fucked nearly to death.

She tried to finger-comb her now wild and crazy hair to no avail. What she'd give to have a brush with her, or anything to get it back into shape. After cleaning her tender and slightly sore pussy lips from the incredible pounding they'd received, she washed her face with a paper towel and soap, put her clothes back on, reapplied her lipstick, and slid on her shoes. When she came out of the small lavatory, Savage stood fully dressed but with his shirt hanging open, exposing his necklace and his jacket off. His sunglasses were propped atop his head. He grabbed his cellphone, appearing to be lost in thought before retreating to the restroom. Not certain what to say, she simply took her seat, feeling a strange tension. That vulnerability washed over her again. How she hated it.

No, I hate myself. This wasn't supposed to happen. I was supposed to have sex and not look back, just like all the others. See? It's happening again! Just like all of those years ago... That motherfucker! I knew better. She chided herself, crossing her legs and staring out the window into blackness. *It's all good. I knew what this was. I was just hoping that... Shit. What was I hoping? He never lied about what he was or what he wanted. But I did...*

The fact of the matter was that Zaire was tired of being alone. She didn't want that—she never had—but she hadn't met the right person. After her last failed relationship, she'd had enough, but her heart wanted to try again. She'd told it 'no.' Now here she was, thirty-seven years old with a beautiful life, pretending she was okay without a partner, someone to share all of her blessings with.

Lies. Lies. Lies.

He's not relationship and DEFINITELY not marriage material. Hell, he admitted it. It's fine. You've had your fun, Zaire... and hey, it was fun, wasn't it? He served you just how you like it...

She smiled sadly as she continued to run the gamut of her thoughts.

He's a great lover... truly one of the best. He actually was probably THE best. Gotta give credit where credit is due. I'll just get home tomorrow night as planned. No worries. I have that Women's Empowerment Conference, and that nice Purple Ladies Brunch in Colorado... Then there's the...

"Zaire."

"Huh? Oh." She smiled nervously, resting her hand on

her chest. "Yeah? I was just daydreaming. What's up?"

He sat beside her, staying quiet for far too long. He looked straight ahead, then began to do strange things with his hands. Cracking his knuckles, flexing his fingers…

"I want uh… I want you to come back to my hotel room with me when we get back to Vegas." He turned and looked at her.

It's very late! My friends will be worried. I can't go back to his room with him and honestly, I don't know if my body can take anymore. His dick game is wicked; he tore my ass up. It was good, but shit, I can barely sit down!

…Bitch, you know you want some more. Besides, it's a long ride back. By then, my pussy will be ready again. I can sleep in the limo and be ready for action.

"Well…" She glanced down at her wrist and realized she'd tossed her watch in her purse. She surmised it was at least four in the morning. She shook her head and laughed. "You know what? Yes! Why not? Fine. I would love to come and spend more time with you. When we land, let me call my friends, okay? Just so they know everything is cool."

"Yeah, yeah, of course. I was going to suggest that." He got up from his seat and made his way towards the pulled curtain. He drew it back and cinched it open. "Thanks. I appreciate the favor," he said in a low voice to the pilot before patting the man on his shoulder.

"You're welcome Mr. Savage. It's always a pleasure to see you."

A pang of jealousy rang out in Zaire at that moment and it shocked the hell out of her.

You're welcome, Mr. Savage? Who else has he brought up here and fucked? Oh, so he just goes all Evel Knievel in airplanes, fucking random women in a single bound! It's a bird, it's a plane! It's ho-ass Savage riding another bitch like a bronco! I bet he has taken hundreds of women to the desert, too! Stargazing like his name is Luke Skywalker. I wish my ass was in a galaxy far, far away! I wasn't special. Always a pleasure to see you, huh? This motherfucker right here! She crossed her arms and huffed. *He probably has a little punch card with this pilot, like the kind you get at the Subway restaurants: buy nine sandwiches, get your tenth one free. I bet I was the free one… that raggedy son of a bitch!*

Zaire, chill! This is not your man… He can do whatever he wants. Relax.

Savage returned to his seat beside her and wrapped his arm around her shoulder.

"What?" he asked after a minute or two of complete silence on her part.

"Huh?" She threw him a brief glance then turned back towards the window.

"You're stiff, and your face is all tight like you've been sucking on lemons."

"No, I'm fine. Just tired."

He nodded and removed his hand from her shoulder. They sat quietly, and she tried her best to smile, to put on her best act. She was good at pretending everything was fine. She'd been doing it since she was a little girl, just how her grandmother had taught her.

"Before we land, which will be in about seven minutes," he glanced at his watch, "I suggest you tell me what the hell is bothering you. I don't have time for a bunch of games. Spit this shit out." Now *his* body had gone all stiff, too, as he played with his smart watch.

"I had a good time tonight."

"So did I. And?"

"I feel like... I feel like I might not be the only one you've done this with and it upsets me."

"It upsets you because you like me and don't want to think that this is just my regular routine?"

"Yes, right."

"And you want to believe that with you it was different, that you were special, but you feel that feeling that way in some way makes you fragile or juvenile?"

She swallowed. "Yes."

"Okay, let's make this short 'nd sweet. I have had sex on a plane before." He stared at his watch. "Several times. Never this one, and never like this." He sat straight and turned to look her in the eye. "I have never fucked a woman against the damn window of a plane though. It never lasted this long, and yeah, that's important. I like to make women have a good time, I want anyone I fuck to cum, but with you, I *really* wanted to make sure I gave you everything you wanted... show you a good time.

"I also don't invite women back home with me, or to my hotel, or wherever I'm sleeping for the night after we fuck. I sleep alone. I prefer it that way. I am usually a 'once I get it, I'm finished' kinda guy. Period." She took a deep breath, briefly closed her eyes, and clasped her hands. "Don't trust your gut this time. It's misleading you. Okay, that's wrong; trust your gut always, don't trust your mind." He gestured to stress his point. "You're different. I told you that. My time is fuckin' valuable. I believe you are worth my time... I'm tryna get to know you better, if you'll let me. Now look." He shrugged. "I don't know what else to say to ya. We met. We ate. We had a date. We fucked. And now, I want more…"

"Okay. I think… so do I."

"If you keep on fighting me though, I'm going to get pissed off. I understood the initial hesitation, but we're adults and there comes a time when you gotta say you're in or you're out. Love is like Vegas. It's a gamble. I don't play to lose. So, either you want to see what I'm about or you don't. If not, fold."

"I do. I just…"

"You're scared."

"Yes."

"I understand that, I do… Don't get me wrong. Like many women, some guys have dogged you out. It's what we do. We're naturally inconsiderate, all right? It doesn't mean we're incapable of caring. We just have to be ready for that shit. We have to want it. I know you've heard horror stories from your friends. Your own parents' marriage was taxing and difficult. You were caught up in the middle of that. I get it. There's a bunch of mental shit going on, but if I," he said, pointing to himself, "with the fucked-up background I've had, Eva, can still have faith in myself, then I need you to have some, too. Any woman who's going to even *consider* getting to know me beyond the bedroom has got to have faith in herself, too… not the façade she shows the world. I need you to buck up and stand up to the challenge. I know who I am, and I know what the hell I want and what I can bring to the table. Now, I'm not the fall-in-love-fast type of guy. I need time… but I'm really interested in you, and that's a starting point. I've already tried to prove to you that I'm not jerking you around."

"I know... you opened up to me. You've been very forthcoming. I appreciate that." She rubbed her hand along her knee, trying to steady her nerves. He was saying what she needed to hear, no matter how rough it came out. It was there for her to latch onto and believe in.

"Yeah. I told you things... personal things. I am just cautious about who I tell my business to... my family shit. That's no one's business but mine. But you asked, so I answered. I didn't do it because I fuckin' felt like it, or because it made me feel good. I did it so you'd feel more comfortable, so you could trust me if and when we got to this point."

"I understand that. I am cautious, too."

"I know you are, so the fact you opened up like a damn clam to me should tell you something." How could she argue with that? "It wasn't because I'm so damn funny, fascinating or interesting, as you've been saying. It's because not only do we have incredible chemistry, we have a connection. I'll admit when I first met you, I just wanted sex. I hadn't spoken to you for any length of time, I didn't know you at all, but as we've talked, I found out I really like you. It's more than that now. It goes beyond sex, though the sex was fucking amazing." She smiled at his words. "Honestly, I need you to believe that I'm worth getting to know or we can part ways as soon as we get back to Vegas. Don't get me wrong, I enjoyed chasing you; it was exactly how I get my rocks off but at the end of the day, Eva, I want you to be as curious about me as I am about you.

"And I want you to admit that shit—not only to me, but to yourself. If you don't, I wish you well." He threw up his hands. "I mean that sincerely. I will kiss you goodnight and that'll be the end. After that, you'll never hear from me again. Shit." He lit a cigar and puffed away. "I'm not promised tomorrow. I realized something as you were pouring your guts out under those stars. We've got a lot in common. I realized that this time, I want somethin' different... somethin' *real* for a change. This drifting shit is getting old! I want someone waiting for me in that big fucking house of mine in California. It's my favorite place to rest my head. Seven bedrooms, three floors, gold fixtures, marble, hardwood floors, state-of-the-art everything and empty!"

He shifted suddenly in his seat, startling her as he clearly filled with emotion.

"What do you truly want, Savage?"

He hesitated for a moment. "I want... I want to smell perfume when I open my damn bedroom door, Eva. I want to see a fucking vanity covered with lipsticks, a hair brush... life in that room. I want to know that a warm ass hug is waiting for me when I walk inside, and some even warmer legs to wrap around my damn waist when I need to be deep in some soft, warm, tight pussy that belongs to a woman who calms me... is my peace. I've heard of this, but I've never had it for myself! I want a woman under that roof who I can respect, cherish and depend on. And I need her to want the same because I plan to give that to her. With this lady, I want us to complement one another and help each other and shit. We'd be best friends! I've never had that."

"Maximus, you said you didn't see yourself getting married though, so… I'm confused."

"I never told you with certainty that I'm never getting married. I told you I hadn't met a woman who made me consider it because this world is fucked up and people don't take marriage seriously anymore. It's not a game to me! To me, my parents are married. No, they didn't have the piece of paper like yours did, but they showed they were married by being there for one another, through thick and thin. My mother didn't leave my father when he got locked up for the hundredth time. My father didn't leave my mother because she was selling herself. I had no idea they weren't legally married until I was like fourteen years old! I just assumed they were. Look, I'm almost forty fuckin' years old, Eva, and I've never had any security, no roots. Nobody to go home to! It hurts!!!" His voice vibrated with emotion. It startled her, in a good way, for it seemed to come out of nowhere. "It was my choice… but now, I've made a *new* choice. And it's because of *you*."

She took his hand and squeezed it, then rested her head on his shoulder.

"I don't know where this will lead. We could end up just being friends or never speaking again after you leave, but I don't want to take the chance of not trying to find out. You've opened the door at least for me even considering this. That says a lot about you as a woman."

"Thank you for telling me what I needed to hear, Savage."

"I didn't tell you what you needed to hear. You're too smart for that. Instead, I told you the truth. They aren't always one and the same."

He squeezed her hand and lay back in his seat. Before she knew it, she'd fallen asleep. She recalled waking up here and there, but going right back into a deep slumber.

When she awoke, she was lying in bed, naked, inside of one of the most lavish hotel bedrooms she'd ever seen. She looked about, taking note of the plush, soft, white sheets, the gold crown molding, a buffet table covered with assorted fruits and flowers, and a large television mounted on the wall. Beautiful artwork hung from the walls and there were several bay windows with heavy cream drapes, as well as a fireplace. Just as her mood lifted, her heart suddenly sank, just that fast. Savage was nowhere to be found.

Did he just put me here and go on somewhere else? I wonder if he's gone…

Before she could call out after him, the man entered the bedroom sporting a white silk robe, tied at the waist. She smiled as she pulled the sheets up around herself and watched him go around the side of the bed, a smirk on his face, and slide under the sheets. He nestled close right beside her.

"Sleeping Beauty is finally awake." He leaned to her and gave her a peck.

"I can't believe I slept the whole way back here!"

"I can. I wore your ass out." She grimaced at his arrogance then burst out laughing. "You woke up a couple of times in the limo but you were out of it, delirious… You say some really silly shit when you're sleepy."

"Oh, no…" She giggled. "Yeah, I've been told."

"Hey baby, I hope you don't mind but I used your thumb to open your phone up. I texted Allison and Kim and let them know that you fell asleep on the way back. I gave them the room number we're in and everything and told them their breakfast was on me, as well as anything else they wanted to do while here." He kissed her cheek, then brushed her hair back away from her face.

"No, I don't mind. If you hadn't, they may have called the police and I'm serious. They know I am fairly good about letting them know my whereabouts when I'm on dates."

"Yeah, I, uh, let 'em know you'd be a little busy today though…" She snickered. Sliding over on top of her, he cradled her in his arms. "Indisposed for the rest of the trip…"

Suddenly, he disappeared under the sheets…

"Savage… Savage?"

Seconds later, she gripped her pillow like a lifeline. Back arched, she whimpered and sighed as he opened her pussy like rose petals with a slide of his tongue.

"Time to eat." His voice vibrated against her pussy. "You're my favorite breakfast, lunch, snack, dinner and dessert. I need to put this pussy in Tupperware for the entire week, save you for later, meal-prep your ass. Your pussy is life. Your pussy is Keto…" She burst out laughing as he made love to her, and it felt oh so right…

CHAPTER ELEVEN

Beg, Borrow or Steal

S AVAGE STOOD ON the huge hotel room balcony, staring out into the distance. The city was alive with the first signs of grinding, hustle and bustle. Sunday mornings tended to be a tad bit quieter than other days in the week since visitors, tourists, and the nine-to-fivers prepared to make their retreat. Meanwhile, the locals relaxed before their work weeks went into full swing—of course, if they didn't work at one of the 104 casinos in Las Vegas. He leaned onto the railing and crossed his ankles, taking a deep breath then exhaling. He took the time to enjoy one of his cigars, sunglasses on even though the daylight wasn't that bright yet. He turned around and looked inside the hotel room, past the blowing sheer curtains that were partially pulled to the side, and noted a hazy, soft image of a sleeping woman…

One long mahogany leg was exposed beneath the white sheets, perfect toes painted bright bronze. Her head turned slightly to the side, eyes closed, she appeared to be in the deepest, most restful slumber. He took another drag of his cigar and blew out smoke from the corner of his mouth. His dick twitched as he took in her image. With one hand, he worked the zipper of his black jeans open and began to stroke his cock as he surveyed his prey…

Long hair framed her in thick, voluminous spirals, tresses scattered all around the pillow and sheets like swirling black smoke in pretty patterns. Such a beautiful contrast. His breath hitched as his excitement increased by the millisecond. He stroked his cock, accelerating his pace, but then thought better of it and stopped pleasing himself before he reached the finish line.

I'll save this for her for when she wakes up. I've got some pent-up energy to expel…

He'd taken a shower and dressed, and she'd slept through it all. The whole time, he kept his eye on her, but Zaire hadn't budged. Their non-stop romping from their time on the plane until a couple of hours ago must have worn her out. Nevertheless, he appreciated her vigor and energy, her attempts to keep up with his manic, insatiable sexual appetite and stay afloat. She'd begged him for rest and he'd begrudgingly granted her wish. Smiling at the recent memory, he pulled his cellphone out of his pocket, taking note he'd missed several calls from unavailable numbers. He hadn't wanted his time with her interrupted.

Savage sat down on a white iron chair on the balcony, propped his bare feet up on the railing, and crossed his ankles, getting comfortable so he could read through several files he'd saved in his specially created dark web email account accessed by TOR and his Orbot account.

D. Miguel. 1.0 – 652 Sector – 64123

A. Smith. 2.6 – 48671 Mt. Freesia – 37012

He had several hits piling up. Kansas City, Tennessee, and more... The names and locations were typed in code, but he knew how to decipher the info. Rubbing his hands together, he stood back up and took in the scenery.

I love it out here, but shit, I'm ready to get back to California. I guess I should've called Mom while here... Nah, I'll just call her later.

It's my luck that Zaire lives there in California, too. Maybe that means something?

Suddenly, his cellphone buzzed. He picked it up and read the text message that had just come through.

Harlem: *Savage, you've got clearance to leave tonight at 8:30 P.M. Your house in California has been cleaned but is still under surveillance by us for the next 48 hours.*

Savage: *Thank You.*

He placed his phone down on a small nearby table. Becoming antsy, he approached Zaire to wake her up so he could drown in her pussy, but he paused when he heard some noise from below. Leaning over the railing, he looked across the street, narrowing his eyes.

A woman was screaming on the street and a small crowd was gathering around her. Interest sparked, he quickly made his way back inside the hotel room, grabbed his binoculars, and returned to the balcony.

What the hell is going on here?

He focused on a man dressed in dark clothing fleeing the scene with what appeared to be a purse in his hand. He returned his attention to the woman and zoomed in.

Shit. I know her. That's Cindy, one of the bartenders in the Black-jack room. Sweet girl. He's on foot. By the time the cops get wind of the incident, he'll be long gone, especially if he knows his way around here. Damn.

Savage's lips curled in a smile and in less than a minute, his shoes and jacket were on. He jammed his gun in his coat pocket, his hotel key and wallet in a front pocket, and headed out the door. Phone in hand, he sent a text message to Zaire using the diction feature.

> *Hello, Sleeping Beauty. Just running a quick errand. I'll be back soon, baby.*
>
> *Order yourself something to eat. Charge it to my room.*
>
> *You'll need the fuel. Be ready to be ripped to pieces when I return.*

Sliding the phone back in his pocket, he bypassed the elevator and raced down the stairs, moving as fast as his damn feet would carry him. Once he got to the front lobby, practically dripping with sweat, he slapped the desk hard, startling the people in line checking in and out.

"I need my motorcycle." He slid his sunglasses on from atop his head and glared at the woman standing behind the counter in her cute little uniform, seemingly lost in thought. "NOW, PRINCESS."

"I'll take care of this, Sarah." The hotel front desk manager, a thin, younger man with a slightly receding hairline, came forward. "Hello, Mr. Savage."

"Hi, Seth."

"We'll make sure it is pulled out in front of the hotel within ten minutes."

"I don't have time for that. Where is it parked?" The manager began to type into the computer while a guy wearing a Hawaiian print shirt bristled up, spouting off at the mouth.

"Awww, for cryin' out loud. Come on! We were here first! This Dwayne 'The Rock' Johnson' wannabe busts in the line like he's the gotdamn President of the United States and demands for someone to bring his big wheel around front. Brat! Get in tha back of the line like the rest of us."

"Be quiet." Savage tossed him a cautionary glance then turned back towards the manager.

"Make me, you son of a bitch!" Red in the face, the squatty buffoon marched over to him, his arms like huge sausages and jammed his short, stubby finger in his face. Savage casually removed his sunglasses from his face and smiled.

BAM!

AHHHHH! People yelled, some screamed and scurried, others cursed, backing up as Savage headbutted the man one good time, knocking the idiot out cold. Someone dropped down to their knees, gently slapping the guy's face, trying to wake him.

"Hey! Hey! Are you okay?!" the guy said, shaking the slumbering bastard to no avail.

"It's parked on C73." The manager swallowed, his complexion growing ashen.

"Thank you." Savage snatched the keys from the manager's grasp, stepped over the poor sap who'd tried him and lost, made his way to the parking lot, slipped on a pair of black leather gloves, and within minutes, was riding down South Las Vegas Blvd.

Once outside the main lobby hotel doors, he looked from left and right, his adrenaline pumping, in desperate need of a damn good bloody time.

"All that wasted time! He could be anywhere by now!" He zoomed about, in between cars, revving his engine, bullying people out of his way. Finally, he spotted an older black car speeding through a red light and people yelling and pointing at it.

Jackpot!

He got on its tail. *I bet that's you… that's the direction you were running and people are on their fucking phones, pointing and yelling. Must've jumped in a car to take off with your loot. Son of a bitch. Nobody robs Cindy in front of me. She's too important. Do ya know why? She doesn't water down my fucking drinks!*

He revved his motorcycle and soon neared the car as they approached another light. Tilting from side to side, he saw a purse strap lying on the passenger seat.

I doubt that belongs to you, ya fuckin' piece of shit! How about a little mood music to send off your little ass in style?

Savage turned on his stereo and the notes of 'Kashmir', by Led Zeppelin, blasted through the state-of-the-art speakers on his candy apple red and midnight black Harley with a huge chrome skull and orange flames on the front. The traffic began to move again. He turned his music up as loud as possible and got on the side of the car. It didn't take long for the driver, a scruffy looking tweaker, to notice him. Savage grinned at the guy and waved.

"Cool purse! Real leather, huh? Niiice!" He showed all his teeth, pointing to the damn thing lying there.

"Fuck off!"

Savage opened his jacket ever so slightly, exposing Mr. Chopper.

The man's eyes bucked in horror. He shifted in his seat and attempted to switch lanes and make a clean escape, to no avail. Savage grabbed a switchblade from his back pocket and waited until they were past the surveillance cameras he knew were present in that area. The guy went in the opposite direction of traffic, causing an explosion of frantic honking and swerving cars. A couple even crashed into each other. Savage stayed hot on his trail, but leaving a slight gap, blending back into traffic. With a steady hand, he tossed his blade at the rear driver's side tire, slid out his gun with the silencer already attached then aimed it towards the back window and shot, shattering the glass.

Within seconds he was back in the far-right lane, his speed normal. He counted in his head, timing it just right.

10. He's not gonna make that turn...

9.

8. Oops! Ya side swiped someone, buddy ol' pal...

7. Ahhh, ya got back control of the wheel but I'm certain you're losing a shitload of blood by now...

6. That tire is losing air and fast...

5.

4. Watch out up ahead...

3.

2.

1.

BOOM!

The car veered back and forth in traffic, zigzagging and fishtailing until the guy ran into a telephone pole at full speed. The sound was so loud it seemed to ripple the airwaves with a cosmic explosion. The splitting of metal was music to Savage's ears as the damn car ripped open like a sardine can on the passenger's side. The front was squashed on contact, resembling an old accordion that had seen better days.

There ya go, sport. Fuck me? Huh? Nah... fuck you, motherfuck-er. This is MY town. The police will be here soon. They'll get Cindy's purse back to 'er and after you're sent to the hospital instead of the morgue because I decided to be benevolent and shoot ya in the shoulder instead of the back of your empty fuckin' head, you can reflect on all of this shit. I guess I'm feeling a little nicer today after getting some magnificent pussy. You got lucky...

Savage glanced at his watch, then quickly turned around, his rear wheel skidding as he raced away, going back in the direction from which he'd come.

The sirens of police cars and an ambulance could be heard through the honking of cars and screams. The ruckus got fainter as he headed to the hotel. The moment he walked off the stairway from the garage and arrived inside the lobby, his cellphone buzzed.

"Did you do this shit, Savage?!"

"Yup." He got ready to disconnect before the officer yelled into the phone.

"For God's sake! You can't roll up on people in the middle of the afternoon and shoot them in the gotdamn shoulder! I *knew* this was your handiwork! You did something similar two years ago!"

"How'd jah know it was me? Did the 'I don't give a fuck' knife in the tire tip you off?" Savage taunted, a big grin on his face.

"Why do you do this crap?"

Savage shrugged and laughed, while the man sounded downright exhausted.

"What's the problem? You fuckers would've let him get away. You're too slow and someone stealing a purse with probably no more than twenty dollars in it is not exactly at the top of your priorities. Just be happy I didn't leave my calling card. You should be thanking me. I can count on one hand how many times I've let someone live. The coroner would've been called, but where's your gratitude?" He walked briskly, eager to get back to his sleeping beauty.

"We've told you about this sort of shit before, Savage! Let us do our jobs! Do I need to call the governor about you again?"

"First of all, fuck the governor *and* you too, if you decide to go 'nd snitch, especially with the info I have on you and your little pals. Two can play that pussy ass tattletale lame game. And as far as doing your job, I *did* let you. You're doing it now, right?" He made his way to the elevator, then slowed when he spotted Zaire's friend Kim sitting at the bar, her back hunched over, staring down into a glass of something that made promises swimming in watery lies. "Hey, make sure that lady gets her purse back. Her name is Cindy Perkins."

"We already contacted her. She's meeting us at the precinct. Wait a minute! How'd you know that? Never mind! Look, Savage, can you at least save me some paperwork and tell me what gun you used?! Don't make us run the damn tests. We have to process this shit. Save the taxpayers some money this time, okay?"

"What did I use? Your mama."

He was met with a frustrated huff.

"You're a real asshole."

"All right." He cleared his throat. "I feel in a generous mood. Beretta M9A3. It's slated for destruction. You're welcome." He disconnected the call and headed into the dimly lit bar.

Sliding on a stool next to the attractive woman, he tapped his fingers against the bar. She didn't seem to notice as she stayed focused on her drink, as if a little television show was playing in the glass that only she could see. A bartender approached, looking sharp in his black jacket and crisp white shirt.

"What can I get for you, boss?"

"Just some water. I'm playing it cool right now." The bartender headed back to the other side of the long counter.

Just then, Kim looked up from her drink and finally noticed him. Her mouth split in a grin.

"I know you." She shook her finger in his direction. "Lavish!"

"Savage... it's Savage." He gave her a gentle pat on the back. "I like Lavish though, too." He grinned. "Thank you." The bartender handed him a tall glass of water, chock full of ice.

"Yes, that's right. Sorry..."

The woman wasn't fully drunk, but definitely tipsy.

"That's all right. No harm, no foul." Running his hand over his beard, he stopped himself from saying the first things that popped into his head. "So, uh, what are you doing here so early? Why aren't you taking in the sights, playing the slots, or shopping before you have to head back to California?"

"I just wanted to sit here and think." She looked away, tucked her long, poker straight black hair behind one ear and stared into her glass once more. "This is gin. I'm trying to get shit-faced."

"Hmm, I see..." He glanced up at the television where they were running live coverage of the 'little tweaker misfortune' that had taken place earlier. They showed the area, now swarming with cops, and closeups of the fucker being taken out of the car, his bloodied body placed on a gurney and his eyes wild and crazy as he mumbled incoherently.

"You know, Allison and I were surprised that Zaire went out with you."

"Shit, me too."

She chuckled at that.

"I'm glad she did though. She's been under a lot of stress lately. You seem like a lot of fun." The woman circled her glass with her fingertip, smiled at him sadly, then looked back down at the drink. "Allison likes you too, says you're funny and nice looking. And rich. She stressed the rich part."

He laughed at that and glanced around at the almost empty bar, then took a sip of his water.

"Yeah? Allison is funny, too. I'm glad she's been having a

good time while here. It's always nice to get away every now and again, meet new people." She nodded in agreement. "So, what about you? Are you having fun?" The woman smirked but remained quiet. "You're just going to keep sitting here alone?"

"I won't be solo for long. Allison will be here in a bit." She yawned. "She had to make a phone call and then wanted to play a bit of Pokeno."

"Pokeno? I never took her as a Pokeno player. That's pretty funny, actually."

"Yeah, she loves it. Uh, I actually had a great time and I'm sad to see it end." She tapped her glass with her nails. "Usually though, the three of us come here and do everything together but it seems that Zaire took a detour. A much *needed* detour, I understand…" Her eyes hooded then she burst out laughing.

"Is that what they call it now? Detours? These kids nowadays and this slang," he teased.

"It's great here… a playground. It wasn't enough time though." She sighed. "But we'll be back. I was able to stretch a bit, you know, relax."

"Good. Zaire stated you were in real estate I believe, right?" He readjusted his watch. "She said you were high in the food chain. Celebrity properties. I bet that can be pretty stressful in Southern Cali. Los Angeles, that is."

"Yes, so true. I love it but yes, it keeps me *really* busy!"

"That means you're successful at it and good at what you do. Nobody stays busy in real estate unless they're kickin' ass."

"So they say!" She winked before taking another sip of

her drink.

Savage got to his feet.

"Well, I'm about to go back to my room but just in case I don't see you again, it was really nice meeting you, Kim." He extended his hand for a shake.

"It was nice meeting you, too, Savage." He noticed her hand trembled ever so slightly as she grasped his palm.

"My first name is Maximus. Some people call me Max." He wrapped his other hand around her fingers, sandwiching her hand between his. The woman was filled with what felt like worry, anxiety. It seemed that Zaire and her two closest girlfriends were all going through something, in one way or another. Such was life.

"Maximus... very nice name."

"Thanks. Goodbye, Kim." He slowly released his grasp and turned to leave. When he took a few steps, she called out to him.

"Mad Max!"

"Yeah." He turned back in her direction, amused by her choice of words. "What's up?"

"I wasn't going to say anything... and it's really not my place... but... don't... don't hurt her, okay?" He cocked his head to the side, feeling a bit confused. "I know Zaire can take a lot and she is the bounce-back queen, so to speak." She dramatically rolled her eyes. "She and I have that in common, but that doesn't give anyone the right to see just how elastic she can be. Look, I can tell she really likes you. I spoke to her briefly a little while ago. Don't say anything about it." Her brows bunched. "And if this is just a fling, that's fine, as long you both feel the same way. But I didn't get that impression."

"Just say what you need to say, Kim. No need to pussy-foot around this shit. What is it you *really* want me to know?"

The woman visibly swallowed and regarded him sternly.

"If you don't want anything more than sex with her, just let her know, okay? I know you two just met, and you're probably scared out of your mind thinking, 'Damn! Her friend is pressuring me now and I just met the lady!' But you have to understand... I don't want to see her screwed over again, Savage. The last time was rough."

The woman slid off the bar stool and disappeared towards the ladies' room, leaving him there, in wonderment. He cracked his knuckles then made his way to the elevator. As he rode up to his floor, he thought about Kim's words.

The gorgeous Hispanic woman spoke with authority, compassion, and empathy for a woman she obviously cared a great deal for. He was happy that Zaire had people around her who cared and loved her so. When the elevator doors opened, he marched down the hall towards his private suite. He hesitated at the door when he heard music playing. It sounded like Herb Alpert's 'Rise.' His lips kinked in a smile as he slid out his hotel door key and prepared to enter. Once it clicked, he opened it and saw the woman swaying back and forth, butt naked as the day she was born, snapping her fingers to the music, her back to him... oblivious of his presence.

Nope. I don't want just a fuck or a fling, Kim. There's a lot to unwrap with Zaire. I know that. She's fucking beautiful. She's complicated. Too smart for her own good. She has so many layers... But that makes her all the more intriguing. I need someone who can understand what the hell I do, what my life is about and be by my side, not in my fucking way. She's half way there… The secret? She covertly likes bad boys. Well, guess what? The Devil knows me by name. She's fucking with the king of the soulless… If she can make me give a fuck, she wins. Let's play a game, and this time, it ain't Blackjack…

CHAPTER TWELVE

Kill Two Lovebirds with One Stone...

WHEN HE WALKED past her and pulled the thick curtains closed with a brutal tug, she wasn't certain what to expect. Something in the way he moved gave her pause. He appeared harder, angrier, more aggressive...

Zaire slowed down, then stopped dancing altogether when he glared at a plant in the corner of the room for a spell, turned the music off, snatching the knob on the stereo as if it had in some way offended him. She stood in a semi-dark room while shadows and light played tricks with her mind. Suddenly, 'White Room' by Cream blasted through the speakers and the lights started to flash around the ceiling as if she'd been transported to a disco. The room grew darker then turned blood red, a pulsing sound and feeling taking over. She felt as if she were spinning, disoriented, caught up in a strange rapture—the love child of a heartbeat and a snare drum...

The sound of something heavy and hard hit wood... perhaps a bag striking a table. She heard a zipper... stomping... Then, his big, rough hands cupped her breasts from behind, and she quivered. The slight tickle of his pubic hair rubbed against her lower back; the hardness of his dick and chest brushed against her while the feel of the gold chain gave her an icy chill.

Warm breath along her earlobe…

He breathed heavy.

In… out…

In… out…

The prickly stubble on his chin made her more aware of his masculine presence, while the strong yet pleasant scent of his cologne sent her somewhere carnal and prohibited. She sighed when he stroked her nipples, lulling her to a state of pleasure and peace, and she rested the back of her head against his shoulder. Every cell of her body awoke at his command, her breasts responding instantly to his ministrations, becoming taut and hard against his touch. Pulling and pinching them as he grinded slow and easy against her backside, he revved her engine, made the kitty cat purr.

She shuddered at the sudden sound of a wrapper splitting open, stealing her out of her lullaby. He pulled away ever so slightly and she could soon feel the head of his dick bump against the crack of her ass. Hands wrapped around her hips; he made her lean forward as if preparing for a good frisk, forcing her to rest her hands on a desk in front of her.

"Shit, shit, shit!"

'Somebody to Love' by Jefferson Airplane now emitted from the speakers, setting the mood as he roughly shoved himself inside her from behind and thrust hard and fast, making everything on that damn desk shake. The smacking of his balls beating her pussy rang in her ears.

"I'm going to make you lose any inhibitions you may have in that head of yours. I'm going to have you doing shit you never imagined!" He rammed his cock deep inside, his fingers pressing into her flesh, so much she was certain she'd be bruised once he turned her loose. Her pussy poured libations, loving the way he handled her and set her on a path of sexual destruction.

Her legs shook when he reached around and stroked her clit, his fingers alternating pressure between soft and rough. "Cum on my dick... cum on it, damn it! Fuck me back! Juicy..." His deep voice echoed and although she started to speak, no sound came out her mouth. She clawed at the desk, her nails scratching the wood as the rain drizzled down from the gaping hole between her legs, stuffed with his pumping, hungry dick, and glazed her inner thighs in hurried trickles of delight.

"Shit!" She hissed between clenched teeth. The maniac yanked her arm, turning her around and making her face him. "Fuck!"

He picked her up with the greatest of ease, forcing her down on his shaft. That all too familiar cocktail of pain and pleasure from his girth and movements made her want to cry in ecstasy. Wrapping her arms around him, wrists criss-crossed behind his neck, she hung like jewelry against him as he marched her across the room. She blinked and turned away when he pulled the curtains open, exposing the back of her to blinding sunlight.

"Now the whole world can see you getting fucked! You like that, huh?!" His eyes grew dark as he jockeyed her hard and fast on his cock, his pace never ceasing.

They were on the 21st floor. She knew any visibility of their illicit affair would be hard to see but then her sensibilities were shattered when he leaned in close, as if reading her mind.

"Binoculars…"

She hated how she grew so much more turned on the worse, nastier and meaner he became. The heat of his mouth latched on to her breasts, his soft, full lips encircling her areolas and making her coo. Burying his head between them, he feverishly sucked and licked her nipples like a madman. She contorted against him as he grunted loudly, the sounds animalistic… a feral brute moving his sword within her, twisting and turning it. His eyes welled with layers of lust and hidden, horrible things cloaked in the blackness of immortality, mysteries she'd yet to uncover. She could feel it all— the coldness of his soul blending with her warmth, the lost little boy within stealing bits of her…

He's two different people trapped in one body… a modern day Dr. Jekyll and Mr. Hyde…

She'd observed him in the short time she'd known him. He'd be beautifully courteous to staff at the hotel, opening doors for older blue-haired ladies, and being a complete gentleman to tourists taking in the sights. But then, sometimes, he'd get reserved, standing off to the side, cigar in hand. He'd sport a crooked smile on his ruggedly handsome face and a darkness would come over his eyes, turning that smile sinister. Downright wicked.

"Always be prepared for the unexpected. Like meeting a motherfucker like me," he whispered in her ear.

She craved his blackness like blazing gold, shimmery silk,

and divine diamonds. He was an incredible heathen, a source of indignity and yearning. Dragging her nails up and down his back with vigor, she fancied feeling his flesh tearing beneath her rush of violence as she met his intense thrusts. She squelched a scream by biting on her lower lip. Sliding his finger in her ass, he rotated it, keeping an even rhythm. Then he thrust his cock slower, but harder and deeper, inside her dripping pussy.

She hated how her voice broke and poured out. Choppy, short… truncated at the root, then amped and loud, desperate… Shuddering against him, she turned into a geyser, the crack of her ass slick and wet as her pussy poured and leaked all over the place. He'd made a fool of her.

"I'm in deep trouble," she murmured, not sure he'd heard her.

"Yeah, you are, but lucky for you, I invented trouble, so I control it…"

In a matter of seconds, she found herself screaming when he flung her on the bed like a suitcase prepared to be packed. He disappeared into the bathroom, returning moments later, the condom off and his bare dick slinging from side to side.

She scooted back on the mattress and he got on top of her, hovering above her, his monstrous cock in hand.

"Open your damn mouth. Suck my dick, and you better suck it right."

She opened her mouth, her heart racing as he jammed his cock closer, bumping the heavy head against her lower lip. He grasped the back of her head, then took a fistful of her hair and drove his fat dick inside her mouth, plunging in short, fast jabs.

"Mmmm!" She moaned, bucking and losing control, stroking her pussy while he fucked her mouth with ruthless abandon. Slurping the muscle that pumped between her lips, she was eager for more of him, thirsting for his special delivery. She rose up on her elbow. Wrapping her hand around his dick, she forced her mouth down on him and back, slurping, licking and sliding up and down it. The wetness of her working mouth against his cock created a loud sound, competing with the blaring music. He groaned, deep and guttural as she fed herself from the bounty between his legs, taking him all down nice and easy. Saliva and pre-cum dripped down her chin, and she was unable to stop herself from devouring him whole. Strawberry Alarm Clock's, 'Incense and Peppermints' played as she came, and came hard.

I've never cum from sucking someone's dick!

Eyes pressed closed, he slipped out of her mouth and gently took her into his arms, cradling her as she vibrated, then went limp. He then shifted his body to rest on his back, one leg propped up and arm behind his head, as she finished the job…

Lying between his legs, she slowly licked up and down his shaft. His eyes hooded, looking much like two long dashes in a sentence… His thick black eyebrows bunched and his long, dark eyelashes fluttered as he made jerky motions. Rising up, he grabbed her head and delivered short, fast jabs again, soon gushing in her mouth. She shuddered when she glimpsed the handle of a gun inside the pillow case, but she kept right on, pleasuring him, giving them both what they so desperately needed. Moaning and groaning, he rotated his hips back and forth, his muscles contorting. He smiled ever so slightly at her as she swallowed his essence, wiping her chin with the back of her hand.

"Let's fuck some more in the shower." Taking her by the hand, he led her into the big, gorgeous gold, gray, and white bathroom. He soon had the water on, giving it a second or two to get hot. She waited while the man meticulously studied various shower gels and shampoos. "Which shower gel do you want? They got some shit called Coconut Hibiscus, and, uh, what's this?" He peered closer at the bottle. "Lavender Fields… some relaxing shit like that."

She squelched a giggle and pointed to the lavender fields bottle. They both got inside the glass shower enclosure, him standing behind her like a protective wall.

How can I feel so safe yet so in danger with him at the same time? My nerves are a damn wreck…

Deep Purple's 'Hush' played through the bathroom all-around speakers.

"So, I see this is all older music. You like sixties music, Maximus? You're an old soul." She lathered up her hands, facing the shower as it beat against her breasts.

"I like all types of music, but yeah, love a lot of classics from the sixties, and some from the early seventies, too. I wasn't even born yet, but those tunes resonate with me. My father used to blast this shit all damn day. He and his friends." His fingers raked gently through her hair, and a soft, cared-for feeling rushed over her, filling her with warmth from the inside out. The big motherfucker who fucked like an enraged monster, talked like a king, and laughed like a hyena was actually washing her hair. He was careful, slow, perfect…

He started to massage her scalp.

"Close your eyes, baby… Don't want it to sting."

When he was done, he grabbed the shower nozzle above them and rinsed her hair out. She then heard what sounded like him rubbing lotion between his palms. He began to separate the strands of her hair with his fingers and apply the substance.

"What are you doing?"

"Conditioning your hair." She smiled and shook her head, accepting this most unorthodox pampering. 'You Keep Me Hangin' On' by Vanilla Fudge started to play in that moment. He pulled away from her, then, in a deep voice full of rusty bike parts, cool dusky days, and the rays of an angry, heated dawn, he said, "Gotta let that set for a minute, so while we wait, I'm going to eat your fat pussy. Spread your legs."

Before she could form a thought, he moved her a bit to the side and dropped to his knees before her, looking up at her as though she were his personal Goddess. She shivered from the intensity in his eyes as he affectionately stroked her legs. The water rained down on his short dark hair, making it look blacker than black. Slicking a few of the slightly longer strands in the front away from his face, he pierced her with a blazing gaze and flicked his long tongue outward, stroking it in a feathery motion against her clit… torturing her. Water webbed in his lashes as he kept his eye on her, his hands cupping her ass and coaxing her closer to him.

"I just love the way your pussy looks and tastes… Brown and pink folds, like Neapolitan ice cream… One day, when I cum in you, my cream will be the vanilla. You taste like peaches and sea salt... sweet and briny... that's what you taste like. It's fuckin' beautiful."

He curled his tongue, jetting it into her slit, lapping her juices rinsed quickly away by the flowing water. Running her fingers over his soft, short hair, she closed her eyes and relished the way he was making her body feel. From the bottoms of her feet, to the top of her head, her nerve endings sang... Her clit throbbed as he flicked and sucked. The look in his eyes said, 'I want to please you.'

Shuddering against him, she crashed into the wall before her, keeping herself steady with one hand against the cold, wet tiles. Crying out, she came hard. He held her to him, still delivering tongue tricks and licks until she was spent, barely able to breathe. She didn't know when he got to his feet, but he was there...

He rinsed her hair with the same gentle handling as before, his touch so intoxicating and kind. Once he was finished, he inched the clear shower door open and grabbed a fresh condom wrapper from the double sink vanity surface.

"Watch me get ready to fuck you..." He rested his back against the shower wall and pulled the rubber down onto his erect cock. "I'm going to slide in you, nice 'nd slow."

He picked her up, positioning her just right as she wrapped her legs around him. He pressed the wide head into her, slightly in then out, over and over, driving her crazy for he went so slow, dragging it out...

"Come on, Savage! Let me feel you," she begged, wanting to feel that beautiful stretch she now craved and loved. He put a bit more of himself inside, and then a little more until he was completely within her sugar walls. Holding onto her back, he moved at a snail's pace, passion in his eyes. He reached up and removed the shower nozzle once again, this time letting it run down between their bumping bodies. He positioned it just so, and she felt the rushing waters massaging her pussy.

"As I fuck you, jam my dick in and out of your warm hot pocket, the water is licking your clit... and I know you like it. Tell me how much you like it..."

"I love it... feels soooo good." Her head lulling back, she batted her eyes and everything became blurry and soft.

"I'm gonna make you cum again, baby... I love making you cum because see, each time you do, it makes you all the more addicted to me. I want you strung the fuck out." He jammed hard and fast inside her, then quickly covered her mouth with his palm, crushing her screams.

"Fuck!" She broke free, the feeling so damn good, loving every broken-souled minute of it.

He grunted loud, his chest heaving, his lips twisted and his brows bunched. Each thrust was rougher than the last. He slammed so hard inside her, he stole her next breath, and the one after that. He pressed her against the wall, and the water rushed over his back and sprinkled her face as he drove himself in jerky, tight jabs, filling the condom with his hot load. His heartbeat competed with her own... both racing away like wild horses. They held onto one another, looking into each other's eyes. She held him close as she kissed him with all she had in her.

"Trust me," he whispered.

What that meant, she had no idea, but she could tell he

needed to say it.

After they dried off, she dressed in one of his T-shirts and he slid on a pair of boxers. The music was still playing, this time 'I'd Love to Change the World' by Ten Years After. The tune made her feel as if she were inside of a time machine, a bubble in life's mystic past. Her body spent, deliciously tortured and captivated by his touch, she felt chills run down her spine from merely looking at him.

Nothing about this could be good for her. But what could she do? He was in her system like a lovely virus. The compulsion was taking effect…

She stood there in that T-shirt, watching him slowly dress. Dread filled her. All good things had to come to an end, but she kept her composure as she sat upon the bed, crossing her leg beneath her. With his back towards her, he slid on his watch.

"Make sure you call me when you get back home." She couldn't respond just yet as she rocked her other leg back and forth. He paused and stared at her through a mirror on a wall, appearing a bit vexed. "Did you hear me, Eva?"

"Yes."

"I'm going to see you when I get back there, too. Seems we live only about forty or so minutes away from one another. I checked. That's good." She swallowed and nodded, feeling confusion and sadness in the worst way. "I have some business to attend to first though, so you may not hear from me for a few days." His jaw tightened for a spell as he reached for his pants and slid them on. He was putting on a gorgeous black suit, as if he was headed to a meeting with some big wigs. She stood when he grabbed his tie, and went to help slide the smooth red fabric around his neck and start the knot. He gently pushed her damp hair out of her face and smiled ever so slightly. She did her best to ignore the incessant throbbing between her thighs... the hardness of her nipples and the hunger within her... Not for food, but for more of *him*.

She gritted her teeth as her hands trembled. Making a loop, fingers stiff, she tightened it some, and then a bit more. He grasped her hands, kissed her knuckles, and winked before turning away, finishing it himself. She stepped back, her body fueled with a sense of betrayal, but he grabbed her arm and kept her close.

"What? I better get going, Savage. I'm just going to call Allison and Kim and have one of them go into my room for me and bring me a change of clothes. Allison has my spare room key," she said in a rambling tone, her brain in a fog of melancholy and missing him already. She tried to turn her mush into magic, her mess into a miracle, but her mind made a fool of her.

"You're not going anywhere until you give me a kiss."

Smiling, she yo-yoed back into his arms and pressed her mouth against his. Gently cradling the back of her head, he slicked his tongue within her mouth and made her melt, fall to pieces right before him. He wrapped his hand around her neck and brought her close, then placed his mouth against her collarbone and kissed, squeezing her.

She blinked and swallowed nervously, but he wouldn't let go... release her.

"Ahhh!"

He slammed her hard against the wall, laughing loud,

darkness in his eyes, his gleaming white teeth looking like fangs, while an invisible heaviness filled the room like fog.

GET. DOWN… he mouthed before flinging her to the floor like a rag doll.

"You mothafuckers must think I'm a moron!" He grabbed a gun that appeared out of nowhere as the closet doors burst open with a loud bang. "COVER YOUR EYES!"

But she couldn't. She simply sat there on the floor, partially hidden behind him, her chest filled with pain as anxiety and fear took over. The man pumped bullets into the assailants and in seconds, left them riddled with holes. She started to scream but covered her mouth with both hands. Their eyes were set upon Savage as they hit the floor like sacks of russet potatoes, blood everywhere. Breathing hard, he glanced at Zaire who was going insane, her eyes full of tears. He snatched his phone, keeping his gun high as he approached and surveyed the bodies. Looking back at her, he shook his head.

"They must've gotten in here after I left, when you were asleep."

"How'd you know they were in here?" Her voice trembled.

"As soon as I made my way into the room, I noticed that plant had been moved. You'd have no reason to move a fucking plant." He pointed to the corner of the room. "I also saw the closet door was somewhat open and noticed slight movement there." He marched over to the plant, messed with the leaves, and pulled out a small black device. With deft hands, he popped it open and ripped out the wires, destroying it. "The plant was bugged. I turned the music up to help muffle anything that might go down. The gun had a silencer on it, I always use a silencer when I'm indoors, in a public place. I closed the window to make them think I was comfortable, so they'd relax and enjoy the peep show. Opened the windows to make love to you just how I wanted to… show you a damn good time. Took my time with you in the shower, just in case I didn't make it out of here alive… wanted to give you something nice to remember. I'd already alerted someone to let them know I had someone in here so they needed to help ya if I got killed… Hold on."

He typed something on his phone, then tossed it on the bed. "Had to confirm."

"WHAT?! Why were these people in here?! Who are they?!"

"I can't get into all of that, but I can tell you this much. You're in my world now." He pointed at himself. "There's no turning back. What you've seen, you can't unsee and you're too smart for me to try and explain this away. This is the *real* world, Eva. Not the fake, cutesy domain that's been sold to people like you, a lie you live by. Only a few know the truth."

"Oh, God!" She got to her feet, unable to stop shaking. She tried to avoid looking at the two dead men riddled with bullets, their bodies bleeding out. Savage had shot them so fast and moved like lightning… didn't even seem human. He was like some machine…

"Someone will be coming to get them in a minute, baby. Don't worry." He checked out his reflection in the mirror, then ran his hand over his hair to fix a few stray strands.

"Don't worry? DON'T WORRY?! I just saw two men jump out the closet with guns and you shot and killed them dead before they even had a chance to say, 'Boo!' I might be next!"

"Nope. They don't know we're involved. In these cases, they just go after the target. Me."

"What kind of shit are you involved in?! You're a criminal, aren't you?! Oh shit!" In shock, she stumped her foot, while praying to God and begging for all this to be some crazy dream.

"Sometimes, bad boys play for the good side, Zaire." He casually lit a cigar, cast his sights towards the dead bodies, then turned back in her direction. "Nah, I'm not a criminal. The police aren't after me, the judges aren't after me, no one you put your trust in is after me. I handle the riffraff. I take out the trash." He blew out swirls of smoke. "I play for the winning team."

"This... this can't be happening." She swallowed hard. "Who are you?!"

"I told you who I was the first time you asked. You just chose not to listen. My name is Maximus Savage. I'm an assassin, Eva." She averted her gaze, unable to look him in the eye, and hugged herself. "Let me give you the cliff notes... My father got in a bit of a jam when I was a kid. The police came to arrest him for a probation violation. He crossed state lines, and they found *me*. I was taken away at age twelve and thrust into therapy with a child psychologist.

"My parents were deemed unfit to raise me and for a short while, I stayed with a foster family. But during that time, Eva, I told the therapist what I could do. She added a remark in my files that I had an unhealthy preoccupation with violence and guns. I told her I could do a somersault and kill someone at the same time, that I could kick a bastard in the neck and destroy his vocal cords in one swoop.

"No one believed me, but I wanted to prove it. The therapist called the police, believing I may have witnessed violent crimes committed by my father and now may be a sociopath since I described in great detail my dreams regarding murder. They weren't dreams. I saw it all happen… The police, intrigued by this and seeing me as some sort of possible informant, a damn rat and freak, decided to test me out when they got me in another room. Alone. They hated my father. He'd made things hard for them, even exposed some of their treachery; so they thought it would be fun to poke the bear, mess with his son. After interrogating me about my dad and comin' up with nothing, they took me to a warehouse. To this day, I don't know exactly where they drove me but it was out in the middle of nowhere. They told me that if I could hit five out of seven targets, they'd let my Dad go. I remember them laughing, having a real good time of it…

"I was given seven knives and seven targets placed half a football field away. I landed those knives, at age twelve, in each of the heads of the damn dummies. In disbelief, they handed me a gun with seven bullets. Yeah, these fuckers did this, gave a gun to a kid, upped the ante. Told me if I shot six out of seven in the exact locations they specified for each one, they'd have Child Protective Services drop the charges and I'd be back home with my family. I made 'em shake on it. I then took that gun, shot one in the head, one in the knee, one in the chest, one in the upper thigh, one in the lower thigh, and two in the neck. I landed EACH. AND. EVERY. SHOT. I was fast and strong, my vision was good and as they say, I was a natural born killer."

She inhaled, afraid to breathe again.

"I do not have that switch in my brain most people do…" he continued. "The one that is grossed out by blood, pain, torture, murder." He tapped the side of his head. "I am not moved by tears. I can't be manipulated by public displays of emotion. I barely feel anymore because I've been doing this so damn long and the life I've had. I'm numb. I remember giving a damn. I remember wondering what it would be like to not have bloodthirst… but that's just not me." He tossed his hands up in resignation and smiled sadly. "Some people are just born… backwards. I don't give a shit about much. I'm cold, dead on the inside. I know how to fake compassion and concern. I wouldn't say I'm a psychopath, I do have the ability to care, it's just not something I tap into often. Caring will get you killed… You're a psychologist by trade. I know you understand this."

"How did you become… what you are, Maximus? Why did you choose this?" Her voice shook, terror taking over.

"I didn't choose this; it chose me. Those same men who'd arrested my father told the FBI about me. They came to the door on my eighteenth birthday and asked me to join a private agency they'd set up as a secret arm of the organization. Their mission was to remove the fuckers that are too slick to get caught up in the prison system and too dangerous to keep around. There are people in this world, baby, who make Charles Manson and any other crazy bastard you can imagine look like a fuckin' cupcake. The *real* bad guys rarely make the news. They're too smart to be caught by the police. I find them. I exterminate them. The end. I'm a highly sought after, government mandated and appointed, artillery expert to the hilt, and a twenty-two-year veteran in this cold ass industry."

"If the government hired you, then why were those men trying to kill you?"

"The prey never likes the predator, baby. Now, to tell ya the truth, I rarely have situations like this. Most of these fuckers are afraid to try anything like this. This is a recent development." He grimaced at the dead bodies and shook his head. "Unfortunately, I am still trying to get to the bottom of it." He slid his gun in his jacket and walked up to her, hugging her tight. For some odd reason, she didn't feel afraid of him. She believed the words he said. As crazy as it sounded, they rang true. She jumped when the hotel door suddenly unlocked and opened. Savage wore a blank expression when two men dressed in white jumpsuits came in. Without saying a word, they gathered the bodies up and placed them in black body bags. Savage turned her away from the scene, made her face him.

"I know this much, and so do you, honey. You're safe, all right?" She nodded, every nerve ending in her body soared. "I'm a walking deadly weapon. I'm trained to hunt, target, and kill. Period. And now, I'm also your lover and protec-tor..." She buried her head against his chest as he caressed her arms, landing a tender kiss against her forehead. "Nothing has changed. You're just no longer in the dark, baby. Sleeping Beauty, you're woke. The blinders are officially off… Welcome to the jungle."

CHAPTER THIRTEEN

A Time to Obey and A Time to Kill

"WELL, YOU GOT it wrong." Savage stared lazily at his neatly made California king size bed in his master suite. Black sheets and pillows covered it from top to bottom, a burgundy throw pillow arranged in the middle. He blinked several times and rubbed the side of his head as the sound of firing guns invaded the recesses of his memory bank. As if in slow motion, he could see the blood flow, hear the screaming, smell the panic all over again... Faded memories of the woman he'd been screwing while the pool party turned into a bloodbath flooded his mind.

"Savage, we had everything on surveillance." His friend's voice broke into his thoughts, making him push the blood-splattered deliberations to the side.

"Evidently not my hotel room. Somehow, that got left off the roster. What the fuck was goin' on?"

"It was because—"

"Look, Harlem, it's been a long ass weekend." He

scratched his forehead, growing tired of the whole ordeal and
pissed beyond belief. The last ten hours had been pure hell.
Calming Zaire down, doing a make-shift debriefing of sorts.
Flying back to California and handling a check-in mandated
by the U.S. Government. And worst of all, still not hearing
directly from Austin. "All I asked is that someone watch
floor twenty-one during the hours requested. If my specifica-
tions had been followed, this would've never happened or at
least, I would have been alerted in time to handle the
situation so our fucking Hazmat team wouldn't have needed
to be called! I had to send them an emergency text to get the
fucking bodies up! What were their names?"

"I have them in the database. We're still running identifi-
cation on the two men though. I should have the full scoop
tomorrow."

"I moved between two floors for my own safety the entire time I was in Las Vegas at the Bellagio, but I told you I
was going to the suite that night. Why weren't my orders
followed?"

"We turned off the monitors."

"What?! Then how in the fuck can you tell me the floor
was on surveillance?!"

"It was, but they were turned off for several hours. The
reason is—"

"Jesus!"

"Savage, stop takin' the Lord's name in vain. You know I
don't like that shit."

"Stop taking the Lord's name in vain?! I almost *met* the
Lord because of *you*! My job is to take out the riffraff, the
pieces of shit in this world that even the local authorities and

FBI are too chicken shit to deal with, and this is the thanks I get—someone in our own circle making my life a living hell! All I ask for your guys to do is watch my back while I do my damn job. The sloppiness is fuckin' unbelievable and I wish you would come back on board, in the flesh, instead of staying behind a computer screen because when you were watching me personally, versus your crew, none of this shit ever happened! You were always on top of your shit!"

He screamed so loud, his damn throat felt sore. "Now I am dealing with incompetent pricks who don't know their asses from a hole in the wall."

Harlem sighed. "I can't come outta retirement, man. I gotta family now." The man sounded sorry and lame.

"What do you mean, retirement? You still work for us!"

The man huffed and smacked his gums. "You know what I mean, Savage…"

"Back to the other shit, what did you mean by you turned the surveillance off?"

"I, uh… picked up a conversation you were having…"

"A conversation I was having?"

"Yeah. Sounded personal…"

Shit. The plane… I called him when Zaire was in the bathroom. How much did he hear?

"What are you talking about?"

"You made some plans with a woman. You were, uh, how should I say this? Tryin' to convince her to let her guard down." *Fuck. He heard everything.* "I knew if I could hear the conversation, others on our team would be able to do the same as we were all connected to you at the time via the app. So I made the decision to cut the connection on my end, since I am the motherboard basically, and that way nobody could overhear. You had called me, remember? But I guess you hadn't turned off the app on your end."

"Damn it... Still a learning curve for me. Dennis had us start using it last week so we could contact each other from remote areas. I thought I had disconnected... I guess not." His face felt flushed.

"So, with all of that going on, I forgot to signal it again for the hotel time you allotted. It totally slipped my mind to turn the connection back on. I could say 'my bad,' but since you had to kill two guys and we missed them entering in the first place, I don't think that would be good enough. I've talked to the team. Man, I'm sorry."

Savage shook his head and slumped on his bed, placing his gun on his lap. The app was new software that had been installed on their phones by their head computer whiz guy. It was invisible, untraceable, secure... However, surveillance mode allowed everyone in the group to hear and see through either cameras installed in a given area, or access the main port—that being Savage's phone—and the microphone or camera. At the time of his call to Harlem, he'd accessed the microphone feature but apparently hadn't disconnected. Thus, he was now busted.

He'd been overheard in hot pursuit...

I get lax with Harlem, and plus, I knew I wanted to invite her to stay overnight with me. I wasn't thinking straight. This woman has my head all fucked up. I never do slipshod shit like that...

"App or not, your instincts saved your life, Savage."

"I'm just glad I realized real quick that something was wrong when I got back to the hotel. I knew not to try and make an excuse for her and me to attempt to leave. That would have been far too risky if they felt made. They would've come out right away and started a war and she was naked when I first came through the door, so never mind…" He shook his head. "It's over with… I survived. All right, so, uh, next week I have the—"

"Wait, man."

"What?"

"We've got an issue here. You have a witness."

"So? I've had them before. A problem arises and I solve it."

"You killed her, too?"

"NO!" Savage rolled his eyes and groaned. "I spoke with her about it. Didn't get into too many details, naturally, but she knows."

"Knows what?"

"She knows what I do…" He was met with silence, on top of more silence, on top of a shitload of silence. Huge heaps and bountiful bounds of silence.

"Savage, you told her you were an assassin?" Harlem asked, disbelief in his tone.

"Yes."

"Un-fuckin'-believable!"

"What?! No one ever believes me anyway and what's the point of lying about it? Who is she going to tell? Who would believe her and even if they did, no one is going to do anything about it, whatever police officer or guard she'd report it to. I have yet to meet a guy in this line of business who is able to keep this charade up as long as I have. You weren't there, all right? She deserved the truth."

"She deserved the truth? This ain't Mother Teresa! It's a chick you've been smashin' all weekend! We need to talk further about this. Did she believe you?"

"Not initially."

"Savage, yes or no?"

"I'm not a fuckin' genie! My name isn't psychic Savage, reader of the stars or some shit! How the hell should I know?"

"BECAUSE YOU WERE WITH HER ALL FUCKING WEEKEND!"

"What difference does that make?! You've been married to your wife over ten years. Can you now suddenly read her mind?!" Harlem huffed. "You've got special powers now that you've put in a decade? Give me a fucking break and how dare ya cop an attitude with me, when you're the reason I'm in this mess in the first fuckin' place and then you—"

"All right, all right! Let's not argue about it. Hell, it's done now. This isn't good. We'll deal with it though."

"Don't worry about it. I had to say something though, man. I had to kill two guys in front of her. It was unavoidable. What did you expect me to do, huh?" He yawned. "Pull out an ink pen like I'm Will Smith from 'Men in Black' and pretend to erase her memory? She's not stupid, far from it, but I was able to calm her down. She and I talked for a long while and she's under the understanding that basically I'm a souped-up cop with clearance to do what I did. I told her to not tell anyone about it, not even her friends."

"Oh, and I'm certain she'd heed your advice…" Sarcasm dripped all over Harlem's words. "You've been tapping that ass of a perfect stranger, and think she is just going to walk away as if she didn't see you put a bunch of holes in two men in a nano-second without blinking an eye. She has no loyalty to you to keep quiet. She's probably been traumatized, and traumatized people, especially women, squeal."

"Not all the time. She doesn't come across that way."

"Remember how I met my wife, Savage? She reported on an assailant and we had to put her in police protection. Sandy was a witness to a brutal crime, just like I told you back in '06, but she was terrified... More afraid of the guy coming after her next, or sending one of his goons if she agreed to testify, than anything else. This woman of yours might fear the same. I have to send someone out to interview this lady. Immediately. We have to do damage control."

"I'm tellin' you, I have this under control. You know I can read people well. And hell, out of all of us, my witness count is low. Roy shot up a crowd at a food festival with an AK-47 in the middle of downtown Chicago, so I dare anyone to try and sequester me about this."

"Please don't remind me. That took months to clean up, get the press off the case. Look, regardless, you have to give me the complete rundown, Savage. We have to start a file on her as she could become a liability."

"If it'll make you sleep better at night, fine."

"It will. No loose ends. I need her full name, date of birth, city and state, all of it. We have to run background information in *our* system, not the police files—the whole nine—and I need to put surveillance on her house for at least the next week or so."

Savage closed his eyes and listened to Harlem give out a long ass laundry list of just how complicated and ugly things could become. He'd been through this before, but never to this extent.

Is it worth all of this? Maybe.

He'd always been able to talk himself out of any situation. Besides, no one would ever believe him if he'd told them the truth about his unconventional occupation. They'd think him a liar or perhaps crazy. Or both. One by one, he answered the man's questions, and each minute felt like an eternity.

"I've already run a check on her. I did it early on," Savage blurted, hoping that would stop the panic, but he was met with a pregnant pause.

"Oh, really? Why?"

Savage took a deep breath and sat up on his elbows.

It was time to come clean. Not everything had been as it seemed.

"Because I became a little paranoid." He swallowed. "Zaire seemed too good to be true. She pretty much ticked all of my checkboxes: She's successful, damaged, has her own business and interests. She's beautiful, classy, intelligent, all of the shit I like… but she's verbally aggressive at times and she doesn't trust me completely. *Yet.*" He smirked.

"Hey, we can't get everything." Harlem laughed. "Why did you mention damaged as a plus?"

"Because I'm an eternally fucked-up motherfucker and if a woman is too perfect, too goody two shoes, she won't understand me… get how my mind works. I don't do this work because it's the only thing I know how to do. I do it because I *love* it."

"I know you do. It's why Longhorn called you a problem last year, said you were out of your fucking mind and a possible threat, and why Austin never wants to lose you… thinks you're the best of the best."

"And what do you think?" Savage smirked. "Do you agree with Austin or Longhorn?"

"Honestly, Savage? I think you already know what I'm going to say. I think you're out of your fucking mind… No, I don't think it, I *know* it, and I'm serious. You're demented. You have continuous bloodthirst and sometimes you view the world through a grizzly lens. Some of that paranoia on your part is warranted though. You've seen way too much in your lifetime." *He's right…* "So, are you a problem? No way, but insane? Yes… but you're a good friend, and I'd trust you with my life before most of these other assholes out here."

Savage laughed. "I've been called an asshole more times this year than in my whole life. I kinda like it now," he teased.

"We're all assholes. You gotta be to survive this long in this business. I've heard you described as heartless, soulless, all of that. But the people that say this, the ones who work in our industry, don't know you like I do. Part of that is *your* fault."

"My fault?"

"Yeah, because you only let a few in, and I'm grateful to be one of those chosen people you trust." He heard the flick of a lighter as the man rested between words. "I can depend on you to do what you're supposed to do and you are excellent at it."

"I *am* excellent at it, aren't I?" Savage stretched, then opened a drawer and placed his gun inside, grabbing his Nighthawk Firehawk in its place.

"Don't get too cocky. You've got one major flaw."

"Bullshit!" He cackled.

"You don't take orders well. You have a serious problem with authority, lone wolf that you are, but you manage to always get the job done, many times better than expected. Now, back to the woman. Why were you paranoid about her?"

"Yeah, about that. I was beginning to think she was there to off me at one point. The thought lasted only a short time, but I had to be sure." He ran his hand over his hair. "Stranger shit has happened. Anyway, I ran a check on her in the system. Not a full one—we didn't have time for that as it would've taken days, but I got the basics. I didn't want to be taken off guard. She came up squeaky clean."

"I still need to run it myself, get a full scope."

"Yeah, yeah, yeah, I know the routine." Savage waited while the man busied himself typing. The silence filling his big home felt odd, as if the extended solitude no longer suited him. He'd never given that much thought up to now. He used to relish being alone, believing it his nature. He imagine Zaire lying beside him on the bed, asleep, looking beautiful just as she did at the hotel.

Long, shapely legs… ringlets of thick black hair… full, soft lips… dark chocolate nipples… beautiful tits… soft, curly pubic hair…juicy, warm pussy… golden-painted toes… curvy hips… the small tattoo of a rose on her right ankle… the beauty mark above her top lip… slightly cleft chin… deep, dark eyes… skin the color of Earth…

She's fucking amazing…

"I know it's not my business but since it's been brought up," Harlem stated, jerking him out of his deliberations, "the bit I heard on the app before I disconnected didn't, uh... didn't really sound like you, man."

"What do you mean it didn't sound like me?"

"You sounded pussy-whipped. Should I call the doctor?" Harlem said, sounding rather serious for about two seconds, then burst out laughing.

"Shut the hell up, man." Savage sneered, not finding a damn thing funny.

"Oh, shit! You're not denying it. You *are* pussy-whipped! Got whiplash from the pussy! You need a neck brace?"

"Are you finished?" Savage asked dryly as he lazily worked his feet out of his white Puma sneakers.

"Savage, I've known you for over a decade. I have *never*, in the history of our working relationship or friendship, heard you even *hint* at being interested in some woman beyond the physical. Last night, I overheard you talking on and on to this lady, pouring your damn heart out. You were laying it on thick!" Harlem burst out laughing once again, this time much louder than the first round. "I thought, 'yeah, he is really trying to make sure this lady gives it up again before he dips.' It was hilarious!"

"Yeah... it's a fuckin' riot..."

"Hey, don't get mad at me because you got caught slippin'." The bastard chuckled. "Savage, you've fucked up, man! I thought that was all an act until you called and said what happened back at the hotel. I had no idea you had her stay overnight, breakfast in bed 'nd shit. Now, I didn't hear all of your conversation with her on the plane, but I heard enough. Over there soundin' like Keith Sweat... 'There you go tellin' me noooo again, there you go... there you go...'" The bastard sang off key, getting his funny bone jollies off.

"Are you finished?"

"She must be some Voodoo Witch or some shit because I could not believe my ears! Please tell me you're just messing with me right now. Tell me it was all a ploy to get sex?!" Savage grinned and shook his head… He'd fallen from grace in his friend's eyes. His few pals, especially the ones that were married, likely lived vicariously through him.

"What do you want me to say, man?" Savage tossed up his hands and grinned.

"I was hoping it was a scheme but you were so damn lovey-dovey and convincing that even *I* for a second thought about dropping my *own* damn draws! That was a smooth ass conversation! You are a sweet talkin' mothafucka, man! Yo' ass need to write for Hallmark. I didn't even know you had it in you!"

"Harlem, go to hell." Savage fell back onto his bed, staring up at the skylight.

"Did you throw your jacket over a puddle for her, and all that shit? Fight off some dragons, threaten a witch? Climb up some hair hangin' from a castle window?"

"All right, and on that note, I'm going to call it a night. Tomorrow is a busy day. I'll hit you up in the morning."

"Make sure you do, lover boy. Oh, one more thing."

"What?"

"Somethin', somethin', somethin', somethin' just ain't riiiight!" The man burst out into another Keith Sweat song, then exploded into raucous laughter.

Savage abruptly ended the call. He lay there for a good ten or so minutes, perhaps longer, falling into a ditch of dark daydreams. Each nerve ending inside his body tingled as his brain launched into an instant replay of the bloody massacre that had occurred in his house…

I'm back home. Finally.

He sat up, debating on whether to take a shower and going to bed, or look over his files, give them a second and third read-over before the evening was through. As he neared a decision, his cellphone rang. Snatching it up, he stood to his feet, anger crawling through him.

"I should've cut your fat fucking head off when I had the chance five years ago."

"Savage, we need to discuss some things. *Important* things."

Savage placed the call on speaker, set the phone down on his bed, and removed his shirt, tossing it onto a chair.

"I have absolutely nothin' to say to you. Your issue is with Austin, not me. The minute you sent your posse after me, in my own home, we were beyond any discussions, Longhorn."

"I was under the impression you had one of my men there."

"So what! Your intelligence was wrong, and I didn't even so much as get a 'so sorry' card and flowers from ya, either. It was a major fuck up at my expense. Kiss my hairy ass!" Savage snatched a dresser drawer open, removed a cigar from a gold container, and lit it with a match.

"Austin and I have a checkered past, that is true; however, I was not coming after you, specifically."

"What the fuck are you talking about? Your guys pointed guns right at me and shot! If that's not coming after me, I'd hate to see what is."

"That's because you had already begun shooting. You are aware, however, that you killed Murdock, took off his tongue, so we're even. This wasn't personal."

"Nah, we'll never be even. I don't give a shit who I killed on your team. They broke into *my* house so the hell with Murdock who was asked who sent him and he refused to answer, so he got what he got I didn't even know who the hell he was before that day and secondly, you came back for seconds!"

"What are you talking about?"

"Don't play stupid with me, Longhorn. You tracked me down in Vegas and tried to explode that party, too. No, Longhorn, this shit is definitely personal now. I am slaughtering anyone you send after me until I can get to *you*. I'm done playin'. This is war." There was a couple seconds of silence, as if the man was trying to collect his thoughts.

"Vegas? I never sent anyone after you in Las Vegas, Savage. I'm telling the truth. I am responsible for the siege of your house in California. That's it."

"That's it?! My pool looked like a vat of strawberry Kool-Aid when your boys got finished! It cost over fifty grand to fix my house and get rid of all the blood and bullets embedded in the walls, broken furniture 'nd shit, and let's not even get into the fact that one of my favorite lookouts was killed by one of your damn roaches! Don't let me catch you out, Longhorn. Austin's orders to not rough you up be damned!"

"Again, it was nothing personal, Savage. My men showed up for a rescue mission. It was due to my agent, Jasper, being missing and spotted there on your premises."

Savage leaned forward and blew out smoke from the corner of his mouth.

"Why in the fuck didn't you just pick up the gotdamn phone and ask if he was here, Professor Dipshit?"

"The profanity and name calling is unwarranted, Savage. I fully understand you and I will never be friends, we do not like one another, but we are work colleagues to some extent. Whether you wish to respect that or not is not my issue. You made an oath. Regardless of you being an independent contractor, you had to pledge just like everyone else. We're on the same team, so your aggression is ill-placed."

"My dear good man, Longhorn, Offended are thee?" he mocked in a faux British accent. "I offer my humblest of apologies and bequeath to you my heartfelt consideration, for you are truly worthy of esteem, reverence, and admiration." Savage chuckled and shook his head. "You fuckin' stuck-up, dingleberry-faced dipshit! How about I stick my size fourteen foot up thee tight, narrow ass?! Or better yet, good sir, a live grenade with flesh-eating bacteria?! Overkill, much?!" He jumped to his feet, mad as hell. "YOU SENT TEN MOTHERFUCKERS TO MY HOUSE, SHOT UP MY PEOPLE, FUCKED UP MY HOME, RUINED MY PARTY. ALL WHILE I WAS IN THE MIDDLE OF A MUCH-NEEDED FUCK! Fuck your feelings, you twit. Answer my fuckin' question!"

He was met with a long, weighty sigh.

"Because there's a bounty on his head and that would've tipped you off. I had no indication that he was not on the premises against his will."

"Don't you get it? He was never here, cum stain! I had to

run off because the heat was on me and I wasn't allowed to lay a finger on you because Austin wanted to investigate. So off to Vegas I went. Running is for cowards. Next time, I am coming after you. Screw the oath, principles, all of that shit. You sure as hell didn't abide by them. You had no business taking your rage for Austin out on me. You two were best friends. Now there's bad blood and you knew damn well this was an excuse to hit him where it hurts. I've had it up to here with this beef you and Austin are in the middle of, and then you have nothing to say for yourself when I tell you that you fucked up! BE A MAN AND OWN UP TO YOUR SHIT!" He angrily smashed his cigar into an ashtray, gnashing his teeth in frustration. "And why should I believe you about Vegas, huh? That's definitely your style."

"Savage, we thought you had a hostage and everything I did was in accordance with our law. We thought he was in imminent danger. As far as Vegas, again, I assure you that wasn't me!"

"Hold on. Let me check this receipt."

"Receipt? What receipt?"

"Nope. I definitely didn't buy any of your bullshit…"

"Savage, for God's sake! I was aware you were in Vegas, yes, but not exactly certain *where*. More importantly, I knew after what had transpired, that everyone would be watching you so it was far too risky. Now, if something happened there, which apparently it did, I will open my records for public consumption and allow you to view my electronic tracking of each and every man on my team—prove to you that I never put a hit out on you. I will even take it one step further and allow you to view my personal tracking as well.

Again, you were not the target at your home, Savage, though I do understand your frustration and disbelief. There was no one from my team after you in Vegas, either. That would've been foolish on our part for reasons already mentioned."

Savage took a deep breath and sucked his teeth. "What the hell do you want from me?"

"A hit had come across my desk, one of the most important ones I've ever seen. Two of my best men, that I'm certain would've handled this with flying colors, are gone. You killed one during the home invasion, and the other is M.I.A. I need this done right. Please consider it."

"Offer declined."

"Savage, I know you hate my guts, but there is something bigger than *us* going on here. If you could get past your ego and pride, that would be much appreciated. Don't you want to even meet and hear details about this? You have to admit that the one time we did work together, it was with positive results. You even received a medal of recognition and honor. Doesn't that mean something to you?"

"I would agree with you, motherfucker, but then we'd both be wrong." Savage ended the call and headed to his master suite bathroom. He opened a panel in the wall and removed a razor blade and shaving cream, setting them on the counter. "Fuckin' Alexa, play 'Calm Like A Bomb' by Rage Against The Machine, bitch…"

I don't even know why I even still have Alexa in this house with all that I know. I am cancelling this service as soon as I get a moment to do so… Total invasion of privacy.

Moments later he was butt naked in his shower, hot water and soap flowing over his tatted up body. His brain was like a race horse on crack cocaine traveling full speed ahead down the track.

If it wasn't Longhorn, then why were those guys in the hotel with me and Zaire? Why did they want to kill me? They didn't want to kill her or they would've...That's a given. They had the chance. It has the way we do business written all over it. Kill no witnesses unless necessary. I was definitely the target. She positively was taken by surprise; no noncombatant could act that well. What the hell is going on?

"Shit!" He slammed his fist against the black tiled wall as he tried to work out the details in his mind, play back the whole sordid encounter, rewind the tapes of time. After rinsing himself twice, he jumped out of the shower and dried off. He picked up the razor he'd placed on the sink counter and began to trim up his facial hair and brows. As soon as he stepped foot back into his bedroom to turn on his computer and do a bit of research, his phone rang once again.

"It's about damn time!" he answered. "I've been waiting to hear back from you. I have left a shitload of messages. Do you have any idea of what happened to me in Vegas, man? And to make things worse, your best friend called me and told me he didn't have shit to do with it!"

"I'm in Tokyo, Savage. I'm sorry about the delay," Austin said, sounding truly exhausted. "I won't be back for another week or so. Yes, I was briefed on what happened... Jesus Christ. Harlem filled me in, and I read the reports."

"Longhorn claims to be none the wiser about the Vegas shit. I don't know." He shrugged as he paced back and forth. "He's a master manipulator so I can't take his word for it."

"As much as I would like to encourage you to do him in at this point, I don't think Longhorn had anything to do with it. I found out quite a bit of stuff while you were away. When I get back in town, we'll need to meet face to face and strategize. I believe you've made your fair share of enemies, Savage, but this one may have to do with a prior hit. This sort of thing happens sometimes, as you know. We'll discuss more later and maneuver as needed."

"Yeah, we *do* need to talk. First on the agenda, I need to set up some new ground rules because as it stands, I'm doing all the work while other people are fuckin' up, making assumptions that could cost me my life. I understand that my job has occupational hazards, but sloppiness is some shit I just can't accept. I am not getting the bare necessities and I'm pissed off."

"Savage, yes, we can—"

"Don't try to sweet talk me this time, either. We had an agreement. I don't think my demands are unreasonable. If I get my own self killed, then that's that. But if I die because you or your guys were not watching my back, then that's a whole different issue. The shit that went down at my house should've never happened. Longhorn's crew should've been wiped out before they even entered the damn house! I reviewed the footage. It's like everyone was on vacation until the last minute. You can't send me on the frontline with no army behind me, man!" Austin gave a loud sigh. "You've got me going after bigshot callers, not corner drug dealers sellin' dime bags. This isn't nursery school. This is no peewee group. This is the big leagues! The money and adrenaline rush doesn't mean shit if I'm dead."

"I get it, Savage. A lot of what you've shared is justified. We'll discuss this further. Try to get some sleep."

The call ended. Savage looked at his phone, gritted his teeth, and groaned. A sinful, hellish heat, born from the mother of resentment and the father of frustration, boiled up inside him and poured out his mouth in the form of a scream.

His phone rang once again, and he cursed... sick of the calls, sick of everyone...

He looked down at the Caller-ID, then smiled.

"You have no idea how glad I am that you called me, Zaire..."

"I was thinking about you, Maximus. In fact, I haven't stopped thinking about you since the moment you kissed me goodbye..."

CHAPTER FOURTEEN

Best Kept Secrets

T HE PAST FEW days had been nothing short of surreal. From the time she'd laid eyes on Maximus Savage, Zaire had entered a dream world up until she'd finally made it home again, her feet on familiar ground.

The podcast show that evening had been successful, without unnecessary shenanigans or P.I.T.A. (Pain in the Ass) interruptions—liked the one with the idiot who liked to call in and curse her out, or send her inappropriate emails, some threatening in nature. Thank goodness she hadn't heard from the imbecile in over a couple of weeks and hoped his reign of stupidity was finally over.

Zaire turned off the last light in her studio and stood, stretching her arms and groaning from sitting for so very long. Her staff was gone, so she was alone. Exiting the dark booth, she grabbed the stairway banister. The air conditioning above her head cooled her as she climbed the stairs, barely able to wait to indulge in a glass of wine, a bubble bath, and some silly TV show. Cell phone in hand, she made her way to her kitchen. She placed the phone on the counter and closed the window as the smell of the salmon, wild rice, and Caesar salad she'd had for dinner was now gone. Heading to the pantry, she found her built-in wine rack inside.

There you are, my love…

She selected a bottle of Cabernet Sauvignon, popped the cork, and poured it into a large glass, to the rim. One wrong move and it would definitely spill all over the place. Leaning back onto the counter, she crossed her ankles and relaxed a little. Herbie Hancock's 'Cantaloupe Island' played through her home speakers, filling her with the rhythm. As she bobbed her head to the beat, thoughts of Savage swam in her head, doing Olympic, tipsy laps. She stared at her cell phone and pursed her lips, remembering the conversation they'd just had right after the show, before she left her booth. From a quick check-in call as she'd expected, he ended up inviting himself over. His excuse: to see her before he got too busy. Also, he'd asked some questions she'd been expecting.

Had she whispered a word of what happened in the hotel room to anyone?

Definitely not…

Was she afraid?

Definitely yes…

Then he'd said something that had sent chills up her spine.

"Zaire, there'll be some men contacting you to arrange to see you. It's protocol. They may even pop up in person, out of the blue. They work for the same agency as me. Don't ask them a bunch of questions—only make sure they give you their names and show you their I.D. It's a special badge, a black and red shield. They'll ask a few questions. Just be honest. You won't see their weapons, but they'll be armed. They won't hurt you..."

What have I gotten myself into?

She polished off the glass and started to trudge outside the kitchen, her bare feet felt cold against the slate flooring, then stopped in front of the photo of her, Kim, and Allison hanging on the wall. Her eyes watered as she dragged her fingertips down the protective glass of the framed image and shook her head in disbelief.

I'm not a good friend. I'm not even a good person...

She'd kept so many secrets from the two women she adored almost more than anyone else in the whole world. Zaire was accustomed to keeping up appearances, to helping others in their time of need while acting all prim and proper in the face of scrutiny, evaluation and adversity.

Lies to self, lies in stealth... What was one more lie? And then another?

The entire road trip back, she'd laughed with her buddies as they teased her, calling her a whore but applauding her at the same time. They talked to one another about all sorts of things, and she kept on smiling, gritting her teeth, keeping secrets, not once letting on she'd witnessed a double murder... that she'd fallen hard for a man she barely knew and that she was addicted to the thrill. That perhaps she was sick. But worst of all, she knew better. That realization made her die a little on the inside.

None of the great music they'd played in the car—Aretha Franklin, Beyoncé, Janet Jackson, and Maxwell's greatest hits—could make the slow, nasty sludge of blood-tinged memories go down any easier.

I'll never forget those two pairs of dead eyes...

Turning off the kitchen light, she stepped out into the hall and was bathed in a soft, warm motion-detecting light. As she reached the staircase, she kneaded on her shoulder, working out a kink. Wicked thoughts swirled within her like dense cigar smoke slipping from the lips of a beautifully truthful, verbally irresponsible, slightly sadistic and complicated individual...

Something about Maximus Savage called to her and would not let go. Allison had seen it, too, and felt drawn to him. He had that sort of power. He was alluring, magnetic, and dripping with the shit. It had now gone way beyond boredom, lust and curiosity for her. She'd gotten way more than she'd bargained for. This was an entirely new scale of 'fuck my beliefs and principles.' She'd graduated into a rebel without a cause.

Her cap and gown were blood red and drenched in treachery.

I am involved with a trained murderer. DID YOU HEAR THAT? He is a fucking assassin. I could be in danger. Everyone I know or associate with could also be threatened. And yet, I still want to fuck him. I still want to hear his voice. I still want to see him. I want to hear all about his life. I want to go out to the movies and dance the night away with this man. I want to lay my head on his chest and fall asleep. Yup. I'm crazy.

She swallowed hard at the notion, beating herself up with several uppercuts to the thoughts in her head, just as she had a million times over recently.

I have given my body, bits and pieces of my mind, and parts of my hidden self to a man who empties clips and knocks the life out of men for sport. I have willingly lost complete control of myself! I am battling within, I am hurting, I am confused, I am struggling here! I tell my callers and readers to never deal with men like Maximus… or do I?

Things had become so weird, she could no longer see straight.

Is Maximus truly like the men I warn against? This is a fair question, right? I mean, I tell them to avoid habitual liars all the time. He's not a habitual liar, or at least doesn't appear to be. No one in their right mind would lie about some of the things he shared. It didn't make him look good. It wasn't a feather in his cap.

I tell the women I try to help to steer clear of cheaters. To watch out for the red flags. Okay, so he's not a cheater either. He was upfront and honest about his feelings regarding us and what he wants. He admitted he has concerns about marriage. I still think he has problems with women, but I wouldn't say he hates us.

I tell my audience to not loan money to a guy, to not be used and financially abused. He's never asked me for a dime and probably makes triple what I do on any given Sunday.

And from what I can tell, what he is doing is not illegal. He is literally backed by our government. How strange! Maybe it's like the army—only he is an army of one? I guess that's how I could look at it. It doesn't sound as odd when I think of it that way. I mean, our Armed Forces, The Marines, the Navy… all of them kill. It's the same thing.

She breathed a sigh of relief as she worked out the complexities of this shit in her mind…

Once she reached her bedroom, she opened the door and walked in. Her queen size bed was dressed in a rich sangria and eggplant colored fabric that gleamed under the small chandelier and recessed lights of the ceiling. She neared the bed, taking note that one of the pillows showed slight ripples, so she smoothed it out just so, then stared at it for far too long, the notions in her head spinning like wheels once again.

And now, I've called this man, after all he's admitted to, the stuff I've seen, and everything he's done. I had the audacity to pick up that damn phone and call him after my podcast, just like he'd asked. Just like I wanted to. As soon as he said, 'Hello?' I was his... I melted. Something is definitely wrong with me, broken inside, because when he said my name, it was over. Much to my surprise, he had invited himself into my girls' weekend, busting it wide open, and now he's coming into my home... It's my choice whether I allow him into my heart or not.

She shook her head, both disgusted and slightly amused with herself. How she wished she had someone to talk to and confide in, but she couldn't go there. It was far too risky. One word to the wrong person could bring everything crashing down, and there was no guarantee she wouldn't be buried beneath the rubble. She was sworn to secrecy. Then too, few would believe her if she spilled the beans. She'd lose credibility at the least, or worse, but even if they believed her, it wouldn't change the bottom line: The fact that Maximus Savage was a true protector turned her on.

The secrecy, the mystery, the smell of the hotel room after the kill...

That fateful day in the hotel room, the adrenaline had flowed so fast, so strong, seeping in her damn bones. All the colors around her seemed more vivid, and the odor of hot gun smoke filled the room. Time remained still though, like the display on a broken watch, the long hand cradled against the short, both jerking every so often to free themselves from their tortured embrace.

She got chills thinking about Maximus, about his voice, about that night… It would forever remain imprinted on her mind.

His face… Jesus. The way the place was cleaned up in no time, as if nothing had ever happened. I felt safe with him. Before anything had even happened, I felt like he'd offered me something I needed; even with all the crazy things he'd say, I felt different with him… It's so hard to describe, but it just felt right, even though I fought it tooth and nail.

She ran her hands along the fabric of her bed, falling even harder into her daydreams. She went somewhere carnal and seedy within, and it felt so amazing…

The way he looked at her with those astonishing, glimmering eyes. The entire weekend they'd spent together, he'd smelled like expensive cologne, burnt Autumn leaves, fresh sprigs of mint, the muted blue smolder of dense smoke, worn leather and musk.

I like how he touches me…

His big, warm hands had felt rough and powerful as they'd glided across her skin. His kiss was all consuming, passionate, and administered with the softest lips she'd ever felt.

Everything that Maximus Savage was, she wanted.

Everything he *could* be, she needed.

She'd do almost anything to fall down face-first into that addictive adrenaline rush she'd felt when he'd wrapped his hand around her throat seconds before thrusting her to the ground… his gun blasting… He'd manhandled her not to hurt her, but to help her and get her out of harm's way.

She jumped, startled by the sound of her house phone ringing. It was so rare for anyone to call her on the landline.

She walked to the vanity and answered the call.

"Hello?"

"Hello, princess." She smiled at her father's husky greeting. He fell into a spell of coughs, then cleared his throat. "Just checkin' in on you. Hadn't heard from you in a while, Eva. How have you been? Your podcast and all of that?"

"Great! Everything is just fine... going well. Just busy," she said. "You sound like you have a cold. Is everything okay?" She leaned against the wall and wrapped the cord around her fingers.

"Yeah, just a little cold. No big deal. I was caught in the rain a few days ago. It started to pour all of a sudden while I was trying to finish mowing the grass. I wanted to get it done but that wasn't the best idea, I suppose. Glad to hear you're doing okay."

"How's Mom?"

"Oh, she's fine... She's fine." Dad's voice trailed a bit, as if he'd stepped away from the phone. "Your grandmother came to visit. Asked about you."

"I'm surprised she left the house," Zaire teased. Grandma was known to be a hermit and enjoyed complaining twenty-four-seven. "How'd that visit go?"

"As good as could be expected." Dad chuckled. "You know how your mother's mom is. I just tried to be accommodating and get her the hell out of my house as soon as possible. Sounds like a contradiction, but you know what I mean." They both laughed at that. "Well, I won't keep you. Just wanted to make sure you were okay. Oh, I spoke to your sister last night. She's going on some European cruise. Isn't that something? I've never been on a cruise. Maybe that's something I'll look into, but with your mom and all, it's not really…"

"I know, I know."

Emotions welled within her. Dad was pretty much a slave to Mom. He had to wait on her hand and foot and he'd become so paranoid of her getting hurt. In the past, she'd walked out in the middle of traffic or accidentally cut herself badly with a knife while making a salad. He was so absorbed with taking care of her, he barely made time for himself.

"Dad, you have to take care of yourself. Would you please consider a psychiatric nurse for Mom? I know you refuse to put her into a facility. I get that. But there were two incidents that I know of when she was pretending to take her medicine but wasn't. That put both of your lives in danger."

"Eva, just like I told you, your mother doesn't trust strangers. The last time I tried to get someone in here for more than a few minutes, she had to be restrained after attacking them, believing they were someone they weren't. The time before that wasn't much better. I… I'd like to do all sorts of things. I miss going to the library for instance and taking walks by myself, but I married your mother for better or for worse."

Zaire slowly closed her eyes and a deep ache radiated throughout her body. A sense of helplessness overcame her.

"Dad, you have to let me and Star help. I'm busy, yes, but I don't have children or those sorts of obligations, so…"

"No. You comin' over a couple times a month so I can run some errands and grocery shop is enough. Star helps when she can." He began to cough again, this spell longer than the first.

She'd offered her money and her time to her father, but he barely accepted either. He'd told her many times that he didn't want her or her sister's life impacted. Their brother's already had been, the consequences irreversible. Dad felt a part of their childhood had been stolen, along with the tattered pieces of Mom's mind. The two went hand-in-hand, but no one was to blame. Her ailment was an invisible culprit, a thief of peace and tranquility, a tyrant who stole family unity and left behind a hole that could never be filled.

This was what mental illness did to families. It wrapped its skeletal claws around decaying window frames, climbed through the slightest cracks in the walls, oozed into one's mind, heart, and soul, and destroyed all who dared to stay long enough to witness it—all who endured and loved the one under its horrid control. It could be put to sleep for a time with medications, meditation, awareness and therapy, but it could never be snuffed out for good. It always fed from the fear of its return.

Zaire had learned this about herself, her family, her mother: it would never end, so she covered it all up any chance she got. Lived in a make-believe world of her own creation. Perhaps though, in some strange way, she wasn't lying simply for the sake of it. Perhaps she wished to also protect her friends from the ugly truth—not because of her own shame, but knowing that then, they'd be more inclined to come to her in their time of need. If they knew of her true struggles, would they bog her down with the nuisances of their life? Their trials and tribulations? Regardless, these sorts of circumstances simply couldn't be controlled but Dad, in his usual protective way, wished to stop the hemorrhaging.

Just then, the doorbell rang. She grabbed her phone to check the Ring app.

There's no way that could be Maximus. That's far too soon.

"Was that your door? I'll let you go, Eva." She checked the live color footage and saw a man standing there, dark sunglasses over his eyes, car key dangling in his big hands, and a huge, shit-eating smile as he stared into the doorbell camera. When Maximus waved, she nearly jumped out of her skin. "Eva?"

"Uh, yes, Dad! So sorry, a, uh, a friend of mine is at the door. He's a bit early. I'll call you tomorrow, okay?"

"All right. I'll let your mother know and then maybe she can speak to you, too."

"That sounds just perfect. Dad?"

"Yes?"

"I love you."

"I love you too, princess."

Her father hung up first, leaving her standing there, listening to the dial tone. She hung up then left the bedroom, her cell in hand.

I haven't had time to change clothes, take a shower or bath—nothing! All I did was talk to my father and drink. I look a hot mess, too!

She huffed as she made her way down the steps to the first floor, unlocked the solid white and frosted glass front door and swung it open to feast her eyes on a male specimen that made her damn near weak at the knees. Six foot five inches of pure, unadulterated delicious fuckery. He burst out laughing, exposing a white wad of gum in his mouth. Casually sliding his shades off his face, he propped them on his head.

It's nighttime and this fool has on sunglasses…

"What's so funny?" she asked.

"You. You weren't expecting me so soon, were you?" He winked, enjoying how she squirmed, no doubt. A mosquito flew dangerously close to his face. Swiping his hand in the air, he made a grabbing motion with thumb and forefinger. When he slowly opened his hand, the mosquito lay in his palm, crushed to death, a shell of what it had once been, and it hadn't even gotten a taste of the Savage blood.

"Are you going to let me in or just have me stand out here under this bright, hot ass porch light servin' as a human buffet for these fucking flying bloodsuckers? If I'm going to be slurped and sucked on, I would prefer it to be by *you.*" Wrapping her hand around his wrist, she tugged hard, dragging the clown inside, then closed and locked the door behind them. "Careful with the jacket. Ya like to get rough, huh?" he mumbled, a greasy grin on his face.

The beast bobbed his head in approval of her digs. She took that time to study his form, get reacquainted with the asshole she'd recently become obsessed with…

His neck is as thick as tree trunk.

But it wasn't short. Everything on Savage was huge, minus his ass, which, if her memory served her well, was cute and well rounded—definitely more muscle than fat. His stomach was also chiseled to perfection, flowing into a lovely 'V' despite his affinity for ample servings of beer.

He tossed her a glance from over his shoulder. "This place is nice."

"Thank you."

"It suits you... all this white 'nd shit." He chewed loudly on his gum. "Like to keep things clean I see." He began to pace around like he owned the place. "But we both know you get down and dirty." He winked at her before plopping down on the couch. Worn jeans covered his long legs, flowing into a pair of heavy black boots. He ran his hands over his knees, one of his fingers adorned with a silver skull ring adorned with dark jewels for eyes. He hooked his finger in a come-hither motion, then patted the couch.

"What?" She toyed with him a bit, fighting a budding grin as she crossed her arms and stared at him.

"Why are you standing way over there like you've never seen a motherfucker before? I bite, but I don't have rabies. Sit your ass down, girl."

"Now I see why they call you Mr. Romance." She rolled her eyes.

"Come on, Zaire." He laughed. "I didn't come all the way over here just to look at you from across the room. I could've done that from the comfort of my own bed on Skype."

She made her way over to him and sat down, feeling a mixture of emotions, including some she hadn't quite sorted out yet. He wasted no time wrapping his arm around her waist and bringing her close. Before she could tell herself once again that she was making bad choices, the devil slid his tongue inside her mouth and gifted her with an all-encompassing, seductive, spine-tingling kiss. Too soon, he pulled away ever so slightly, smelling delicious and looking good. With a twinkle in his eye, he gently reached for her chin and made her look him directly in the eyes.

"So, you want to talk first, then fuck? Or fuck then talk? I'd prefer the second option, but I'm trying be a gentleman 'nd shit, trying to show you that I don't have to be selfish."

She snorted. "You're impossible, you know that?"

"I know."

He gave her a quick peck on the lips, then she got to her feet. He followed suit, taking off his jacket and flinging it on the couch. She took his hand and led him toward the staircase. All she could hear was his heavy boots behind her, his slow and easy breathing and her own damn heartbeat practically beating out of her chest…

CHAPTER FIFTEEN

Purple Prose & Women's Work

"IT SMELLS LIKE vanilla and amber in here. Sweet, alluring..." Savage murmured as he quickly disrobed, but was duly distracted by the woman's flair for the color white that dominated the furniture, matching décor and accessories. The bedclothes and curtains offered the only contrast of color, both in rich shades of purple. He wasn't a fan of purple, but the shade suited her just fine. Rich. Lush. Regal.

"Probably the diffusers." She pointed to a corner glass vanity with a silver and diamond crusted frame and two vases filled with what appeared to be oils. Long straw colored sticks poked out of the vases, responsible for creating the scented oasis he'd entered.

Women were strange creatures indeed. Their trappings were essential to them, especially when it came to pedantic ladies like Zaire. He too enjoyed his homes, from his minimalistic apartment in Manhattan to his cabin in Tennessee, so he understood. His eye needed to be fed on a daily basis and beautiful accoutrements, beautiful women, and beautiful violence made his fucking day. Still, his own digs were definitely stamped with pure testosterone. Those were his personal tastes.

His place was a bachelor pad on steroids, with a hell of a lot of money thrown at it to emphasize his greatest desires. Zaire's femininity, on the other hand, was poured into her hideaway as if she'd been melted into the liquid gold that she was… but there was a catch.

This was the side of her that viewers didn't see. The plentiful, fragrant flowers in every room, rich silks and satins, oversized abstract minimalist paintings in clear frames, and the whole estrogen driven display would've been enough to drive him crazy, but right now, he had a one track mind. He stayed focused on the prize: the honey pot between her long, shapely legs…

He sat down on the edge of the plush, high-poster bed, nearly slipping off the slick sheeted son of a bitch while Zaire took her sweet time removing her ho-hum, oversized gray ensemble. Honestly, if she were wearing a plastic grocery sack with holes in it, she'd still look good, but his showing up sooner than anticipated afforded him a luxury. He got to see her in a relaxed, no-frills state, inhibitions down. Not all dolled up with her mask on.

"Where's your studio at? I thought you told me it was in your house?" He looked about in wonder, then cracked his neck and knuckles, beginning to unwind.

"It's in the basement. Yes." She slid her bra straps down

her smooth shoulders. He'd kissed them a hundred times… "I have probably one of the few homes here with a full-sized basement. I asked for it when the home was being drafted to build. My intentions for the space were already clear in my mind… thinking ahead."

"I have a basement, too." He ran his hand along his jaw, eyeing her, unable to control the lust bubbling within him like a pot simmering on high for far too long.

"Oh, you do? What do you use it for? Storage?"

"Persecution. It's a torture chamber." She chuckled at his words, but her smile soon faded once they locked eyes and his expression remained placid.

"Are you serious?" Her brows bunched and her mouth dropped open, pearly white teeth fully exposed.

"Nope… I'm just fuckin' with ya."

She grimaced, then huffed. Wiggling out of her panties, she tossed them at him in a fit of irritation. He burst out laughing, catching them midflight. He closed his eyes and brought them to his nose, inhaling her feminine aroma. "Shit, you smell so good, baby." He let them fall onto the hardwood floor then scooted back towards the massive headboard, waiting for his meal to be hand delivered. His rock hard cock twitched in anticipation. In a sexy sashay, her round hips swinging with each step, her naked body glorious, she inched closer—a thing of pure beauty.

Her eyes gleamed with something dark, gentle feelings replaced with seedy seduction and yearning.

"Yeah… bring that ass over here." His heart beating hard, he snapped his fingers for her to hurry the hell up. He wanted her in the worst way… had practically chased cars off the road trying to get his lips pressed against that sweet snatch of hers, to taste her fountain and drill her pussy with a dick pulsing at the mere thought of her. His head resting on one of the soft lavender scented pillows, he kept his eye on her teasing movements.

"I'm growing impatient with you."

Ignoring his angst, she climbed onto the bed slow and easy, tiger-like, torturing him. When she was close enough to be made into an example, he lunged at her with full force. She screamed out and chortled, grasping at air. He turned her around and lay back down, dragging her with him like prey.

"Sit on my face." The woman hesitated as she cast him a glance from over her shoulder, then arched her back and ass like a cat preparing for a good old-fashioned fuck. He grabbed her by the waist, his fingertips sinking into rich, soft flesh as he positioned her just so above his mouth. Zaire leaned slightly forward, her elbows resting on the sheets in the space between his thighs, her knees on either side of him as she straddled his body. With her pussy up close and personal, he used two fingers to open her up for a better look and taste.

The pussy lips were slick as he rubbed them gently, his heart now racing out of control with lustful hunger. Her heady scent of arousal fell upon him and his mouth pooled with anticipation and hunger.

"Do you know how fuckin' pretty your pussy is, baby?" he said, his voice cracking. "It's fuckin' perfect."

With his tongue, he teased and toyed with his feminine reward, administering the lightest and most feathery of caresses, driving her clearly insane by the way she cooed, begged, and tried to garner more of his oral touch by shoving her love harder against his lips. Gathering momentum, he began to feast, holding her steady so she couldn't move and take control. He slid the tip of his tongue up and down her pussy, licking and applying pressure, sucking the glistening, overflowing valley that oozed a creamy stream, drenched just for him… Taking his sweet time, he made it his duty to show her what wet dreams were made of.

It didn't take long for her guttural moans and light and airy sighs to fill the room as she clawed the sheets and cursed. He yanked her impossibly closer, practically suffocating himself with her honeyed essence and loving every second of it. His arms wrapped around her stomach, he drew her in, made her use his face as a chair to bring her closer to an explosion of passion. Her floodgates opened from his touch, and he circled the delicate, soft fleshy folds with a tilt of his tongue to the left, then the right. She shuddered ever so slightly as he increased his pace, his lips and chin coated with her sweet, drizzled caramel center that dripped from her delectable cookie.

"Smother the fuck outta me! Where tha hell are you goin', huh?! Get your ass back over here! I said sit on my fuckin' face!" She began to bounce and twerk against his lips, driving him insane as she bucked from his grip.

He welcomed the wonderous waves and rolls of her body; the roundness of her ass and hips felt like a pillow from Heaven as his hands roamed every inch of her within touching distance.

Her skin is like mahogany velour and umber velvet… I can eat her silken pussy and taste her wet dreams… Her vivid visions told me she

SAVAGE

wants to be eaten from the outside in, her walls torn down, her pretty little world destroyed by a wrecking ball of a motherfucker like me… I'll keep going until I suck her soul out of her damn body, claim it as my own since I have none and swallow it whole… She'll feel empty like a broken vase once I turn her loose, and she'll have to fuck me with all that she has in her to get it back…

Opening her wider with his fingers, stretching the pink flesh until her pussy hole was fully revealed from behind the fleshy curtains of her fat lips, he sucked her tangy juices then twirled his eager tongue within the love tunnel he craved to engulf and penetrate with vicious tenacity.

"SAVAGE!" Her voice cracked like lightning and leather whips. It was earthy, the ends tattered and the tone untamed.

"I love how you sound, baby. You're breathing so hard…" he said between feverish licks and the smacking of his lips, savoring every single drop as she came. She screamed and shuddered against him as her honey released into his mouth. His dick was hard as a damn brick as the woman panted and cried out and moaned, slowly coming down from her high. The sounds of her orgasm made him all the harder. Made him want to destroy her then rebuild her all over again. Before he could finish having his way with her, she slid away from him and off the bed, her thighs coated in her slick, clear cum, then paused at what appeared to be an orgasmic aftershock taking her over. She leaned against the dresser for support, her temple under orgasmic siege…

His oral prowess had defeated her. His mouth had once again been her undoing. He smirked with pleasure at her temporary disability, loving how her body succumbed to him, proving he was a bastard with a vicious tongue, in more ways

241

than one.

"You've got some good pussy, baby. Damn. Tastes incredible." He licked his fingers with relish, sighing, then sat up, making himself comfortable.

"So I've been told." Her voice was shaky as she attempted to keep her cool.

"But only *my* opinion matters. Get back in the fuckin' bed. I want to beat that fuckin' kitty up. Make ya call PETA."

She chuckled at his words.

The woman left the dresser, almost tripping over herself. She leaned up against a wall, her back towards him, breathing heavily, then walked gingerly toward a MacBook computer attached to Bose speakers. Within a minute or two, The Weeknd's, 'What You Need' played in the room. When she turned to get back to the bed, he reluctantly left his comfortable spot to grab a condom from the wallet in his pants pocket.

In no time flat, they were wrapped in the sheets like mummies, kissing, laughing, hugging, rolling around, playing and falling all over each other like feathers from a busted pillow. He couldn't recall ever being so enthused, enjoying such a good time. Perhaps he'd never laughed during sexual encounters before. Never deviated from the singular mission of pounding some pussy then removing the female from his sight as soon as possible. Right then, he couldn't recall a time when he'd put all of himself into it—like now. It was simply happening. They were two wild waves in an ocean, merging, becoming one.

He hooked his hand around her neck and drew her in for a kiss. Their mouths touched lightly, then pulled back... then came back together again like prayer hands. Plumy touches, lip licks, and seductive caresses...

He swallowed when he looked into her gorgeous ebony eyes.

"You taste yourself when I kiss you?" She nodded. "Salty sweetness... so beautiful. I could just eat you up."

She quivered beside him, then lay her head against his shoulder as he sat on the bed, her hand on his lap. Brushing her hair out of the way, he kissed her once again.

"You have the softest fuckin' skin..."

"When you speak, you make my entire body vibrate, Savage. I finally figured out who you remind me of."

"Who?"

"You sound just like Sam Elliott, you know that? He has a slight twang to his voice. You don't, but that's really the only difference. I imagine if thunder could talk, it would sound much like *you*." He kissed her forehead.

"I've heard that I sound a little like him a few times in my life." He grabbed the condom from the dresser where he'd set it and sheathed himself, then straddled her and hooked her long legs over his shoulders. Their eyes locked as he grabbed his erect dick and slid it all the way inside her like a runaway train. He couldn't help but smile, getting off on the way her face twisted from the ruthless intrusion and pleasure he was determined to deliver. He delighted in how he took her damn breath away with each rough pump of his hips.

Her full pink lips parted, her breaths shallow then fast as he stroked her pussy with his thumb between thrusts, relishing every sensation, every sound, every second. Grabbing her calf, he paused for a spell and kissed her ankle.

Her smooth flesh against the unevenness of his palm felt like such a contradiction… but just as it was meant to be. *Where* it was meant to be. He increased his pace, going deeper, and she moaned. Placing her hand against his thigh, she tried to control his manic, bottomless thrusts.

He slapped her fingers away, making her scream as he leaned forward, his body flush against hers to force that same arm above her head. Keeping his pace, he jabbed in and out of her slick, hot pocket. Their groans dated and married one another, wrapping around each other tightly, filling the room in overlapping echoes of indulgence. Ankles crossed around his neck, chest to chest, his lips against her ear. He breathed hard, hearing his own oxygen escape his mouth as he fought for the next breath, and loved how she cried out and pleaded while he delivered blow after blow.

"Shit! You're killing me… too deep! Feels so good!"

"Never too deep, baby…" He snatched her chin and made her look into his eyes. "I always have to make sure you remember my name, so I'm going to fuck it inside of you, leave my imprint in this motherfuckin' pussy forever, like a gotdamn tattoo!"

He rammed into her hard, back to back, making her yell so loud, his ears rang. He loved that deafening sound as he tore her to pieces, making her cry, shudder, cum, curse and love him all at the same time. His phone began to ring but he ignored it. He wrapped his hand around her neck. As her eyes bore into his, there was no denying it…

Their connection was different, special. Something was happening between them—something severe and in need of attention. It wasn't just her pussy, her body, her sophistication, the way she gave herself to him in between those sheets and became his greatest wish. It wasn't that he was able to turn a resistant woman out, one of his favorite past times… All of that definitely helped, but that wasn't the main reason why he couldn't stop thinking about this incredible woman. Couldn't stop wanting her… needing to please her…

It was the way she touched him, the way she listened, the way she was genuinely curious about his life, and the way she looked at him…

The way she tried to understand him after what had happened in Vegas… She was scared as hell, but open to the conversation. She wanted to know the truth, a plausible explanation. He had no choice but to tell her. This wasn't someone he never wished to see again; he had to handle this differently, for so many reasons. He was enchanted with her. She ran circles in his mind as if she were an Olympic runner. She consumed his thoughts with the way she opened up like a flower to him, showed him bits and pieces of her shattered life, and exposed herself to him—not just her body, but her very soul, in all of its broken glory. He felt something for her, but she'd unlocked so much more. She'd grown up in a house of craziness. How could she not pretend to be stable, ordinary? She needed it like a child needed love.

Burying his face against her neck and shoulder, he shivered when she lightly caressed his hair, as if she were reading his mind.

"I'm about to cum…" he murmured. "I want to hold it off though…"

"I want you to cum. I *love* how you look and feel when you do. You don't have to wait."

"I'm waiting for *you*... Cum with me." He rose slightly, slipped his finger against her clit, and grinded on her with each thrust. He watched her intensely, gauging her reactions. She seemed to not only get off on his lovemaking, but she also enjoyed being the center of his attention. She liked the way he observed her... fancied her... desired her. Pressing her back into the mattress, arching her body beneath his, eyes wide open... she filled him with something indescribable. Together, they gasped, releasing simultaneously. He held tight to her, his body convulsing, muscles stiff, barely able to breathe as his climax came in harsh waves.

Sweat rolled off every inch of his skin, tickling his flesh. His dick throbbed and twitched in the condom, expelling the last bits of ecstasy. They lay together, breathing hard, holding onto each other for dear life. After a while, he reluctantly let her go and got to his feet to retrieve his phone.

"Do you have to go?" She sat up, wrapping the sheets around her body.

His missed call was from Harlem. He glanced back at her. Her eyes were big and wide, like a doe's. The whites reminded him of pure snow.

"Why do you ask?"

"Because... you don't, uh, you don't have to yet if you don't want to." She blinked a few times, as if nervous to even say it, then she turned her gaze away. He realized at that moment that they both were stuck. They were struggling. Neither of them expected this, and damn sure weren't looking for it. They were falling for each other. Fast and hard.

He must've stared at her too long as he sorted his

thoughts because all of a sudden she turned her sights back on him, shook her head, and looked away again.

"It's okay. You can go, I was just, uh, extending the offer. It's no big deal."

"No big deal, huh?" He smirked. "What if I don't want to go? What if I just have to?" He placed the phone down on the bed, grabbed his underwear, and slid them on, his dick still hard and covered in her essence. He had no desire to wash her scent off. He wanted to keep her all over him for a bit longer. "Huh? Did you hear me?" She said nothing, her attention on her cuticles, as if they were of particular interest. "I want to stay, Zaire. I'm *going* to stay. Want to... shit... I have no idea what the hell I'm doing, all right?" He shrugged. "I'm not a dater. I don't "do" relationships, all right? I don't even know how this really works so I guess we could go out for breakfast, maybe a movie later, some shit like that? Is that what you want?" He smiled, hating the confusion he felt, not sure how to put one foot in front of the other with this whole awkward thing.

"Savage?"

"Yeah?"

"I want to know what you want from me. I want you to tell me again, like you did on the plane, but give me the updated version because a lot has happened between then and now. I feel like we've almost lived an entire lifetime in just a few visits. I'm scared. I care... about... I care about you, okay? I'm intrigued... and uh..." she paused for a moment, "I am admitting that I'm interested in you, as a person to date... to be with. I want to get to know you better, beyond the bedroom."

He nodded, then reached for his pants and put them on.

"All right. I understand. I don't feel the need to try and lay it on thick as my friend said again, so I'll just come out straight, okay?"

"Yes, please do." She crossed her arms over her chest.

"I wanna be with you. Like, together… just us. I want the same thing you want, to get to know you. I still want to fuck a lot though so that outta the bedroom shit kinda threw me for a loop but…" She laughed at that. "Yeah… I think we're on the same page."

"I don't want to be with you though, Savage, if you're going to be having sex with other women at the same time. If I allow myself to get emotionally attached to you, I can't share you with other women."

He swallowed. After a brief hesitation, he moved closer to her, shoving his hands in his pockets.

"Yeah… I can appreciate that. So I will make a promise to you that I won't fuck any other women while we're tryna see where this goes, okay? What about you? Is the pussy locked down now? It's just mine, right?"

She smirked at him and nodded. "Of course."

"All right. Get cleaned up and dressed. Let me take ya out to get a late-night dinner or early breakfast from one of these twenty-four-hour joints. I'm starving."

"No, no, no." She shook her head, waving her finger in his direction before flinging the sheets off herself and sliding off the bed. "I'm going to prepare for you a home cooked meal if you're hungry, okay?"

"You can cook?" He couldn't help but be surprised. She didn't seem like the type.

"Hell yes I can cook. I can throw down! Now come on, have a seat on the bed. I am going to take a shower, throw on a nightgown and my robe, and we'll go down to the kitchen together. The remote for the television is right there." She pointed across the room before disappearing into the master suite bathroom, closing the door behind her. He sat there for a spell, scratching his head.

The woman was full of surprises. And he liked that shit. He liked that shit a lot...

CHAPTER SIXTEEN

From Hell to Breakfast

Z AIRE PULLED HER robe up for what felt like the one hundredth time. The silky silver material kept falling from her shoulder and gathering around her elbow as she moved about, spatula in hand. She maneuvered the utensil back and forth in a butter coated skillet of scrambled eggs while the bacon sat on a nearby plate, the grease absorbed by a few layers of paper towels. The fluffy homemade buttermilk pancakes patiently awaited the fried apple topping she'd prepared from scratch and the hash browns, seasoned with onion and green pepper, were still warm enough to melt the cheddar cheese she'd sprinkled on them. She'd sliced strawberries and an assortment of other goodies as well. Truth be told, she hadn't cooked a large banquet like this in eons. There was no reason to; she lived alone, and she wanted to watch her weight. Today, however, was special.

She glanced at the man who'd turned her into a puddle of giggles and joy, and smiled. His back was towards her and though she couldn't see his face, there was no doubt he was smiling, too.

In the open living room on the white couch, Savage sat bare chested, hunched over with the remote control in his grip and his glass of orange juice on the clear coffee table before him. His coffee was right alongside it, steam still rising from the cup. He was watching a rerun of the obnoxious hit show, 'South Park'. She'd seen it a time or two, and that was a time or two too many. The crass, outlandish adult cartoon was enough to make her head explode, chock full of absurdity, sheer stupidity, and political incorrectness, but he appeared to be enjoying himself nonetheless, chuckling every other minute or so. She imagined from his line of work that the senselessness of it all was a welcomed reprieve.

"Are you hungry, Maximus? It's almost finished!" she called out. It sounded odd at times calling him by his first name. She ping ponged between it and 'Savage', just as he did with Zaire and Eva. Perhaps they were both acknowledging their double personalities—something else they had in common.

"I'm fuckin' starvin'!"

She turned off the eye of the stove, grabbed two stone-colored square plates, and placed everything on them just so. After garnishing with a sprig of fresh mint and a slice of tomato, she made her way into the living room and handed him his plate, along with a napkin folded over a fork and knife. "Oh shit... Wow. This looks amazing, baby."

His eyes glazed over with wonder and before she could even get situated next to him, the man was digging into the damn food like some ravenous maniac. She watched in amazement as he chewed and smacked his lips, occasionally chasing the bites with a hard gulp of the tangy, fresh squeezed citrus delight.

"Now I know you've had good food before. You took me to a nice restaurant in Vegas. You probably even have a private chef. Why are you acting as if this is the first time you're eating something decent?"

"Yeah." He jammed a forkful of sliced strawberries into his mouth, his gaze roaming over his plate like a nomad who'd come upon an oasis. "I have good food all the time, but I don't..." He paused to swallow. "I don't have a private chef, nothin' like that." The sound of his fork clinking against the plate sounded vicious, as if he were stabbing everything to death. She placed her hand over her mouth to keep from laughing. "I need my privacy. I mean, I have people come in and clean 'nd shit, but always with a security guy watching. As far as food though, I usually just get take out. This is incredible!" He burst out laughing when one of the characters on the television explained something about an anal probe.

She studied his arms and chest covered in tattoos, still reeling at how much ink covered the man. He was hairy, tanned, broad shouldered, intimidating as fuck... and she grew wet just by looking at him. He looked exactly how he behaved, there was no guess work with this one. "Baby, to tell you the truth though, I can't remember the last time I had a home-cooked meal."

"Really? Was your mom or dad a good cook? Wait, hold that thought." She got to her feet, retrieved her glass of juice that she'd left on the kitchen counter, then returned to his side. "I asked about your parents cooking for you when you were a kid. Did they?" She sipped from her glass then set it down next to his.

"Nah." He stared straight at the television, chewing sloppily and seemingly distracted—perhaps not interested in delving deeper. "My mom pretty much just threw some shit in the microwave and when my dad was home, sometimes he'd just pick up somethin' from a fast food place or food truck, somethin' like that. My mother made coffee, cereal, and lit cigarettes." He chuckled dismally. "I only saw my father make me hot dogs and pop tarts every now and again... oh, and bowls of chips and pretzels on special occasions, with dip. On my birthdays I got pizza, cake, and ice cream—store bought. My mother wasn't much of a cook."

"What about holidays? Thanksgiving? Christmas?"

"We'd go to the Chinese buffet or over one of my dad's friends' houses."

As she sat there looking at the man with the thick brows, long dark lashes, and heavy muscles, she realized he was more of a feral animal who'd somehow made it out of not only an unusual wilderness of a childhood, but one that was missing essential pieces to his past puzzle. Savage was definitely a fitting surname.

He's like Tarzan...

"You practically raised yourself, didn't you?" she asked as she bit into a piece of lightly buttered toast.

"Nah, I wouldn't go that far. You're jumping to conclusions based on what I said about the food 'nd all. There are other ways to nourish a child... and they definitely fed my mind." She nodded in understanding. "My parents raised me for sure. The thing of it was, they had a lot of faith in me. After they showed or taught me somethin', they knew they didn't need to waste a lot of time going over it again. I was shown very early on how to take care of myself. Remember, my mother had to do the same. She was a survivor. Her parents had abandoned her because so she ended up in an orphanage. She was abused in there, and figured out ways to endure."

"That makes sense. What did they teach you?" She took another bite of her toast.

"She and my father taught me how to get up and get ready for my day, how to make a bowl of cereal and fry an egg. I washed my own clothes, cleaned my shoes, ironed the collars on my shirts, walked down the street to a friend's house. His father would cut my hair until I learned how to cut my own. I was good with dogs. I could train them because my father taught me how. We had some pit bulls and mutts, and would sell the puppies. I was a good teacher that way, just like my father.

"My dad took me over his friend's house who was a Jiu-Jitsu fighter. I found out, after messing with him and his kids in their garage, that I liked fighting. My dad had another friend who was a body builder. I also discovered I liked lifting weights. My dad lifted weights, too, so between the two of 'em, I bulked up pretty quick. I liked it. It took my mind off... some things."

She wanted to ask him what those things were, for he seemed to fall in deep thought then. His expression turned into a scowl. But she decided to hold off and just wait.

"I liked racing my friends, you know, to see who was the

fastest. Most of my friends back then were biker kids, just like me."

"That makes sense. We usually become friends at that age with whoever we attend school with or the children of our parents' friends. It becomes an extended family." He nodded. "Did you play sports in school?"

"Yeah. I played football and basketball. I liked athletics, period. I was pretty good. It was just somethin' to do. I tried to be a part of everything, ya know? I was even in the debate club but got kicked out of it for always cursing." She shook her head and couldn't help but laugh. "Anyway, school bored me, but my mother would be on my ass if I missed too many days. I did just enough to get by. The kids there were square or involved in stupid stuff for no reason. I mean, why be in a life of crime if ya really didn't need to be? Just dumb. So, uh, back to your original question. No home cooked meals...

"I got raised, but the other stuff just wasn't a daily thing. They didn't nag or get on me unless I wasn't following the rules. They'd tell me something once and I was expected to do it. If I didn't, there were consequences." He took a sip of his juice.

"Consequences? Were you physically abused?"

"I was disciplined. Not a beating that almost cost me my life or anything crazy like that, but maybe I was grounded, ya know? No friends over, no bike, no allowance, shit like that." She nodded in understanding. "So." He picked up his cup of coffee and tasted that. "Since you're all in my business, let me get into yours. Who taught you to cook?"

"My father." She couldn't help but grin.

"Are you real close with him?" He smiled. "Seems like it

from what you've shared with me so far and that big, pretty smile on your face."

"Very much so." She adjusted her robe once again and crossed her legs. A strange looking character with a rotund shape apparently named Cartman was speaking about some equally funny looking character named Kyle stealing his girlfriend. Savage took her plate from her grasp, set it on the table, and started to massage her feet. He watched the television, laughing so hard, his complexion deepened and the vein in his neck protruded. She leaned back on the couch and slid a hand behind her head, staring at him.

"What are you smilin' at?" he asked, sensing her gaze.

How'd he know I was smiling? He is who he is, that's why...

"You..."

"Why? You like what you see?"

"Of course I do. You don't like being stared at?" she teased.

"It depends on the reason why. What are you thinking about? I'm supposed to ask that, right?" He paused, his fingers on the balls of her feet, no longer delivering the wonderful touch she'd already grown addicted to. "I mean, when you're dating someone, you're supposed to ask about their day, how they feel, shit like that."

She sucked her teeth and shook her head at him.

"I refuse to believe that you have no compass as to how to navigate this, Savage. You're pulling my leg. I know you've had relationships with women before I came onto the scene. I've had plentiful conversations with you. You know how to hold your own."

"Yeah, this isn't a first, but you're the first woman I really wanted to impress." He shrugged, seeming a tad nervous as he began to rub her feet again. "I just want to make sure I'm doing this shit right, that I cover all the bases." She was duly impressed. "Maybe I should read some articles online, take some of those love surveys, corny shit like that." She burst out laughing, and he tossed her a hooded glance.

"Let's just have a conversation, okay then? A simple one," she offered.

"All right."

"First of all, when you're talking to your lady, you should look her in the eye and not continue to watch television."

With a huff, he reached for the remote control and turned off the television. He then turned towards her, a silly smirk on his face.

"Better?"

"Much. Now, you tell me at least two things you really enjoy doing."

"Oh, that's easy. Fucking and work."

"Savage." She pursed her lips in disapproval. He burst out laughing.

"All right! Let's see... Well, just so you know, that was the truth though, okay? I'm serious. Sex and my job are really important to me." She grimaced. "But I know what you mean. I, uh... Oh, I've got it. I like gambling at the casino and swimming."

"Great! I knew about the casino, obviously, Blackjack being your favorite and you being quite good at it, too. As for me, I like cooking, traveling, and reading. I threw in a third one for good measure. Are you a good swimmer?"

"Yeah, really good. When I was a kid, I used to have a gig

as a life guard one summer. You? Do you like to swim?"

"Oh, I can't swim." A wave of embarrassment washed over her as he regarded her with wide eyes and pupils steeped in judgment.

"Can't swim? What kinda shit is that?!"

"What do you mean what kind of shit is that? Lots of people can't swim!" She tossed up her hands.

"You were born and bred right here in California, in Los Angeles! Beach baby, for God's sake!"

"So! I wasn't born underwater and I'm not a mermaid!"

"We were *all* born underwater. Does the amniotic sac ring a bell?"

"I don't recall mine," she snapped. "And chances are high, you don't recall yours... you know, the whole being born part."

"Our bodies are made up of over fifty percent water." She couldn't help but roll her eyes. He was a showoff. "Let me ask you something. Is it true that Black people don't even like to swim? Like, get into a swimming pool? I thought maybe it was just a myth but then there's *you*!"

"Now how the hell can I speak for all Black people, Savage?! Can you speak for all White men with too many damn tattoos, buzzed military haircuts, and beards? What if I stereotyped you and said all guys who look like you are national terrorists, have been to prison, are camo lovers, racists, and gun zealots?"

He raised a brow in response.

"But I *am* a gun zealot. I very well coulda ended up in prison when I was out in the streets. Everyone is a little bit racist if we want to be honest about this shit, and camo clothes aren't half bad."

"You know what I mean!"

"We've gotten off track. The important issue is that you can't swim."

"So here we are again." She crossed her arms. "Why's that so important? I don't plan on dancing with any sharks, unless you know how to do the tango."

"I happen to be a great dancer, too. I know how to tango, salsa, a lot of shit." Now THIS did surprise her about the man. "This Latina chick I used to bone taught me." She grimaced. It all made sense now. "I'll show you later."

"No, thank you. Wait, dance lessons? Okay."

"No, the boning. Back to the swimming though. What if you went on a cruise and people had to jump overboard for their own safety due to a serious mechanical issue, huh? It's not guaranteed that there's enough time to get everyone life jackets and even so, that may not be enough to get you to shore safely. What if you saw your friend or sister's child drowning in a pool and there was no lifeguard on duty? You gonna just stand there and watch the kid drown?" She swallowed. The morbid scenarios were not terribly farfetched. "Your car could swerve and go into the ocean or some ravine with high water. There's all kinds of things that could happen and go wrong, and besides, it's great exercise, it's fun. Fucking under water is the shit, and it's just a good life skill to have."

"Are you done, Smokey the Perverted Bear? Only YOU can prevent forest fires and drowning. I get it! You've made your point. I agree with you. Now, let's talk about something else."

"This isn't over. I'm teaching you how to swim soon."
He casually reached for his wallet and removed a cigar. He lit
it and took a drag, blowing out dense curls of smoke. "I can
get you sorted in just a few days. I'm that good."

"You know those cigars are bad for your health, right?"
She began to cough, laying it on thick as she waved her hand,
trying to dispel the smoke in a dramatic fashion. "Since you
want to sit there on your high horse and talk to me about not
knowing how to swim, talking about safety and all." She
frowned. "I bet your lungs are black as tar."

"They might be." He shrugged. "But you can bet your
pretty little ass I never get winded…" He looked her up and
down. "I dare ya to say otherwise. In fact, you tap out way
before it even crosses my mind. Considering my age, I run
circles even around teenagers and have the speed of an
Olympic athlete. My strength is one of my best assets. I have
an extremely high pain threshold and I can breathe for two
minutes and thirty-two seconds underwater on my worst
day."

"Do you ever get tired of discussing how great you are?"

"Rarely. So black lungs or not, I can go toe to toe with
most men my age and younger. But your ass *still* can't swim."

She walloped him with a pillow, which only caused him
to laugh all the louder. Standing to his feet, he took her hand
and helped her up. He was so tall, so overwhelming. Before
she knew it, Savage was pushing her body back, then drawing
her close, spinning her and counting steps.

"This is how you salsa."

"I like it! This is fun. Maybe we should turn on some
music?"

"Nah, just feel the rhythm. See, everything has a beat, a song. Friendships have a song that only those friends know the lyrics to. No one else can hear it. Killing has a song. When I'm on one of my missions, I listen closely to it. Only I can hear it, and I like it, especially since I'm the DJ." She swallowed and drew serious. "Realizing you like someone as more than just a fuck buddy has a song, too, so… I'm just here, you know, tryna learn it… waiting for you to teach me all the lyrics. I'm trying to hear what your mind and heart are saying to me, Zaire. I know your body well. We've got that part down pat. Now I'm trying to do that shit lovers do… romance you, dance with that thing my friend Harlem calls soul. He told me one time, when he and I first met, that I was soulless, but then, he changed his mind."

"What made him second guess that?"

"He spent more time with me. He said I've got plenty of soul—I just show it to a select few." He pressed his lips to hers. "Soul sharing makes you vulnerable, baby. Be careful."

"Speaking of souls, do you believe in God, Savage?" He sported a quizzical expression but kept moving and showing her the steps, holding her close.

"Don't they say God is within all of us?" he asked.

"Yes."

"Then yeah, I believe in God. I have to because I know Satan is real. He's in me, too." The man's eyes grew dark and hooded, sending chills up her spine. Goosebumps covered her arms. She felt the same sense of urgency and panic when he'd tossed her about in bed, the steel metal of his gun within sight, sticking out of his pants splayed on the ground in her bedroom. He'd manhandled her in the shower after their session in bed earlier, and she loved how rough he was when he had his way with her. He was an infectious gorgeous disease, a horribly seductive addiction, and she prayed she never got well. "I can't believe in one without the other. Good and evil must co-exist. They depend on each other. They have no definition without that reliance."

"I never really thought of it that way. I suppose you could be right."

"So no, you're not dancing with a shark, baby. You're dancing with the Devil... Thing is, Eva, I like hurting people. But you? You like helping people. I wanna protect you, and in your own way, I think you want to protect me, too—from myself." *He was right...* "I know a part of you is afraid of me, but believe it or not, a part of me is afraid of you too."

"Why?"

"Because you motivate me. You compel me to examine myself. I've never met anyone like you. You're making me think about the things I do—pushing me, making me want to see if I can have my cake... that's you... and eat it, too. Settle down for a change. It was never tempting until now. I still have to be me, you seem to get that, but maybe, just maybe, I can take all this shit off... the heavy shit that sets on my shoulders and weighs me down while I'm with you. Maybe when I walk through your door, I can just be Maximus. I am Savage, I am both, but Maximus doesn't get as much airtime, and maybe he needs it." He shrugged. "There's something inside of you that I want. That I *need*. You can teach me some shit I don't know how to do."

"What's that?"

"To fall in love graciously..." She closed her eyes and

blinked back her emotions. "But I have to earn you, right?"

"Yes. We both are trying to earn one another, and that includes trust." She leaned in close and kissed his cheek.

"So here I am, the Devil in the flesh. I've been cast away. I'm a black sheep, a proud member of the discarded, revered and feared. Wasn't Lucifer a fallen angel?" She looked at the imp tattoo on his wrist, the whipping tail and the two sharp black horns along the top of the beast's head. "I'm extinguishing my flames for just a moment so you can get close to me, Zaire, without getting burned. This shit is hard for me because I like being on fire and destroying everything that comes my way. Now, I have to consider someone else. Something tells me that you're worth it…"

CHAPTER SEVENTEEN

Don't Touch My Shit

…Two weeks later

S AVAGE TOSSED ANOTHER blade into his army green duffle bag then slid the bag strap over his shoulder. His phone planted to his ear, he cleared his throat as he made his way down the stairwell, out the kitchen, and opened the garage door.

"So, it was just a matter of time, you know?" Austin said.

Savage half-listened to the man rattling on. Setting his bag onto the concrete ground, he tugged at the black tarp covering his midnight blue and jet black Boss 1969 Ford Mustang. It was one of a kind, rare and coveted. He'd been offered so much money for it he could have purchased another home, but he refused to part with it. His father had gotten it from a dump, fixed it up, then given it to him for his eighteenth birthday. He'd never let it go. He took care of the damn thing like he would a newborn, ensuring she stayed in good health.

"And so I appreciate you taking care of that for me. Your assignment is complete," Austin added, bringing whatever the hell he was saying to a close.

"When do I get the other half of my money?" Savage picked up his bag, slipped his car keys out of his pocket, and unlocked his prize, anticipating the purr of the engine as he sat down on the soft white leather interior. He tossed the bag in the back of the car and rested the phone on the dashboard.

"You always get it within forty-eight hours. That's been the protocol for years."

"Yeah, well, I have some business to take care of so it never hurts to ask."

"You're definitely not living pay check to pay check. You're rich!" Austin chuckled, though his laughter was tinged with confusion. "What's gotten into you?"

"This is business. Nothing has gotten into me." Savage drummed his fingers on the steering wheel, feeling antsy, then turned on the special stereo system he'd had installed. His Prince cassette was still inside and the tune of 'Uptown' came through the state-of-the-art speakers.

"That's a bit loud."

"Huh?"

"That's a bit loud, Savage!"

"Really? Loud like… fuck it!"

"You seem a bit, I don't know, edgy lately, Savage. Is something troubling you?" Austin inquired as he turned the volume lower.

"Yeah. A lot is troubling me, Austin. Yesterday, I had my tires slashed. What a bitch move! What grown man slashes another man's tires?! My jeep was parked out in front of a liquor store."

"Well, maybe it wasn't a man. Did you piss off one of your many women?" the man teased. "You've been known to break some hearts."

"Nope, it wasn't a chick." Savage closed the car door and gripped the steering wheel, trying with all his might to not lose his cool. "I asked the store to see their camera footage, and showed 'em my government I.D. The man was dressed in black from top to bottom. Couldn't make out shit... The video was grainy, too."

"Well, who do you think did it? What's the motive?"

"Someone is trying to kill me. It was a warning. The timing couldn't be worse."

"Someone is *always* trying to kill us, Savage. It goes with the territory. You've said it yourself—you're the doorkeeper, you take out the trash. Sometimes the trash has trashy friends, and they want a piece of the action."

"No, this is different."

"The incident in Las Vegas? I thought we had that resolved," the man stated with a long sigh. "Longhorn had nothing to do with that situation, Savage, and we figured that the two guys in there were tied to the assignment you did last year in Miami. We could never get their real names, only aliases. No fingerprints, nothing. They're not in the database which is strange, but they'd been spotted in Miami several times by eye witnesses, so that had to have been it. That was a heavy case, the Toret Crew. They were connected, remember? It was a revenge thing. You and Dimitri took out three of their kingpins within eight hours. Unheard of. Come on.

You have enough *real* life bullshit to worry about than to bother yourself with suspicion."

"No, I'm not convinced that isn't what this is about. My gut is tellin' me that's wrong, *all* wrong, and it's not paranoia. It's called being proactive... smart. Yeah, they were from Miami, the same area I was in last year when Dimitri and I took out Miguel and his squad. And yeah, they may have known Clinton and Miguel, who really knows? But this had a different feel to it and if that was the motive, why isn't Dimitri getting people jumpin' out of closets on his ass, too?" He was met with silence. "Exactly. Why would they wait in the closet to confront me in the first place?

"They had a clear shot for at least ten seconds before I noticed the plant was moved. My defenses were lowered. I was walking into that room to be with a woman, not to strategize, not to get more ammo. I had just been outside on my motorcycle serving a little street justice. I was amped. Why would they sit back and watch me fuck someone, for over an hour I might add, then shower, all of that shit? I was ready for them in case they came in the shower, too, but they didn't know that. It's like they were waiting for a signal. For someone else to show up, to give them the go ahead."

"You're reading too much into this. They wanted a good aim, no doubt. They knew if they missed, you'd take them out. You're known for your shooting accuracy."

"Are you aware Harlem was supposed to come and join me that day?"

"No. Why would Harlem come?"

"Because I hadn't heard back from you and I was concerned. He said he would arrange to come, especially after the heat was on me regarding me mowing that fuckin' meth head down who stole that woman's purse and it was all over the news. But this just isn't adding up, Austin. Something stinks."

"I don't think anything suspicious is going on here, Savage. We've all looked at this extensively but I tell you what, I will have the intelligence crew look over it again, okay?"

"Yeah." He pushed the button on the car visor and opened the garage door then started the engine and lit a fresh cigar. "You do that."

"So, what are your plans today? I hope you don't plan on heading off on vacation. Don't get too comfortable because next week I need you... Very important task. It just got signed off on."

"I don't work for you, Austin. You're on *my* time, not the other way around."

The man sighed. "I know that, Savage, but this is important. I need—"

"It's always important, isn't it?" He quickly rolled the window down. "Like the fact Longhorn keeps blowin' up my gotdamn phone, demanding to talk, even after the bullshit he pulled. And it was also so super fuckin' important that you sent five fuckers to my girlfriend's house sporting full metal jackets to interrogate her and didn't even have the fuckin' common decency to give me a heads up so I could warn her!"

"So that's what this is about..."

"So that's what this is about?! Like it's no big fuckin' deal! She's not one of us! You can't do that! She was scared out of 'er mind! Her friends were over there, too. Do you know how fuckin' bad that looked?!"

"They waited until her friends vacated the property," Austin stated dryly, as if the entire conversation was a waste of his time.

"You want a cookie?! SO WHAT! They weren't even down the street before your guys were pounding on her door in full gear! These interviews are supposed to be just that—interviews, not arrests! She's a fuckin' relationship podcast guru, not a saboteur! The only thing she is out here killing is a runway during her annual domestic violence fashion show fundraiser!"

"You were on assignment and it was protocol, Savage."

"Protocol or not, you shoulda said somethin', man! Damn! Is that too much to ask? We're better than this!" Savage jammed his finger into his chest, feeling some kind of way.

"Look, I understand why you're upset but I am not supposed to tip you off. She could have become a flight risk."

"Where would she go, Austin?!" He tossed up his hands in disbelief. "We are everywhere! She can't go to the police. They'd report back to us. She can't go to the governor, send Gavin Newsom an email. She can't go to anyone. She can go nowhere because we'd always find out. Besides, she's innocent."

"Not anymore. She's seen far too much and unlike your other conquests, you're keeping her around, like a pet. You also told her too much. We had to come in and address this. You left us no choice."

"I blew away two people in front of 'er! What the fuck was I supposed to tell her, Austin? 'Oh, Zaire, that was pretend. Hee hee hee, so funny! See, the red shit is ketchup, not real blood. We like to play like that.' Do you see how stupid that sounds? She's not a fuckin' moron! Two dudes got smoked right then and there and she was about to piss her pants. Do you remember your first kill? Do you remember seeing your first dead body?" Silence, only breathing. "You told me you got sick... threw up. I don't have that trigger. I don't get queasy, I don't get scared, I don't get sick. Never had it, never will; as Harlem jokes, I was born broken. But I can imagine how you must've felt that time. Now, it's old news to you.

"You don't bat an eye at bloated bodies floating in the river, putrefied gangsters in trashcans, the stench of decomposition, dismembered escape high-risk felons, guys with their guts pulled out yet their hearts are still beating. None of that phases you. You've seen it too many times now. Zaire, on the other hand is not in our world, okay? She will never be like us. Not everyone is built for this shit, and I like her even more because she's not, man. It makes her human. She's not in the street, she's not around drugs, she's not in our sphere. She still has a heart, unlike the rest of us sons of bitches who are completely desensitized and don't give a fuck. She's not a savage... Don't confuse her with me. Don't make her a monster, man. She's not."

"I don't believe she is at all. That's not the issue and for the record, her interview went well so I have no reason to believe we'd need to address this again unless something else transpires in her presence. However, you understand the risks, Savage. All of our men have had things like this happen. It's common. We have sex lives, I get that, but then you have unexpected visitors, too. Depending on the person and what transpires determines how we handle it."

"And you handled this wrong."

"Savage, you're killin' me, here." Austin sounded exasperated. "No, we didn't. That still doesn't change the fact that we followed the rules."

"Well, here's a Savage rule for you. Write this shit down. If one of your motherfuckers pops up over Zaire's house again with no warning, no call to me, no text, not letting me know what's up, I am going to blow his fuckin' head off. No hesitation."

"Savage…"

"No… No! I mean this! Since you want to talk to me like everything I say is an over-reaction and this situation should be swept under the rug and you did no wrong, then we'll be finished talkin', all right? And I'll just handle it hands on. You just make sure you have that same energy when I protect what's mine, okay?! Try me! Not much into conversing anymore about it. All I know is one thing, and one thing only: You better leave her out of this, you hear me? If you need to speak to her, you speak to me *first*. You got what you needed. Don't ever do that shit again without giving me a heads up."

"I can't promise you we'll never have to speak to her again, especially since, according to the interview, you two are seeing one another. You should know me well enough by now to understand that I would have alerted you regardless had I known it was scheduled while you were in South Dakota, Savage! You're pissed at me for something that needed to transpire, regardless of how your dick feels about it! Get your head back in the game… the *big* one."

"I believe I've made myself clear." He took a puff of his cigar and hung his arm out the window. "Now, if you're feelin' froggy, motherfucker, then jump. Do that shit again, then you just make sure it's worth it to ya. If you cross that line, you should never call me again. For shit. I won't be at your son's graduation, no more parties, no more nothing. I definitely won't be taking any more assignments from you. You'll be dead to me. It'll be like you never existed. There are plenty of agencies who want me should I feel so inclined to stop my solo act. They'll ask me about Austin, and I'll say, 'Austin who? I don't know that motherfucker.' I mean that."

Tense silence stretched between them for a few moments.

"How in the hell did we get here? How did this happen, Savage? You and I don't argue! We get along great. A woman has come between us. Why am I surprised?" He chuckled. "Anyway, I have to admit I find it interesting that this is so serious… you know, between you two. You never told me she was your girlfriend. When did this happen, if you don't mind me asking?"

"When was my private life any of your business? Besides, the answer is in the interview. She was grilled—even had to tell them how many times we had sex. Unbelievable."

"It *is* my business if you'd like me to lay off and tell the others to step back. Look, I know how you are. We've known each other for a mighty long time, Savage, and not only are you one of the best; I consider you a friend. This disagreement is disheartening to say the least."

It truly was. Savage enjoyed Austin as a person, but

things had happened, lines had been crossed, and now he was cross, too.

"If you think I'm enjoying this shit, I'm not. There are just some things I won't stand for, Austin. From anyone."

"I know you don't trust many people, Savage, and you don't discuss your life unless it pertains to the job, but in the line of work we're in, we just don't... have successful relationships, okay? It can get messy..." Savage leaned his head against the back of the seat. He stared up at the roof of the car, feeling a million things, thinking a billion thoughts as Prince serenaded him. "But I'm not going to try to deter you. I know that this must be pretty important... *she* must be pretty important for you to proceed forward. Now, back to the original discussion. Do you want the added security or not? You can't be in five places at once, Savage."

After a rolling it over in his mind, he came to a decision.

"Yeah... But I don't want her privacy invaded, okay? No cameras in her bathroom, nothin' like that. Don't enter her house without knocking, no recorders. Just drive-bys and check-ins. She's got... never mind."

"No, what? She's got what?"

Savage sighed, not certain he should say anything just yet. "She's got some fuckin' looney toon callin' her show, emailing her and harassing her."

"Looney toon? What's going on?"

"Yeah, a fuckin' nutjob." He ran his hand down his face. "Some cracked in the head asshole is pissed that she told his wife to love herself again, basically, and leave his ass. See, Zaire is like this women's empowerment expert, Austin. She gives tough love. It's entertainment but a lot of her advice is on the money. It's part show, part truth. She acts overly dramatic and shit to keep the ratings high. People like drama, goes with the territory, but she still has integrity. She tells them what she believes to be true, and gives good advice, ya know?"

"Yeah, so what happened?" He could almost hear the man's brain churning—a leverage tool to get him to do his bidding. Austin was always trying to run deals and trades. This time would be no different.

"So, the wife, her caller, eventually did kick this guy to the curb and has a whole new life now. New boyfriend and shit and this guy blames Zaire for it all. This has been going on for over a year, but he's getting more manic. The wife has a restraining order against him and moved across the country with their kids. Zaire said he stopped callin' for a long time but the other day I was listening to her show and heard him call in. He said some pretty foul shit."

"Is Zaire concerned now?"

"Actually, she didn't bring it up to me at all about this latest incident, but I'm not surprised. She and I have spent a lot of time together and she's pretty much caught on that I don't like shit like this, that I could do something. I haven't told her I'd heard the call, but I don't like this shit. I don't like it at all."

"Okay, we need to do something about this. These issues rarely just go away on their own, you know? I want to help."

"Sure you do… and then you have me in the palm of your hand again, out there chasin' another bad guy while you sit back from the comfort of your office and watch."

"Savage, Jesus! Get the stick out of your ass and just talk

to me! We have a good relationship. If you're angry about something else, something you haven't relayed, just say so!"

"STAY AWAY FROM HER!" he yelled so loud, his own ear rang. "You kept talking about rules, but I can't let this go! I need to hear your promise. You keep those motherfuckers away from my girlfriend, Austin! You've caused disruption! I am trying to gain her fuckin' trust, and then as soon as I turn my back, the A-Team crashes into her fuckin' house! She didn't want to talk to me about it and had to get herself calmed down. You're fucking with my life!"

"You're relentless, Savage! You're like a dog with a bone. I cannot believe we're back on this shit again!"

"Because it's not resolved!"

"I told you that you weren't home and I damn sure wasn't about to call you during a sting! You were apprehending the suspect!"

"You've given me a million reasons why you did this, and none make sense. First, I wasn't around. Then it was you would've told me anyway, but I was working. Then it was, you can't tell me because it would compromise the interview process and that would make us all subject to an interrogation. Next you'll say it's because she planned to go to Disneyland and give Minnie Mouse a hug! Fuckin' clown behavior…"

"We're going to settle this once and for all. We had to do it right then, Savage. You know how these schedules work!" He looked at himself in the rear view mirror. His nostrils flared as he shook his head in disbelief. His heart was beating nearly out of his damn chest.

The fear he'd felt when she'd called him and told him

what had happened… and then she wouldn't answer her phone when he'd called her back. When they did speak again, he could tell she was beyond concerned. How could he have this woman all to himself if he couldn't even build a foundation for her to stand on? He needed time to do that… but so much had happened.

"Austin…" He hated how his voice cracked. "I can't risk her runnin' off because she's afraid of what I do, or of me! The first time, in Vegas, it took me hours to calm her down, to make her understand. This is the second time some fucked up shit has happened around her because of her involvement with yours truly, under her own roof, the one place she is supposed to feel safe. If you mess this up for me… I FUCKIN' SWEAR!" He beat the armrest and rocked about in his seat, seeing red. "She didn't sign up for this. Don't do this shit again. Promise me, Austin! If our friendship means that much to you, if you really honor our professional affiliation even a little, promise me that if you ever need to speak to her again, before you send them in like stormtroopers, you will tell me first."

"Savage, I can't just—"

"PROMISE ME!" He hit the steering wheel.

"I promise." They both drew quiet for a spell. "Now, back to what we were saying. We can put a tracer on her show phone, the one she uses for her podcast. Would that be okay?" Savage blew out puffs of smoke and looked about his garage. Everything was where it should be, put in its special place. Sometimes he came out there just to think, tinker around with one of his bikes, or sit back and listen to music.

"I already did…"

"Oh. Does she know?"

"Nope. She'd tell me I was over-reacting probably, over-stepping my bounds." He shrugged. "But I do want some of your equipment. I'll rig it myself. What do you want in return? Let's get to the part where you start askin' for extra shit, like an extra hit for half the price."

Austin laughed on the other end.

"Believe it or not, Savage, I just want you to continue to keep working some of these assignments for me. I'm honest enough to say some things just need a special touch, and only you can deliver it. So, until I find someone as good as or better than you, you are the one that comes to mind when I need assurance that one of the more challenging jobs that I come across will be done correctly. We can't have any mishaps right now. The FBI is down our throat." After a pause, he added, "I've never had the threat of losing you before."

Savage sniffed, feeling a bit of a cold coming on, then took another puff of his cigar.

"You won't. All of this comes with the territory. I can't stop doing this; it's who I am. I haven't stayed single this long just because I'm a commitment-phobe. I mean, yeah, that played a part in it, but I had never met anyone to even make me consider settling down. She's... she's different."

"I know it hasn't been long, but with your irritation over the interrogation schedule and what happened in Vegas, do you believe you love her?"

Savage took a deep breath and turned off the music.

"Maybe... Hell, I might... time will tell. I don't know what that's supposed to feel like, really, Austin. I've never loved anyone before." He shrugged. "I mean, I love my mother and my father. I love a couple of my friends, wouldn't want anything bad to happen to 'em, but that romantic love? Nah, I have no fuckin' clue. It seems a little silly to me. Well, it at least it did."

"Doesn't seem so silly now, huh?" Austin laughed forlornly.

"Nah, it doesn't. I was blindsided. This wasn't supposed to happen, ya know? But it did. It's never funny when it's happening directly to you, is it?" He smiled sadly as the realization set in.

"Savage, I'm struggling here."

"With what?"

"My own self-interests versus what I know is right." Austin cleared his throat. "I have been in love many times. I'm a bit older than you, so I've seen a bit more shit. One woman though, she was the one that got away... the one I think about to this day. I should have never let her go." Austin's breathing became louder. "She understood our line of work. She was a cop, so she wasn't surprised that organizations like ours existed. But what did I go and do? I imploded it. I made excuses, Savage. I was afraid I would put her in the line of danger. I was also afraid of being saddled down. I mean, if we're really honest, we're around beautiful women all the time. We travel the country, sometimes the world. We're high on adrenaline, no one can touch us... It's a dangerous life. An exciting life. A fucked up life." Savage nodded and sighed. The man was right. "I already had a young son at the time from my brief relationship with Meredith. Anyway, I lost her, Savage. She got tired of waiting. She married someone else.

"This happened over fifteen years ago. Now, she's got two kids. The oldest is like, thirteen, I believe. I ran into her the other day, and all of those feelings rushed back. She looked even more beautiful. But I was too late. She gave me a kiss on the cheek, told me she was happy, and wished me well. I'll never be well though, Savage... because I let my work come before my heart. If you can find a balance, do it. If you're ready to try to commit, go ahead with it. It's not going to be easy. If Zaire's easily offended, squeamish, has a big mouth, any of that, your goose is cooked. Cut her loose. But if she can hang with you, Savage, if she can learn and listen, if she has true interest in you as a man and not just the fact that you're a legal killing machine, she can be, as the young kids say, 'your ride or die.' So you should fight for that. I mean it."

Savage hung his head, feeling the man's words deep in his soul. "I hear you, Austin..."

"We all need love. I don't, uh, I don't think we're supposed to be in this world alone..."

Inside, Savage felt like a time bomb. He refused to confess everything that was on his mind and in his heart. Zaire had become such an intricate part of his life that he allowed her to see bits and pieces of him he'd kept under lock and key for years. The sex was becoming more intense. The words they shared were serious. The time they spent together meant everything to him. When they weren't together, he was thinking about her, and when he was working, he couldn't wait to finish the shit up and get back to her. His first love had always been his gun and the intended target. Now, his bloodthirst had competition.

"I want her, Austin. I'll do almost anything to keep this going with her. It feels so good. She makes me feel like I've never felt before. That's all I want to say about it. Maybe that was even too much."

"You've confirmed my suspicions. You're in love. It's too late. That's why you became so angry with me. I get it now. Look, you have my blessing—not that you asked for it, but you have it all the same. Now, get your ass over here as soon as possible for your next assignment. Pick up that equipment tomorrow for your little project. I'll have it waiting for you." The call ended abruptly.

Savage placed the phone in his lap, then turned the music back up. Prince belted out, 'Why You Want to Treat Me So Bad?'

He picked up his phone again and went through the camera roll, looking at the many photos he'd taken of Zaire, some of which she wasn't aware of…

He loved studying her when she slept, especially if she was snuggling against him. He found a photo of her asleep in the bed, the purple sheets all over their naked bodies. Her head lay against his chest and she was completely zonked out. He'd taken that photo because he always wanted to remember what her peace looked like, and to ensure he never made her life more difficult than it had to be, to rob her of her serenity. He placed the phone back down and ran his hand over his head, vibing and bobbing his head to the music.

Shit. Austin is right. I've fucked around and fallen in love…

CHAPTER EIGHTEEN

The Deep End

"COME ON."

"No." Zaire looked down into the large indoor hotel pool. She stared at the 3ft. mark written in black paint on the wall, then at the deeper parts. Her nose itched from the intense scent of the chlorine that filled the room.

Savage had jumped into the pool and waited with his arms outstretched, as if she were some bouncing beach ball soon to be tossed his way. She scratched her arm, her nerves a wreck as she devised a plan for how to get the hell out of there.

"Get in the fuckin' pool, Eva," he stated dryly.

"No."

The sounds of Loco, Hwasa (MAMAMOO) 'Don't' played from a small mp3 player shaped like a battery-operated radio, which the fiend had brought along, trying to get on her good side, no doubt. He had everything set up just so, and she couldn't help but give him credit for that. The son of a bitch had rented the space for just the two of them, bringing with him two thick brand new gold and white beach towels, a couple of bottles of iced tea, some flip flops for her, a boogie board, arm floaties, goggles, and even a swimming cap for her though it was way too small so it remained on top of the duffle bag he'd brought stuffed with more odds and ends.

"What's wrong? You on your period or something? You can swim on your period, you know."

"No... No! What would make you think that?"

"Because you're refusing to get in the fuckin' pool like you didn't know what this was about, like we didn't discuss this days ago—and honestly, you've had some mood swings lately, like lady type shit. I have a mother, sister, female associates. It's the same ol' shit with you people. I know the signs."

"You people?!"

"You're also a little bloated."

Her eyes practically popped out of her head. "Bloated?! You're amazing, you know that? Screw you, Savage."

"Look, we're not leaving until you learn how to swim. I'm not dating someone who can't swim. That's a deal breaker."

She rolled her eyes, sucked her teeth, and crossed her arms over her white bikini top.

"You really have some audacity, Savage. If I were in your shoes, I'd think really carefully about tossing around ultimatums. I don't want to date someone who—"

"Don't say it..." He placed his finger to his lips. "We're out in public. I have no idea what is being watched and filmed." His eyes narrowed as he pointed towards what might be a camera hanging up high in the corner of the room.

"Fine, but don't talk to me about deal breakers or 'lady shit'."

"I shouldn't have to talk to you about anything right now because you're supposed to be in the water. This is my last time asking you. Get your ass in this pool."

"No." Before she knew it, Savage was walking towards the steps. "Shit!" She rushed toward the pool area entrance. Perhaps she could exit in time, run through the hotel lobby and back to the car—hell, anywhere to get away from that place—but when she got to the doors, she tugged and beat on them frantically. The damn things were locked.

"Noooo! Oh, God!" She tried again and again. They rattled like chains, but didn't budge.

"See, I knew you were going to try some shit like this, woman. You pretended to be on board, and now you're chickening out." He drew closer, his body dripping wet. Her nerves were wrecked, yet she was turned on at the same damn time. She tugged a bit more, then made a mad dash across to the other side of the pool area.

I'm fast... and I'm scared! I will tire him out, he'll be chasing me so long!

She looked back a time or two. Savage kept his pace, a smirk on his face, never running, but walking briskly, his calf muscles tightening as his feet slapped against the concrete floor.

"Take me home!" she hollered out as she raced around the pool. He was quite a distance away, so she paused to regain her breath.

"After we have this swimming lesson, I will take you wherever you want to go, but you're getting in this pool." She took off running again, her breasts aching as they bounced about in the tiny bikini top. Before she knew what hit her, rough hands wrapped around her waist and yanked her back as though she were a mere rag doll. Dropping a kiss on her cheek, he held her as she squirmed about, begging for release.

"Come on, pleeeease! I'll do it next week, I promise! I want to go home!"

"You're coming with me." He hoisted her in the air and tossed her over his shoulder as she kicked and screamed to no avail, her empty promises falling on deaf ears. Beating him about his shoulders and back did no good. He might as well have been made of granite. In a split second, she was up in the air, flying backwards at warp speed.

"AHHHH!" she yelled when the rush of water smacked her back hard and tossed her about. Her fears realized and bursting free, she flapped about helplessly, getting sucked deeper and deeper into the water, her head barely above the surface. She looked up helplessly at Savage who stood there, his form hazy as she strained to keep her eye on him. He was looking as if he'd been hired to watch paint dry.

"How's it feel?" he asked with a smile, hands on waist.

I hate him! I hate his stupid face!

"Heeelp… Help me!" Panic set in.

Taking his sweet time, he dove into the pool and snatched her from the grasp of the water. Hauling her towards the other side of the pool which was far shallower, he stood her on her feet like some mannequin.

"I should slap the shit out of you!" she gasped, barely getting the words out. She trembled from the rush of cold air hitting her wet body. She held herself, feeling sorry for herself, worried and full of rage. His expression impassive, Savage crossed his arms and eyed her with his amber gaze.

"You do have the natural instinct to try and stay afloat at least. Not everyone has that, believe it or not. You didn't do as bad as you probably imagined."

"I almost drowned! Fu-fu-fu-fuck you!" Her teeth chattered.

"Mmm hmm," he said dismissively. "First thing we're going to do is learn to breathe correctly. Then I'm going to show you how to kick and move your arms. Look, baby, this is for your own good. Let's just bite the bullet, get it over with, okay? You don't have to ever be the best or fastest swimmer, I'm not trying to turn you into an athlete. You just need to know how to stay afloat, okay? Remember how we had that talk the other night about facing fears? I said I had none, and you said we all have at least one? You were right. Don't let this defeat you. You're stronger than this. Respect the water and it will respect you back. It has to move when you come into it, not the other way around. You're one of the strongest people I know, but you're allowed to be afraid. Just don't let it control you. That's what you tell your loyal listeners and callers. Practice what you preach. I have faith in you."

She nodded, now dedicated to at least trying after his words of encouragement. Fifteen minutes later, the man had her in the middle of the pool, his hands under her stomach as she kicked her legs about. "That's good, baby! You're doing well… Keep going."

Yuna's '(Not) The Love Of My Life' played through the speakers. He truly had made a playlist of all her favorite songs. She glanced at him out the corner of her eye, and her heart raced like rain flowing down a mountain. Her stomach fluttered like black moth wings against the brightest star…

His long dark lashes were webbed with water, his chest gleamed with the wetness covering the intricate tribal tattoos along his tanned frame. Suddenly, her muscles relaxed as she fell into a state of peace.

I feel so safe with Maximus. I feel like I don't have a care in the world. He makes me breathe. I can exhale and inhale around this man. I can swim, not just in this pool, but also in my life. My problems are the ocean, and he helps me move around them, navigate them, encourages me, helps me get out of my own way. He's not intimidated by me. He makes me feel like the little girl I was never allowed to be. We laugh, we play… I can float, I can be free… I can be me! He loves me for me… and I love him for him. We accept one another, but keep pushing each other! I can let my guard down. He doesn't judge me. He has no expectations except for me to be myself and try my best. I am not always sure who that is sometimes since I've been pretending for so long!

Her eyes watered and she quickly turned away, overcome by the unexpected emotions. Without saying a word, he calmly gathered her into his arms and embraced her. Wrapping her arms around him, she rested her head against his chest and sobbed.

"I don't know what's come over me, Maximus. This is embarrassing!"

"Why is it embarrassing?" He gently stroked the wet strands of her hair.

"Because... I'm emotionally exposed right now. My moods are all over the place. I'm crying and I don't know why... Well, yes, I do. I'm not on my period right this second. It's due though."

"So I was right." They both chuckled at that. "Nah, it's cool, baby." He kissed the top of her head. "I don't know what's going on in that complicated head of yours, but I can tell you this much: I'm just glad you allowed me space in it."

She slowly lifted her head and looked him in the eyes.

"You're like me—no one gets close. We don't allow it."

"The only difference is, Eva, I remain who I am, the same man in all situations. You put on a show and present an image that's really nothing like you. That's actually what intrigued me about you when we first met. It's like you knew I was onto you, but instead of running, you let me undress your façade, layer by layer."

"Maybe I was tired of acting."

He shrugged.

"Anything is possible. We all get tired of things... running away, running to shit that doesn't serve us well just because we're used to it. I accept who I am. It's not pretty, but it's me. There's freedom in that."

"You excited me. I was attracted to you for all the wrong reasons, Savage, but then I realized you were far more than meets the eye. You're smart and, believe it or not, you're also kind."

"I'm not nice, baby. I'm just nice to *you*."

She swallowed. She knew he was telling her the truth. There was no way she could twist and turn this so that it went down easier. Savage was a hard man. Hard to love.

Hard *not* to love. Impossible to forget.

"Well then, aren't you putting a show on now, too?" she asked.

"I guess you could say that, but it's not really a show. It's an evolution."

"Ahhh, I like that." She nodded, smiling before kissing him on his soft, perfect lips. The water made a slight sloshing sound around their bodies as they slid against one another.

"My changes aren't fake. My existence in your world is real. You motivate me to want to be nice to you because you allow me to be, desire for me to be, and I know that if I'm not what you require, I won't get what I want from you. I can relax around you, not look over my shoulder every damn minute, worrying about what the hell you might do to me when my eyes are closed. I can tell you anything, baby." He ran his thumb against her cheek and smiled. "I may not be ready to tell you all of those things, but at least that door is open to me. I can't do that with just anyone, let my guard down... and best of all, you can offer advice when I need it. Not to try and change me, but to help me be a better man if I so choose to be. Think about it."

He shifted her body to bring her legs around his waist. She held on to him as he walked slowly through the water, like a giant crossing a river.

"Remember when I asked you last week about wanting to visit my father? I told you as he ages, our conversations get a little strange, uncomfortable, so I'd been kind of avoiding him. That's been on my mind for a while. I had no one to talk to about that until you came along. Do you remember what you said?"

"Yes. I said we all go through stages in our lives. If we have no witnesses to those stages, that doesn't make them any less real. We can either go through life with our eyes wide shut, or open them and watch the splendor, even in the most painful of transformations. All things under this sun have beauty. It's up to us to find it," She said.

"And that was so damn profound to me, baby. You gave me books, and I read them on the plane when going on my last mission. Some of them made me think about this in new ways."

"Yeah, I remember. You were in my little library and looking at all the movies on the shelves, the DVDs, my old collection. You saw all the books placed next to them in alphabetical order. You started pulling some out, one by one, and asked to borrow them. Of course I said yes. You selected 'How to Win Friends and Influence People,' 'The Secret', 'The One Thing', and 'The Art of Happiness.'"

"See, they all had gems in them, making me question myself and my relationship with this person in my life—a guy half responsible for me being born. This man raised me, watched me grow up." She kept her eyes on him, keeping him engaged, attached to her. When Savage showed himself to her, revealed the inner workings of his private thoughts and the secret rooms inside his heart, she was all ears. These instances came in spurts, totally out of the blue, and she relished them, for they meant that he trusted her… and she trusted him, too. "If he could watch me go from being a whiny, crying baby all the way to a grown man, then I can get over myself and extend him the same. Like you seeing your mother. It hurts you to visit her sometimes, but you do it.

You inspired me. Your courage helped me."

"Exactly. We encourage one another. It's hard, but we can do it, Savage."

"You know, he's not going to always be strong and tough. He's getting older... That was the basis of my concern."

"I figured as much."

"Baby, years of wild livin', alcoholic binges, three cigarette packs a day, occasional recreational drugs, and just a hard life have caught up with him. He's still a hard-headed, hard-hearted motherfucker, but he's slower now. Things are different. My mother, on the other hand, seems to avoid me." He chuckled sadly, averting his gaze.

"Yeah?" She ran her fingertips against the back of his neck, then gently nudged, forcing him to look back into her eyes. "You were telling me a while back that she hasn't returned your calls and you're getting worried. Is that totally out of character for her?"

"Nah, not really. She does that sometimes, goes kind of into hiding. My half-sister, Shauna, said she was over there a couple weeks ago though and she claims they're both fine."

"I almost forgot you had a sister. Do you see her often?"

"When we were kids? Not as much as I would've liked. Now? We talk often. See, here's what happened. Never mind though... you don't wanna hear this shit."

"Yes, I do! Tell me."

The man hesitated, but then decided to go on. "Well, I mean, because her mother raised her and had custody, things were difficult. She didn't live in Los Angeles until the last four and a half years. Shauna is good people, ya know? I used to ask about her all the time and my dad would get pissed. Not at me, but at the fact that he couldn't see her when he wanted to. He would always send money when he could and visit her, or at least try to see her, but from my understanding, and my sister pretty much vouched for it, her mother didn't want my father around.

"So, they were in and out of court until the judge ruled that her mother have full custody and he only get supervised visitation. It was due to his criminal history and motorcycle gang affiliations and my father swears up and down that her mother lied and said he abused her. He said he never laid a hand on her, that he doesn't beat up women. I know he never touched my mother, even during some of their loud arguments—though that was rare that their fights were so loud that I could hear them. My father was really upset about this, you know, about not seeing his kid, but he tried to make the best of it. He used to warn me about getting the wrong woman knocked up because of this shit."

"Oh... you got someone pregnant? I know you don't have any children. I just didn't—"

"Nah, that's not what I'm saying. He was talking about don't do it." She nodded in understanding. "He'd tell me I needed to make sure I didn't get anyone pregnant if I couldn't see spending the rest of my life with them. I knew it was serious then, even as a kid. Now, yeah, I slipped up sometimes when I was young and stupid, risked it by not always strapping up, but more times than not, because of his warnings and what he taught me about women, sex, and how I was basically raised around it due to my mother, I was careful more times than not. As I became an adult, the warning stuck with me, not just due to what my father had gone through regarding his daughter, but because I don't know if I even want to be a father. I struggle with the idea of it."

She cocked her head to the side, feeling a wave of disappointment.

"Why are you looking at me like that? I told you this already. I was upfront."

"Not quite in this way though. I thought you said your father was a great dad? You also told me a while back that you like kids."

"He *is* a great father and I *do* like kids, baby, but if I have any, it means that they'll be someone else in the world that I'm responsible for. That's huge to me. I know it sounds selfish, but I don't think everyone having children should be having them. Some people don't deserve to be parents, or sometimes they just aren't ready."

"True…"

"There are so many unwanted children out here. They didn't ask to be here. It's not right."

"I have to agree with you about that." She sighed, still reeling from his confession.

"You're upset, aren't you?"

She shrugged and looked away.

"I'm disappointed, not necessarily upset. I just, well, I must've assumed from some of your previous comments that you wanted children. I misunderstood, apparently."

"Listen to me." He made her face him. "I don't know. I can't say either way. Since I'm not sure, I refuse to do it until I *am* sure. Do you get that? It's not that I'm trying to mess up your plans or anything like that, and I don't want to waste your time. This is something that has to be discussed further is all."

"Yeah, I get it. I know that one day I'd like to have at least one child though. But I would never want to make someone have a baby by guilting them or anything like that, if they're not totally on board with it. Nothing worse than feeling unwanted, or like a mistake." She shook her head. "No child wants to know that their mother or father was tricked or manipulated into parenthood." They pressed their foreheads together and swayed in the water to the music. A sense of peace fell over her, a blanket of love.

"I'm sorry, Eva… just being honest, baby."

"I know… I know." She pressed her lips against his. This was not the swim lesson she'd expected. The old her might have ranted and raved, stating she'd been misled, but in fact, she'd simply heard what she'd wanted to hear. When she played back their prior conversations, she had to admit he was right. He was on the fence. Liking children and wanting them were two different things. Was this a deal breaker? That concept seemed to be floating around quite a bit this afternoon… She wasn't certain.

I'm being silly. I don't even know if I am going to be with this man for an extended period of time. Hell, we may break up next week. Who really knows? I can handle his job, I can handle his over the top personality, I can handle him, period. But there are plenty of reasons why we might part ways, and not all of those reasons would be the result of some calamity. It could simply be a decision based on the realization that we're seeing life and our personal journeys in two different ways. Him being the best lover I ever had is not enough to sustain a relation-

ship… though I know damn well we have so much more than that. I hope we'd always remain friends, but I am putting far too much emphasis on this one thing. Funny how you never know how much something means to you until the threat of it being snatched away comes into the picture. I knew I wanted kids eventually but it's not something that occupies my thoughts day and night. But now.. after this, it worries me… I'm falling in love with him! That's why this jarred me…

She shook her head, confusion taking a seat inside her. What could she say? She rested her face against his chest once again, hiding herself. She didn't want him to see the disappointment on her face, now morphing into so much more.

"Baby, you can't trust me about this."

"Huh?" She slowly faced him again. "What do you mean I can't trust you about this?"

"I'm still trying to sort it out. I didn't want a girlfriend either, remember? You weren't necessarily looking for a boyfriend, yet here the hell we are. So who the fuck knows what the future holds, right? Shit, this time next year I might say, 'Fuck this condom!' and go up in you raw without a care in the world! Just bust wide open! Nut all up in that pussy, shootin' sperm in you left 'nd right! POW POW POW!"

"You are so nasty!" She chuckled. He looked so proud of himself.

"My pull out game with you would be weak as fuck, Eva. I couldn't imagine trying to pull out of you. Trust me, it's good that I always strap up. You'd be pregnant every ten months fuckin' around with a motherfucker like me if condoms didn't exist."

They smirked at one another then burst out laughing.

"You're so stupid and crass."

"I'm serious! I can only imagine what you'd feel like flesh to flesh... especially since you feel as good as you do *now*, when I'm wearing a Magnum. I think about that sometimes, you know that?" His smile slowly dissipated. "I can't wait until we can make love without barriers. Shit, I wanna feel your pussy grip me, baby, and those soft, wet walls squeeze my dick so fucking bad, you have no idea. That takes time though... for you to feel comfortable enough to let me do that to you, be inside of you like that..."

He gripped the back of her head, brought her close, and snatched a kiss from her very soul. When he turned her loose, the intensity in his eyes was tenfold. "This connection is something I've never had with any other woman, but with you, I want to experience that, making love in the purest of ways. I plan to have you just in that way because I love you, baby..."

His eyes turned to slits as the love and lust poured from him into the air. Her pussy pulsed at his words. He'd never told her that before. The 'L' word had never escaped his lips.

"All the bullshit and jokes aside, Eva, I have no idea what the future holds. I think I'd make a good father if and when the time comes, so I'm not doubting my abilities. That's not the issue. I just have to be ready, ya know? I have to truly want it."

"Definitely."

"Who knows what the future holds, right?"

"You said that already." She smiled.

"And I'm saying it again." He grew serious again. "Give me time. Let me figure this out. This is all new to me. But I can tell you this much: if I *did* get someone accidentally pregnant before I felt I was ready, I wouldn't be mad if that person was you. In fact, that would give me some peace." She smiled at his words. "I wouldn't have to worry about whether the baby would be wanted, loved, and cared for. You'd be a great mother. There's no doubt in my mind."

"Thank you."

"You're welcome. Now, back to your lessons. Enough of this shit… How in the hell did we even get into this heavy discussion in the first damn place?! My father gettin' old, unprotected sex, my mother avoiding me… what tha fuck?!" They both burst out laughing as he waded about in the water. He dipped under the surface and popped back up a few seconds later, shaking the excess water from his head. "I want you to do a lap around the pool. I don't care if you doggy paddle—just move without me."

"Oh, I'm not ready for that. I can't!"

"Yes, you can. You're ready. Come on."

Ten minutes later, much to her surprise, she was doing it. Sure, she had adult floaties on her arms and she was certain she looked like a damn fool, but she was giddy about her progress.

"I'm swimming! Look!" she yelled.

"Yup. You sure are. A few more lessons and you'll be exactly where you need to be."

"Oh, let me get this straight right now. I know what usually happens when we go back to my house after a day out. Don't expect to swing by my place for any nookie. I can feel cramping and I *am* about to come on my cycle any second now, so I should probably get out of this pool."

"Right now?! I mean, we don't even have a few hours, you think?"

"Nope." She winked at him and giggled, delighted with how irritated he suddenly looked. She loved to annoy him.

"Not so fast. This isn't a surprise to me but I *will* be coming over because your mouth isn't broken. My dick is rated P.A. M. – pussy, ass, and mouth open for business. It'll take *any* of those at any time, cashier's checks accepted, too."

"Go to hell!"

"I'll be expecting another steak and a BJ then tonight. Medium rare with a baked potato, loaded. You don't get off that easily. I expect service."

"See? You're taking advantage now. I cook naked for you *one* time, and now you've been ordering food and sex left and right! So far, you've gotten steak and shrimp from me, chicken alfredo, and homemade deep dish pizza. You're spoiled!" She loved it though. She truly enjoyed cooking for him and watching him scarf it all down... then her, too, right afterwards. She rarely had leftovers when Savage hit the dinner table.

"And don't get it twisted, baby. I won't eat it when it's covered in hot sauce, but I will fuck that red sea into oblivion in a New York second! You know what I am. A little blood isn't going to scare me away!"

"You make me sick, Savage!" She suppressed another bout of laughter. The man was ridiculous.

"So, either way, you still owe me a blow job and some ass if you are adamant about not giving me the snatch tonight," He glanced down at his watch. "Let's finish this lap... you're almost there... and get out of here. It's almost time for lunch. I can take you to that Chinese place you like." He made his way towards the pool steps. "Hey!" he called out, pausing as he held onto the rail. She looked over her shoulder at him.

"Yes?"

"I want you to spend the night over at my house sometime soon. It's time."

"Really? What made you change your mind?" She reached the end of the pool, then pulled herself up, resting on the side to take a breather.

"I know I said that there are a lot of cameras and shit, things that might make you uncomfortable, but you need to see where and how I live, okay? This is just how it is, so you might as well get used to it."

"Okay, I definitely agree. I'd love to come by." Excitement filled her. The man had pretty much made it clear that his home was a practical fortress after some disturbing altercation had gone down on the premises. That incident had driven him to go to Vegas in the first place. After giving her the Cliff's Notes of the situation, she had tamped down her desire to see the place. But, as time passed, her curiosity got the best of her. In fact, she'd become paranoid, sometimes wondering if he could be hiding a wife and kids, but after running a background check on the bastard, as she encouraged all her callers to do when becoming serious with a new fellow, she found out he was clean as a whistle. No marriages, no domestic violence charges, no felonies, no children, and the property in question was in his name. Exclusively. He'd been telling the truth.

Minutes later, they were dried off and dressed, walking

hand in hand to his Ford Mustang. It was a gorgeous vintage car; she'd never had the pleasure to ride in one until that day. He opened her door for her, like a true gentleman, then leaned in close. Biting his lower lip, he looked her up and down before snatching his sunglasses off his head and shoving them on his face.

"You know they say a good fucking relieves cramps. I've got just what you need to turn that pain into pleasure."

"This again?" She smirked as she ran her fingers along his chin. He grabbed her hand and kissed it, then slid one of her fingers into his mouth, licking and sucking it. The heat of his mouth and the softness of his tongue sent her into overdrive.

"And I change my mind. I'd eat *your* bloody pussy in a heartbeat. Call me gross, I don't give a fuck. There's nothing on you that I wouldn't devour, any time of the month, and don't you forget it." He slammed her car door and walked off to the other side. Soon, they were speeding down the road, their hands linked, entertained by the sounds of Danny Brown screaming his sick lyrics of 'Die Like a Rockstar…'

CHAPTER NINETEEN

The Bee's Knees...

...Three weeks later

THE AIR SMELLED of desperation and revenge. Savage was only familiar with the latter, but the first had a distinct stench he was becoming accustomed to.

This is the stupidest shit I've ever done.

Savage stuck his head out of the car window as anger set in. He placed one of his guns at his side, just in case someone decided to grow a pair and try something dumb and dangerous. Up ahead on a hill, a white and slate stone mansion towered, a black iron gate barring the way to it. The structure made his house look like an ant hill in comparison.

He pressed his finger on the buzzer once again, knowing damn well the bastard behind the Wizard of Oz curtain was well aware of his presence at the front gate. He swiped his hand across his brow then smoothed it along his wrinkled black Iron Maiden wife beater as he waited for what felt like a lifetime. As he checked his surroundings, he pulled his shades down from his head to shield his eyes from the sun, which had started to set behind the mountains. There was no guard at the post; perhaps the entire crew was inside waiting for him like well-trained wolves salivating for a soon-to-be slaughtered lamb.

"Come on, fucker..." he murmured, jamming his finger over and over on the red buzzer, out of pure annoyance at this point. "Longhorn! I'm leaving! You're not doin' me any favors!" He tried the buzzer one more time, then kicked his car in reverse. Before he could pull away, the scratchy crackle and snap of broken soundwaves carried on the wispy wind, and an aged voice tinged with a slight British accent came through. The tone held a twist of snobbery and a dash of arrogance.

"I apologize for the delay, Mr. Savage. I was on a call. Thank you for accepting my invitation. I'm certain you recall the routine, but just in case, place your right hand against the panel next to the signal for scanning. Then you will gain entry and the gate will open, allowing you to drive up and park. You've been cleared for entry."

"Accepting your invitation?" Savage smirked as he followed the instructions. "Why so formal? Is this a party or somethin', Longhorn? Should I prepare for some line dancing? A birthday party for five-year-olds? Gonna be red balloons and shit there, too?" He heard a loud sigh, but he'd had about enough. "We all float down here, motherfucker... Look, Pennywise, ya fuckin' clown, I didn't come all this way to boogie with you and what do you mean I've been cleared for entry? You removed my clearance from before? You're a sensitive motherfucker, aren't you? Do you rub your nipples in the shower? How petty can you be?" He stared at the damn speaker, wishing he could just rip it from the wall and stomp the hell out of it, just because.

"Mr. Savage, this is not really—"

"You keep me out here waiting so gotdamn long I could've grown out a full head of hair, shaved it off, and sewn it into a fuckin' sweater just in time for Christmas. And then you have the fuckin' audacity to come on here actin' all pretentious and hoity toity. Let's get something clear. I haven't been calling you; you've been calling *me*!"

He was met with silence, but wasn't a bit surprised. Disgusted, Savage slid a cigar out of the pocket of his leather jacket and lit it.

"You appear to be agitated so I am giving you the floor. Is there anything else you'd like to say, Mr. Savage? Any other senseless rants you wish to get off your chest?" the man asked wryly, sounding as though he was tempted to yawn at any moment.

"Nope, I'm finished for now. Just open this fuckin' medieval fortress of a gate of yours and the front door once I drive up in this bitch and if you or your little weasel-faced sissies try anything, have the coroner on speed dial."

"Very well. Mr. Savage, are we finished with this discussion now so that we can proceed?"

"Nah." Savage puffed out loops of solid white smoke from the corner of his mouth. "I'm just getting started. I got back from Jamaica a short while ago. Can you believe it?" He chortled. "That's not even our fucking territory. They sent my ass out of the country to do their bidding. I'm telling you that because I'm irritated, Longhorn. I don't have the time for any of your shit right now. I'm tired. I'm hot. I'm bothered. So the last thing I feel like doing is adding you and your little buddies to my list of DOAs. But I will if I have to. I'm never too tired to lay a motherfucker out."

"There is truly no need for any additional threats or paranoia, Savage. We're all on the same team."

The gate slowly swung open, revealing an elaborate garden with perfectly trimmed vibrant green bushes, an assortment of colorful flowers in full bloom, ostentatious twin stone fountains, shaped like children, in the center of two ponds, and a double stone staircase leading up to massive red and frosted glass double doors. Savage hadn't been by Longhorn's place in years, and that had been for a dinner party where he'd been whisked away and questioned about an incident regarding a bow and arrow. Ah, the memories...

Savage put his gunmetal and black Porsche 911 GT2 RS in drive, and made his way up the long, winding driveway towards the incredible estate. In a flash, he was parked and jogging up one side of the stone staircase. Light classical music could be heard pouring from inside. Once he reached the front door, he gave it a hearty tap, though he was fully aware that at least five men would be surrounding it, watching his every move.

The doors clicked and opened, and as soon as he stepped one foot inside, two men in dark suits and red ties reached out for a pat down.

"Don't touch me," Savage stated gruffly, tossing the butt

of his cigar on the floor. He waited for them to stop. They didn't. He raised his gun and swung it.

"Ahhh!" one of them screamed, blood splattering from his nose. The men drew their weapons, locked and loaded.

"He broke my fucking nose!" the poor sap cried out.

Savage could see Longhorn way at the end of a very long hall, standing in his dark gray suit with a matching dark gray scarf wrapped about his turkey-like neck.

"Mr. Savage," Longhorn stated calmly, his loud footsteps echoing on the granite floors… "Please relax."

He knew the bastard didn't order his hounds to double down only because he needed him for something. Whatever it was, it must've been the motherload.

"Call them off before someone gets hurt. Again," Savage ordered.

Longhorn paused in his steps, but said nothing. The men's eyes glowed with anger as they kept their weapons drawn.

"They need to check you. Surely you can understand that."

"Check me for what?! Didn't you just say we were on the same team? How quickly we forget. I don't like people touching me, Longhorn. I didn't give any of these fuckers permission to touch me." Savage studied all the guns pointed his way, assessing the situation.

3…

2..

1.

BAM! BAM BAM BAM!

In the blink of an eye, he shot three of the men in the

knee cap and they dropped to the floor like flies, writhing about. Savage held another in a brutal chokehold. The one with the broken nose had hobbled away, out of sight, still whimpering and cursing.

"Mr. Savage," Longhorn stated dryly. "Is there a reason why you've shot my guards in their legs and you're holding Mr. Rodriquez here hostage? I've had about enough of this."

Another man came around the corner, his gun drawn.

"Motherfucker, I will break this bastard's neck and toss your ass out the nearest window with your own gun jammed up your ass like a gotdamn flagpole if you keep pointing that thing at me."

The young man blinked a few times. His hands shook, but he held the gun steady.

"Derek, please put the gun down," Longhorn ordered.

"This is how you treat your guests, you piece of shit? Pat them down, put guns in their faces? You're lucky I aimed for the legs. I see you didn't tell them about me, *my* rules." The man in his grip gurgled and groaned as he squeezed him harder. "If you're a pretty woman, don't take off your clothes unless you want to get fucked. If you're a man, no touching. Period. Don't point a gun at me unless you plan to shoot." His adrenaline shot through the roof.

"I…. I can't breathe!" the man he held captive gasped, his face turning tomato red. Savage released his grip, dropkicked the dirtbag to the floor, then stepped over him as if he were a mere inconvenience. Tossing up his hands, gun still in his palm, he laughed.

"Nice place, Longhorn. I see it looks exactly the same as the last time I was here. Me and my boys bought you all of this, huh? All of our hard work, putting our asses on the line while you live the highlife. You've done well for yourself!"

Longhorn offered a tight smile, grabbed his cane from an umbrella holder and laughed in a forced tone.

"You've forgotten that Austin and I were once in your shoes. Our bodies are retired, not our brains, Savage. We've earned our stripes, our riches, our trappings. Now, follow me." The man motioned for him to follow, likely to some private room where they could discuss some shit Savage was hellbent on not doing. "Why did you finally agree to come and meet with me? Believe me, I was thrilled, but my curiosity needs to be fed."

The man's wiry black and white eyebrows bunched then relaxed, his lips curled in a slight smile. The guy's expression reminded him of a black abyss, just like his innerworkings and deeds. That mouth was equipped with a wicked tongue known to order executions left and right at the slightest infraction from anyone who got in his way. He wasn't above corruption and playing dirty, but in some odd way, he'd placed himself on a pedestal without impunity. The man's bloodthirsty nature matched his—that much they had in common.

Perhaps this similarity was what caused their confrontations. Austin had alluded to such many year ago. Savage had rolled that around in his mind a time or two. Could the Devil not stand to look at his own reflection?

They walked side by side down the hallway, their steps in sync. Longhorn was only 5'10, but built solid. He'd been a feared man back in the 1970s and '80s. He'd been nothing but muscle and was known for his strength, mental agility, and fluency in various languages. He'd been a bodyguard and head of security to not one, but two United States presidents. Savage would've given the two headed serpent his props had they actually enjoyed one another, yet Longhorn was a thorn in his side. Sneaky, always slithering around under the cloak of the night.

He didn't care for his personality, his checkered, questionable history with Austin, or his criticism of Savage's at times unorthodox execution of his hits. Savage didn't care though. His mission was to get the job done by any means necessary. Sometimes protocol simply didn't fit into the equation.

"No answer for me?"

"What?" Savage asked.

"I'm not worthy of knowing why you changed your mind to speak with me?"

"At this point, I doubt it actually matters. All you really care about is that I'm on your turf and now you can lie and scheme in peace."

Longhorn chuckled as he opened a large, glossy black door by hooking his cane around the silver doorknob and twisting. They entered a room with a high, domed ceiling and dark oak walls, one of which was covered with bookshelves and the other with a large painting of a military man from the past.

"That's King Leopold II," Longhorn stated as he rounded his desk and took a seat, pointing at the chair before him. He settled and cleared his throat. Two prescription medications sat there, which he quickly grabbed and tossed into a desk drawer. "That man was one of the most savage, pardon the pun, rulers of the world. He was—"

"The King of the Belgians…"

Longhorn's brow rose as Savage pulled out the chair before him and took a seat, his legs wide apart, feeling like a fucking king amongst peasants.

"So." Longhorn placed his cane down against the desk and rested his elbows on the wood and his chin on the back of his hand. An obnoxious smirk formed on his pale face. "Though I'm surprised about your knowledge of such things," He pointed to the painting. "I really shouldn't be. You didn't get to where you have in life by being an imbecile. With guys like you, there's always more than meets the eye. It all makes sense."

"What makes sense? That I can read and write and know how to use my opposable thumbs?"

Longhorn tittered and shook his head, then reached into his drawer and pulled out two large liquor bottles— Bowmore Whiskey, a bourbon—and two shot glasses.

"You're a rather interesting person, Savage." The man poured the whiskey in both of the glasses, then the dark liquor. "I would—"

"Can you please tell the walking pubic hair behind us to leave? I'm not going to sit here talking to you with a gun pointed at me." Longhorn's brow rose as he clutched one of the glasses in his hand. "Yeah, here we go again. Are you *that* afraid of me?" Savage smirked. "Long live the memory of the great Longhorn! Scared of little ol' Savage… How humiliating." Longhorn quietly finished pouring the drinks.

"Siiiimon!" the older man finally called out. "You can leave. It appears your presence makes Mr. Savage here uncomfortable." The man came out of the shadows, and their eyes locked briefly before he left and closed the door behind him.

"You know, Longhorn, I debated on tossing a knife at the middle of his fuckin' forehead, but I like this knife and didn't want to have to wrangle it out of him and clean off the bits of brain matter… you know, the usual." Savage removed the bone dagger from his waistband and twirled it about.

Longhorn gave one shot glass a gentle nudge in his direction and took the other for himself.

"It's a nice piece, Savage. You don't see too many bone daggers these days." He chugged his drink, then poured himself another. "Would you classify yourself as old school in weaponry of choice?"

Savage shrugged as he picked up the glass and studied the liquor from various angles.

"I got it while in Rome a few years back."

Longhorn leaned back in his seat, and the chair squeaked.

"Savage, I want to hire you for a job."

"We've already discussed this and I haven't changed my mind."

"Hear me out first. Just so the secrets are out," he said, raising his hand so his simple gold wedding band shone in the light, "Austin was given this task first." Savage paused. Now his interest was piqued. "He refused it. He had his reasons. So now, it's in my hands. It has to be done."

"Who is it?"

"I can only tell you if you at least promise to consider the job."

"Now why would I do something as foolish as that? I'm

not going to make any promises without having all of my ducks in a row." Savage crossed his legs and steepled his hands.

"You'll have to trust me."

Savage burst out laughing. He couldn't believe his ears.

"No, it doesn't work that way. You sit here in your glass house throwing stones, telling me that Austin refused a job, and we both know that's practically unheard of. You dropped a bomb then hid your hand. That means either it's a woman, a child, or someone he feels is far too risky to even go after. Someone has an 'X' on their back, but it isn't the usual suspects. He wanted nothing to do with it, and since he actually has scruples, unlike you, this makes me question the whole damn thing. Now tell me or I'm outta here."

"Okay, meet me half way." The man pulled out a drawer and removed a cigar wrapped in black then handed it to him. He then took out one for himself, lit it, and swiveled slowly back and forth in his chair. "What you said a bit ago? It's the third option…" They stared at one another for a long while. "This is coming directly from a former president of the United States. The laundry list is long. This individual is a threat to national security. I looked over the information. He's got to go."

"He's a threat to a legacy then and probably has some ties to leaking information. A spy for another country…" Savage ran his fingers along his jaw, feeling the dense hairs of his beard. "The president who ordered this… Skull and Bones affiliation?" Savage grinned as he took a small taste of the whiskey, pretty certain he was right.

"I am not at liberty to say, but you're a smart man. I'm

sure once you agree to the job and read over the report, you'll figure it out along the way."

"I don't play hide-and-seek. I know my objective and where the fun is being had before I step foot in any mother-fuckin' assignment, period. POINT. BLANK." Savage tapped his finger on the desk. "No blind shit. You're banking on my curiosity, but curiosity killed the cat and I'm no pussy... so put up or shut up."

Longhorn shook his head, a greasy grin spread across his face, then rested his cigar in an ashtray shaped like the world.

"Temper, temper... Let's play it this way. I just so hap-pen to know you've been in the company of a lady friend. It appears to be rather serious from what I'm told."

"I've been told you like to fuck pigeons." Longhorn burst out laughing and briefly closed his eyes. "I see you've got your flying monkeys all over my shit. Snoops."

"You never make things easy, do you now, Savage? My reason for bringing this up is because, perhaps, I can be of assistance." The man cocked his head to the side.

"I don't need any assistance from you and definitely none for my love life."

"Well, maybe *she* does..." The silence built between them like walls. "You see, I understand she is a very beautiful woman with a rather successful podcast show. I mean, that's not much." He shrugged. "But she's gotten a bit of a name for herself. She ran a successful practice at one point in time. I suppose she can always return to that if so wishes. She has a couple of self-help books that have had fair success. They're barely a blip on the radar, but she's not exactly unknown either. Seems to me, she just needs a little help."

"We don't need your fuckin' help. Why don't you worry about how to get it up so you can please your fourth wife, you know, the twenty-five-year-old who's probably fuckin' your pool boy and swallowin' his load as we speak?"

The man sucked his teeth before continuing, ignoring Savage's vicious jab. "Your lady friend's family is rather interesting, wouldn't you say? It appears her mother rarely leaves the house... a recluse. She has some interesting mental challenges. Pretty serious, too. I imagine some expensive home care could make a great difference. Top of the line specialists who can give this woman the attention and treatment she so deserves. Do you know how many solutions are out here that cure all sorts of diseases, but the medication isn't yet FDA approved? This woman's schizophrenia symptoms could be practically gone within a matter of months."

Savage's jaw tightened as his anxiety and angst revved up.

A flash of Zaire on the phone with her father the other day flooded his mind. The man was at his wits' end. Her mother had destroyed the kitchen in a fit of paranoid rage. As if reading his mind, the man took another jab at his fragile stack of mental cards.

"Her father is a hardworking man, a pillar of the Black community. Articulate, handsome, kind." His lips curled in a heinous smirk. "And yet, he is hardly recognized for his past bravery as a firefighter for the city of Los Angeles. What a pity. I could change that, too...

"She has a half-wit sister who isn't nearly the woman she is, but they are making lemonade out of lemons. Eva Zaire Ellington is also a witness who will be forever under some form of surveillance thanks to the likes of you, Mr. Savage. It's the name of the game. Regardless of that, I could assist in her career to bring it from so-so to skyrocketing notoriety. Now you, of course, being the prideful man that you are, will deny my help, but perhaps she will not. Sometimes it's not the money that makes the world go around, which you have plenty of. It's who you know." The maggot of a man picked up his glass and chugged it straight back. "Would you like her to receive the assistance I put into motion? It's only a couple phone calls away. If so, let's make this deal."

Savage picked up his glass of whiskey and polished it off.

He placed the empty glass back down onto the desk, then shoved it aside with a swipe of his hand and leaned forward.

"Longhorn, let's talk... do some business." The man gave an eager smile. "You see, the business we do doesn't concern my girlfriend, the members of her family, her friends, her fuckin' stuffed teddy bears, none of that shit. Now, I know everything there is to know about Eva Zaire Ellington, you son of a bitch. You're not schooling me on anything." Longhorn puffed on his cigar, his smile all but gone. "From the top of her fucking head to the bottom of her feet, I know my woman almost better than she knows herself.

"There isn't shit you can school me on to try and manipulate me into feeling like this is the deal of the century, offer the Devil's gold in order to entice me. You can't sell heat to a demon... I invented fire. This woman is important to me, and you just tried to play on that. I can't fault you for trying. It's normal to find a man's weakness and poke at it to get what you want."

"I've received a report, Savage. There are probably some things you're not yet aware of, some information that—"

Savage raised his hand to stop him.

"Didn't I just tell you there isn't shit you can tell me? I know the mundane about her to the serious! I know about her breast reduction in her twenties! I know about her run in with a serial rapist on her college campus, which she narrowly escaped, and the memory still leaves her shaken. I know about her ex-boyfriend who beat the living shit out of her in a jealous rage and she in turn got in her car and ran over his fucking foot. She doesn't do what she does as a career just for sport! She's trying to save other women from doing the same shit she did! I needed to know why she was the way she was, and she's told me some things, but me being the nosy fucker I am… I needed the whole fucking picture! No public record exists of some of this shit so whatever little report you have doesn't even scratch the surface. There's nothing I don't know. Nothing that will surprise me or make me change my mind. I know who I'm kissing at night… who I am confiding in… who I am in love with. Don't play with me, Longhorn, because I also schooled her about motherfuckers like *you*!

"She graduated at the top of her class and she's got street smarts. She loves her father to pieces, to the point she'd do anything for him, a true blue Daddy's girl. And she has a thing for men that come from the wrong side of the tracks. It's her damn downfall, but this time, I am going to make sure she doesn't regret it. I found a diamond in the rough, a woman who'll be loyal to me and loyal to herself, too. I don't need you tinkering around in our business so let me make somethin' real clear, you slimy, underhanded fucker." Savage hissed, jabbing his finger in the air. "Whatever she needs to elevate her career, she can get it herself or from me.

"She doesn't need shit from you, especially since we both know the price far outweighs the service. Since she's been involved in an investigation as a witness in Vegas, unfortunately you got wind of her presence in my life. It's in our database, public knowledge amongst us, but don't you for one second think she's a bargaining chip. This isn't the casino, and she's not up for grabs. That sort of thought process will get you killed, motherfucker."

Savage gritted his teeth as his heart pounded and his temper soared. "You know I'll do it. I've done it before. Since you played a game with me and lost, two of your men are dead and now several more may need knee replacements. My parents didn't raise no punk! Now." Savage leaned back in the seat, clasping his fingers over his lap. "Let's get to the part that matters..." He snatched a toothpick from a dispenser and shoved it in his mouth, twirling it about. "I see you're desperate since you tried to go there with me, so that means this must be a hell of a lot of dinero. A lot of cash on the line. How much money are we talking?"

Longhorn hesitated, a mixture of confusion and anger on his face, but then his expression smoothed out and he leaned forward.

"Twenty-five million."

"Yippee ya yay! Your cut?"

"Twenty percent, per my usual."

"So, winner takes twenty million, and you snatch five mil for a finder's fee, all tax deductible thanks to ol' Uncle Sam giving special blind eyes to assignments such as this."

Longhorn nodded. "Yes, it's all yours after we do the light accounting work."

"Hmm, interesting. And why me? You coulda got Stevens, Germane, or Johnson. They're all pretty damn good, if I say so myself."

"They are, but let's be honest here. I don't exactly enjoy giving you a compliment, but I must give credit where credit is due." The man chuckled, darkness shining in his small blue eyes framed with abundant crow's feet. "With you, Savage, I know exactly what I'm getting into. No surprises. You deliver. First, the timing would be short; you are an in and out kind of man, much like me. Second, the procedure will be clean. No messes beyond a short clean up, no fingerprints, no paper trail. And thirdly, the mission will be completed. Here's why I am not as inclined to hand this off to some of your suggestions mentioned. Stevens is slower and more methodical than you. This target may not take kindly to that if he's tipped off and the slower you are, the more chances of that.

"The target moves around a lot. He's erratic and though he doesn't have a ton of people around him, protecting him, he is quite paranoid and will bounce if he has the slightest suspicion that he is under surveillance and being hunted. Germane also has collected too many enemies from this same city; he wouldn't make it across the first line of defense. This target's line of work is quite familiar with him. They'd spot him a thousand miles away. He is a marked man amongst their ilk due to some prior dealings that, shall we say, didn't end well. Johnson is amazing. There's no denying that. He is a talented young man with amazing accuracy. He could be your biggest competitor, but I think, for this, I simply need to go in another direction. Therefore, you're my first pick."

"Oh, lucky fuckin' me. You got any of those little chocolate mints you had last time? I don't want this visit to be a total waste." He pointed to an empty crystal bowl on the table and placed his toothpick down. Longhorn quickly opened another desk drawer and hastily tossed about ten of the sweets onto the desk. Savage grabbed a few, putting them in his jacket pocket, and scarfed down the rest.

"Ask Johnson."

"Savage, you have more experience than he does, and that will work to your advantage." The man shrugged. "I must call it as I see it. So, please stop pretending you're not rolling this over in your mind. It's a big jackpot, a big fish. If you ever wished to expand your horizons, as they say, it's right up your alley, too." Chewing loudly, Savage looked about the room, noting more paintings of old White men wearing gold crowns or military garb. The paintings were grand, featuring stern-faced generals, warriors, kings and tyrants, and they seemed better suited for the walls of a history museum.

"There's nobody Black in here."

Longhorn cast him a confused expression. "True. So what?"

"Well, I just find it curious is all. The first people on the planet were African. You seem to enjoy history, leaders that ruled with iron fists." Savage got to his feet and began to pace the room, scanning the pieces of art once more. They seemed so lifelike. "Over here you've got Joseph Stalin, for instance. Right there is Attila the Hun, I believe." He reached into his pocket, unwrapped another chocolate, and tossed the wrapper on the floor, smashing it with the thick sole of his black boot. "That looks like Vladimir Lenin over there and right here we have George W. Bush, Sr. Now, I'm not one to criticize anyone for their, shall we say, artistic leanings, but you seem to be drawn to who's the best, who's on top, regardless of how ruthless they are. Anyway, I'd like to suggest you expand your collection. Maybe read up on, say, Behanzin Bowelle, also known as "The King Shark." Interesting shit. Check out, Marcus Garvey, Richard Allen, and Benjamin O. Davis, Sr., just to name a few. Those are some real O.G.s."

"Very interesting commentary, Savage. Are you interested in such people due to your current romantic leanings?" Savage shrugged as he walked about the place. "There's no need for us to beat around the bush, though you became rather irritated when I mentioned your lady friend previously. We know that she's Black and it seems this has possibly sparked you to diversify your interests."

"It could be, but I've always included everyone in my history lessons. See, like you, I'm a history buff, too. I like to learn from the past, and if I can learn from another mother-fucker's mistakes, regardless of their race and gender, then I will. If they're doing some shit right, I want to learn how they did that, too. I can't live in a place without color, because I'm from Hell. Some of us just pretend to be demonic, but I can spot an imposter... Have you ever been to Hell, Longhorn? Ever looked in the eyes of evil? Everything is gray down here…" They locked eyes. "So." Savage approached the desk once again, placed his palms on the smooth, polished surface, and leaned forward. "If I accept this offer, I want ninety percent, not eighty."

"That's absurd."

"That's my final offer. I'm the one on the front line, not you, and if that much money is being placed on this bastard's head, then it is serious and he's a hard target. You obviously know how dangerous this mission is or you wouldn't have offered any extra icing on top of the shit-cake, so I deserve every penny. Not to mention you want to send me in there solo. And lastly, I demand that you have a sit-down with Austin before the end of the month to air out your differences. You two temperamental little girls having a fit at a tea party are affecting the entire organization, and we're all sick of this shit. I lost a good man because of your bullshit. I will never forgive you for that."

He snatched the cigar, took a hearty puff, then smashed it right into the man's desk, extinguishing it. "If you don't like my counter offer, that's not my problem. Now, if you'll excuse me, I have some other business to attend to." Savage turned around to vacate the premises but paused when Longhorn called his name.

"I accept your conditions, Savage. Do you accept the assignment?"

"Yes. Send me the details. I'll follow up with you in the morning. Oh, and one more thing." Savage turned on a dime and shot out the window right above Longhorn's head, causing him to honker down, the damn thing to shatter and a group of men to race into the study, their guns drawn.

"Don't mention my woman again. That's a real big pet peeve of mine. She's not a toy, something you can play with to get your way, toss on the table like dice. I don't play when it comes to my money and my pussy. You just tried to fuck with both. First and last warning. Tell your boys to not have any more kneejerk reactions."

He chuckled as he headed out the door, snapping his fingers to Beethoven's Symphony No. 4…

CHAPTER TWENTY

Cross My Palm With Silver

THE SOUNDS OF a drill going full throttle blended in with the blaring music of 'Cherry Pie' by Warrant. The scent of stale cigarette smoke, oil, and smog clung to the air like snot to a wall, and the humidity made it all the more pronounced.

The older man, wearing soiled jeans held up by a leather belt and a dirty denim vest smeared with emollient on bare skin, was busy working in the garage. His broad, bare chest, covered in gray hair and crude tattoos, strained against the material of the old garment. Savage entered the open garage attached to the large ranch style home. The sound of his footsteps, or perhaps his shadow, caused the old timer to rise from behind his 2015 Harley-Davidson Wide Glide with a drill in his hand.

The man donned a black bandana around his sweaty forehead. Long, thin strands of hair, dark blond with auburn, silver, and light brown running through it, twisted into a long braid draped down the center of his back. Sunburned flesh, abundant wrinkles, and a shitload of freckles adorned his face from years of riding hogs in the blazing sun. His body, especially the arms, were completely covered in prison tattoos and a few professional ones during his stints out for a taste of freedom during his youth. For many years, he'd never returned to jail unless it was to visit one of his many incarcerated brethren. He'd been determined to stop stressing Mom the fuck out, and be there for his kids. They wanted him home, where he belonged.

"There's my boy!" Savage's father called out, his grin sporting a black hole on the side where his left incisor tooth had been knocked out in a fight years ago, before he was even born. His dad turned the radio off and stood like the tower of power he was. "Get your ass over here!"

Savage approached the old man and stiffened when the guy wrapped one arm around him and brought him in for a tight squeeze. He could feel the man's strength in that simple embrace. Dad had remained physically strong, despite a couple of health scares. They stepped back and eyed each other. The old man's ice blue eyes looked straight through him, as if he could read his mind.

"Hey, Dad, what's up?" Savage slid his hand in his pocket and rocked back on his heels. Dad returned to his bike and continued to work on it.

"Same ol', same ol'. Same shit, different day." The old man chuckled hoarsely. "I'm glad you stopped by... haven't seen ya in a couple of months. The text messages are fine, but sometimes I'd like to look my only son in the face."

"Yeah, been real busy. So what's up with the bike?" Savage crossed his arms as the man tampered with it. The sound of metal hitting metal echoed in the air.

"Not a damn thing, believe it or not. Just a routine oil change. Haven't had many problems outta this bike at all. That's nice for a change." Savage nodded. Dad tended to purchase fixer-uppers. Not always because he had to, but he enjoyed the challenge. This time, he treated himself to something that required nothing more than a good time.

"Need some help? I can finish it for you." Savage quickly tore off his leather jacket and tossed it on the hood of his father's old Plymouth, prepared to get his hands dirty.

"I've got it under control but you can hand me that bucket over there," Dad said, pointing toward the other side of the garage. His large silver Indian chief head ring glimmered as he moved. Savage returned to him with a small black bucket. Setting it beside him, he looked closer at what he was doing. "Thank you."

"You're welcome. Where's Mom? In the house?" Dad grabbed a filthy rag from the back pocket of his jeans, swiped it across his grimy, ruddy face, then jammed it back in its place.

"Yeah, she's in there. Might be on the phone."

"Is she okay? I've had trouble gettin' a hold of her lately. No response to my calls, one-word answers for the text messages. I started getting worried until I spoke to Shauna and then you."

"Yeah, she's fine. She's your mom." The man laughed, though his voice had a tinge of something in it, something Savage couldn't quite describe. "You know how she is, Max." True, the woman kept everything inside. He'd learned that early on. Repression was her middle name. "Anyway, she told me the other day she was going to stop by and see ya." Dad grunted as he toiled. "She must not have gotten around to it yet."

Typical…

His father paused to take a breather. Dirt was smeared along his cheek and on the bridge of his nose. His scruffy white and blonde beard was soiled, too, but a mischievous twinkle gleamed in his eyes.

"How's work been?"

"Good, not too many complaints. Well…" He shrugged, "I could. But it wouldn't make a damn bit of difference."

"I'm sure you're right. I hate that you can't really ever tell me much about what you're doing."

"Like you really want to know." Savage smirked.

"Hell, I do! When I do what you do, I go to prison. When you do it, you get a check and a pat on the back! What kind of bullshit is that?!" Savage burst out laughing. "My son is a hired gun, but I shoot that fuckin' bastard, Roy, in the groin, and get sent away… It was self-defense!"

"Losing a card game was not self-defense, Dad. Poker just isn't your calling. Admit it."

"He cheated!" Dad snarled. "He deserved to lose his left nut, stupid son of uh bitch! And don't you snub my gambling skills. I taught you everything you know! Why do you think you're so good at it?"

"I dunno. Lady luck? She must not like you. Mom must've run her off in a jealous rage," he teased, drawing a dirty look from his father. "Blackjack is my thing, you know that. Poker doesn't give me the same rush."

Dad nodded in understanding.

"Oh, Max, before I forget, would you do me a favor?"

"Yeah, what?"

"Tell the president to go fuck himself."

"I don't talk to the president and something tells me he's oblivious to what I do, how it's done, the logistics, all of it. He's not exactly in our group, the way some past presidents have been. If you're hellbent on giving him a piece of your mind though, I'm sure you could tweet it."

"Fuck the Internet. Nothing but bad porn and fake news stories." Dad went back to work. "You could just tell him for me. But that's kinda your boss, I suppose, so it wouldn't work out, now would it?"

"Probably not."

"You still helping out that one guy? What was his name? Dallas?"

Savage burst out laughing and shook his head. "Austin… His name is Austin and yeah I am."

"Can he get my man James outta prison, yes or no? You told me you'd ask, have it looked into. Did you?" Dad gave him a stern look, as if he somehow believed his thoughts alone would in some way influence the situation and make all of his wishes come true.

"Oh, believe me, Austin looked into it all right, Dad, but James killed two cops. You neglected to tell me that."

"They were chasing him. It was none of their business."

"I can't believe some of the shit you say sometimes." Savage couldn't help but smile, for he knew his father meant every damn word. "This was James' fault, Dad. Come on now. Remember all the shit you told me about taking accountability for our fuck-ups?" His father rolled his eyes.

"Not only did the police incident happen, but he's a well-known member of your Outlaw Vagos Motorcycle Club, which you know is a 'no-no' in the political circles."

Dad glared at him. "That's your family. Show some respect."

"I am. I am not bringing it up to down them; they had our backs. I show the utmost loyalty. The problem is, Dad, it doesn't bode well politically. Strings can't be pulled as easily if a guy has basically shown the middle finger to the system. I figured maybe Austin could work around that but then there's the pussy sales… That was the nail in his coffin."

"The whores? Well, hell! Half of that entire police force is fucking the same women! The hypocritical bullshit is why I would never join in any gotdamn army, a police force, the Boy Scouts, hell, even what you do! You're still helping. If it weren't so sweet of a deal, I'd call you a traitor."

"No, you wouldn't."

Dad chuckled. "All right, I wouldn't, but you know exactly what I mean."

"I tried though, regarding James, and Austin couldn't get anyone to budge. He's been tied to running a couple pretty big prostitution rings, Dad. It wasn't a woman or two—we're talking across state lines, none of them legal. His ass is grass, old man." Savage slid a cigarette out of his father's little tin cup that sat on a counter in the garage covered with sullied pieces of cloth and tools, lit it, and blew out a gust of smoke. "He's not going anywhere."

"Well, shit. That's some really fucked up news. I wish they'd hear this out. That shit he did was a long time ago. It amazes me how they'll toss him in prison and throw away the key, but won't discuss their cocaine habits. I hate those cunts in the White House. The entire government is ass backwards. What happened to the Republican party from my era?! We were proud! They're going to try 'nd take our guns, too… fuckin' assholes. I don't give a shit that I'm a felon. I'm keeping some heat on me at all times and I dare a mother-fucker to come in my gotdamn house and try to tell me otherwise." Dad hawked a wad of spit and went back to working on the bike.

"No one is taking your guns, Dad, trust me. I have inside information. Anyway, back to what we were saying. Accord-ing to James' records, it was only three years ago that he had those prostitutes. Some were interviewed and said it was against their will so he got some additional charges, like kidnapping, and don't forget he also got wrapped up in that extortion case. He's not a good candidate for Austin to rally for."

"I don't care what they say. He's a good guy—turned a new leaf."

"Unless you're talking about a marijuana leaf, no he didn't."

"Anyway, the lawyer he had wasn't shit, Max! I did take that money you gave me though and we got him another one. Hopefully it'll make a difference. Anything else going on in your life? Cool trips planned? Gotten any women preg-nant? You're not blowin' blanks, are ya?"

They both chuckled at that.

"Not that I'm aware of." Savage scratched his head. "I just got back not too long ago from Missouri."

"Missouri, huh? Not too bad there. Your birthday is

comin' up. Gettin' long in the tooth there, fucker."

"I am." Savage smiled.

"When are you going to put some roots down some-where, you handsome son of a bitch?! You got your looks from your mother, that's for damn sure. You look like a fuckin' GQ model. You're an embarrassment to the Savage name!" Dad quipped. "If you had long hair, Danny might try to fuck ya, pretty boy."

Savage burst out laughing again, this time until his stom-ach hurt.

Danny was a good friend of the family, an Outlaw and a well-known pervert. He'd been caught whacking off in his ex-wife's flower garden and trying to fuck a literal hole in a wall.

"Time to find you someone to continue your fucked up last name, Savage. Where's the pregnant girlfriend, huh? I've heard about you…"

"You've heard about me, huh?" Savage rolled his gold skull ring around his finger.

"Yeah… lots of women. Just like your old man back before I settled down with your mom. You're a fuckin' jack rabbit but your days are numbered. Time to get married maybe? Move in with someone at least… Dump some Savage sperm in the well of life we call pussy and hope the baby doesn't turn out like Chucky, you sick motherfucker."

Savage took a drag of his cigarette.

"Funny you should mention that, Dad, you know, settling down. I met someone."

"Did ya now?"

"Yeah. We've been seeing each other for a little while

now. I like her. I like 'er a lot."

Dad groaned as he rolled over to his other side and grabbed a screw driver. "What's her name?"

"Eva. I need to tell you something about this though. Something important."

"Yeah? What?"

"I know that some of your pals, some of my uncles, as I call them, basically wouldn't approve but you know I don't live for other people. My decision is made but I am giving you a heads up because you might catch some heat for this."

"Heat? What's wrong with her?"

"Nothing is wrong with her. She's Black."

Dad stopped working and looked up at him. "Black?"

"Yeah."

Dad sighed and rolled his eyes.

"Max, what the fuck are you tryna do here?"

"What do you mean, what the fuck am I tryna do? I met someone I like, and she happens to be darker than me. So fucking what?" He shrugged. "I'm not going to stop seeing her."

"I don't expect you to. You haven't listened to a damn thing I've told you in years."

"I expected better from you, you know that? I was only telling you this because I know how the Outlaws feel about this sort of thing, despite the club having Mexican roots and they're over here at the house a lot. I didn't want you blindsided or being the last to know."

"It's not me that's the problem, you little bastard you." Dad pointed to himself, his brows furrowed. "I don't give uh flyin' shit if she was purple with green polka dots. If ya told me her father was a Hell's Angel, *then* we'd have a problem! Fuck who you wanna fuck. I've had my share of black pussy back in the day; I kept it to myself of course, but so fuckin' what?! Look how dark your mom is! She's mistaken for Hispanic all the gotdamn time so it's got nothin' to do with complexion, or even race for that matter. I don't want you in any trouble is all. That's it. We're Outlaws, gotta stick by the code, but you're family. The newer guys are the ones bringing problems like this to the table, turnin' everything into a gotdamn race war. It's not us, but it's been a struggle because we're passin' the baton. Regardless, I'm sure your mother would want to meet her, but you can't bring 'er around here until I explain the situation to the guys, you hear me?"

"Yeah..."

"The last thing I want is to have to shoot a motherfucker in the throat for talkin' shit about my fuckin' son and his ol' lady! I gotta ask you though, before I go through the effort, are you really serious about this?"

"Yeah, it's serious or I wouldn't have even brought it up."

"All right then. I'll take care of it. No sweat." Dad shrugged and went back to the bike. "So, tell me about her. What the fuck does she look like? Does she work and if so, where?"

"She's fuckin' beautiful. About average height... long hair..."

"Is the hair hers? You know a lot of these Black chicks have fake hair. Hey, as long as the pussy is real, I guess that's fine, but ya know."

"She has naturally long hair but has this shit called weave tracks in it to make it thicker sometimes. I found out a lot of White girls' do it too, especially the Vegas performers and entertainers."

"I can believe that. It looks nice, I guess. Your mother bought a wig last month." Dad chuckled. "She wanted to try out red hair. It looked good actually. I fucked tha shit outta her after she put it on. Felt like I was having an affair with Jessica Rabbit."

Savage snorted. "That's way too much information."

His father snickered. He'd forgotten how obsessed the man was about long hair on women. It was his thing. The longer the better...

"Eva would be beautiful if she were bald headed. I think you'd like her. Real smart, classy."

"I asked about her job, too."

"Yeah, she used to work in a clinic with patients. She has a podcast show, wrote some self-help books, strong woman... like Mom, but sweet, too."

"How's the pussy?" He shook his head. The old man was a real piece of work. "Must be primo since you won't even answer. I remember... Black pussy is good. I used to love how it looked when I'd fuck them, you know, the difference in color."

"Oversharing again... I don't fuckin' care about your past sex life or what you're doing to my mother."

"Hey! I'm an old man! I like to talk about it. Cut me some slack! Makes me feel like I'm still young. Can you just humor me? Jesus Christ though, Max." Dad began to turn a bolt. "You've always done shit like this!"

"Done shit like what?"

"You can't just do shit the easy way. You're like me—a total and complete bullheaded fucker." The man rolled over to sit upright. "Gimme that." The man waved his dirty hands at the cigarette. Savage handed it over and watched the orange ember sizzle and brighten as the man took a drag. "I thought you stopped smokin' cigs?"

"I did. I left my cigars in my car. Saw it sitting there." Dad took another puff.

"Thanks for the house, by the way." Dad brought his knees up and rested his big arms across them.

"I don't know why you keep saying that. There's no reason to keep thanking me. This is what I was supposed to do. Why would I have my parents livin' in a piece of shit while I was living well? That's bullshit. You two deserve this... all this land. Mom has a garden; you've got a big ass garage and great scenery. Now you both can be at peace."

Dad nodded.

"I am. I still think saying thank you is important. You're not obligated to do shit. The people that make ya aren't always the people that love ya. Your mother knows about that all too well." Dad's eyes narrowed. "Speaking of which, go in there and say hi to her. She might be off the phone by now. I think she said somethin' about going to In-N-Out Burger. Ask her to get you some, too. I'm starving. Hopefully we can eat soon." Dad tossed the cigarette.

"All right, I'll be right back." Savage maneuvered around him and entered the house. He immediately smelled Mom's nail polish and pungent perfume, and could hear one of the ceiling fans going full blast. His mother was still on the phone, talking in Russian. He approached her open bedroom door and found her sitting half naked on the edge of her bed. Black stockings covered her long legs, and her robe lay open, exposing her black lacy bra. Long ebony hair flowed down past her ass, with a bit of gray on the left side.

"Привет (Hello)," he stated in Russian. The woman looked over at him, and her amber eyes lit up like stoked flames. Full pink lips framed by naturally tanned flesh curled in a proud smile.

"*Moy syn zdes.* (My son is here.)"

He leaned against the door frame and crossed his ankles as he waited for her to wrap up her conversation. She ended the call, got to her feet, and immediately covered up with another robe, this one a bit thicker. Then, she rushed to him and wrapped her arms around him, giving him a kiss on the cheek. It took him a bit off guard.

"You look good," she said. "Very healthy. Nice glow. How have you been, Maximus?"

"Fine. Why haven't you called me back, Mom? I've been trying to get a hold of you for a while now." He wiggled out of her grasp and leaned against his parents' ivory bedroom dresser. She lit a cigarette and went to sit back on her bed, crossing her legs. She seemed a bit nervous, perhaps perplexed.

"I just needed some time. I was upset… didn't want to worry you."

"What's going on?" He crossed his arms, though he had a damn good idea now.

"My family keeps asking for money." *Big surprise.* "I give them some, just like I had told you, but they ask for more…

on and on it goes." Her slight accent still held tight to some of the words as she spoke.

"We've discussed this."

"Just a little more, Maximus."

"This is the same family that abandoned you, basically threw you to the wolves but popped back up when they found out that you were living well here in the States, right? Are we talking about the same fuckers? I just wanna be clear." She lowered her gaze. "Did you tell them you get the money from your son? That you're retired?" She swallowed and nodded, fidgeting.

"I did. They don't care, you know that. That was my sister, Milena, on the phone. You've spoken to her before. She adores you."

"She doesn't adore me. She doesn't even know me. I'm just a bank to her. Yeah, she's a fuckin' loser and user. I was on the phone with her thirty seconds a few months ago when you made me talk to her, and she started asking me about visas, green cards, gambling, if I can fly her and her family down and take care of them. They didn't give a shit about you when you were out here sellin' your ass to make ends meet!"

"Max, please…" She closed her eyes.

"Max, please, nothin'! Mom, you've got to stop this. They only call you to ask for this fuckin' money and I told you to change your number. To stop taking their calls."

"I can't. They need me. It's very dangerous and they have nothing."

"Where you were at was dangerous, too… and you also had nothing. They don't love you, Mom. Can't you see that?

Now it all makes sense why you've been avoiding me. You know this is wrong. You wanted to ask for more money but didn't want to argue with me because I'd tell you the truth!"

"They're not bad people, Max. It was a bad time in our lives!"

"You and Dad struggled. There were many bad times in our lives as well." She bit her bottom lip, then brought her cigarette to her lips. "No one cared when you were in that horrible orphanage as a child but now that they can use you—BOOM! You may as well recite those song lyrics: 'I heard you bitches was lookin' for me, bitch! Here I go!' Ahhh, we're family now, all of a sudden! 'We love you, Karina!' That's what they say. It's all fuckin' bullshit! When Dad was in prison that one time and you got beaten up by that asshole, that guy who was trying to turn you out, pimp you, where the hell were they?!"

The woman rested back on her elbows and looked away.

"I'll remind you. You were in the hospital for five fuckin' weeks, that's where. Dad got outta prison and settled the score, killed that motherfucker, but you called your family to come and help, send money, anything... reminded them you had a little boy. And they didn't do *shit*! They knew you were alone with a child to raise and they had amnesia when it came to remembering the fact that when you and Dad had little, you still gave. When they had abundance, they did nothing. With the little bit we had, you and Dad still sent them money and gifts every now and again but when you were in your time of need, they were nowhere to be found. Does that sound like love to you?"

"Love is expressed in many different ways, Maximus."

"Love is an action word, Mom. The Outlaws took care of the situation with action. That's real love. They said, 'Hey, Mad Dog is in the pen doing a one-year bid. Let's help his boy, send his daughter and her mom some money and watch over his old lady.' Dad's buddies, their women came and surrounded you, cooked for you, took care of me, took care of *us*, nursed you back to health, made sure I got a ride to school and my homework done. Your *real* family, Mom, is right here!"

"You see how you become? Hot and crazy! This is why I did not tell you! Maximus, you do not understand!"

"I understand just fine. We know what the next thing is you say is going to be. 'Max, please give me a couple thousand dollars to send them.' I am not sending them shit!"

Mom hissed, a look of disdain on her face.

"Do you know how much money I have doled out, and hated it, but I did it for *you* because you convinced me it was just a one time, two time, three time thing to help them out of a jam? But it was never enough. I have given over fifty-eight thousand dollars in the last six months to these motherfuckers I don't even like, Mom! Blood is thicker than water, my ass! That's fuckin' outrageous! These people wouldn't spit on me if I were on fire. They're calculating, manipulative, lying users. You've got like fifteen of these fuckers asking you for shit at any given time, and the number keeps growing. They keep churning out babies like roaches, and expect you to foot the bill. Why don't they put 'em in a nasty ass orphanage that smells like rotten piss and shit, just like they did to you? What's wrong, huh? That place not good enough for their children but it was all right for my mother?!"

"Max... you're out of line."

"I'm out of line, am I? But it happened! You were raped at the age of seven because of them! Your parents didn't get rid of you so you could have a better life. You need to face the truth. They *sold* you! They sold their seven-year-old daughter to a grown man who ran that orphanage to rape their child whenever he got good and ready. And they did it for the equivalent of a measly thousand US dollars. I looked into it, remember? I found the paper trail!"

Mom started to shake, looking so pitiful.

"*Fuck* these people! Your entire family. Even the members that didn't do it knew about it and did nothing. They hate Dad because he's not rich and he told them to basically go kill themselves, because he hates 'em too. And they only tolerated me because I'm yours and I am where the gold is. No more money for these fuckers, ya hear me?! We're done with this!" He waved his hands in the air. "And to ensure that you don't, I will be making out the checks myself for your bills for a while instead of handing over cash. I can't trust you to stop the bleeding." Mom's eyes grew dark as she glared at him. Her chin held high, she played with the fabric of her robe. "Did you hear me? They're cut off."

"Fine, Maximus," she stated coldly.

"Now Dad said you were gettin' some food, is that right?"

"Yes."

"Get some clothes on. I'll take you."

Mom nodded, clearly shaken but unwilling to speak further. He stepped out of the bedroom and closed the door, making his way to the garage. Dad was standing against the wall, his vest off and a beer in hand. He lifted the bottle and took a swig.

"These walls aren't soundproof," he said. "You just told her everything I told her more than once. Goes in one gotdamn ear and out the other, Max." He took a deep breath. "I fuckin' hate those people. I wish they'd all just die and leave us the hell alone."

"If you tell her that, she'll never forgive you."

"I don't give a flyin' fuck. They've got your mother wrapped around their finger, like she's under some spell. We're fighting an uphill battle, son. They are promising to give her what she always wanted."

"A family? But she has us! She has the Outlaws, too."

Dad shook his head.

"No, son. Your mother has always wanted her family's love…"

CHAPTER TWENTY-ONE

Savage Truths

"**Y**OU'RE NOT GOING to do what you're supposed to so there's really no point in us even having this discussion. Get out, and I mean it." Zaire shook her head as she pulled out her studio chair, sat down, then took a sip of her wine. "I should've locked the door, treated you like an animal that needed to be caged away."

"I'll be quiet! I promise!" Maximus was all smiles, standing there in a pair of black silky boxers as if he were about to go into a wrestling ring and knock someone the hell out.

"Yeah, right! You can't help yourself. Last night, at dinner, you promised to not make a big deal about your steak. Instead, you went the hell off."

"I didn't ask for beef fuckin' jerky and that's what it tasted like. I gave that fucker several chances to get it right."

"Did that include you going back into the kitchen, pulling out a skillet, and barking at the chef about how a prime rib is supposed to be prepared? You then had the absolute audacity to cook it right there on the spot!"

"He should've thanked me. That was a free lesson, on the

house! I'm not even a good cook, but I know how to not overcook a fuckin' steak! It was a fuckin' romantic dinner, tryna take my baby out for a good fuckin' time, and even your steak was tough and rubbery, so I had to defend your honor."

The gall of the man.

"Maximus, I'm serious. I'm not trying to play with you tonight." He slid his dick out from the slit of his boxers and shook it at her. She hated how her body betrayed her, her pussy instantly getting wet from the sight of the semi-hard cock with its thick veins and bulbous head. She still hadn't quite gotten over how huge the man's manhood was. She salivated, as if she were standing before an amazing buffet, and she was starving, needing nourishment in the worst way. "Put that damn thing away. I have work to do."

"Can't you suck it during commercial breaks?"

"Get out." She swallowed a giggle, not trying to encourage the son of a bitch. Before she could utter another warning, the bastard was all over her, leaning her back in her seat. "Savage, no!"

"You don't mean that!" He lifted her nightshirt, exposing her breasts, feverishly licking her nipples and sucking them hard and fast. Big hands explored her flesh as he covered her body with kisses from the waist up, his cock now pushing hard into her stomach.

"The show starts in five minutes! Stop it!" Her chair nearly toppled over when he dropped to his knees, yanked her panties out of the way, and licked her pussy, pushing the lips open with his vigorous maneuvers. Gripping his head, she gyrated into his kiss, losing her damn mind. Her orgasm stole her breath away, curling her toes, drawing wild curses and promises of retribution. She hadn't even noticed until it was far too late that he was off his knees and practically sitting on her lap with his big, throbbing dick in his grip.

"I've got the *real* steak, some grade A beef right here! It'll be a speedy delivery, and trust and believe, mine is prepared to perfection." She screamed when he lunged deep inside her, knocking her walls down in a single thrust. The monster grabbed a fistful of her hair, and made her take his powerful plunges one by one, staring at her lustfully, possessively. A look full of love and desire. He slammed into her with the quickness of a cheetah, making her shudder.

"Fuck!"

"You said you needed it fast, right? Any regrets?" He smirked, the Devil in his eyes. "I'm fucking the hell out of you! Fucking you so hard and fast, you look like a bobble head doll during a tornado."

"I hate you!" She laughed, her body desperately addicted to him. "Why… why would you do this right… right now?!" She could barely get the words out as she trembled, another climax sucking out her very soul.

"Because I was horny. And you're going to give me this pussy whenever the fuck I want it!" He groaned and thrust again, his voice low and guttural. The little red light began to flash.

"One minute until the show!" she screamed, her thighs burning from being spread so far apart. Her pussy squeezed and pulled at his dick as multiple orgasms took her asunder. He grunted loud and deep, pulled out, grabbed a nearby tissue and released into it, his body jerking, filling the

Kleenex up in hard, quick spurts. Her head spinning, she pushed his thigh aside, or tried to—It was hard as rock, and the damn thing barely budged. He finally stepped away from her as she made quick work to pull her nightshirt down and hide their dirty deeds. Her wet pussy pulsed and throbbed from his intrusion. It was fucking delightful.

"I think that deserves a chance to stay. I finished just in time." He grinned as he tossed the cum filled tissue into the trashcan.

"Fine, you crazy lunatic. But let me tell you something, Savage," She pointed her finger in his direction and cued another button to play an advertisement. "If you say one word during this broadcast, there will be repercussions. I'm a one woman show tonight. I told my engineer and producer to stay home so you and I could spend more time together but you are not following the rules. You were supposed to stay upstairs."

"It's more fun underground."

She worked the controls to begin the theme music as he headed into the small lavatory and washed his hands.

"Do you have any more of those potato chips?" he whispered as he walked back in, drying his hands with a paper towel.

"Shhh!" she snapped, sick of him already.

The man began to walk about and explore. He checked out various files and books, being generally nosy, and grating her last nerve down to the nub. Once the theme music grew louder, he began to shimmy, doing silly dances with his dick bobbing about inside his boxers, free and loose. He made it bounce from right to left to the beat of the music, then helicoptered it.

Oh my God, I can't stand him! He's a big kid!

It took everything in her power to keep from bursting into a fit of laughter at his antics but she fought it with all that was in her. She sure didn't wish for him to have the satisfaction. But she almost lost her shit when he waltzed over and downed the rest of her merlot.

He did NOT just drink my wine!

Leaning down, he gave her a kiss, then disappeared back up the steps with the glass.

Oh, thank God, he's gone… Don't come back, either!

"Hello, Los Angeles and beyond! This is Dr. Zaire Ellington with, 'Confessions of a Better You'…" The callers began to pile up in the queue, and she started out the show with a young man by the name of Bruce whose boyfriend had taken a new job out of state and was now seemingly avoiding his calls. Zaire got comfy in her chair, swiveling back and forth in her long, oversized navy blue silk nightshirt that was now slightly wrinkled due to a delicious attack from her lover. She ran her fingers through her loose waves that framed her face. The rest of her hair was piled high atop her head in a lazy bun.

She listened intently to her caller, taking a few notes along the way. Things were going smoothly. In fact, too well. She surely should've been suspicious. Savage was at times like a child. If he was quiet, you knew he'd gotten into the cookie jar…

She jumped nearly out of her seat when she heard the damn basement door slam and loud footsteps approached. She closed her eyes and counted to ten in her head, trying to keep her cool and not go off into an early commercial from one of the ad revenue sponsors so she could bop him upside of the head in peace.

This man! As she turned, ready to put herself on mute and tell him off, he set a fresh glass of wine before her and a small plate of red and green grapes, the fruit glistening from being freshly rinsed. Next to those were thin square slices of cheese, a few sesame crackers, and a couple pieces of rectangular pieces of chocolate they'd taken from the restaurant they'd eaten at the previous night. She offered a smile of appreciation when he lifted her chin with two fingers and stole a kiss. Moments later, she was back in the throes of her conversation, doling out advice, while the man of her dreams—and dare she admit it, nightmares—sat across from her, his feet propped up on the table, ankles crossed and wiggling his freakishly long toes every now and again. He flipped nonchalantly through a magazine, but kept fairly quiet. She hoped it would be like this for the duration of the show.

"I agree, Octavia, and that's why I stated should you return to school per your original plan. There's no reason why your husband can't watch the children if he is home during those hours. That's unfair. You're trying to better not just yourself, but your family." The woman went on about the selfishness of her spouse, and how she'd tried to better their financial situation but he seemed content with doing the bare minimum and at times even making things harder for her. "Yes, I see. The other thing is that… No… No! Stop it! Oh my God! You are horrible! STOP!"

"I'm… I'm horrible?"

"Uh… no! Not you, Octavia, we're having… a… problem here!" The tug of war between her and Savage over the microphone was a thing her worst nightmares were made of. He wrestled it from her grip, snatching the microphone away, forcing her to place the caller on mute before further damage could be rendered.

"Take it off mute," he barked.

"No!" she yelled, barely able to catch her breath from the altercation. "Stop playing. This isn't funny!"

"I'm not playing. Let me talk to her."

"You're not qualified to talk to these people! Maximus, I am going to kill you!" She lunged towards the microphone as he pressed the mute button twice, releasing it.

"Sorry about that interruption, Octavia. You don't know me, I'm a guest speaker you could say, but I just wanted to weigh in on your situation, from a man's perspective. Is that all right?"

"Uh… yeah, I guess so," the woman stated, sounding confused.

"Dr. Zaire feels as though your husband doesn't want to pull his weight and watch the kids while you go back to school but from what I heard, the man is working thirteen hours a day and is tired when he gets home. All he wants to do is eat, relax, maybe get a little ass and go the hell to sleep."

Zaire slowly closed her eyes and started to hyperventilate.

"This is the end…" she murmured. "Sponsors are going to pull out. I'll be a laughing stock come tomorrow morning…"

"So, what you two should do is come up with a schedule, ya know? Put that shit on the refrigerator with chores you do, school, work hours, all of that stuff. Sometimes the man isn't always the bad guy and let me tell you somethin', I don't have any kids, okay? So I can't speak on shit I don't know about, but I can talk about the mind of a man and how we think, so if you show you want to compromise and it's not an all or nothing situation, he might listen. If you keep makin' it seem like he doesn't want to spend time with his kids and is trying to hold you back from going back to school, you'll put him on the defensive. That's not right. You said he was a good father, but when you tell him that, it shows you feel differently. You both are tryna do the right thing, busting your asses, but you gotta think of the kids and also try to be fair with each other. I'm not a relationship expert, either; far from it, so you can take my advice and toss it out the window if you want. I really have no room to give any advice, and that's just me being honest, but I felt like you could use some help and insight into how us men think and how you can get what you want from us—well, him, in this case."

"Okay, I get that. I have tried to be fair though, and I've spoken to him countless times. We've had arguments about this. I yell until I'm blue in the face."

"Has yelling at him about this worked? Have ultimatums worked?"

"No…"

"Exactly, so why the hell are you still doing it? You come to him yelling and going off, and that's what you're going to get right back. Do you understand?"

"Uh, yeah. Actually I do." The caller seemed to perk up, as if that was a novel idea. Perhaps Savage had worded it in a way that made sense to her.

"Unless he's a wimp, he's not going to allow you to tell him he's a bad father all because he doesn't want to come home, clean, and watch the kids all night after working long hours in a hot ass warehouse. So, to help get you both out of this financial situation, look into alternatives. Like, can ya find a way to take some of your courses online and set a schedule with him, just like I said? Also, to help him feel appreciated, fix him something to eat. Don't keep dinner from him out of revenge, as you admitted to doing. If he sees you being nice, he is going to try to be nice back. I'm serious. The only way he won't is if he is an asshole and doesn't want you to progress and better yourself. You said he had been great up until this issue, right?"

"Yes. This honestly has been the biggest problem we've had and I didn't mean to imply that he wasn't a good father. It's just that lately... I don't know. I'm not sure what to say, but you know what I mean. I need his help and he's not giving it, but I understand what you're saying."

"Yeah, look... We men are simple to please, okay? Don't complicate this. All we want is some sustenance," he said, counting off his fingers, "some sex and some space. The three S's, and that's it. Well, there are other things too, but those are the three main things. We want our egos stroked, too, sometimes. We want to be able to talk to you even if we don't feel like talking—just nice to know you're there. We want to come home to peace and if something is wrong, yeah you definitely should be able to talk to us, but just let us get in the door first. That's what my father used to say and my parents have been together for over forty years. Look, I don't have a degree," he said. "I'm no expert on this shit like Dr. Zaire.

"All I have are my own observations, my own family growin' up. Zaire is the expert, and I can't take that away from her. Now, I know I contradicted some of what she said. I'm not sayin' she's completely wrong about this. I am just saying she might be right, but she might not be. I'm glad she let me weigh in on this and asked for my opinion. That shows she's not intimidated by another perspective because at the end of the day, it's not about her ego. It's about helping her callers."

He tossed her a wink. She gave him the middle finger.

"Thank you so much, and you too, Dr. Zaire. I appreciate your perspective! I have a lot to think about. What's your name?"

Zaire sat there seething, but when he glanced at her again, her defenses came tumbling down. He looked so... innocent. So wanting to please her... to help... She toyed with a grape on her plate and whispered, "It's fine. Tell her."

"My name is Maximus, but that's not important. Everyone listening in tonight, you're lucky to have someone like Dr. Zaire to call and talk to. This isn't some gimmick for her. She brings a wealth of information to the table, and I hope one day she shares more of that with you from her own personal perspective. We should never be ashamed of anything that's happened to us, especially if it was out of our control. All of the bad shit that has happened to each and every one of you out there has in some way helped make you who you are today... made you stronger. It takes true strength to even admit that.

"Nobody has to pretend to be anything they're not. It never works out anyway, because the true you will always come out eventually. The real us refuses to be ignored; it's going to have its way sooner or later. Whether it's telling your husband you wanna go back to school but you can be patient and make it so that it works for both of you, or it's trusting someone who honestly scares the shit out of you— someone you met practically on a dare and then… your whole life was turned upside down, although you know they can give you the love you deserve. You know you finally have a man who would turn the whole fuckin' world inside out for you, baby…" He stared at her, and her heart felt as if it were going to burst out of her chest. "Someone who will love you, cherish you, and have your back like no other. We have to take risks in life. We have to compromise or nothing will work out. That's just the savage truth."

She took a deep breath, and looked into his eyes.

"I'm going to give Dr. Zaire the microphone, but before I go, I want everyone in the listening audience to know that this lady's heart is pure gold, people. She's the real deal. She cares. When she was made, they broke the mold. That's why I love 'er… I know I could trust my life with this woman. It took a shrink to make my own ego shrink and see that if I second guessed this special connection we have, I was going to lose out on the love of my life… and I don't lose bets, I don't lose games, and I damn sure wasn't going to lose her. I will keep her with me, keep her happy, by any means necessary."

He dropped the microphone onto the desk, stole a grape from her plate, kissed the top of her head, and made his way back up the steps, softly closing the door behind him…

ZAIRE HELD THE handle of her favorite burnt orange leather purse with both hands while standing on the porch of her parents' gorgeous home. It was always in pristine condition, even the blinds and curtains often cleaned from top to bottom. The light wind flung the heavenly scent of pending rain about, teasing her with the promise of a good storm.

That's good making love weather…

She smiled to herself, envisioning her man ravishing her.

It hadn't rained in so long, the thought of it doing so gave her comfort, slightly easing her knotting stomach.

I never know what to expect when I come over here. I hate feeling like this.

Moments later, she found herself staring into her father's Ring Doorbell camera. She smiled and waved, just in case he was looking at her. The front door swung open and the sound of the television and the smell of fresh ginger immediately poured from the place. The front screen door squeaked as she stepped inside and he wrapped his big, warm arms around her. Nudging her chin into the crevice of his shoulder and neck, she closed her eyes and turned into a little girl, releasing her demons.

"Hey, Dad." She closed the door behind her and locked it.

"Hey, baby. Come on in." She walked into the living

room and paused. There mama sat, her eyes lifeless yet glued to the television. She was dressed in a white blouse, a pair of loose jeans and white socks. Her gorgeous honey brown curly hair that Dad would dye on her behalf was pulled back in a thick ponytail.

"She's just watching some movie on Lifetime or one of those dramatic women stations." Dad chuckled as he made his way towards the kitchen. "Go and make yourself comfortable."

After a while, the older woman looked up at her, then scowled. Before Zaire could say anything, that scowl turned into a smile, and Mom's eyes lit up.

"Eva. Hi, baby."

"Hi, Mama." She made her way over to the woman and sat next to her on the couch, immediately reaching her hand out and clasping her mother's.

"You look so pretty, honey."

"Thank you, Mama. So do you."

"I really like your lipstick. What color is that?" Mama gently ran the pad of her thumb along the edge of her lower lip.

"It's called 'Bad Reputation.' It's by NARS."

"It really pops against your skin. Us Black women look so good with bright red lipsticks. I wish more of us wore these shades. You having such a lovely red undertone that really brings it out... I always loved your rich, brown skin, baby. Do you think it would look nice on me, too? I have yellow undertones. It might clash."

"We can see. How about I buy you one of your own?" Mama grinned wide.

"Oh, I'd like that, baby. I'll give you the money back. I'm sure it wasn't cheap. You've always liked nice things. Your cosmetics I'm sure are no exception."

"Mama, you don't have to pay me back. It's just lipstick." She kissed the woman's cheek settled on the couch.

"How's your show?"

Eva cocked her head to the side, surprised her mother was so lucid, flowing with the conversation so well. Oftentimes, Mama barely spoke to her when she came by. She was either zonked out on her medication, asleep, or in a sullen mood.

"It's going well, Mama. The ratings are high. I got me two new sponsors, too."

"That's good, baby. You've earned it. I listened to it yesterday." *What? She listened to my show? I've never heard her say that. She must've heard Savage then, too...* "Your father has been 'round here cleaning. He did about three loads of laundry, too. I helped fold and put them away. He's been so helpful." Her cheeks flushed. "He made some ginger tea, and he picked up some sushi. Do you have sushi left, Mitchell?" Mama called out to Dad.

"Yes, Iris!" Dad responded from the kitchen. "Do you want some more?"

"No, just offering some to Eva."

"I'm fine, Dad. I'm not hungry, but I'll take some tea if you have any left."

"You bet. Do you want sugar in it?" he called out.

"No, but if you have some stevia, one pack will suffice." She soon heard the clatter of drawers and closing of cabinet doors.

"You look so happy, Zaire... just glowing." Mama tapped her hand.

"I... I am, Mama." A few stilted seconds passed, neither saying much.

"I'm so proud of you and your sister. I should tell you that more often." Zaire's heart beat faster within her. Not once in her life had her mother ever told her such a thing. "Star has started a jewelry company. It's doing well, too."

"Yes, she told me! She sells most of it online. I bought some earrings and two necklaces from her. They're beautiful!" Mama nodded. "I'm glad she found something else to pour her energy into that not only helps her relax, but earns her money. Have you spoken to Timothy?"

Mama's glow slowly drained from her face. She turned towards the television and went quiet for what felt like an eternity.

Guess I shouldn't have brought him up...

Zaire had been hoping Mama would say something kind about her brother too, something out of the ordinary. It was apparent by the woman's expression, that wasn't in the cards.

"One day, I had visited my grandmother in Baltimore. There was snow on the ground and it was blowin' around in the air, getting all over me. I felt like I was inside a snow globe, so beautiful..." Mama's voice went low, her eyes glossed over as she withdrew within herself. Zaire had seen that expression far too many times to count. It often preceded one of her episodes. Her stomach tightened with anxiety. Dad handed her a cup of warm tea, startling her out of her thoughts. The mug felt good between her palms.

"Thank you, Dad."

"You're welcome, Eva," he stated it in an almost robotic way, his face serious. He patted her shoulder then walked away, leaving them alone once again. Time passed, and Zaire scooted a bit closer to her mother, bracing herself.

You can't let fear of her reactions and outbursts stop you… You have to take risks, Eva… Stop running from this.

"Mama, you were talking about the snow."

"Oh yes… the snow. That snow was so white, it glowed that day. I hadn't seen snow like that before. Born and raised right here in L.A., it just isn't something we get. I guess, some may like that, some may not." Mama shrugged. "I hadn't seen much snow, period, over my lifetime but this snow looked like white diamonds, Eva. It looked like a blanket God had laid down from Heaven, covering the whole state of Maryland, you know?" A twinkle showed in Mama's eyes as she moved her arms about, expressing herself, falling face first down into the soft, white memory. "I was walking down the sidewalk, putting one foot in front of the other, my boots sinking into this heavy snow, and along the way I saw one bright red drop in that snow, then another… then another until there were so many, I was shivering.

"Not from the cold, but from fear… Fear of what was bleeding like that, leaving a trail, the dots getting bigger and closer together. I then saw a hand forced up like a daisy bursting through that snow. It looked frozen stiff. The fingers were long and dark. Red tinged the knuckles and was embedded under the nails. That hand was attached to a body curled up real tight in that snow, right there on a lawn in front of some apartments. It was a man, Eva. His jet-black eyes were wide like an animal's that had been shot in the back. I didn't know if he was dead or alive until I screamed... then he blinked. He gasped for air, and a curl of his breath caught the wind and drifted away. I yelled for help, but it seemed nobody heard me, baby. Nobody came...

"Timothy is like that, Eva. Not that man lying there hurt in that snow, but those blood drops. You know something bad is going to happen if he keeps on going down that same road. You know if you keep walking and watching him, if you don't turn away, you are going to run into something horrible. I'm responsible not for his snow, not for his blood, but for no one hearin' him call out when he needed help."

"Mama, we are adults now! We have to accept responsibility for our own actions!"

A tear streamed down Mama's face.

"I know, baby," She patted her knee. "But you see, I was his mother and he'd been yellin' for help since he was a baby. Today I woke up and for some reason, I remembered things I hadn't thought about in years. It was a routine day. Your father woke me up and fixed me some coffee. I brushed my teeth, took a shower, got dressed. I made my oatmeal, and he and I talked for a bit, then he ran down the way to get lunch. I promised him I'd be okay. He's so afraid to leave me alone." She dropped her gaze. "While he was gone, I took my medicine. I looked at those pills in my palm."

Mama outstretched her hand, riddled with fine lines, proving years of life lived. "I said, 'God, you didn't make me crazy; I just am. Right now, I feel mighty guilty though. I had three babies and don't know their names. I know the names I gave them, but I don't know who they are, not on the inside.

When your father got home, I told him these things. He reminded me that I used to keep journals. Most of what I wrote was a bunch of crazy nonsense," Mama shook her head and laughed dismally. "But not all of it was crazy talk or gibberish. Some of it made sense. I'd written stuff about my babies, all three of you... and now, I am starting to remember who you are on the inside. I know you don't come around much because your father doesn't want you upset. And I know you're kinda happy about that, because then you don't have to see me."

"Oh, Mama, that's not true."

"It *is* true, Eva... and that's all right. I wouldn't wanna come and see no crazy old lady, either." Another tear came down Mama's face, tearing her apart. "No matter how pretty the snow is, how it sparkles, honey, it's ruined because somebody is bleeding and dying on the inside, even if it's from their own mind. My mind stabs me in my heart every day. It plays tricks on me, never gives a treat. I don't know what tomorrow is going to bring, but right now, today, I'm okay. And I know that *every* day, I love you."

Zaire squeezed her mother's hand. She swallowed back the tears that threatened to fall, but could barely hold on.

"You ever seen snow before, honey?"

"Yes, Mama." The woman sported an odd smile now. "When I travelled to Chicago and New York for business I did see it sometimes."

Mama nodded, but kept her eyes glued to the television. Soon, Dad joined them and they said nothing for quite some time. She took her father's hand and squeezed, and he squeezed back, while she sat there shaking, falling apart inside. Mama exhaled, as if awakening from a long slumber, but still, she kept her eyes on that television, the tears coming down like a river…

I wish I could talk to you like this every day, Mama. So many people take for granted being able to pick up the phone and have a chat with their mother. I wish I could tell you how much I need you, and that you could understand. I wish I could explain how your approval when I was growing up meant everything to me, but I guess that doesn't matter anymore. I'm trying to heal the child inside me, and sometimes, you give me glimmers of hope that one day, I might be able to sit down with you and tell you I'm sorry for being ashamed of you… Sorry for not forgiving you… Sorry for blaming you for the bad choices I made… Sorry for at times wishing you were dead!

Zaire shook her head, unable to fight the tears any longer. She both chastised and hugged her inner child within, beating her up and loving her at the same time…

As we sit here, together, a family… yes, a family, I am reminded we don't get to choose our parents, but in some strange way, we do. Perhaps on a subconscious level we believe we can learn a lesson from them. I know those blood drops in the snow could've been me or Star, but Timothy was the sacrificial lamb. We all have our vices, don't we, Mama? Star has been in denial and sticking her head in the sand. Timothy had drugs and blamed the world. I had shame and a superiority complex—a deep desire to be needed and held in high regard. A need to feel like I was better than you, Star, Timothy, my friends, my callers, everybody, all to hide the fact that I really believed I was a nobody! I didn't think I was pretty like you and Star. I didn't think I was as smart as Timothy. I didn't believe I was as brave and strong as Daddy, either! I felt like nobody wanted me! NOBODY! All of this shit has been a silly act. I was sitting high, and everyone else was way down low in my twisted-up mind…

Her heart broke.

Somebody though loved me enough to tell me the truth. He came into my life and forced me to look at a mirror. He wasn't afraid to be his authentic self, to show his defects, craziness, bumps, bruises and all. He wasn't ashamed of his family, no matter what they did or said. I was in awe of his strength! I was mesmerized at how comfortable he was in his own tattooed skin! He said whatever he wanted to say, didn't care that it didn't sound refined or jazzy. He dressed how he wanted to dress, did what he wanted to do, went where he wanted to go! HE WAS FREE! He was everything I wanted to be! That's why I loved the bad boys… because they didn't care what anyone thought, and I wanted some of that magic! Some of them are twisted, and should be avoided… but then there are others like Savage, who doesn't allow himself to hurt the people he loves. I knew then that I wanted him, and had to have him.

I wanted a man who could protect my inner child, like my father. I wanted a guy who could make me feel good not just inside my body, but in my heart and mind, too. Oh my God! The truth is savage! It rages! It will be heard by any means necessary.

She looked at her mother. The woman had zoned off, seemingly trapped in a daydream.

I want to be able to tell you this, Mama, to look in your eyes and say, 'Hey, I'm in love! He gets me. He understands me. He's good to me… so good to me!' One day, I pray I'll be able to.

Zaire smiled, sniffed, and didn't pull her hands away from her parents to wipe her eyes. Instead, she turned to her father and realized he was staring at her. He, too, had tears in his eyes, and a big smile on his face. She leaned in close to him and whispered, "Mama had a good day."

"Yes, she did. It's been real nice."

"Guess what, Dad? I met a wonderful man. I finally decided to try again, to take my own advice. I took some time out for myself, as you know. That helped. This time I believe will be different. I think I found someone who truly appreciates me."

The man looked thrilled, and proud.

"That's beautiful, Eva. You're a good woman, and I'm not saying that just because you're my daughter."

"I have to warn you though, Dad. He's a bit rough around the edges."

"So was I, and your mother loved me anyway..." He kissed her cheek. "I can't wait to meet him. Bring him over soon, okay?" She nodded, her heart exploding as she explored the hard-to-navigate valleys of her truth. Somehow, she knew deep within that even within the cold, hard walls of sickness, there was health and hope. Even within hope, there existed at times a dash of dreadful fear.

It had to be, for life was not always about being the strongest, smartest, or wisest. Sometimes it was about the most beautiful of mistakes, and the savage risks one was ready to take...

CHAPTER TWENTY-TWO
Tongue Tied, Hog Tied, You Decide...

"Y EAH, HE WAS definitely trailing me. Black pickup, one guy this time," Savage stated as he approached a red light. Harlem could be heard typing on the other end.

"The license plate is bogus. Doesn't even show up."

"So, looks like they're not as stupid as I'd hoped."

"Where are you now?"

"Still on 405, headed to LAX."

"Whose job?"

"Austin. I accepted Longhorn's assignment though, but I told Austin as a courtesy, friend to friend. I owed him no explanation, but I'm tryna do as my lady says, and treat people how I'd like to be treated." He cracked up, thinking it sounded rather corny.

Harlem laughed.

"Sounds like some chicken soup for the soul shit, a hazard of dating a psychologist I guess. What did Austin say when you let him know you were moonlighting for Longhorn of all people?"

"He wasn't pleased but hey, he accepted that it's my choice. Besides, I reassured him that this is a one-time thing and I want them to kiss and make up. Not for Longhorn's sake, but Austin's. Longhorn can go fuck himself, but you know I can't refuse a boss ass challenge like this. The last assignment that got my blood pumping was from a turncoat. This motherfucker has bodied over twenty-five of his own crew. He was fuckin' nutso. Anyway, though I can't get into any details, I want to go for it. The money I'm getting from this is secondary at this point. I hate motherfuckers like this… a fuckin' traitor, Benedict Arnold to the country. Of course, Longhorn played on that but I had to let him know he wasn't getting over. I understood exactly what was going on."

"Where is it? When do you plan on heading out for it?"

"I have to stake the area and target first. You know I can't tell you the location; this one is top secret. They don't want anyone being tipped off accidentally. It took them over two years to even peg this guy down. Anyway, I won't be leaving for a few weeks. I don't like rushing in with no prior personal surveillance that I conduct on my own, if I can help it. There's always the rush jobs, the calls in the middle of the night but I have a bit of wiggle room with this one. I read the files, but this is a slick one, man. I really need to be on top of my shit. One false move and my ass can be on a slab."

"I wish I knew who it was! Wow, man…Those are the kind that get your blood pumping! You've got me missing being back in the game."

"I promise to tell you after he's wiped out."

"I'll know by then, motherfucker. You'll probably get an

award for it and it will be all over the server. I doubt you'll be humble about it, either."

Savage placed his Glock 19 in the glove compartment. The guy was gone; there was no need to keep it out on the passenger's seat any longer. "Okay, so let me look further into these guys following you. You still believe they were the same people that showed up in Vegas?"

"It has to be, man. This is all tied together. Yeah, I've got enemies, but they move weird, man. They move funny. Something isn't adding up. I was in the middle of rush-hour on the 405 so it wasn't exactly conducive to doing anything unless he looked as if he was going to shoot. I was ready, but he didn't make a move. That's not like us. We don't pause. We take out the target as soon as we get a positive I.D. and the coast is clear. Anyway, about the truck, I did slow down then move faster, zigzagged a bit, got on his side but he took off. Ran like a chicken off the exit once I raised my gun." He sighed. "He had on a hood. White guy, dark shades."

"Got it. They can't go on like this for too long. Eventually, they'll fuck up. Especially if they're amateurs."

"All right, if you do pick up anything else, let me know. I have surveillance kicked up a notch. All of my cars have cameras, and the Harleys, too. I'm really tired of this shit. I'm convinced now it really isn't Longhorn; they wouldn't go around slashin' tires like some bitch and follow me and not try to attack. This is some crazy shit. I don't think they're professional, they're a bit clumsy, but like I said, they're not dumb, either."

"Definitely not. Even the truck he was in, that make and model, there's literally thousands of them. I'll keep checking though."

"All right. Catch you later." Savage ended the call and decided to tune into his baby's podcast. He knew she'd been working rather hard lately on a forum she was hosting the following month and he'd had to fly out to Denver to take out some trash. The last few days they hadn't seen one another, but they did text and call when time permitted.

"Thank you for calling! Okay, now, we're taking Gina from San Bernardino. Gina, you're now LIVE with Dr. Zaire Ellington."

"Hey bitch, it's me!" Savage's brows rutted as the deep, gravelly voice came through. "My wife won't remove the restraining order because of you! I CAN'T SEE MY FUCKIN' KIDS! I'm going to kill you, you Black bitch!" the guy hollered.

Zaire immediately ended the call.

"Okay, sorry about that, callers. Sometimes people get a bit too much alcohol in them before calling here." Zaire laughed, though he knew she didn't find a damn thing funny. A series of honks ensued as he busted a U-turn, crossed over opposing traffic, and barreled towards the exit.

He pulled up the surveillance on his phone of her podcast call logs.

"Trace! Where's the last trace? Come on, damn it. I need the last number traced!" He waited for a few moments while the information populated on the special app on this phone. It was an interesting set of events that had transpired. Much to his surprise, Zaire kept her studio locked when she wasn't inside it.

Back when he was still at her place, he'd tried twice to get down there while she was asleep after their romp, but she seemed to have an active sixth sense and would call him out as soon as he'd pick the door open. This had been of course after extensive searching for the key which he'd presumed was hidden so well, she may have even forgotten where it was. Picking that lock had taken much longer than he wished because he had to be as discreet as possible. To make matters worse, leave it to Zaire to have some special handle on the damn thing—nothing run of the mill. He'd had to go forth with Option B…

This time, he'd made sure to be present during her show so he could take care of business there and then. He'd looked at some books and magazines in her studio as she spoke to her callers, placing a few bugs here and there to record the words shared. He'd then taken the microphone from her during the show and decided to talk to one of her callers in hopes of distracting her. It had worked like a charm. She'd been so busy trying to prevent him from making a fool of her, she hadn't noticed him slide a tracking and recording device onto the phone call console, as well as her computer. It would record the location of origin for each and every call that came through that line from that point forward. Within a matter of a minutes, he had her entire studio bugged without her being none the wiser.

A man's gotta do what a man's gotta do. This fucker is in Savage country now…

"Coordinates confirmed," said the robotic voice.

"Perfect. Dial Harlem." His phone immediately dialed his friend.

"What's up? We just spoke. You miss me already, lover

boy?" Harlem teased.

"I have some coordinates that I need a direct address for. Can you get it to me?"

"Yeah, send it over." Savage hit the forward option on his special app and sent it to Harlem. After a couple of minutes of silence, the man came back on the line.

"3021 Magnolia Drive, Bettendorf, Iowa."

"Cool. Cows and manure it is. Look, I'm making a detour. Find me a later flight for the assignment for today that I was headed to. I need to get over to Iowa first. Got something to take care of."

"Will you make it in time though, Savage? Iowa is three hours away and depending on what you have up your sleeve, it could take a long time. Austin wants this done in forty-eight hours."

"I will have time to spare. This crew is small potatoes. Escaped convicts who murdered a retired government official in Milwaukee."

"All right, piece of cake for you then. As far as your request, I will take care of it. Do you need a private flight since you seem in a hurry?"

"Yup. Going over to the base right now. Call them up, please, and let them know I'm on my way. Looks like I'm going to the corn state for a second, Harlem. This mother-fucker's chickens have come home to roost..."

THE THREE-HOUR FLIGHT proved uneventful.

Savage received several text messages from Zaire, and wasn't the least bit surprised that she hadn't mentioned the fucker who'd been harassing her. He knew his baby's nature. She wasn't afraid of this guy, though perhaps, she should've been. He was a loose cannon, and he was clearly coming unhinged.

Richard Anderson... 38 years of age... 5'8... 170 lbs... Caucasian, brown hair... blue eyes...

One hour later, Savage pulled up to the residence in his Jeep Cherokee rental car, and got out. A small white 1999 Honda Accord was parked on the gravel in the driveway. The tires looked in desperate need of air. The old vehicle was caked with dirt and the windows looked as if they'd been smeared with dry kisses from a dust storm. It was a drizzly, rainy day and the air in Iowa was clean and new, unlike the smoggy shit he was used to. He'd seen his fair share of cows on various properties during his short stint, and the locals seemed nice enough. The people were paler and a bit frumpier than he was used to seeing. Not so flashy, their voices more monotone, their speaking a bit slow. This was middle America, where wholesomeness and nostalgia met and married, then gave birth to hypocritical laws and ideologies that danced along the line of the Bible belt but held tight to the hope of the North.

There were no palm trees and grand oceans to ride the wave, no calypso music pouring out the open doors of a posh watering hole that served colorful cocktails for twenty bucks each. There were no big-time casinos and magic shows to wow the most skeptical of men, but there were however several neatly stocked and well-maintained corner stores with flashing neon lights advertising a couple different types of beer, freshly made sub sandwiches, and lucky lottery tickets. Police officers waved to people here and weren't feared. Clean-faced children grinned while clutching their shiny lunchboxes and getting off school buses to race into the arms of their mothers. And the most ass he'd seen thus far was from a heifer shaking her skimpy tail along her wide, flat, shit-covered ass as she moseyed about a lush, green pasture, eating as she sashayed. He hated to admit it, but he thought the place was kind of cool, neat and comforting in its own down-home way.

He'd even stopped at a small Mom and Pop store and had a piping hot cup of coffee and smoked a cigar, taking a breather before setting off to turn their little town upside down. The hot drink was good—no, it was great. They threw in an apple fritter, made him feel at home, asked his name and tried to delve into his private life—so he simply stated he was there on business. He cracked a smile and left a hundred-dollar tip for the hell of it. Now, the only thing cracking was his fucking Remington rifle.

Bella, as he called her, shook the air like a snake rattle. She was ready, willing, and able. Always hot. Always loud and abrasive, aged to perfection. Stomping in muddy puddles, he made his way to the small, dingy white house with several plastic planters surrounding it, all of them housing half dead foliage. A small stone angel with a chipped wing sat at a strange angle on the front lawn, and a rusted rainbow colored wind chime blew in a sideways motion on the porch, as if beckoning him while he ascended the three steps. He promptly knocked on the door three times.

"Who is it?!" came the gruff voice he'd now heard too many times to count. Savage had played that recording on the plane over and over, such that it did nothing more than pump him up. He was on fire for revenge.

"You can call me M.S. I'm from division number 721, Unit A.A., when on assignment."

"What the hell are you talking about? Alcoholics Anonymous?"

Savage smirked and sucked his teeth.

"No. Apocalypse Assassins..." He ran his hand along his jaw, time ticking like miniature bombs within him.

"M.S. from the Apocalypse Asians? What the fuck?" The guy chuckled.

"Assassins, Mr. Anderson. Assassins."

"How'd you know my name? You're some wierdo! Whatever you're sellin', I don't want it. Get tha fuck off my porch and go home."

"I'm not sellin' shit, not a gotdamn thing but believe you me, buddy boy, you're buyin' the farm!"

BOOM!

Savage kicked the door in and burst into the foyer that smelled like weak weed and boiled hot dog water. "This is on the house, motherfucker! I'm givin' away free ass whoopings, but national travel charges do apply!"

"WHAT THA FUCK, MAN?!" Richard yelled.

Savage grabbed him by the collar before he could make a run for it. Hoisting him up in the air, he used the bastard as a human shield as he went from room to room, kicking in each door, ensuring they were alone. All he saw were a few bongs here and there, some old beds with ratty sheets, a television tuned in to Jerry Springer, a murky fish tank, and a bathroom in desperate need of a good cleaning and repair.

The coast was clear. He led him back into the small living room, lifted him high with one arm, and shook him like he was trying to get change to fall out of his damn pockets.

"Who are you?! What do you want?! I don't have much money but you can have what I've got though! My wallet is in the bedroom!"

"I don't want your little piddly money, Mr. Anderson. There's nothing you can give me, but there's some shit I'm going to *definitely* take. Now, open your mouth wide."

"Huh? What?!"

"OPEN YOUR FUCKIN' MOUTH!"

The man did as he asked. Savage aimed the tip of the rifle at his throat. The man's complexion turned dark crimson as he gagged, and his blue eyes filled with tears. He wiggled about like a desperate worm on a hook.

"Yeah... why aren't you keeping that same energy you had to pick up your phone, call a podcast, and threaten someone, huh? Your mouth was wiiiide open, then, now wasn't it? You fucked with the wrong one this time. That Dr. Zaire Ellington you keep calling? You know, the one you called a Black bitch not too long ago? Guess what? That Black bitch, you inbred, illiterate, unpleasant piece of shit, is my fuckin' woman! Shazam!" The man's eyes grew impossibly larger. "It's time you learned some respect, motherfucker. Class is in session."

The man tried to talk, but he could only make incoherent sounds, his face turning odd shades of green.

"I know what you've been doing." Savage's eyes narrowed. "For over a year, before I was even on the scene, you've been harassing her." The man shook his head vehemently, denying it. *What a coward...*

"No... No! You'b got tha w'ong guy!" he said as the rifle slid in his mouth.

"Oh no, I've got the *right* one, baby! Yes! It was *you*, motherfucker. No doubt about it. I need to see your tonsils! Put your mouth back on the front sight... SUCK IT!" The man whimpered and wrapped his lips tighter around the gun. "You wanna act like a fuckin' bitch, call and threaten women like some pussy, then I'll treat you like one! You're going to give Bella here a nice blowjob. Chicks with steel dicks!" Savage cackled. "Hey, whatever you like! Whatever floats your boat; I'm not one to judge. You just don't know when to quit though, do ya? You've been fucking with your ex-wife, too, making her life a living hell. I found out you have a loooong history of this...

"Let's see, domestic violence with some ex-girlfriends, threatening to kill a stripper, all sorts of crazy horse shit. Looks like you constantly strike out with the ladies and instead of trying to find your mojo, you blame the women for not wanting your ass after they discover what a lame you are. You make me fuckin' sick! Going around threatening someone you don't even know, all because your ol' lady took her advice, woke up and didn't want your stinking ass anymore. It was about damn time!

"You can't let go... can't handle rejection. You lie around here with no job, collecting checks from the government, joining little websites that encourage men like you to harass and stalk women. You're pathetic! You're not a man! You cut your own balls off and tossed them in the fire! You silly motherfucker," Savage snarled, getting off on how afraid the bastard was. "I gave you a chance, tried to see if you'd stop, but you didn't. You just kept on calling… kept on bothering my baby. So now, you're having a visit from your worst nightmare and unlike the local police who tried to coddle you in years past, I didn't come all this way to play. I'm angry, motherfucker. You've disrupted my schedule. So, here's what's going to happen. I want you to think long and hard about all of this shit, the dumb things you've done. Etch it in your mind right before I blow your brains out." Savage grinned wide, practically salivating.

"No! P'ease! P'ease!" the man begged, the gun in his mouth preventing him from pronouncing the words correctly.

"Peas! Peas!" Savage mocked. "You want some peas and carrots with your tombstone?" He dropped the man to the ground, then yanked him back up, tossing him on the couch.

"Where's your phone?!" The man pointed to the kitchen counter. Jamming the gun in the back of the bastard's head, he made him march over to it and grab it. "Now, call your ex-wife."

"I… I don't have her number… the restraining order."

"That's a lie. You just called her last week and threatened her and her boyfriend." Savage wrapped his hand around his skull and squeezed. "I could crush your dome with my bare hand!"

"I don't understand why you're doing this! I can't—"

Savage yanked him off his damn feet, slammed him back

down onto the couch, and jammed the gun against the bastard's ear. "Can ya hear me now?! Understand me now? Can. You. Hear. Me. Now?!"

"Yes! Yes!" the bastard sobbed.

"It was in the police report! WHO THE FUCK DO YOU THINK YOU'RE FUCKIN' WITH, HUH?! I SAID CALL HER!" The man shivered and went limp for a second, then pulled her up in the contacts on his phone. "Put it on speaker..." The phone rang and rang, then went to voicemail. "Leave her a voicemail telling her you're sorry for everything and you're going to leave her alone," Savage stated quietly, his chest about to burst with rage. The introduction greeting from a sweet, feminine voice ended and the man began to speak.

"Hi... Hi, Ash... Ashley... This is... this is Richard..." His teeth chattered. The man pitched Savage a glance, then continued, "I just wanted to tell you how sorry I am, and... and that... I won't call or bother you... any... anymore... okay? Just... take... take care of our kids. I—"

"Hang up."

"I love—"

"I SAID HANG UP, MOTHERFUCKER!" Savage snatched the phone and ended the call. "This isn't any love song dedication! The damn request line on Hot '97! Playing all the classic jams... There is no, 'And IIIIIIIII, will always, love yooooou, Whitney Houston moment here to be had, you silly fuckface, you! FUCK THAT! You had *years* to give a shit! Don't start pretending to do so now. Now get up..."

Moments later, Savage had the bastard hogtied on his bedroom floor.

"Pleeeease, don't hurt me! I'm beggin' you, man!" the guy pleaded, looking so feeble and stupid.

Savage smacked the shit out of him with the stock of his gun. Blood sprayed in all directions, and the man moaned and yelled so loud, it was music to his ears.

"Say, 'I'm a whiny White bitch,'" Savage taunted.

The man looked at him with blood all over his face, hatred glowing in his eyes.

BAM!

He hit him again, starting a series of curses and cries.

"Say it!"

"I'M A WHIIITE BITCH! I'M A WHINY WHIIIITE BITCH! MAN, PLEASE STOOOOP!"

BAM!

"Say, 'I like to hit women because I'm a punk ass waste of cum!'"

"I... I like to hit... women 'cause I'm uh puuuuunk ass... ass waste of cuuuum!" Spit and blood dribbled out of the man's mouth, soaking his white shirt.

"You really don't love your kids. Because if you did, you wouldn't be doing what you're doing to their mother. Now, you should count your lucky stars. Your ass got lucky today. I actually have some other shit to do." Savage glanced down at his watch. "So I can't stay here and play with you all damn day. Before I leave though, I'm going to cut out a piece of your tongue to make sure you can't make any more calls to my woman, or your ex—well, you could, but you won't be sayin' much." He cackled. "And since you like to beat up women, I'm taking that right hand, too... So, you get to live, but you'll look a bit different. Now that's a bargain. Do we have a deal?"

"OH GOD, NO! HEEEEELP! Somebody heeeeelp me!"

"I'll leave the left hand so you can at least jerk off. See? I'm a compassionate son of a bitch today. I guess love can do that to ya, huh? Now be still…"

"AHHHHH!" Savage shot the fucker in the shoulder.

"Didn't I tell you to be still? Now your left shoulder is all fucked up because you don't know how to follow instructions. Tsk, tsk. How are you gonna masturbate in peace, man? It's all in the wrist though, right? You should be just fine."

Savage pulled out a sharp blade from his back pocket. The man's eyes grew big as he blubbered and begged, cursed and wiggled about, trying to break free. "Let's have a little small talk, you know, like how they do in the dental office during a root canal. Let's see, oh I know what we can talk about. What do you like to jerk off to? Pictures of corn fields? Maybe chickens 'nd shit? Bawk! Bawk! Cock-A-Doodle-Doo!" He burst out in tears from laughing so hard.

"FUUUCK! Help! God!!! HEEELP! Oh my G—"

The blood quickly poured, pooling into the matted carpet fibers as Savage sliced off the tip of his tongue. He tossed the bit of flesh across the room then sliced the fiend's right hand off with one swift chop. The wails of pain practically vibrated through the walls of that house. The moaning and shivering was a thing of beauty. Richard turned ghostly white. Savage pummeled the bastard's chest and stomach with both his fists, tenderizing him, pouring all of his angst, hatred, and ugly desires into each blow. After he'd grown tired of the human punching bag, he stepped over the almost lifeless body and made his way to the door.

"After your very long recovery, Mr. Anderson, if you decide to contact your ex-wife, my lady, or any other woman and threaten them and I get wind of it—and believe me, I most certainly will—I will be back to finish the job. I hate loose ends anyway. Don't make me return and strangle you with them..."

CHAPTER TWENTY-THREE
Charity Begins At Home

E ACH ROOM HAD its own vibe. Every space in the Spanish style mansion was bursting with layers of texture, paired with sleek design. Attractive contrasts abounded with all the muted earth tones balanced with pops of unexpected flair and color. Zaire's heels clicked against his glossy wooden floors as she took it all in. It was exciting to stand in Savage's home for the very first time. Definitely long overdue.

"Maximus, who is your decorator? Your house doesn't look anything like I imagined it would."

"His name is Paul François," he answered, his back towards her as he poured them each a glass of the good stuff, even though he wasn't a fan of dry white wine. Perhaps he just had a bottle around for her. "How'd you expect it to look?" He placed the glass down before her as she slid onto a gray barstool, one of four that surrounded a polished glass and white breakfast bar.

"Less... I don't know..." she shrugged, "put together.

Definitely not like this. I really like it even though it isn't to my personal taste."

He stood for a while watching her, a strange fire in his eyes, his expression thoughtful. Sipping from his glass, he grimaced at the taste. He set the glass on the bar next to a bowl of glass fruit.

"I don't know how you can drink that shit. Too dry!"

"Only classy people like it. That's why it makes you sick," she teased, poking fun at him.

He rested his elbows on the counter, getting in her personal space, invading her boundaries and observing her like some specimen. She relished his natural scent mingled with the slight lingering aroma of cigars, the mints he often devoured, and his cologne. She brought her wine glass to her lips and took a sip.

Damn. He always smells good. I wouldn't mind taking a sip of him, too...

She inhaled, then exhaled, overdosing on his fragrance.

"If you ever run low on that cologne, you let me know. You smell so good."

"Are you flirting with me?" He winked.

"Of course I am." She winked back.

His signature musky, rich cologne surrounded her like sun rays, warming her emotions, giving her a sense of comfort. He looked good and relaxed too, in an open silky black button-down pajama shirt. A thin gold chain hung from his neck over his tattooed chest.

"Just so you know, baby, I have an assignment I need to leave for in the morning. I told you about it last week, but you may have forgotten." He picked up a crumb from the counter and tossed it in a silver trashcan.

Assignment... He really kills me calling it that. Wait? Did I really just say kill? I am certain I could have chosen a better word.

"Okay. How long will you be away?" She crossed her legs and tried to ignore the way he slowly licked his lips like a hungry lion.

"A couple of days, three tops." He took another sip of his wine and winced... an obvious glutton for torture.

"Why do you keep drinking it if you don't like it? I'm not going to look at you all evening making that face. That's just silly."

"I paid two hundred for that shit! I have to drink it!" She rolled her eyes and smirked. "So, how'd it feel to know you're a pro at swimming after only six lessons with me?" He grinned and crossed his arms on the breakfast bar, obviously proud of himself. She raised an eyebrow and kept sipping on her wine.

He's a damn fool... This is delicious.

"I'm far from a pro. It feels good though. To be able to at least not drown is a blessing, and hey, no floaties!" She raised her left arm and made a muscle pose, causing him to laugh. He walked leisurely to the refrigerator. "Maximus..."

"Hmm?" He opened the door and peered inside, check-ing out the contents.

"We need to talk."

"About what?"

"When you came over the other night, it was, uh, strange between us."

He retrieved a bright green apple from the refrigerator and faced her.

"What do you mean?" He bit into the crisp fruit and chewed noisily as he made his way back towards her.

"You'd been out working, and you came over... You didn't say anything but you had blood on you." His eyes grew darker as he took another bite. "You went into my shower and stayed in there for over an hour."

"So what?"

"If you let me finish, I'll tell you what!" she snapped. He kept on biting and chewing, clearly not giving a damn. "When you came out of the shower, I could see bruises on your arm. You didn't say much... We... made love, and you were quiet... so quiet. That's not like you. You didn't smile, laugh, joke, say sexy things... You were simply... simply... fucking me." He bit into his apple once again, the crunch loud and rude. Just like him. "It was rough..."

"I always fuck rough," he said around a mouthful of fruit. "That's how we *both* like it. Don't you think I know that about you by now? You want to be taken, not toyed with. I like to be in control, take over. I want to be felt... remembered. I want your pussy to scream my fucking name whenever I come near it. I want to possess your entire damn body." He swallowed.

She blinked a few times, momentarily taken off track from where she wished to drive the discussion.

"Um, yes, it was passionate, but something was missing. Something was off. There was death in your eyes. Your lips offered no confessions, but I could see it. Tell me, how many people have you killed, Maximus?" The man's eyes turned to black slits, and he looked like he was about to go off the rails with his wide stance and hard lines. A chill ran up and down her spine, and her breathing hitched. This was the demon he'd spoken of and warned her about. He said it lived inside him, but she hadn't seen it yet. He took another bite of his apple and inched closer, scaring the living daylights out of her. His brows bunched and his nostrils flared. She averted her gaze to gather strength and courage, then stared him back in the eye.

"Let me ask you something, Eva. How in the fuck is that information going to help you?"

"I don't know. I'm curious though. I understand what you do, I get it, but I believe it takes a toll on you. I believe that it's killing, pardon the pun, your humanity, Savage, and I have the right to tell you such."

"Really?" He chuckled mirthlessly, licking the corner of his mouth to chase a drop of apple juice. "And how do you even know that I *ever* had any humanity in me at all?" The room temperature dropped to freezing. Those eyes of his glowed as he smiled at her—a foul, beastly smile. His head was cocked to the side, and he looked vexed and amused all at once. He stood to his full height. "Do you want to change me, baby? Make me, I don't know, confess my sins and purge my lust for assassination? Treat you like a priest? I can't. I'm good at what I do for a reason. I'm no choir boy. I can't be tamed and anyone who believes anything else is an idiot. I do what the fuck I want and how I want to do it. I'm just lucky that I found a legal way to do it."

"I'm not trying to change you. I'm simply—"

"The hell you aren't. This right here is why I never wanted to be in a relationship! You're on that bullshit!" Iciness seeped from his voice, into the air. He tossed the apple core in the trash, then pointed his finger at her. "I knew, eventually, the molding attempts would begin. You'd turn me into a fuckin' patient. 'Oh Maximus, maybe you should drink less? Maximus, maybe you should smoke less. Maximus, maybe you should cuss less. Maximus, maybe you should stay at home more and kiss my fuckin' ass! Maximus, stop taking assignments and just become a square. Be miserable just so I can be happy. Sell yourself out because now, you love me, and I *must* have my way."

"You're overreacting," she stated calmly. This hadn't been her first time engaging in an exchange with a wounded animal parading around like some beast. "I never said *any* of those things."

"Yeah? But you've wanted to. I've seen how you look at me, Eva. The worst part of this is that I *care* that you look at me that way. That you're appalled by me. Oh heavens to Betsy, whatever shall she do?!" He mocked, pushing her buttons. "Poor little Eva fell for a dude that's bad news! You don't want me to do my job, to kill, but you're intrigued by me, so you stick around. For now. Your pussy keeps you close, doesn't it? You don't really want me. Your body does."

"That's not fair…"

"Nothing in life is fair, now is it? You just like how I make you feel. You like how I push my big, hard dick in and out of your pussy. Fuck the shit out of it. You like to suck my dick and taste my cum. You like both my unpredictability and reliability at the same fucking time, but really, you can't handle me, can you Eva? You tried and failed. And now." He tossed up his hands and turned his back. "I'm stuck, right?! You know I'm in love with you!"

"And I love you, too!"

"No, you don't. You've got me in a jam. So now, what am I going to do?! It will start like this. This is just the beginning. First, it's you asking about body counts, then it'll escalate to us arguing and not speaking at all as you manipulate me, probably even withhold sex like a punishment. Then, before I know it, you'll be gone! There'll be an exit investigation in which I will have to explain *every... fucking... detail...* of our breakup to my authorities and then you'll have to be cleared so they never have a fuckin' reason to interview you again. But only if you're lucky, because now you know too much. There will be a smear on my record because I took a chance with my heart and come to find out, this woman is the wager I bet on! I gambled and lost everything. I chose to lay it all on the line for you, and you can't even handle it! Damn! How could I have been so wrong?!"

"I *can* handle it!" She shot up from her seat, tired of his shit. He was a classic case, and too smart for his own good. Savage didn't want to have the real conversation, the deep conversation, the one that would change everything. Make him reflect and remember. He could feel what she was gearing up to do, and though she hadn't planned it, it was happening. She had to keep pushing forward, to get it out of him. She loved him, and she refused to let him out of the hot seat.

"I didn't ask about a body count to change you, Savage! I accepted this situation a long time ago! I understand that people like you exist, and I understand *why* people like you exist! That still does not mean you can skirt around self-healing and reflection. What you do messes with the brain! It

fucks up the mind! This all started from somewhere, and if I
love you the way I say that I do, I am going to find out what
is truly going on inside that head of yours and make you
purge and cleanse. You can't keep killing all these motherfuckers and not talking about it! Without thinking that it
changes you!"

"And what would you know about it?! You couldn't even
stop some punk ass pussy from callin' and harassing you for
over a gotdamn year! It takes people like *me* to step in and
handle that shit. You try to ignore anything you find ugly or
embarrassing, pretend it isn't true. Or you can mind fuck it
to death and then people like me have to strap up, show up,
show out, and I fix it. Period!"

Oh my God. No wonder the calls stopped...

"I am telling you, Savage, that I am worried about you
and I want you to start processing what you're doing, not just
going through the motions! I never told you to stop your
work. I told you to slow down and think about it or you will
go crazy. Now you can stand there and keep lying to
yourself, telling yourself that you're some robot, but you're
not! I fell in love with you because you know who you are,
yes, and you accept it. You're not ashamed of who you are,
but there is another part of you that is a scared little boy!"

"Oh, bullshit!" He rolled his eyes. "Here comes Sigmund
Freud in a dress!"

"You're a child. One of my favorite bible verses is, 'When
I was a child, I spoke as a child, I understood as a child, I
thought as a child: but when I became a man, I put away
childish things.' It's time to put away the childish things, the
hurt, the pain... You're a child that is afraid to get too close

to someone because you think they'll run away or emotionally abandon you, like your mother!"

"Don't you listen? My mother didn't abandon me, Zaire. She's been there the whole time! Try your little brain tricks on someone else!"

"SHE *DID* ABANDON YOU! She didn't mean to. It was her way of trying to protect you; hell, it may even be a cultural thing, I don't know, but what I do know is that it affected you, baby. You're so... so cold! It's not natural. I've seen the light in you. That child plays with my heart, my soul! He wants to be acknowledged, not just swept under the rug and only used for humor! Your mother was never taught how to love. She had to learn on her own. I'm not saying she doesn't love you. In fact, I believe she probably loves you so much that it frightens her. Like me, you leaned on your father for some semblance of normalcy, but there was only so much he could do, especially since he was in and out of prison so often."

"Oh, so now you want to take a bite out of him, too? You wanna go down the entire fuckin' family tree? Don't forget my cousins, aunts and uncles then, they're available for dissection, too!"

"Maximus... listen to me. I am no longer talking to Savage. Savage, please step back for a moment. I am talking to Maximus..." He sucked his teeth then looked away. "You've had to wrestle with the fact that your mother sold her body. The same body you were born from, the same body you fell asleep against when you were sick or worried as a child. She did it to help you have the kind of life she never did. Her body is sacred and it was desecrated because that was all she knew how to do! It hurt you! Deep down, you were ashamed of what she was doing! You knew that if she put her mind to it, she could do something else though. She was smart and beautiful, but she was hurt because her little girl within was broken, too! That little girl inside of her was taught that her vagina was the only thing people cared about. She'd been raped and abused! It was wrong! Her spirit was destroyed! A part of you just wanted a normal family, and you hated her for that! Admit it!"

"Shut up." His eyes became wild like those of a frightened horse. He took a step back from her, then another. He put his hands up, practically balling up, retreating.

"No. I won't shut up, Maximus! Your distrust of women began with *her*! I told you when we first met that you had a problem with women. You denied it! You're forty years old and never been in love. Stop blaming that on your job! That is the *real* reason why you've avoided commitment. That's the *real* reason why you put yourself on autopilot and just go out here and do your job and aren't phased because you learned a long time ago that when you become emotional, when you become attached, when you hope for the best and refuse to expect the worst, you become a victim.

"I learned that lesson, too. I remind you of your mother. Strong! Frontin'! Playing make believe and pretend! You told me yourself that I came across as aloof and a workaholic. Now why would any man in his right mind want to get involved with me? I had purposefully put up barriers, but you saw through all of my bullshit immediately because you grew up with the same bullshit in your home! I was familiar to you. I made you feel, comfortable. As crazy as it sounds, there's a parallel and you know it! You wanted her to just tell you that she loves you. I did. You now are reminded that you *still* want the same from her. Was that too much to ask?"

"Stop it." His voice cracked.

"You know she loves you, but you're ashamed to admit that, even to this day, you still want to hear it. That's okay. You have the right to feel that way."

"I'm not doing this shit with you. Leave me alone, Eva!!!" He roared like a lion, his anger and fear palpable.

"No, I won't leave you alone. That's the problem. Too many people have left you alone when they should have been surrounding you with love! You are callous—not because you were born that way, but because you were *made* that way!"

"You couldn't wait to do this shit, could you?! I'm not one of your callers!"

"No, you're not. You're my man, and that makes this even *more* necessary. You made me swim. It's time for you dive into the deep end, too. Come here... let's talk, baby." She went around the breakfast nook and tried to wrap her arms around him. He fought her, pushed her arms away, shoved her back. His strength nearly took her breath away, and yet, she knew he was trying to be careful and not hurt her.

Rage filled his eyes as his face twisted. An unholy evil poured out of him and confronted her, but she wasn't afraid.

"Come here!" she screamed, backing him into a corner, her fist balled tight.

She pressed her body against his and he refused to look at her. Refused to give her any eye contact at all. Placing her hand against the back of his head, she rested her cheek against his chest. His heart was beating so fast, she thought it might explode. He went stiff, barely breathed. They stayed locked like that for what felt like an eternity.

She'd found it. His little secret, his one and only fear.

Slowly, he began to move against her. She felt his arms come around her and squeeze. His body shook against her as he fell apart. She smiled and closed her eyes...

CHAPTER TWENTY-FOUR
The Key to Her Heart

...a few minutes later

"SAY IT."

"Say what, Eva?"

"Say what you're afraid of. I promise it'll make you feel better. I want you to say it out loud. Confess."

Seconds ticked by. No sound... His heartbeat slowed to a normal pace.

"I've... I've been afraid to get close to a woman, to allow myself to fall in love... because... then she'd have power over me."

"Power over you to do what? Come on... say it."

"To hurt me."

"And how could she hurt you?"

"By not really wanting me, not even really liking me as a person at all..."

"And as a little boy, you sometimes felt like your mother didn't want and like you at all. As you got older, you realized that wasn't true, but the pain that it caused when you were unsure did irreparable damage." She ran her hand along his shoulder, soothing him.

"I didn't want to spend my time tryna convince someone to love me, that I'm worthy of them, ya know? I know I am, but it seems bad to feel like you have to make someone else believe it."

His voice broke, and she waited so he could regain his composure.

"How did that fear from your mother's rejection translate into your romantic relationships?"

"I'm afraid of bein' in love and that person not lovin' me back." He sighed. "It scares the shit outta me. So, I just never let it happen." She heard him swallow. "But I wanted—"

"Say it…"

"I wanted to meet someone like you for so long. And I'm still scared. I hate being afraid. It's the worst feeling in the world."

"No, it's not, baby. The worst feeling in the world is what your mother experienced as a child—knowing for a fact that no one loves you."

They stood there, holding one another, feeling the pain, the joy, the love. She sighed when he squeezed her tighter, picked her up in his arms, and set her down on the counter. His cheeks were wet, taking her off guard, making her fall apart at the sight of him. Shuddering, she wrapped her arms around his neck, holding tight while he jerked her leggings and panties down. The cool air hit her exposed nature. Moving fast, he dropped his pajama pants, revealing his erect member.

"Ahhh…" She hissed when he drove himself inside her. Deep. His big hands cupped her ass, bringing her close for each thirsty plunge. They moaned together, shaking and calling out to one another with need and desperation.

"I'm balls deep, baby. Feel me… feel *all* of me…"

"Oh, God… yes, I feel you, Max…"

"I wanna be so deep inside you that my thoughts become yours, and your thoughts become mine, baby. I want to be one with you."

Clawing at his back, her breath hitched as she came, her orgasm a thing of beauty. It floated within her like fluttering butterflies set free. He pumped harder and faster. Her head bumped against the cabinet behind her as he had his way with her, fucking her with brute determination. His growls were deep and throaty, his need relentless…

"I love you so much, baby." He groaned and she clutched him close.

"I love you too, Max. So very much."

He picked her up from the counter and she crossed her ankles around his back. Holding on tight, he kept fucking her while he walked, pausing every few steps to keep the rhythm. They reached his staircase and he kept her steady as they climbed, using her pussy for his therapy…

What he didn't say in words, his dick said in deep, nasty plunges. She held onto the railing, and when they reached the top, he navigated the hall to his master suite. She barely had a chance to take in her new surroundings before he gently deposited her on the bed, pressed his muscular body against hers, and pounded her pussy with such vigor, the large bed shook beneath them. She held on for dear life as he layered her breasts with kisses and pumped ferociously within her."

"Yes! Fuck me, baby!" she purred, getting off on the fire in his eyes.

"Shit, baby, I'm about to cum!" he roared.

Instead of easing his way out, as he typically did, he went impossibly deeper, jerking and pumping like a piston. Within seconds, she felt the warm rush of his appreciation fill her vessel as he succumbed to fast spasms, his biceps and calves locking and releasing. He groaned and trembled in her arms. The last of him slipped away inside her, so she wrapped her legs tightly around him, not wishing him to go away just yet. They lay together, breathing hard, relishing the silence. Warm breath caressed her shoulder. He hugged her so tight, his big, juicy dick throbbing inside her.

"Damn! That was good..." he said breathlessly.

"You really aren't shit, Maximus," she teased.

"What did I do?" he asked lazily, his eyes closed.

"All I can say is, good thing I never forget to take my pill. You didn't even try to pull out this time." She laughed and shook her head as he carefully slid out of her.

With a chuckle, he disappeared to his en suite bathroom, then returned to her with a warm cloth. He gently cleaned her pussy and gave her a kiss on the lips, then bent down to kiss her inner thighs and pelvis before crawling back up her body.

"I don't know why you're mad. You've been lucky because I told you already that my pull-out game with you would be weak. I predicted this. This time, I proved that true. It was just too warm in there to leave, you know?" She rolled her eyes at the man. He was full of it. "Hey, don't hate the dick. Hate the soft, wet pussy you used to seduce me."

She hit him with a pillow and he fell back on the bed beside her. He wrapped one arm around her, dragging her close. Love lingered in the air, filling the room with happiness. He pressed his lips to her forehead.

"I love it when you give me forehead kisses. They're the absolute best." She leaned in and landed a peck on his lips.

"Why? It shows my tender side?" He reached for the remote and turned on the massive television on his wall.

"Maybe that's it, I don't know… I just like it." She took a deep breath and lay on his chest, looking around the bedroom while he channel-surfed.

"I think I know what it is. It's just one of those things where it's like affection, you know?" he said. He stroked his chin as he stared lazily at the screen. "It's just pure. I don't think about it. I don't believe it will lead to more or get me somethin' from you that I want. I just do it when I feel like it… because I love you. You're my VIP." His voice sounded deeper than usual, gravelly, amping up his sexiness to the nth degree. She glanced at the television, too, running her fingers along his chest. He paused on a channel where some old cowboy movie played.

The screen was huge, the bed like a king's throne. It all fit him to a T. His left leg, covered in black hair with a little scar on the knee, lay exposed outside the sheets, almost as if he couldn't fit in the bed beside her. Her man loved big furniture, fast cars, expensive cigars and cologne, and anything that got his adrenaline pumping. His home was like *him*— overwhelmingly beautiful, and full of hard edges and sharp turns. Silly, yet serious. It reeked of masculinity, but there were two whimsical gold and green abstract statues in his bedroom by an enormous window with thick white and black curtains. They gave an interesting contrast to his otherwise testosterone-driven trappings. On the wall hung a majestic crest shield painting with a lion. A perfect touch.

Soon, she felt her eyelids getting heavy but was quickly snatched out of the clutches of sleep by his sudden movement.

"Sorry, baby." He moved from beneath her and stood up.

"Damn... boy, you sure are fine!" she teased. She couldn't help it; he *was* fine. Savage's body was something she simply couldn't get used to, not even after all this time. She took in his naked body and blew him a kiss as he reached for his phone on the nightstand. He smiled. "How do you stay in shape? You don't always eat healthy and I never see you work out."

"I work out all the time." He swiped his finger across the screen. "I run and lift weights at home. I just don't like the public gym. You think with the way I drink, smoke, and eat I could catch these fuckers if I didn't work out? You have to be fast and on top of your game. There's a reason why you never see eighty-year-old assassins."

"You've got a point there. So where are your weights at?"

"I have a home gym. That works for me."

He put his phone back down and approached a large black dresser. Pulling out one of the top drawers, he removed something small that fit in the palm of his hand. He returned to the bed and stood before her.

"What?" She looked up at him with a smile, then reached for his dick to give it a lick. Instead of taking her up on her offer, he jumped back and laughed.

"Now hold up, wait a minute. We've got something important to discuss."

That definitely got her attention. She sat up, resting against the black headboard.

"You're refusing a blowjob? Oh yes, this must be dire."

He smirked, showing his gorgeous teeth. "Open your hand."

"Nope."

"Why not?"

"Because you love to play practical jokes on me! Just last week when we were at the theater, you put a whoopee cushion in my seat and made all of those people think I was farting!" The man burst out laughing. "It wasn't funny, Max. Then, another time, you put marshmallows all over my damn house, like millions of them! I am still finding them to this day! Who knows where you got that many marshmallows from!"

"You had told me you wanted me to be more loving and soft! And I delivered." His face turned red with mirth. Oh, how she loathed him right then.

"The list is long of the mess you've pulled: the fake coffee prank—it was actually warm root beer. Uh, let's see, the plastic vomit in my car… It's always something childish with you! So no, I won't open my hand. You're about to do something immature like put a damn bug in my hand, and then you're going to find yourself cursed out and me gone, out the door! I mean it, too."

He now seemed both amused and frustrated. "Come on, Eva, I'm serious. I'm not going to do something like that."

"Don't try to stand there and act like you're hurt, as if that is somehow beneath you."

They both laughed that time.

"Trust me. Open your hand." After a brief hesitation, she did as asked. The man placed a silver key in her palm. "This is the key to my house."

She gasped.

"Why did you give this to me?" she asked softly.

"Because every queen should have the key to her castle…" She swallowed and ran her fingers along it, in awe. "I won't be upset with whatever you decide, baby, but, uh, I'd like for you to move in with me. Even if you don't want to right away, that's cool. Just come over a lot more then, okay? I don't want you to ever feel like anything that belongs to me, is a part of me, is off limits to you again. I was doing a lot of thinking about how I'd never had you over here, and the reasons I gave you were legit, but it's time for us to move forward."

She placed the key down onto the bed.

"What about my house?"

"My house is like three times the size of yours, and don't get me wrong, your home is beautiful. I love it, Eva, and that would be perfect if it was only going to be the two of us forever, but it's not. We'll probably have a family." Her heart began to beat hard and fast. "I have a lot of land. You could do all sorts of stuff here. The possibilities are endless and as far as your studio, I have two free rooms right now that have nothing but storage in them." He paused, closed his eyes and ran a hand over his head. "It sounds stupid, doesn't it?"

"No… No!" She shook her head.

"I don't know what I'm doing. I don't know how to do this, I'm winging it, but eventually I want to get married to you and yeah, I've been thinking about the whole family and kids thing, too. It's now or never. I've made up my mind. You're the one for me, and I want us to be together, a *real* family. I could die tomorrow, baby."

She looked down at her lap and shook her head.

"I can't believe this. I am in shock right now, Max."

"Well, that makes two of us. No one could've told me twelve months ago that not only would I meet the woman of my dreams, but I'd fall in love with her too and ask her to move in with me. Life is short. I was lying here thinking about that, you know? This wasn't planned. I keep that spare key there for myself but as I was lying here next to you, smelling your perfume, feeling the warmth and softness of your body against me, thinking about the fight we had downstairs and how you really *do* know me, how you see through me just like I see through you, I realized something.

"I realized I'd practically give my right arm to have this feeling all the time… to know you're by my side. I'm not promised anything, and neither are you. Everyone is going to die, including us one day. My father is gettin' old, and I told you that bothered me. It reminds me that… I won't have him forever. My mother is aging, too, obviously, and when they're no longer here, I don't think I'm going to take that too well. They were all I had." She nodded. "I look at that man, my dad, and basically see a blond version of myself in thirty years, Eva. I don't want to look like that, moving slower, aches and pains every day, and not have something else to hold onto besides my material goods and a prescription medication.

"My father needs my mother, and I understand that more and more. Not to take care of his ass, but to have someone to talk to, someone who accepts him for who he is. What the fuck is a million dollars going to do for me if I don't have anyone to enjoy it with? I have all the money I need. And don't get me wrong, I love money, but I love you, more." His words filled her with warmth and joy.

"Money can't buy me what you've given me since we've been together these last few months, Eva. I need something comforting beside me, with a fuckin' pulse... a woman who understands me and just... wants to love me. I pushed you away, and like a trooper, you came right back. You weren't afraid of me. The savage in me was trying to make you retreat, to make you live up to my fears... but you didn't. You literally backed me into a corner! Your little ass stood up to me! I've got grown ass men who drive tanks and practically piss themselves when I walk onto the yard. I am one of the most feared men in our unit, but you..." He swallowed hard, his eyes sheening, and he blinked back the tears. "You confronted me, you let Maximus come out to play... I need *you*, baby."

A tear streaked her face.

"What's wrong? What did I do, Eva?" His voice shook. He actually sounded afraid that he'd offended her. It was the sweetest thing...

"You didn't do anything wrong, baby. I am just surprised is all." Relief washed over his face. "And happy... It's all a bit overwhelming."

"Look, I'm not trying to rush you." He threw up his

hands in resignation, maybe frustrated with himself. "I know it's not what you were expecting. Is it the house?" He looked around. "I know the décor here may not be your thing. You can do whatever you want; you and the decorator or whoever can have at it!" He waved his hands about. "Just no pink or purple, please. Nothing like that."

She smiled at his words. Speechless.

"Baby." He took her hand in his. "I just want to see mail coming here in your name. I want to see your clothes next to mine in the closet… your lipstick on the dresser, your robe hanging on the bathroom door hook. Just think it over. I need to get ready to go."

He bent down close, framed her face with his hands, and delivered a passionate kiss. Before she could form another thought, he was out of her sight, in the bathroom with the door closed behind him. Soon, she heard the shower and music playing. She turned back towards the television, smiling, feeling giddy, silly, scared, out of sorts…

Picking up the key, she brought it to her chest and pressed it against her heart. She wasn't certain what had happened, but apparently she'd dozed off. She found herself waking up to the sound of an automated robotic voice and what sounded like buttons being pushed. Rubbing her eyes, she looked around the bedroom and spotted a red rose on the bed. She smiled and picked it up, then noticed Savage standing in front of two large doors she'd thought lead to a closet, but boy had she been wrong.

They opened up, revealing a bright room. She watched in disbelief as he stood there dressed to the nines in a black Dolce and Gabbana suit. His shoes gleamed like black gold, catching the light of a small chandelier within the long closet. Black, red, silver and white dressers lined the walls inside the room and, one by one, Savage pulled out various drawers, exposing an assortment of big and small guns, knives, ammunitions, and other weapons she'd never seen. One side of the room revolved, revealing additional storage and a safe. On the wall hung several axes, bows and arrows, and a number of swords that looked deadly enough to slice a house in two with the greatest of ease.

"Are you scared? You can't be scared now, baby. It's too late," he said, obviously feeling her stare. She was too stunned to answer. "Yup. You're scared." He chuckled. "Come here, Eva." He bent down and opened another drawer. She slowly slid out of the bed, a sheet wrapped around her body, and made her way over to him. "You see these guns down here?"

"Yes."

"These are perfect for a small hand. You told me a while back that your father taught you how to hold a gun, right?"

"Yes, he did, and how to shoot, too. He was always worried about break-ins and things like that at the time. He had a lot of friends who were police officers since he was in the fire department, and they'd tell him things… He was worried about his family."

"Do you still remember how to use a gun?" He looked up at her from his stooped position.

"Uh, yeah, I believe so."

"When I get back, I can give you a refresher course. I'm glad you've already taken self-defense classes, so there's no need for me to start from scratch with that. It's not that I think you'll necessarily need it, but I believe in being more safe than sorry." She nodded in understanding. "Everyone should know how to protect themselves, especially those people society sees as more vulnerable. The elderly, the mentally and physically disabled, children and women…" Her eyes glued to his every move as he stood and grabbed weapon after weapon, opening and checking out some of their chambers. With a somber expression, he counted the bullets, placing some in a large briefcase. Her pulse raced, her adrenaline soared. He grabbed a knife and jammed it into his suit jacket pocket, slid on a ring with a sharp blade embedded in it, and wore a watch that had some sort of odd timer. It went on and on…

He looked so sexy, beautiful, dangerous… smelling good from his freshly shampooed hair, cologne, and dark machismo. He fixed his cufflinks, then grabbed a pair of shades from a small eyewear display and placed them atop his head. Picking up the suitcase, he took her hand and walked her back out of the room. As soon as they exited, the doors closed with a loud locking noise. He placed the briefcase down at his feet and wrapped his arms around her waist, pulling her close. He gazed at her as though Heaven lived within her.

He didn't have to say it; his eyes told on him.

They said, *'If I don't make it back here, know that I love you…'* He kissed the tip of her nose, then her mouth.

"I'll be back in a couple of days, baby. Three days tops, okay?"

"Okay."

"The alarm code to this house is 7239154. You'll need to remember that. If you leave this house and don't lock it up and set the alarm, it will lock itself up and set the alarm after five minutes of you exiting any of the doors. And then it will require you to enter two more codes and answer a series of security questions. You don't want to have to go through that. Say the code back to me."

"7239154."

"Very good. Now, you can stay here for the rest of the weekend if you like. Invite your friends over, have a party. You deserve it." He winked at her. "I'm sure Kim and Allison would enjoy that. They won't be able to get into anything they aren't supposed to, so don't worry about that. The only area off limits is where my weapons are stored. You saw how I retrieve my stash. No one can get in there but me. This place isn't a prison; it's a home—just with special features for a man of my nature… Now look, my bar is fully stocked. Order whatever you want to eat. Go swimming in the pool, watch Netflix, whatever. Just enjoy yourself and relax."

"That might not be such a bad idea." She got the words out, despite the fact she was anxious as hell. She watched the man she loved go off and do what he was destined to do. She raced to him and threw herself in his arms. He hugged her, a firm, protective hug. "I love you, Savage!"

"I love you too, baby. I'll call you when I can." He pulled back from her, gave her a quick peck, then headed out the bedroom door.

She listened to him going down the steps, and then she could hear him no more…

CHAPTER TWENTY-FIVE

The Cat Burglar

S AVAGE HIT SEND on the text message to his parents. It was a simple message that simply read: '*I love you.*' It had taken him over thirty minutes to type it, but it had to be done. It had been a long time since an assignment had had him this revved up and concerned. He loved the adrenaline rush, it was addictive, but things could turn ugly, and fast. Everything he did from that point forward had to be utter perfection. There was no room for error; even the slightest misjudgment or mistake could send him to an early grave.

At least, if this is it, I met and found the love of my life…

He smiled as he envisioned Zaire in his mind. He closed his eyes and kept her image close to his heart. He'd left a folded letter for her on the seat of one of his cars in the garage should he never be able to look into her eyes again. Moments later, he was back in the real world…

He turned his burner phone off and took a deep breath. The filthy gas station bathroom he stood in smelled of vomit and a terrible case of the runs. The toilet was stopped up with a load of urine and shit in it from God knew how long. A trashcan was filled with rotting foods and used condoms, the base of the receptacle covered in sludge and piss from years of bodily fluids collecting around it. It was a hellhole, and it suited him just fine. The demon within him was itching to get out, scratching right below the surface. Maximus was disappearing, trading places with the monster known as Savage.

It's showtime, brother…

He looked into the mirror, breathing slowly in and out. Thinking, scheming, planning…

He'd found out not too long after accepting the assignment from Longhorn that the fucker had asked a couple other guys to do it after his initial refusal. So much for him being the one and only choice. They wouldn't touch it. After he received the file, he realized why. The person in question was on their internal top ten of worst motherfuckers. He was being sent after a man by the name of Anthony Hickson.

The FBI had been trailing the crazed lunatic for over two years. The twisted domestic terrorist was too cunning, too slick to be caught red handed while under surveillance. What some criminals possessed in physical brawn and agility, Mr. Hickson made up for in pure intellect. He'd always managed to get away and play it cool until the coast was clear, time after fucking time. He also knew his rights. No searches without warrants. Period. This cat and mouse game had gone on for far too long, and at this point, no one was interested in an arrest and trial. They wanted him dead.

The bastard now lived cooped up in his deceased parents'

home—parents that the locals rumored were murdered by their one and only son. It had become a story like one of those creepy tall tales narrated around a campfire on Halloween night, but truth was, they weren't too far off. The police believed he'd done the heinous deed, too, but with no evidence or bodies, they could do nothing about it. Perhaps the parents had gotten in the way by trying to intervene, to convince a mad man that he was not fit to continue living in his paranoid bubble. There were often consequences for forcing people such as Hickson into a corner.

Zaire had almost gotten the horns for doing the same, but somehow, she'd convinced the Savage within him to stay low, to not come out and tango and fuck up the best thing he'd ever had.

I guess we have a little in common, huh, Mr. Hickson?

Hickson had been toying with the police, taunting them with his threatening electronic messages and hacking into their systems with his impressive computer skills. In fact, it was this talent that had landed him on their Hit List. First, he'd accessed top-secret, encrypted files and demanded millions in exchange for not sending sensitive information to the nation's enemies, putting US national security on the line. Then, he'd also sent threats to several high-ranking government officials. Hickson was not only skilled in hacking, but he was also a talented explosives expert. He used his knowledge for evil, creating bombs and then keeping the authorities on their tiptoes by messing with the intricate software systems protected and used by the government.

Clearly, this was nothing more than a game to Hickson, and he was growing bolder by the minute. Oftentimes, in cases of this nature, there would be two assassins assigned with the task of dealing with the problem, but Hickson had somehow discovered he was being followed by one of their own a year prior, and he'd blown the poor man to kingdom come. Proof had been hard to come by, but everyone knew he'd been the one to send the bomb to poor Patrick's house in retribution. It had wiped out his entire family, including his mother who'd been there for a visit.

If you were made, you had a small window to take a target such as Hickson down. If you missed that window, you could pretty much kiss your existence goodbye.

Savage grabbed his briefcase and made his way out into the gas station parking lot. A few cars were parked there. A buzzing, flickering light caught his attention with a bunch of insects gathered around it. The annoying sound blended in with light chatter from right outside the storefront. Two intoxicated individuals stood there holding brown paper bags stuffed with cheap bottles of liquor and cigarettes in hand, eyeing him.

"Got any money you can spare, chief?" one of them called out, a waif of a man with a long, pockmarked face that betrayed picked scars from meth use.

"Nah, you get better, you hear?" Savage made a thorough inspection of his rental car, looking for any vermin hell bent on surprising him.

"I'm tryin' to… need money to do it… goin' to the clinic."

"Ya know, druggies are the worst liars. I hate liars. I'm not giving you anything. You'll spend it on that bullshit." He rubbed a cloth along the front of the car, removing a smudge. "You're going to be dead in a month. Get some help, and I'm not your chief."

"Fuck you!" the man responded, then started muttering under his breath.

The sky darkened as the sun began to set over Minneapolis. Savage got in the car and made his way over to his destination. The traffic was rather light for a Friday night. He'd been in town for a little over twenty-four hours, getting his bearings and doing the pre-runs to scope out the target's place of residence. Savage had performed some of his typical maneuvers, such as walking two different dogs past the hit's home.

The dogs were adopted from a local shelter and would be gifted to someone deserving after the venture. That was how the intelligence gathering worked. For now, the canines proved the perfect prop for him to get close enough to the house and get a better feel for the layout. The dogs' collars contained a special signal that alerted Savage of crucial information, letting him know if any occupants were in the house by detecting warmth. It also identified metals that were commonly used in weaponry. The technology wasn't flawless and still in the testing mode, but it was definitely helpful.

He simply needed to get at least within fifty feet of the property to have a decent read. It would be a rough assessment, but still a good start. The animals at various intervals would snoop around in a yard nearby, or on the curb. The old school stakeout was never a good idea in such instances. Sitting outside of the house in a car with binoculars would be a dead giveaway. Guys like Hickson were old pros and would notice right away, seeing something like that as pure entertainment. In addition, with all of the cameras around the bastard's house, he'd be made within five minutes.

On foot was the way to go, in various disguises, never walking the exact same way, with the same dog or in the same getup. Savage was even able to alter his height and build by wearing shoes with lifts, or low sandals, hats, broad-shouldered jackets with extra shoulder pads, the works. He'd gotten pretty good with covering his facial hair, learning an amazing trick to do such from a drag queen in Vegas. It took forever but was well worth it. He'd learned during training a long time ago, the wigs had to be high quality, made with real human hair and never synthetic. The idea was to look the part and blend in with the surroundings.

He never looked directly at the house while in front of it, and always pretended to be preoccupied with the dogs, on his phone, jogging, carrying shopping bags from the nearby convenience store, or engaged in some other normal activity as a passerby.

Night fell and Savage sat in the vehicle, drumming his hands against the steering wheel of the rental car parked two blocks away from the target's home.

He started the countdown in his head, feeling a rush of excitement. From the research, it appeared Hickson rarely came out of his house. He was a hermit, unhinged, delusional and paranoid. His anti-government sentiments would only have worsened his condition, and his level of genius denoted a sick mind. He was also a stealthy killer with at least five murders under his belt, had an unhealthy obsession with dissection of furry creatures. A textbook killer—he'd been known to hurt animals since he was a child. Savage couldn't call Harlem for any insight; no one should know he was there until the job was complete. Not even Longhorn was privy to his schedule. He was on his own.

He removed several guns and two blades from his brief-case, strapping them to his body in various locations. Beneath his hoodie he wore a bullet proof vest and inside his black Reebok sneakers he'd put a couple additional blades. Placing his hood over a black baseball cap, he began a slow sprint, as if he were taking an evening jog around the neighborhood. The wind blustered—not the sort of thing he enjoyed after being spoiled by California sun rays, but the chill kept his senses heightened, so he couldn't complain. He listened to his own breathing, falling into a rhythm, then turned his earbuds on, soothed by the sounds of, 'Psycho Killer' by the Talking Heads at high volume.

His heart pumped faster…

His mouth pooled with saliva like a monstrous beast on the hunt for hot prey…

His feet pounded against the concrete, all of his weight slapping along the ceiling of Hell as he drew closer to the house of cards…

He fisted his hands, tight-knuckled, then released, then fisted them again, hungry to wrap them around a fucker's throat and squeeze or slice another tongue…

Stealing someone's voice was one of his favorite maneu-vers, one of many reasons why Longhorn abhorred him, stating it was overkill. But oh, how wrong Longhorn was. Stealing one's voice, removing their tongue, was power. No talking… Shhhh… Die in bloody silence. People knew it had been a 'Savage kill' for certain when he got that fucking tongue.

Flashes of the members of Dad's motorcycle club pulling into the house one summer, fifty deep, entered his mind as he kept moving, sprinting slowly along... music still blasting...

He couldn't have been more than ten when it had happened, and he'd been mesmerized. Dad had been clad in all leather, gun in hand. They'd all parked their bikes along the road. Dad's long blond hair had waved in the wind as he'd approached, a big ass smile on his face. The big man had stood tall, leading his brethren into his modest home for supper, good times and drinks. They'd just attended a funeral of one of the Outlaw One-Percenter fallen soldiers, a dude by the name of Easy Bee. His other friend, the now deceased Crazy T-Bone, had been right by Dad's side. Crazy T-Bone had shoulder length black hair, a thick scar that ran the length of his chin, and dancing, bright blue eyes. He'd been stocky and muscular as fuck, garnering respect, just like Dad, but known to be a loose cannon. In the fucker's gloved palm he'd glimpsed something pink and slimy—a tongue. He'd cut some bastard's tongue out for calling him a motherfucker, allegedly one of the Hell's Angels...

Savage had never been the same after that. That scene had indelibly marked him, tattooed his soul...

He tossed the thoughts out of his mind, for they'd obliged their purpose... fed his monster a hearty dose of delightful dysfunction served piping hot.

Hickson, what's for dinner tonight? I'm coming to eat...

He fell in love with the chase...

Run, run, run...

Savage is comin' for you…
And there's not a damn thing
You can do.
Run, run, run…
The big bad wolf wants prey…
He'll huff, and he'll puff
And he'll blow you away…

His body turned into an inferno, his chest heaved, eyes burning with bloodlust as he spotted the house in the near distance. The song ended just in time. Turning off the music, he set his plan in motion. The air smelled like a twisted Autumn—burnt leaves, a dull sweetness reminiscent of rotting apples, and the pending stench of death.

Savage walked right past the house until he'd gotten past the camera's view. Like the damn pro that he was, he circumvented the house's alarm system with an electronic signal that disabled it with the push of a button. The home-owner seldom realized this until it was far too late. On their end, everything would look fine, but if a window was opened, a door cracked, the alarm would not beep or blast. Sizing up the area, he cut into the back of a neighboring yard, and crawled on his hands and feet towards Hickson's small backyard. He noticed two motion detectors. Moving at a snail's pace, not his typical fast 'grab and go' style and making no sudden movements, he made it to the far side of the property, just out of reach of the motion detectors. He slid right beneath them, in the blind spot, staying low until he was past them completely. That was the thing about these contraptions; there was *always* a blind spot. A professional could figure out how to spot them. He cut the wire of the

SAVAGE

one closest to the door once he'd managed to maneuver around it.

Time for the next phase of the operation.

Sliding up the steps, staying as low to the ground as possible, he reached the back door. Down on all fours, he removed a laser beam glass cutter from his sock and carefully cut through the window of the ratty and splintered white painted door. Keeping his gloved hand pressed against it to catch the pane once it was completely dislodged, he watched his footing, too. He'd done this operation countless times before, but this time he knew there would be no second chances should he fuck up. He smiled to himself as the pane came undone like a dream, and he softly placed it down onto the neighboring grass.

Crisscrossing his arms over his chest like a mummy in a pharaoh's tomb, he twisted his body and climbed through the narrow window, using his legs for leverage, and gritting through the pain when a jagged piece of wood scraped his shoulder, drawing blood. Once he was inside, he got his bearings. A horrid stench hit his nostrils immediately. It was pitch black inside, but he could tell it was the kitchen. An old stove and refrigerator stood in the cramped room. Pulling down a mask over his head that he'd tucked in the hat, he crept on. The muted sounds of a television came from an upstairs area—he presumed a bedroom based on the blueprint he'd seen of the property.

Placing the infrared scope light goggles over his eyes, he navigated slowly out of the kitchen. He now stood in a small living room that smelled of rotting flesh, the odor more pronounced with each step. Upon further inspection, he noted several dead cats and squirrels in various stages of decomposition, all of them laid out on silver medical trays alongside blood-tinged scissors and knives. He watched his step as he pulled out his SilencerCo Maxim 9 equipped with an optic.

Slowly rounding the corner, he saw the staircase. He was once again hit with the overwhelming odor of physical deterioration. He'd investigate that when time permitted. He assessed the area, watching his breathing, careful to not make any unnecessary moves. Just as he suspected, there was another motion detector light placed in a corner of the room. The alarm was disabled, but knowing Hickson, he had a back-up plan for his back-up plans. Any hit tripped out on the heavy dose of paranoia often went overboard with such things, especially since he knew the FBI was after him. Savage dropped down to the floor and slid against the wall along the blind spot. Careful... careful... done.

He stared at the staircase. It was a fucking nightmare. There was barely any light. He suspected the man hadn't paid the light bill and had rigged the electricity that did exist in the house. Grateful for his night vision goggles, he noticed old newspapers and magazines strewn along the steps, along with debris such as paper cups, ripped pieces of paper, and old potato chip bags.

There's no way I can use these steps without making a bunch of noise. They're like a booby trap. There's shit everywhere. Not only that, they look old... they'll crack under my weight. But the banister...

He edged up to the second floor on top of the thing, inch by inch. Upstairs, he spotted two more motion detectors.

Fuck. Here we go again.

Back pressed firmly against the wall, arms and hands spread out along his sides and his gut sucked in, he made it past the first blind spot. The sound of the television grew louder, and the bedroom door was slightly ajar. He could see the light from the screen, as well as several computer monitors sitting side by side.

Then, he paused, his heart skipping a beat. He could've sworn he heard movement. It could've been an animal, or it could be... *Shit.*

Something isn't right. I need to get out of this hallway.

Trusting his instincts that had yet to fail him, Savage gently tugged on a doorknob close by, praying he wasn't about the enter an area that would throw the entire operation off. He carefully opened the door and slipped into a dark room that smelled musty and dank. He could hear water dripping, likely from a faucet.

Bathroom. I'm in a bathroom.

Soon, he heard heavy footsteps approach and quickly stepped out of view, hiding in a narrow space barely big enough for a few brooms. It was dark and tight and gave an unspectacular view, but it would simply have to do. The bathroom door creaked opened and the light switch was flipped. Standing about six foot two and thin as a rail, Hickson made his way inside, his skin covered in prominent blue veins that practically pulsed under his pale flesh. He wore only a pair of white briefs, and they seemed two sizes too big. Savage knew not to mistake his scrawny frame for weakness, though. Others had done the same and lived to regret it.

It had already been noted that he was physically strong,

and had no issue overpowering men much larger than himself. There had been fights with security guards in stores, an incident at a strip club, and a laundry list of run-ins that proved mental illness gave some dudes the strength of a million men. The guy flipped up the toilet lid and began to piss. Savage didn't move a muscle. His eyes narrowed on a dead dog's carcass which lay in the filthy tub along with several cups and baggies filled with what appeared to be coagulated blood, pieces of bone, teeth, and fur. The distinct scent of embalming fluid stung his nostrils, blending in with the sickeningly sweet bouquet of decay. Savage took a deep breath and counted to three in his head as he placed his gun on his hip...

Moving like a bolt of lightning, he charged the mother-fucker, grabbing him from behind. They dropped to the floor. Muscles and bones slid against him, assaulting him with a pungent body odor and bad breath. They struggled, each trying to gain control of one another, but Savage soon overpowered him. Grabbing him from behind in a death grip, he positively identified the guy as he looked down into his eyes—making sure, just in case. The man's eyes rolled as he gasped for air, kicking his long legs, fighting with all of his might. The man jeered forward, attempting to rock his head back for a brutal headbutt, but it was far too late...

Savage snapped his neck, then scrambled to his feet, slipping over something slick, oily, and blood all over the gotdamn floor. The man lay on the floor, looking like the trash that he was. The man looked up at him, still holding onto a bit of life, his eyes dancing like those of a crazed lunatic. A strange grin creased the bastard's face. Savage pulled out his gun.

"Had to make sure it was definitely you first, Hickson. I'm doing you a fucking favor. Goodnight." Savage grinned back, then shot the fucker twice in the middle of his skull...

Thanks to his silencer, it proved a quiet killing. Blood sprayed on the floor and his shoes. He reached down and felt the man's pulse. Slow... slower... then it stopped.

Savage drew closer to the tub, pulled out a small camera from his jacket pocket and began to take pictures. He then checked out each room, gun drawn, only to make more grizzly discoveries. There had to have been at least a hundred animal carcasses in that house. The FBI would have to sort it all out. Making his way back to the room with the television and computers, he flicked on the light and began to snoop around.

Sitting down at one of the computers, he pulled out a special stick drive that was programmed to circumvent any necessary passwords for logins. Within five minutes, he was in Hickson's database. And what a treasure trove he found. Hickson had a hitlist of thirteen prominent politicians, and a few local folks were mentioned, too. He also seemed to have a creepy obsession with a stripper named Candy, for the man had collected over two thousand photos and video clips of the woman, most of them seemingly without her knowledge. He found a folder icon simply labeled 'M.D.' When he opened it, he discovered various files including scans of hand-drawn maps, deranged ramblings, and photos of his parents, many of them altered with odd drawings over their faces... He then found a real map of a vacant lot nearby, with R.I.P. written on it, right over a big black 'X'.

I bet that's where he buried them. Jesus… The media is going to have a field day with this…

He finished scouring the premises, taking photos, making notes. Though he was paid handsomely, in some ways, Savage realized that this was a thankless job. No one would ever know, besides the people in his organization, that he was the one who took this fucker down. The FBI and local police would take credit for the world wasn't ready to know that real-life assassins existed, and sanctioned by the government to boot. They were cold blooded killers, hired to do a job. Nothing more. Nothing less.

After about twenty more minutes of investigating, Savage pulled out his burner phone and sent Longhorn a text. Only two words were necessary…

MISSION COMPLETE.

CHAPTER TWENTY-SIX

If You Think I'm Pussy...

"**H**E JUST SENT me a text, finally. He'll be home in a couple of hours, y'all. Come on, help me get all of these wine glasses and cotton balls off the counter! Why in the hell did we have cotton balls in the first damn place?!" Zaire rubbed on her forehead. Her skin felt gritty, like sand. Her memory was foggy, and for all she knew, she'd danced naked out on the front lawn.

"Your guess is as good as mine," Kim offered wearily while she helped gather pieces of popcorn from the floor, her hair all over her head. "And I don't remember this. Who had this hot sauce? I could've used some on the wings last night." The woman picked up the half empty bottle and shook it in the air.

"The hot sauce was for the pizza we'd ordered. I always put hot sauce on pizza, Kim." Kim shot Allison a look as she tried to explain her unique tastes. "We gave each other facials and painted each other's nails too. That's why those cotton balls are out, Zaire." Allison looked down at her toes. From Zaire's vantage point, the bright pink polish was uneven and smeared. "You'd think we were sixteen-year-olds. We lost our complete minds last night. It was fun as hell… Let's do it again."

The three paused and looked at one another, then burst out laughing. Zaire caught her reflection in the microwave.

Good Lord.

She vowed to never use a glitter bath bomb again. The three had used the thing in Savage's hot tub, of all places. It smelled like bubblegum, and left a hell of a residue, too. It had taken her over thirty minutes to get the sparkles out of that tub. She surely didn't want to chance Savage seeing it; he'd have a fit. She hadn't even known he had a damn hot tub until the three had gone snooping about and discovered his small, well-equipped gym and the black and silver basin of joy. Allison had attempted to climb on the elliptical—bad move. Her forehead had paid the price.

Zaire was hung over and had a horrible headache, yet she still reeled with elation.

"Girl, you look like a disco ball!" Kim drew closer, dust cloth in hand, and burst out laughing. "Look at Zaire, Allison!" They both turned in her direction and fell into fits of laughter. "Doesn't she look like a disco ball?"

"Yeah! One that exploded!"

"Thanks a lot." Zaire poured a mug of flat beer down the drain.

"None of us look all that great." Allison giggled. "Kim, you look like your hair got stuck in a blender—a damn troll doll. Zaire looks like a cheap hooker with all of that glitter on her face. And I look like I'm going to the airport with these two damn bags under my eyes. I just hope I am flying first class. It was well worth it though!"

Good times...

Allison and Kim were clearly in just as bad of a shape as she was, and yes, in hindsight, it had been worth every damn ridiculous second. The 'Girls' Night' at Savage's home had turned into a true pow-wow, accompanied by way too much drinking. Once the liquor had loosened her tongue, she'd opened up, discussing her relationship with her mother from the very beginning to recent developments.

As her two best friends helped her get her man's place back in order after an evening of absurdity that had involved silly putty, softcore porn, Uno, and chocolate triple decker cake, she was surprised to discover that not only did they shower her with support to encourage her relationship with Savage, but they also expressed genuine admiration for her efforts to accept her truth and share it with them. She'd never forget this night.

Pressing her foot on the steel pedal of the trashcan, she tossed in a plate of chicken bones.

Bones... Skeletons in the closet...

Discussing her childhood in any depth had been taboo for her, a rule she'd stuck by. She'd made her secrets her fortress, not one of lies, or so she'd believed, but one built from a lack of admission. Telling only half the truth was acceptable right? Savage though had taught her through his actions towards her how she'd been dead wrong about that and so much more. It was tradition to turn the other way in her family, to keep up appearances. The elders in her clan had encouraged her to pretend, her maternal grandmother especially, but it had to stop.

And it'll stop with me.

Someone had to unplug the generational curse and rip it clean out of the socket. Mental illness was nothing to sweep under the rug. Her own mother was afflicted, and she would no longer throw a towel over the matter, and pretend half the time that she'd been hatched from a golden egg. A variety of mental challenges and illnesses affected millions of people around the world. Brilliant people, compassionate people, worthy people who deserved to NOT be alienated, but helped and loved.

She picked up a plastic spoon and tossed it in the trash, smiling. Just a week prior she'd been under the weather, a 24-hour flu bug. Savage had brought her some soup and even fed it to her. The sweetest thing…

"Giiirl! That mothafucka had it going on, too! I should've slipped him my number!" Allison hollered to Kim, the two women still working on the mess left in the living room. They'd talked about men all night too…

Naturally, they'd wanted to know where her man was. That was a normal question, certainly, but with a man like Savage, the answer was never cut and dry, or something she could delve deep into with mixed company. She explained that he worked for the government, and his job had to do with a bunch of classified information. Unsurprisingly, her friends had even *more* questions after that, their curiosity turned up a notch. Every time she tried to redirect the conversation, it came right back around like a Frisbee. They were completely intrigued by everything Savage.

She couldn't blame them. So was she.

"Dude's house is amaaaaazing, Zaire! I would love to live here," Kim stated, the real estate agent in her overdosing on his digs.

"Funny you should mention that. He asked me to move in with him." Zaire grinned wide when both of her friends turned towards her, their jaws dropped with utter disbelief on their faces.

"Oh. My. God! That is crazy! I love it! Are you going to?" Kim grabbed another trash bag and threw a big ball of used, tear-drenched Kleenex inside it. That therapeutic cry had done them a world of good, too.

"I don't know." Zaire shrugged as she grabbed a sponge, spritzed it with bleach cleanser and began to clean the countertop. "I mean…" How could she say what she really meant? "I always envisioned myself being married first, then sharing a home with a man. I'm concerned because the one and only time I moved in with someone beforehand, broke that idea in hopes that it would all work out, well, you know the rest of that story."

"Stop overthinking everything. They aren't the same person," Kim offered as she fluffed a pillow.

"Yeah, Kim, but if she wants to get married first, then that's fine, too," Allison said. "Some guys never buy the cow if they get the milk for free."

"That's so old school." Kim rolled her eyes. "That's not how the world works. Besides, marriage is overrated. You of all people should know."

"It might be old school, and it sure isn't for everyone, but if that's what Zaire wants then she has the right to experience it. Marriage, house, then baby… In that damn order!"

"What is this? 1955?"

"Nothing new changes under the sun, Kim. As soon as a woman moves in with the bastard, they never propose but have no problem getting a woman pregnant. It's crazy to me. So, you won't enter a marriage, but you'll make a whole new motherfucker walking the Earth! Backwards ass thinking, if you ask me."

"Okay, you have a point there, but different strokes for different folks. Well." Kim sighed. "I know we aren't around him a whole lot, but I like Savage, Zaire."

Zaire felt good about her friends' approval. Though she didn't need their blessing, it always felt good to have it.

"I do, too. I've even spoken to him on the phone a couple of times when I called Zaire when they were out and about together," Allison said. "I think he's a really good guy. I like his vibe, ya know? And I know I haven't always had the best judgment either when it comes to men, but you are aware how this works! We can choose for each other better than we can for ourselves."

They all nodded for that was on the money.

"That's so true." Zaire laughed. "Somehow, we can tell if a man isn't shit for each other, but in our own lives, it's a crap shoot!" Giggling, she opened the microwave and began to clean it out too.

"Exactly. So, since Kim likes him, and you know that I do, Zaire, and that's a rare thing, we've basically formed a triangle of agreement. My only thing is, if that's not what you want, then you shouldn't do it."

"But she didn't say she didn't want it, Allison! She's just

rolling it around!"

"She did too say that's not how she wanted it to be. She also said…"

And on and on her two friends went, nipping and pecking at one another like tiny birds. Zaire drifted away into her own thoughts, mulling over the possibilities. Savage had said to take her time deciding to move in, but she knew his impatient ass would want an answer sooner rather than later. Honestly, a change of environment might be helpful. She'd begun to feel like she was stuck in a rut. If she lived with him, she'd be a bit closer to her parents, as well as Allison. If they did get married and have a family down the line, the school system in his area was definitely better, as well as the hospitals, parks, restaurants, the whole nine.

"Let's turn on some music!" Kim picked up a large empty wine bottle and tossed it into the recycle bin.

"Yeah, but not too loud girl. My head is killing me." Allison ran her fingers through her hair and winced.

"Does he have Alexa, Zaire?"

"No, not anymore. Maximus doesn't trust it."

"Why?"

"He says it records private conversations and gives the information to Google or can be hijacked by foreign intelligence. He believes it's like bringing a stranger into your house and letting them record your every move as long as they clean up a little and cook you a meal or two. The invasion of privacy is dangerous and nullifies the advantages, in his book. He also says it emits frequencies that encourage certain behaviors, such as over-spending and other mind control tactics."

Her friends' expressions read something like, '*Bitch, both of y'all crazier than a nun dancing in Hell.*' Brow raised, Kim moseyed over to one of Savage's drawers in the kitchen.

"I know I saw an mp3 player lying around in this drawer last night when I was looking for a bottle opener." The woman rummaged through a junk drawer filled with stationery. "Here it is. Let's see what songs are on here. Hmmm… Oh, shit!" Kim screamed, dropping the damn thing on the floor. They turned in her direction to see the mp3 player spinning about, one side of it flashing and snapping pictures fast.

"What kinda shit is this?" Kim picked it up and studied it.

Shit! That must be one of his little government gadgets!

"Uh, give that to me, please!" Zaire snatched it out of the woman's hands. Allison came over quick, wanting a closer look.

"What the hell is that? That's no mp3 player!" Kim put her hand on her hip.

"It's just a little camera. He likes cameras," Zaire offered with a goofy smile. Her friends clearly didn't buy what she said, both crossing their arms over their chest, giving her *that* look.

"Zaire, you're a damn liar." Kim grimaced. "That looks like some shit from a science fiction movie. First, we see an axe on the wall in the guest room, and you can't tell us why in hell Savage thinks he is He-Man. Now, this. This little thing almost sliced my damn thumb off, too. That's why I dropped it."

"What?" Allison said, "It cut you?"

They would never let this go.

"Yeah, girl! There was a little blade when I pushed a little lever on the side. The damn thing popped out like... kapow!" Kim did a silly karate chop motion, drawing a giggle from Allison.

"Look, I don't know exactly what this is." And that was the truth. "Probably just some manly fun gadget thingy. Anyway, I'm glad you're okay. Let's finish cleaning up, please." Zaire busied herself with her task, her back to the two.

Hopefully, she hadn't said too much. If she did keep running off at the mouth, the men with the big guns, black suits, and dark glasses would come and visit their asses too, and that was the *last* thing she wanted. Their stares bore into her back, but she did her best to remain cool and calm. After a while, they finally began to clean up again, talk and carry on. Zaire sighed with relief. Allison started playing music from her iTunes playlist on her phone, and the three danced around to 'Good Vibrations' by Marky Mark and the Funky Bunch.

Just then, her cellphone buzzed. She pulled it from the pocket of her oversized sleeping jumper and smiled. Savage had sent a text message:

Savage: *Baby, I'll be home real soon. I'm about an hour away now. Tell Allison and Kim I said hello if they're gone when I arrive. I love you.*

Zaire: *Was worried. I love you, too. Are you hungry? We've got food left here.*

Savage: *No, I don't want any food. I saw you made use of my Grubhub account. Looks like you guys partied like rock stars. Glad you had a good time. I want something else though.*

Zaire: What? 😶

Savage: You know what I want.

Zaire: I can't. Have a terrible headache. Drank too much.

Savage: But I'm not trying to fuck your head.

Zaire: You are selfish. LOL

Savage: Me? That's YOU. The pussy isn't drunk too, is it? Only you. The pussy doesn't drink anything but cum, and I've got plenty of that. I make COCKtails all damn day.

Zaire: I'm not having this ridiculous conversation with you right now. Goodbye. LOL

She slid her phone back into her pocket and ran water in the kitchen sink to wash up the dishes. Her friends were laughing and dancing, having a damn good time.

"I love y'all so much!" She placed her hand against her lips as tears welled in her eyes. Kim shook her head and laughed. "I'm serious! You always have my back, even when I don't deserve it. I'm going to be a better friend. No more acting like my world is perfect. You both mean way too much to me."

"This girl still drunk, Allison. Out here showing affection, being all soft 'nd shit." Kim winked at her, while Allison swiped at her eye, smiling. "Seriously though, we love you too, sis. And you're a great friend; you always have been. Just because you didn't tiptoe around me and could be abrasive sometimes didn't mean you weren't a good friend, Zaire. Your heart was *always* in the right place and we know you'd give us the shirt off your back."

Zaire blinked back tears and raced over to them. They huddled together, embracing one another.

"We love you for you," Allison said, her voice choked up. "The hard-nosed you, and this softer side, too. We'll take both, and girl, you never have to worry. We'll always have your back..."

SAVAGE HISSED AND tossed his phone back in the holster as he navigated bumper-to-bumper traffic.

Talking about she has a headache... What the fuck does that have to do with my dick?! I know she better take care of me when I get in there. That's what the hell I know...

Traffic moved a bit, at a snail's pace.

How in the hell can three women eat six meat lovers and cheese and veggie pizzas, two baked chickens, a large pasta salad, an entire loaf of garlic bread, three tossed salads, four orders of twelve piece garlic pepper wings, three meatball hoagies, and all that other shit they had? Let's not forget the birthday cake they ordered. Who eats a birthday cake when it is nobody's fucking birthday? Eva, that's who. My liquor cabinet is probably wiped clean, on top of it all. When I told her to have a girl's night, I didn't mean a girl's food extravaganza! They were eating as if they were all nine months pregnant with triplets! She better give me that pussy when I hit the door. I am fucking her on sight.

He was horny and cranky, an awful combination. Austin had contacted him that morning and, much to his surprise, congratulated him on his completed mission. The news stations were swarming around the Hickson home before he'd even gotten out of town. After he'd spoken to Longhorn, he contacted the local police, as their policy required. He was glad it was over.

His phone rang. He snatched it up, smiling.

"Hi, Mom."

"Hello, Maximus. Your father said you are coming back home soon, yes?"

"Yeah, on my way now. Anything wrong?"

"I must ask again, though you told me not to, for money for Erjon, Jetmir, Kreshnik and—"

"You can name all of my fucking uncles, aunts, cousins, the man on the moon, whatever, Mom, but I am not giving them any more money!"

"Maximus, please! They are homeless!"

"How are they homeless? I saw photos of the building they're staying in a few years back. It was decent."

"No, I just found out last night that they've moved here, to Miami. They had to flee, no jobs, nowhere to go... Please, just help me get them settled."

Alarm bells rang in his damn head like a fire drill.

"Miami? How long have they lived in Miami?"

"Mirarber said they've been there a while, but illegally... he didn't want to tell me. He was careful who to tell about it. The rest of the family is still in Armenia according to my sister Milena. Now, you see? This is very important! Just enough money so they can get their papers, pay for a lawyer, things like that."

Savage's head began to pound in shock and disbelief. He swerved his rental car and pulled over to the side of the highway, trying to regain his composure.

"Mom, I need you to answer a question for me."

"Yes, son? What is it?"

"Have you told anyone in the family what I do for a living?"

"Of course not! Never! I just say my son has a good job and makes very good money. Very proud of him."

"Mmm hmm, okay… Next question. Have you told anyone, and I mean anyone, that you're my beneficiary in case I die?"

There was a brief silence.

"I don't know. I may have. Let me think…" He sighed and plopped his head on the car seat. "I don't remember, Maximus. I may have in general talk, you know? No big deal."

"Mom! Do you have any idea what… fuck! Never mind."

"What? What is the matter?!"

"Nothing… Look, how much money do they need?"

"You changed your mind? Oh, thank you!"

"Yeah, yeah, yeah. How much money are they asking for? I want to give it to them in person if they're here in the States, in Miami. I need to go there soon, anyway, for an assignment…"

"Saban told me they need forty thousand dollars."

"Forty thousand! Are they out of their fucking minds?!"

"A lot of money, I know, dear. I sold the television you bought us to give them a thousand, you know, to help. I sent it through the Cash app, but I explained that you pay all our bills directly so I cannot give them more."

"You sold that television you wanted for your birthday last year? Why in the… never mind, Mom." He felt like he was going to burst from pure rage. "What about your jewelry?"

The woman went silent. Mom loved her silver and gold bangles, her pretty rings, but he'd noticed she hadn't had them on the last few times he'd seen her.

"Gone."

She was in deep. The emotional blackmail, lies and manipulation these people had her under was overwhelming. They toyed with her, playing on her need to be loved by them and be finally accepted into the fold. Dad had been right. Mom was easy pickings. Savage and his father gave her everything she wanted, though she had never asked for much and had even refused higher priced gifts in the past, deeming them too extravagant. Her relatives had been milking her like a cow to get to his assets and his death would be the big prize, the pot of gold at the end of their rainbow. She'd get the insurance money and, knowing her, she'd give them a huge percentage of it, if not everything. She wouldn't be able to help herself.

Mom wasn't an affectionate person. She wasn't emotionally demonstrative, but Zaire had been right, too. Inside her lived a desperate little girl still trying to be loved. Mom was very generous, that much was true. She wouldn't tell him she loved him in words, but she'd always showed it by getting him the little toys he'd desired as a child, whenever she could, and making a big fuss over his birthdays. Too bad that giving nature seemed to end with her and not extend to her leeching family.

These animals would have it made in the shade. They'd be instant millionaires as soon as I kick the bucket. Fine then. I've got something for their asses...

Stroking his chin, he smiled.

"Mom, here's what I want you to do. Get me their Miami address, okay? I am going to furnish their entire apartment, pull some strings to help them get residency, and a car or two so they can get around, too. I have some connections with immigration, okay?"

"Oh, Maximus! Thank you so much! This is their American dream come true! Mirarber is going to be thrilled! Can't wait to tell him the news!"

"Let them all know that I will also be bringing lots of cash, so it isn't traceable, okay? Loads of it."

"Beautiful news! I cannot wait to tell them!"

"Yeah… you go on and do that. Tell them I will be making it there very soon. I just need to get my schedule in order." He grinned, the savage within him amped and happy as could be. "I'll talk to you later, Mom. Send me that address as soon as possible."

"I will! Thank you, son!"

"Uhh huh…" He disconnected the call. "Call, Harlem," he told his phone.

The man picked up after the fourth ring.

"What's up, champ?! You fucked Hickson up, my man! Why didn't you take his tongue out though? I was a little disappointed to hear he was intact once I got the bio report." The man chuckled.

"It was a disaster. I wasn't in the mood."

"A disaster? What do you mean?"

"He had some sort of strange ass infection, man… Look, I've seen it a few times. Sores all over his mouth and inside it, too. It could have been from a number of causes but getting my prize wasn't important to me anymore after I peeped it. He was into some really strange shit, too. We're talking rampant animal dissections, bestiality, a bunch of shit. A real sick, dangerous fuck. That's not including all the evidence I uncovered of bomb attacks he was responsible for. There were two bombs in the house, as well, as I expected. Thankfully, one was a dud and the other was removed without incident."

"Shit, man. No wonder Austin didn't want to touch it."

"Exactly. Pay out was pretty, but let me tell you, my adrenaline was through the roof. Anyway, we can talk more about that later. Right now, I need your help."

"What's up?"

"Apparently, blood isn't always thicker than water."

"Huh?"

"I've figured it out. My mother's family has her hemmed up in some bullshit. I believe they've been the ones trying to kill me."

"What?! Come on, Savage. That doesn't make sense."

"Yeah, actually it does. Hear me out. Remember how everyone was sayin' that these guys knew the Toret Crew down in Miami, so they figured it was retribution for me taking out their boss last year?"

"Yeah."

"Well, they're from Miami all right. These bastards relocated there! They came here to California to take me out, and made a pit stop to Vegas after finding out I was there, probably because of my mother since only you guys knew. She's been running her mouth, supplying them with all the information they need without realizing it. She was doing what mothers do: brag on their kids. Well, that was a mistake."

"But why would they want to kill you?"

"Oh, I'm getting to that part. Here is where it gets juicy. I have no wife and kids. She's my life insurance beneficiary."

"Ho...ly... SHIT."

"Yup. It's her name listed first, then my father's. She and my dad would also get everything I own, not just the insurance, if I kick the bucket. The houses, the cars and bikes, the boat, the casino I've invested in. They'd get my share, and that's over 500k on its lonesome. All the money in my accounts, stocks, the whole shebang. They started small, asking for five hundred bucks here and there, so I didn't think anything of it and handed it over. Now they've pumped her up to ask me for forty thousand. She's the heir to the ponderosa... She knows it, they know it, and now I know it. She isn't capable of sayin no to their demands, no matter what my father and I tell her. They get rid of me, then they're in."

"Shit, man... Damn! All right, so what do you want me to do? What do you need because you know I'm on it, I've got you man? Family ain't shit sometimes! As soon as one of my brothers calls me with some shit, tryna borrow some money, I hang the phone up. I learned a long time ago that throwin' money at people who are users only feeds the tiger to have a taste for you."

"Tell me about it." Savage rolled his eyes. "I'll give you all the details later, but I've got a plan." He pulled away from the curb, merging back into traffic.

"I bet you do." Harlem chuckled. "Lay it on me."

"I had other assignments to take care of man, but it looks like ya boy is headed to see Don Johnson and Philip Michael Thomas." He bit into his lower lip, trying to contain his enthusiasm. "I'm the new Miami Vice! It's a family fuckin' affair!"

CHAPTER TWENTY-SEVEN
Bullies, Bullets, and Brides

ZAIRE STOOD IN the grocery store line, yawning. It had been a long, eventful day. Although it was just eight in the evening, it felt more like midnight. She'd been the keynote speaker at the Los Angeles Women's Outreach Conference that day. They'd served coffee, tea and croissants, a full luncheon buffet, and dinner had been catered by a popular local barbecue spot. The topics had ranged from education to international travel, anything to help empower the Black women of L.A. to be their best selves. She'd been enthusiastic and energetic, but now her battery was drained, running on E.

I wonder what's taking so long?

Two people stood in line in front of her, and it seemed time was moving at a snail's pace. Soft music played in the store, the sound mingling with that of the beeping cash register.

"Try this coupon..." the woman at the front of the line said.

When coupons where involved, it could mean an exceptionally long wait.

I should've done self-checkout.

She yawned once again and picked up a gossip rag from the display to entice last minute needless purchases. Flipping through it, she landed on an article about Brad Pitt, detailing his life after divorce, his new spiritual leanings, and how he was dealing with his past demons. The handsome, talented actor was dressed in a bluish gray suit and white shirt, looking amazing. Her lips curled in appreciation.

He still looks good... Good for him. It was a mess what he did to Jennifer, leaving her for that other woman who looks like a whole ghoul, but he seems remorseful. We reap what we sow, don't we, Brad? No one is perfect. Just learn from your shit and move on. I'm not going to even lie though; if I were single, I might have to look you up. I heard you've dated the chocolate a few times.

She chuckled to herself, being silly as her exhaustion set in.

"I understand, ma'am, but that coupon is expired so I can't accept it."

"Shiiiid! Just by one damn day! Y'all make me sick! How much is the total then?!"

"Your order comes up to $43.75. Your EBT card also doesn't cover that brand of milk, those candies, or the crackers you selected. Would you like to replace them?" the cashier said softly.

Zaire poked her head past the man in front of her and began to eavesdrop.

"No, I *don't* want to replace them!" the woman barked. "I don't understand this shit. It ain't like I have a big steak dinner sittin' here. I've got four kids I'm tryna feed! I ain't have these problems at Aldi's, I tell ya that much! Wait a minute..." The woman huffed. "Let me check my change purse. Might have a five-dollar bill or two rolled up in there."

Zaire this time peeked around the red-haired man ahead of her to get a better look.

A tall, thin, light brown skinned Black woman in a taupe turban wore a scowl fit for Halloween on her face. Her expression conveyed anger mixed with embarrassment. Zaire couldn't quite blame her. She recalled how mortified she'd been herself years ago when her brand new VISA had been declined because of some error on the bank's end.

For what felt like an eternity, the woman kept digging in her purse, while everybody gawked at her. The woman paused and looked at people behind her, and she and Zaire locked gazes.

Oh, my God. I know her...

The lady quickly turned away, frantically searching in her worn, oversized denim purse. She gathered a few coins and slapped them in the cashier's hand. Several people in line began to huff and grumble at this point, tired of the dog-and-pony show, voicing their frustration.

I have to do this. This is a teachable moment. I just spoke all damn day about us Black women owning our choices, not making excuses for our behavior when it does us more harm than good. I discussed elevating ourselves, getting with mates who appreciate us, regardless of their race or ethnic background, and encouraging travelling abroad. I talked about obtaining higher education, the importance of reading, and not having children with men who can't even take care of themselves—the whole nine. I also argued about us confronting our demons and making amends. I guess this is God's way of trying to make me literally put my money where my mouth is. Here goes nothing...

"Excuse me," Zaire spoke up, wishing to bring this all to a close. The cashier and the woman turned to her. "How much does she owe?" Zaire reached into her pocketbook and pulled out her debit card.

"Her total is $43.75. She has only $31.15 that covers this. The rest she'd need to pay some other way. That makes a difference of, $12.60."

"I'll pay it, okay? In fact, put the entire amount on my card. Excuse me, just let me get past you for a second here." Zaire walked in front of the man preceding her to stand between him and the woman trying to get her groceries, then put her card in the card reader. The woman crossed her arms over her chest, chewing nervously on her lower lip, fidgeting, and stealing surreptitious glances at her. Through it all, she never said a word.

"There you go." Zaire smiled at her before she quickly gathered her bags and placed them inside the cart.

"Thank you," she muttered, then rushed away.

"Damn, she sure was ungrateful," the man she'd stepped in front of stated as she went back to her original spot in line. He placed his carton of orange juice down and shook his head.

"It's okay. Sometimes our pride causes that. She may have been very thankful but just didn't know how to express it."

The cashier nodded in agreement. "That was very nice of

you to do."

The cashier began to ring the next customer up.

Zaire, this is not over… A little voice in the back of her head began to nag her. *You did not confront your demons completely. GO. AFTER. HER. Come on now, live by your teachings. Don't be a hypocrite. Stop putting on airs and TELL THE TRUTH!*

"Uh, excuse me, I'm so sorry." Zaire stepped out of the line. "Let me put my stuff over here to the side. I'll be right back." Placing her groceries back in her little plastic basket, she set the thing next to another cash register that wasn't in use. She then hurried out of the store, her heart beating a mile a minute. Looking all over the parking lot, she didn't see the woman at first, but then caught her sitting on a bench, perhaps waiting on a ride. Zaire approached her. The lady was toying with her cellphone. She suddenly looked up in surprise, her eyes large.

"I didn't mean to shock you." Zaire smiled. "But I re-member you from a long time ago…"

"What do you mean you remember me from a long time ago?" the woman asked suspiciously, her eyebrow raised and her forehead creased. "I don't know you."

"I had actually—"

"What else do you want? I said thank you," she barked.

"It's not about the groceries, and it's not even about you acknowledging that someone helped you or not, Deanna." The woman's eyes turned to slits. "That's right. Deanna Brooks is your name. We went to high school together."

"Hmmm, I don't remember you, baby. Sorry." She pulled out a cigarette from a little pouch and lit it. Crossing her long, skinny legs, she began to swing it back and forth and turned her head, dismissing her. "What are you still standin' there for?" she asked, blowing smoke out the side of her mouth.

"You know what? The old me would've relished this moment, seeing you down and out like this, Deanna. I would've been sitting high and looking down. I would've figured karma caught up with you, too. You know who I am. Don't play stupid. I came out here to let you know how I felt, and to tell you that I forgive you and wish you nothing but the best. I wanted to have a conversation with you to see what's up in your life—not to gloat, but to see if I could help. From the looks of things though, you have the same mentality as a seventeen-year-old. You never grew up. You made my life a living hell in high school."

"Lady, I don't know what tha fuck you're talkin' about. You must be crazy. My ride'll be here in a second so please turn yo' siddity self around and leave. Shit, you make me sorry I accepted the money." She sucked her teeth and rolled her eyes.

"Oh, are we still playing that game, Deanna? You still want to pretend like you don't remember me? Let me help you out. Jog your memory, if you will." Zaire stepped a bit closer, her hand on her hip, her blood boiling. "You tormented and tortured me about my mother. You see, you already didn't like me. You'd accused me of thinking I was better than you and your friends, which was an absolute lie. All I wanted to do was go to school, have a good time but also get my work finished. You wouldn't let that happen! I allowed you to make me feel like shit because I was young and didn't know how to deal with it. I allowed you to step on me!

"My mother had come up to the school and caused a scene more than once because she had an undiagnosed mental illness. One time, unfortunately, you and your little crew witnessed it. Rather than show some compassion or just keeping your trap shut, you and your band of mean girls called me all sorts of names, said my mother was, and I quote, 'fucked in the head', and I was probably just as stupid as her. You made fun of the way I dressed because I liked to wear more conservative clothing than most of our peers. You called me a nerd just because I did extra credit, and you also said I must've been the mailman's baby because I wasn't as pretty as my sister, Star, who you were also jealous of! My sister was popular, while I was not. You said it to hurt me."

"Look, nut, I don't remember none of that shit you talkin' 'bout," Deanna hissed, waving her cigarette about. "And if it *did* happen, so what? Kids do dumb shit. That was a long time ago. We grown now. You need to move on... like for real." She sized her up, her expression one of disdain.

"I *have* moved on, Deanna. That's the beauty of this." Zaire shifted her body weight from one foot to the other. "I didn't pay for your groceries because I wanted to feel better than you. I did it for my own peace of mind, to put closure to this and face how you made me feel—how I allowed you to make me feel—and try and make amends! I came out here with a clean heart," she said. "I am not better than you because of my job, my clothes, my home, my man or my family, but I am better than you, at this moment in time, because I am *trying* to accept responsibility for my decisions and grow as a person! You're right, we were children, but you're a grown ass woman now, still doing juvenile shit!"

"Get outta my face." The woman waved her hand in a dismissive gesture. "You ain't better than me on my worst day, Eva. Just 'cause I got food stamps don't mean shit. I still look better than you. That ain't even probably yo' real hair." The woman chuckled as she tapped the ashes onto the ground.

"I knew you were lying." Zaire smirked. "You *do* remember me, just as I suspected. Needing a helping hand is not a sin, but sitting on a bench, filled with all of that hurt, all of that rage and anger of a million women, then turning it around and blasting it out like a fire hose at everyone who walks your way is not cool at all! We've *all* been hurt in our lives! We've all been in need! We've all been lied to, played, abused, played for a fool! The problem is, you haven't grown. You enjoy being this way because it's easier than looking deep inside yourself and finding out why you stay in this vicious cycle. Regardless, your children shouldn't be punished simply because their mother is a damn fool. I am done with you. Demon has been faced and destroyed and I'm going to sleep just fine tonight. Enjoy your groceries…"

Zaire turned to walk away.

"You ain't better than nobody 'cause you wrote some damn books and went to college!" She cackled. "Yeah, I know who you are, you dumb ass bitch! Yo' mother was up there talkin' to herself and sayin' all kinds of crazy shit! It ain't my fault, bitch, and you probably don't fall too far from the tree! Don't be mad at me 'cause she out of her fuckin' mind. That shit was funny!" Zaire kept walking, the smile on her face getting bigger and bigger… "You damn near forty fuckin' years old still talkin' about that shit. You maaaaad?" The sad woman burst in a forced fit of laughter as she raged on.

"You walkin' away 'cause you know you ain't shit! You can't beat me, bitch! Swing on me, mothafucka! I want you to! Just 'cause you got nice clothes don't mean a damn thing, bitch! You *still* ain't all that pretty, even wit' all that makeup and hair and shit! You still ain't nothin'!" The woman's voice got fainter, harder to hear, while Zaire's weight on her shoulders got lighter. "Silly ass bitch! I done fuhgot yo' name already!"

Zaire spun around, a big, proud smile on her face. Her man was all in her ear, in some strange way, telling her what to say. It was time to deliver the truth, Savage style...

"Bitch, I'm famous!" *(Thank you, author Phoenix Daniels for saying this at an author's event. I salute you, heffa! Readers, go check out Phoenix's work if you haven't already. I had to pay homage! Okay, back to the story...)*

She went back to the store and found a little old man in line, all by his lonesome.

Oh, he is adorable! Look at his little checkered shirt and over-alls... He can't be more than five foot two!

One by one, he placed ten tiny red apples on the convey-er belt, a tub of margarine, some cinnamon and brown sugar, a pre-made pie crust, and a canister of whipping cream. She approached him from the side.

"Ohhh, someone is making a pie! Yummy!" The old man smiled wide, his little wide wrinkled face flushed in hues of red and pink.

"I make them. It's for my wife." He folded his knobby

hands together and faced the cashier. "She hasn't been feeling well, but loves apple pie. I figured it would make her feel better."

The ringing of the items began and Zaire got back in line.

"Well, isn't that a nice thing for you to do! I hope she'll be okay soon."

The old man's jovial expression faded.

"She has terminal cancer."

"Oh... I'm... I'm so sorry." The wind was knocked out of her sails at the unexpected reply. She'd been on cloud nine after seeing how unhinged Deanna had become, but this was a real bummer.

"It's okay." He nodded, his smile slowly coming back. "We've known for a while." He shrugged. "Edith and I been together sixty-two years..."

"Wow! I admire you two so much! That's beautiful."

"I'm just appreciating each day that comes because we never know when our last will be, you know? Just appreciate today, young lady." He tapped her hand. "Let go of all that ol' silly fuddy duddy stuff." He sighed. "Who did what to you, what you did to them. Tonight, I'm baking a pie for my wife. That's all I want to focus on. Life's too short, you know?"

"It most certainly is." Zaire patted the man's shoulder. As his groceries were being packed and put into the canvas sacks he'd brought, she called out to him. "Sir, I have a podcast."

"A podcast?" He paused.

"Yes, it's kind of like a radio station. Would you be interested in being interviewed? See, I talk about relationships, things like that. You're just so inspirational and I think my listeners would love to hear your story! You really inspire me!"

"Oh." He blushed. "I don't get out much."

"Oh no, no, see, you wouldn't have to come by. I could just call you on the phone and we'd talk... have a conversation. That's all it is but others would hear us. I don't do podcast interviews but I am thinking I should start with those. You would be perfect as my first guest. I'd love to hear all about your wife, and if she is up to talking, I'd like to chat with her, too! I want to hear about your family, and all about you, your journey in life!"

The man's cheeks plumped as he showed that adorable smile once more.

"Well, that sounds just fine! Could be fun!"

The two exchanged telephone numbers, and she watched as he walked out of the store, slowly pushing his little cart. The cashier began to ring up her few items, then paused.

"You're a really good person, you know that?" The young woman's expression grew sullen. "So many people come in here and get mad and impatient, but you made my night. You're like a breath of fresh air."

"I wasn't always... I was full of hot air." They both got a good chuckle from that. "Let me tell you something, young lady, and you're the real young lady, not me..." The woman grinned. "The way you handled that situation with that unhappy woman cursing at you and making her problems yours was very mature and professional. You're so much further along than I was at your age, believe it or not. You keep setting goals for yourself and *never* settle. Be your authentic self. Don't put on airs. Be savage about what you deserve, what is owed to you, and go get it!"

SAVAGE WITNESSED THE fireworks blasting off a neighbor's yard from the vantage point of his master suite terrace. The breeze blew gently through his white button-down shirt and pants and cooled his bare feet. Enjoying his beer, he crossed his ankles, smiled and waved at his guests below, all of them seeming to be having a good time. He hadn't had a party since Vegas, so this had been long overdue. Some people gathered around the pool dancing, many of the women in revealing attire.

Several people lifted their glasses in the air and downed the shots, partying the night away as the DJ spun records and the waiters served drinks and nibbles.

He'd decided to throw this party out of need, not want. His bouts of isolation due to his work at times wore him down, the schedule draining. Depending on the assignment, he could be forced to spend weeks or more without human contact, his mere thoughts for company, as well as his guns and a penchant for killing. So now, it was time to relax and reconnect.

Things had been so hectic, he hadn't seen Harlem face-to-face in what felt like an eternity. In fact, he'd not even spoken to many of his closest friends. Things had changed unexpectedly. He'd been swallowed into an entirely new world. Uncharted territory.

He was madly in love.

After telling his guests he had something to take care of, he came upstairs, needing a moment alone. He stared at the small black velvet box he held in his hand, the one he'd been nervously checking and patting all evening. Popping it open, he smiled down at the striking scalloped pavé diamonds that encircled a huge round center gem with an intricate band. He grabbed his phone and dialed Zaire.

"Hey, baby," she answered. He could barely hear her. "Where are you? I was looking for you."

"I needed to come in the house and get something. Hey, can you come upstairs to the bedroom please?"

"Huh? Baby, I can't hear you!"

"COME. INSIDE. UPSTAIRS."

"Oh, okay! Be right there." She disconnected the call.

He waited, so anxious, he contemplated sitting down before he risked passing out.

I can't believe I'm nervous like this! I don't get like this about any fucking thing! My knees are buckling... Oh, God...

He gripped the railing with all of his might and waited forever for his baby to arrive. Zaire finally entered, wearing a white one-piece bathing suit and sheer cover-all robe. She looked absolutely stunning. Her long, wet black hair hung in loose waves down her back as she sashayed over, sporting a pair of faux diamond adorned slides.

"Let me tell you, Allison and Kim are flirting with every good-looking man here. They both should be ashamed at how thick they are laying it. I encouraged them though," she quipped.

"It's all good, let them get their groove on... Hey, baby, I need to talk to you for a minute. Come over here and sit with me."

"I'm wet though… I was swimming! Did you see me?" She grinned wide.

"I sure did, baby! Looked like a damn mermaid. It's all right that you're wet. This is important. Just sit down please."

She gave him a quizzical look, but took a seat in a plush black chair, one of two he had set around a white table. Standing before her, he took a deep breath, then exhaled.

"Everything okay?"

"Yeah… look, uh, Eva," He tried to convince himself he could get through this shit without falling apart. "I love you."

"I love you, too."

"Here's the thing… I… know you said you're going to move in with me soon. You also said you didn't want to sell your house just yet, and I get that. I was just happy you've started to prepare for the transition. But see, I know you… I know what you want, what you need. You need to feel secure, and I get that."

"Where's all this coming from, Maximus?"

"I'm getting to it… I am." He swallowed, taking a moment to gather his wits, then continued. "When we first met, then started dating, I told you a lot of shit, right? Like, how I felt about marriage, kids, all that shit. And I meant it at the time, but see, when you fall in love with a person who exceeds your expectations, one who isn't perfect but is perfect for *you*, you kinda… change. You evolve. My reasons for the whole marriage thing had nothing to do with lack of desire, per se. We've already discussed what was going on with me and I hate the brain picking you do to me sometimes, but I have to admit you were right about this.

"I had a problem with women… didn't trust you people. At all. A lot of shit was goin' on with me in that regard. I'm a grown man so I do accept my actions as an adult, like the fact I haven't always treated women with respect, seeing you all as something to just fuck and dismiss… and I'm not blaming her, but the cause of some of that was my mother." She nodded and crossed her ankles, remaining quiet… giving him the floor. "I love my mother… I love her a whole fucking lot!" He got choked up, needing a minute. Zaire took his hand in hers and he closed his eyes, fighting back tears, dealing with the emotions…

"She sacrificed a lot for me, and my dad, too… But see, there's a hole inside of her, Eva." He finally opened his eyes and looked down at her. "And I and my father can't fill it. You were right about that, too. She's in a lot of pain, always has been, but she doesn't talk about it. Like you though, she holds that shit inside, though you've started to change. You've started to share more of yourself."

"Yes…" she said quietly, a sad smile on her face. "It will kill you, holding that kind of sadness within you."

He nodded.

"Well, see, here's what happened. Let me explain. My mother contacted her family when she was pregnant with me. That was forty years ago and she'd been living here in the States for at least a few years by then. She hadn't spoken to them in forever and for all they knew, she was dead. Once they began to interact with her, talk to her, it was like she felt she needed to do anything she could to keep them around. They never showed any real interest in her wellbeing.

They've just been using her the entire time, trying to see what they could get from her.

"She came from a very poor family, Eva. They struggled, but unfortunately, sometimes that extreme poverty turns men into monsters. My mother's challenges gave her an escape route—as you say sometimes, the disaster became a blessing. Had she not been in that orphanage, been sold, she might have remained there, barely surviving. Instead, she got the motivation to find a way to get out of there and legally enter the United States. She's an American citizen, and proud of it. Eva, I have come to realize that my mother really needed that validation, you know? And since I'm not a woman and wasn't in an orphanage in Armenia and going through the shit and abuse she went through, I have accepted there are parts of her mentality that I will never be able to understand.

"I just have to accept my mother for who she is, ya know? Now, there's more to the story. There's some shit going on that I can't get into right now, but it's kinda brought this full circle. My mother always wanted a family, security, love from her bloodline. Culturally, for her, that's a big deal. She doesn't understand my father and me trying to make her understand for all of these years that we've created our own family, that not everyone in our clan has our back. Blood doesn't mean shit if there's no respect. My mother just wants love from them, like you said. That's normal, right?" Eva nodded. "It makes her feel secure, and gives her purpose. And that brings me back to you. I know you didn't sell your house so you'd always have some place to go should what we have fall apart."

"That's not true, Max."

"Yeah, it is. You may not realize this, but it is. You want

to be with me, you want to make me happy, but you don't want to put yourself in a position where, if something crazy happens, you have no safety net."

The woman took a big breath, but said nothing this time. Didn't try to protest. "I've heard you talking on your podcast about things like that, about women making smarter choices. You probably asked yourself, 'What do I look like moving in with this guy and we've not discussed marriage seriously?' I know what you want... you've made it clear. And I'm just the man to give it to you, baby. You don't need anybody else to fill those shoes but me. I want this, not because you want it, but because I know you'll take it as seriously as me. I know you'll be by my side through thick and thin, so there's no need to drag this out any longer. The safety net won't be that house. It'll be *me*."

He got down on one knee, staring at the floor, and heard her gasp. Digging into his pocket, he removed the box and opened it. When he looked at her, they both were quietly crying. He smiled through the tears.

"Eva Zaire Ellington, would you please marry me? Will you be my wife?" His voice trembled, more than he cared for.

"Yes!" He took her hand and slid the ring on her finger, then she caught him in a tight embrace. Wrapping his arms around her, he kissed her cheek and squeezed. Her body jerked, for the woman was crying her eyes out. He ran his hand up and down her back, soothing her, unable to quell the wave of joy that took him under.

"I can't even tell you in words how much I love you, Eva. This is it... we're getting married!" He kissed her once more, this time on the lips, and stood to his feet, helping her up.

"Oh, my God! Max, you were so slick, I had no idea you

were planning this. I am in shock right now!" She giggled, then eased her left hand from his grip to study the ring. "It's beautiful! It's exactly the type of ring I would have wanted, too! How'd you know?" He led her to the terrace, where they stood hand in hand, observing the guests.

"When I took you out to the desert on our first date, I saw how you loved gazing at the stars." He pulled a pair of binoculars out of a bag and handed them to her. "Look up there, at the sky. What do you see?"

She brought the binoculars to her face.

"I see a bunch of stars."

"That's how I saw you when I first met you…" She slowly lowered the binoculars from her eyes. "I said, this woman is amazing. She's so damn smart, bright and sexy… I was wowed by you. So, whatever type of ring I got you would have to match the stars we saw that night. The night of our first date. But what really helped me the most was a paper trail you'd left. See, when I was in your studio while you did your show that time, I saw a couple of bridal magazines. They were dated, at least a few years old, but you had a couple of dogeared pages. I saw those rings, so I made a mental note of it. Then I went down there again after that, while you were asleep, and took notes about the images you'd marked.

"I knew those rings had nothing to do with me; like I said, the magazines were old. They'd been for your ex, the guy before me, the one you thought you were going to marry before he cheated and put his fuckin' hands on you." She dropped her gaze, her face flushed. He reached for her and gathered her close to kiss the top of her head. "I'd never do anything to you like that, Eva. I'd never try to hurt you in a million fucking years!"

"I know." She wrapped her one free arm around him.

"Look, tonight went better than I expected. I honestly thought you might say no."

She frowned. "Why would you think that?"

"Because... see..." He took a deep breath. "I know I can be a bit much sometimes, so I just wasn't sure what you'd say, you know. But I had to take that chance. Anyway, despite me being the happiest man in the world right now, we have to keep this on the low-low."

"Oh, no!!! Why?" She pouted, looking downright pitiful. "I want to tell my father. He loves you, by the way! You made a big impression on him by showing him your bike." Savage chuckled lightly. "And I'm glad you weren't phased by my mother saying your arms looked like a newspaper with all your tattoos. She can't help herself."

He grinned. "No, baby, all of that was cool... no problem. The reason why you can't say anything right now is because I can't let anyone get wind of the fact I'm getting married. I promise we'll be able to tell people soon though, okay? Just give me a little time." She nodded. "So, before you go back outside, slide that ring back into the box. It's on the floor by the chair over there. Then I want you to put it away in your purse. Put it up somewhere safe, but whatever you do, don't wear it."

"Damn! Okay... Soon though, right?"

"Yeah, I promise. Trust me, I'm just as excited as you to tell the world, but we need to hold off for a bit. I'll explain later. It's complicated. It'll be resolved though." She pulled him in for a kiss. "Go back out there and dance. I like seeing you shake that big, fat ass of yours!" She winked and walked away, her expression bright as the sun. Picking up the box off the floor, she slid her ring off and place it inside. She blew him a kiss, and exited the bedroom, leaving him there by himself.

Yeah, I wish we could tell the whole world this amazing news, but if somehow these motherfuckers find out I'm getting married and the beneficiary to my insurance and estate is no longer my mother, but Eva... then they may try to hurt her when I'm not around. I can't let that happen...

Savage slid his phone out of his pocket, and began to text:

Savage: *Dad, I can't come by tomorrow. I have a business trip.*

As he placed his phone back into his pocket, he was surprised to hear it vibrating. Dad rarely returned his texts that fast.

Dad: WTF.

Savage: *LOL. Not now. I need to take care of something.*

Dad: OK. You owe me. I told everyone you would be here. You're a coward. Come face Tommy like a man!

Tommy was one of Dad's MC pals, a brother. Savage had known him since he was a kid but Tommy had scared the shit out of him way back then. He was a good guy, but had a rare birth defect that caused his hands and feet to look like lobster claws. Tommy would chase Savage around, making pinching motions with them like a crustacean, making him cry, and Dad and all of his drunk friends would laugh at the antics until Mom stepped in, demanding they stop.

Ahhh, good times...

Savage: *I'll make it up to you, promise. Love you, crazy old* *man.*

Dad was having a get together he'd promised to attend. His bros were all going to be there, and he'd invited him to join. Savage hadn't seen some of his 'uncles' in a long ass time. He regretted missing it, especially after Dad had let them all know, in no uncertain terms, *'Max is fucking a sister. He's knee-deep in some Black pussy and he isn't coming out of her snatch anytime soon. He loves her. Say anything about it and I'll split your fucking skull open with a rusty razor blade and toss your ass in the Pacific Ocean for shark food. Now, let's get shitfaced.'*

He placed the phone back inside his pocket and smiled at the sight of Zaire and her friends drinking, dancing and acting silly. She glanced up at him and he waved, then blew her a kiss.

Moments later, he checked online for his flight information. Tomorrow morning, he'd be paying some relatives a nice little visit.

It's almost showtime, boys 'nd girls. My mother may care about your acceptance, but I don't give a single fuck about any of you motherfuckers. I'm not a doctor like my soon to be wife, but I sure as hell make house calls. Dr. Savage is about to be in the motherfuckin' building and I know you love money, so I'm about to make it rain...

CHAPTER TWENTY-EIGHT

It Runs in the Family

ALLAPATTAH, MIAMI WASN'T a place where people drifted about late in the evening just for the hell of it. Notwithstanding its rough reputation, Savage felt right at home amongst the grime and grit. Spanish music blasted from the various open windows of the project buildings surrounded by dying palm trees. Some cars were parked in a liquor store parking lot, all of them filled with party people trying to make a dollar out of fifteen cents. He kept on driving, his burner phone in hand, taking in the sights. The strong aroma of cooking pork and blunts full of weed filled the air as he drove past a little general store. A large BBQ pit emitted hazy, fragrant smoke alongside one wall, making his mouth water. He met eyes with a pretty woman, her long dark brown hair covering half her apple-shaped face.

A sizeable group of Dominicans stood huddled together in front of a small store advertising Arizona Iced Tea – buy one get one free. Savage slowly turned the corner in the tan Chevrolet Impala he'd rented at a rather unusual rental car store near the motel he'd checked into under an alias. They specialized in older models, and the place was actually illegal. Their license that was taped haphazardly on the wall was expired, their prices ridiculous, and the car he was in smelled like a million drunks had had a pissing contest inside it. Perfect for his needs.

He traveled closer to the address his mother had given him. His cousins were expecting him, or so they said. He'd feigned excitement twice on the phone, speaking with the bastards in Russian, expressing his jubilation to meet them at last. He was literally driving to his death. Nothing was more beautiful than a meal being brought to a starving lion... no hunting required. Their previous efforts had failed, so now they probably felt like they'd won the lottery. That the God they worshiped and cursed had finally allowed their ship to set sail. He slowed down a bit and glanced at a picture of him and Zaire. Running his thumb along it, he smiled, though his joy was tinged with frustration and concern.

There could be no happy ending. Either there would be a bloodbath, or he would lose his life in the process. He weighed his odds; this was simply the nature of the beast. There was no way they wouldn't try to rob him right then and there and beat his fucking head in, or perhaps they planned to get it over with quick and dirty and simply attempt to shoot him in the face. They'd then bury his body... but not in a remote area. They'd need him to be found so the death certificate could be issued.

I gotta hand it to you motherfuckers, you bided your time, didn't you? You planned this out to the letter. That takes patience and talent. I damn sure can't knock the hustle... Moved to Miami... easier to get in and out of here than California and the price of living is cheaper. Kept your foot on mom's neck, pumping her for information… Sending money back to Armenia and investing the rest in your little project. Saved up enough money to fly a couple of you out to Vegas. That didn't end well though, did it? Tried again with the guy in the van, but whoever that was got freaked out and took off. You were probably devising another plan and couldn't believe your luck when I fell right into your lap. I have to do this for my mother. She deserves to be set free. I have to do it for Zaire and Dad, too…

He leaned over and grabbed the one and only cigarette he had. His lucky cigarette. The poor thing was slightly bent in the middle. He'd decided to stop smoking them several years prior, and this was the last one from the Parliament pack he'd bought back then. He wasn't even quite sure why he'd made that decision. Could have been his father's bronchial issues, the tightness in his chest he'd once felt during a workout, or the thought that, without his health, his job was as good as gone. Regardless, he couldn't completely divorce himself from the flames…

What was the Devil without his inferno-filled lair? Blazes were simply a part of his life; they were painted on two of his motorcycles and etched upon his body. His cigars, on the other hand, he refused to part with; they'd become second nature, his shadow in need of the light. Twisting and turning the lucky cigarette about in between his fingers, he grabbed an old BIC lighter and flicked it.

Let's see what's on the radio… He blew swirls of smoke out the corner of his mouth, turned the knob on the transistor and out of a scratchy speaker came 'International Players Anthem' by Outkast and UGK.

I haven't heard this in a long time. Let me turn this shit up.

He turned it up to full volume, pulled his dark shades down over his eyes and bobbed his head to the music. Taking his time, driving slow, he passed a bunch of whores and drug addicts who were eyeballing him.

He ran his hand over his low-cut black waves and smiled when he spotted two people begin to dance to the music pouring out of the car. Soon, the song switched to UGK's 'Diamonds and Wood'.

Only in Miami. They're playing a bunch of UGK songs from yesteryear... Wow.

Nasty, beautiful memories flooded his mind of some of the orgies he'd had to such music. Harlem had introduced him to some of these hits. He'd never been a big rap fan until he started to travel more. Then, some of the songs felt so damn good to his soul, he kept them close to his heart.

That shit was fun back in the day. I've moved on though, gotta beautiful ass woman who knows how to fuck the shit outta me... makes sure I get my dick wet when I need it...

As he drew closer to the address, he assessed the area, his eyes moving about like tiny cameras, snapping his surroundings in a series of memory shots. He parked between two cars, one of which was on blocks.

It's dark as hell here. Perfect. The street was dark, and that included the apartment buildings and small houses around him. He raised one of his cellphones and used the Flashlight app to illuminate the area. A car door opened up the street, allowing some light to streak the road like a line of piss. He sat there for a moment, then grabbed his phone and called Harlem.

"If you don't hear from me when you're supposed to, drop that dime."

"Got it. Ride out, mothafucka."

Savage ended the call, grabbed a small suitcase, and got out of the car. Black boots on his feet, dark jeans, metal chain belt, and a leather jacket over a white wifebeater, he made his way towards the apartment building, cigarette dangling out of the side of his mouth. A few people yelled to get his attention. Ignoring them, he kept his mind on his money and his money on his mind. Soon, he was at the door, crushing his cigarette beneath his boot. He gave the door three big bangs and waited a moment or two. A short guy with straight black hair, light tan skin, and bright green eyes answered it.

"Ты семья? (Ty sem'ya)? (Are you family?)"

"Я твой двоюродный брат, Maximus Savage. (I'm your cousin, Maximus Savage.)"

The man's face lit up as he reached out to give him a hug. The guy smelled of oil and sweat. He called out to everyone in that tiny space and walked him inside the small, crowded room filled with cigarette smoke. A studio apartment, one space housing a living area and bedroom combo, a small bathroom in the corner, and a kitchenette no bigger than the inside of a mid-sized truck. The television was playing commercials, and about five other men, all with dark hair, sat at a table on folding lawn chairs, eating fries, burgers, and a shitload of ketchup packets. The other men in the room smiled and waved, talking over one another to vie for his consideration. But one in particular drew his attention. His eyes turned to dark slits as he chewed a burger slowly, hatred drawn all across his face. The man placed the food down, never saying a word. He lit a cigarette and drew on it, the scowl on his face growing bigger by the second.

I have to keep my eye on him. He's going to cause me problems.

All of them introduced themselves, offering their names.

"How was trip?" the man who'd answered the door asked in broken English, offering him something in a red plastic cup. Savage accepted it and pretended to take a sip, then set it down on a nearby stool.

"It was good."

"Down to business now," the tall, big man with anger in his eyes stated, cutting the little happy-go-lucky party short.

"Down to business we go…" Savage smiled. "So, uh, my mother, your Aunt Karina, told me everything. She's been talking to several members of the family and understands the situation. She made me aware of it." He rocked back on his heels, playing his part in this ridiculous after school play. "As I told you on the phone, I can help. We're family." Two of the men quickly nodded in understanding, eagerness in their eyes. The one with the evil glare kept his eyes on the suitcase in his hand, barely blinking. "I don't think it should take too long to get you guys squared away."

"Karina say you rich." One of them chuckled. "How nice. She not say what job… Can we work where you work?"

Most of them burst out laughing, including Savage. He shrugged.

"I work in investments. Property, casinos… things like that."

They oohed and ahhed, as if impressed with his answer.

"Very good!" one said, showing a missing tooth. "Karina's living good life." The man sounded as if he, too, should be living a good life simply by association.

"Yeah, things are good. So, uh, let me explain something to you." Savage hesitated, pretending to not know what to say next. "You got into the country easy, but moving around the country, from state to state or even right here in Florida, won't be as easy without getting I.D.s. Eventually, your luck will run out. What we can do is—"

"Where is the money? We need the money. Show money, talk later," The brooding one set his cigarette down in an ashtray, wiped his hands on his pants and stood to his feet.

"I have the money, but we need to go over some things first."

"I want to see it. Now." The other cousins began to yell at the guy, speaking all over each other in Russian and telling him to be patient, that his behavior was no way to treat a guest. A bunch of bullshit, when Savage knew damn well they all felt the same.

"Why are you in such a hurry, Grigor?" Savage asked with a smile. "Money won't solve your problems until you know how to ensure you won't be busted by immigration."

"No trust you."

"Well." Savage crossed his arms and smirked. "I don't trust you either, Grigor, but luckily, trust doesn't really have shit to do with this. It's about family, and doing what's right by our loved ones… making sure they're not abandoned and forgotten like trash." His eyes narrowed on the big motherfucker that kept his gaze on him and his suitcase. "Now, as I was saying, we can—"

Suddenly, the man pulled a gun out and aimed it straight

at Savage's head.

"Put case down on floor."

Savage assessed his options in quickfire spurts, then slow-ly placed the suitcase down and lifted his hands in the air as the man drew near. The man picked up the case and studied the lock, then dropped it back down on the floor.

"Open case."

"I'm fucking sick of you, you know that? You should be thanking me, mate. Since you know so much, jolly Albanian giant, *you* fuckin' open it." Grigor slapped him across the face with the butt of the gun. Savage tasted blood in his mouth, and throbbing pain came when he rubbed on his jaw. He never backed down from the man's gaze. The others kept silent. In fact, being the betting man that he was, Savage surmised they were seeing exactly what they all wanted. A nice little show before the final blow.

"Grigor." Savage spat blood out onto the floor. "You're makin' me think you don't really want my help. What happened to the welcome wagon? I feel like you may just want to take the money and run, end our happy family reunion. I thought we were семья (family)?" Grigor cocked the gun against his head and the click of the trigger echoed in the room.

"I kill you. Open case. Final time."

Savage finally nodded. "I definitely don't want to rattle your chain."

Snatching his chain belt off, he hooked it around the gun and swung it across the room, hitting the wall. Then, in a flash, he lassoed the chain around the big fucker's neck with one hand and grabbed one of his guns with the other.

"AHHH! FUCK!"

Suddenly, two other guns were pointed in his direction while the guys hurled threats in Russian.

"I will snap his fuckin' neck! Did ya get that, fam? I'm certain you understand those words loud and clear! Now, put the motherfuckin' guns down and kick 'em towards me or I will rip his head clean off his shoulders, and give a whole new meaning to a 'head start'!"

The fuckers did as instructed, fear and confusion on their faces. He yanked on the chain wrapped around the bastard's neck and spun him around to face the crowd, causing him to turn a deep shade of purple and choke as he kicked the guns behind him.

BAM!

The big man fell back, causing pandemonium in the room as he yanked him then shot him three times in the back. Savage grabbed his two Glocks from his jacket and began to blast everything in sight. It took no time for the place to be bathed in splashes of red. He killed everyone before they even had a chance to process what was happening.

He checked inside the bathroom, ensuring no one was waiting to pop out of there and surprise him. The coast was clear, minus a porno magazine and a bottle of lotion lying by the sink across from the stopped-up toilet. He found a middle-aged man cowering in the corner in the kitchen, his face bloodied, shaking and waving his hands in surrender. Savage stepped over the bodies, one by one, riddling them with bullets as he walked past, making it rain...

"There's the insurance policy, motherfucker. I just made

sure all of you got dead as doorknobs," he muttered under
his breath.

When he reached the sole survivor, the one with chatter-
ing teeth, he looked down at him and shook his head.
Stooping low, he brought his face closer until they were at
eye level.

"Maxzeemus... I know nothing, my friend... nothing!"
the man blubbered.

"Shhh, it's okay..." He patted his head. "Antonjo, just
listen," Savage stated quietly, placing a finger up to the man's
dry and cracked lips. "For forty years, you've destroyed a
woman. That's my fuckin' mother!!!"

"Ahhhh, no, no, no!" the man cried out.

"A woman who in desperation reached out to her family.
She forgave you, but forgiveness should never be free. That's
a lesson my mother has to learn and she will once I let her
know how her fuckin' family tried to kill me. That's the
funny thing about death, ya know? Her parents are dead, the
grandparents I never met, the same ones who sold 'er, so she
clung to her sisters and brothers, once she found them.
Really, anyone who's in the family over there she held tight
to... Even though I suspect deep down she became skeptical
of you all sometimes, her need to be wanted and loved by
you all overshadowed that doubt. Once she told you all that
she was living in the States, had food on the table, a decent
home – your interest was piqued.

"You would get a bit of money here and there from her,
just enough to take the edge off. It was a good deal. For forty
years, you've lied, tormented, manipulated, stole, guilted, and
robbed from her, her son, and her husband. My parents

never had a whole lot of money, but they had way more than you all. You've robbed her of her hopes, her dreams, and replaced them with silly fantasies. You've caused friction between my parents because my father is a realist, and my mother has bought into a delusion that you convinced her was real but was actually fool's gold. You played on her insecurities." He leaned over and flipped on the radio then removed the silencer on the gun. The tune of 'Get Throwed' by Pimp C was playing.

"I wanna hear this shit... Not the song, but your screams from my gun rippin' you to pieces. You ever think about how good fucking sounds a lot like someone losing their life?" Savage laughed. "You know, when you're really drillin' a chick, right? Giving it to her, pumping that pussy until her back busts out, and she's screaming her head off and begging, pleading, but she loves it so fuckin' much, right? It feels so fucking good and her yells just turn you on... I love that shit, and I love it when people like you beg me to not do it... to not kill them... You scream and yell, beg for your life. I love the sounds of a good kill and fantastic fuck. It's a beautiful thing.

"I want *every*one to hear me fuck you *all* the way up. I don't give a shit about anything else right now... Gotta get my fix. I'm addicted to murder." He winked at the man. "Anyway, as I was saying." He snatched a cigarette out of the bastard's shirt pocket and jammed it in his mouth. "For forty years, you motherfuckers plotted, schemed, and planned to destroy my mother, to take all she had. The final blow would be slaughtering her son."

"No! We weren't... we weren't going to kill you, friend!"

"I'm not your fuckin' friend. I'm not your family. I'm your foe, and don't you forget it. See, you'd earned my mother's trust, did and said just the right shit to get her to believe in you. Then, by the time she got my assets, she'd slide you all some, give you a bunch of my money because you'd trained her well." Savage placed the gun under the bastard's chin and forced his face upward, eyes towards the ceiling, then lit the cigarette and blew out rings of smoke in his face.

The man's eyes sheened over and he swallowed hard, his Adam's apple bobbing. He appeared to be hanging on to his sanity by a slippery thread. "See, though my maternal side of the family is very resourceful, I'm actually quite impressed with what you all managed to accomplish. You guys forgot though that your blood runs through my veins, too. I'm *just* as calculating as you, times one hundred. I'm just as ruthless and dangerous as you, times one thousand. I have no conscience, too, like you, times one million... See? You played yourself.

"Guess what? I *do* have investments, but my main ones aren't properties, shit like that. I'm an assassin." The man shut his eyes and winced, knowing damn well it was a wrap. There was nothing he could say or do. "I'm not bragging when I tell you that I'm one of the best ones in the country. Hell, the world. No one can shoot faster than me, mother-fucker, or think as fast on their feet and cover their tracks in seconds. I'm like a damn cat with nine lives. In your own way, you all created me. It was the perfect recipe. I'm a trained and sanctioned killer runnin' rogue, this time on a mission of my own."

"No… No!"

"Oh, yes, yes!" Savage cackled. "It's true, loved one! See, I can make *all* of this disappear, this little blood bath here. It'll be like none of you ever fucking existed and if for some dumb ass reason any more of you decide to harass my mother, pay her a visit or seek revenge for my having to wipe out this entire rotting branch of the family tree, then they'll get worse than you, as hard to imagine as that may be. When the bough breaks, the fuckin' cradle will fall…" Savage shrugged. "I have special connections, people you have no clue about who know a whole lot about you, and they'll keep tabs on every one of you people back in Albania that decides to get any crazy ideas. Forty years of bullshit, my man… And now, the time is finally up." He jammed the gun harder against his chin, ready to pull the trigger.

"Please! Please, my friend!" The man shook as he lifted his hands in the air. "I did nothing. I promise you! Never receive money, I just came! We're family, you're my friend! I'm small, small piece, small man. Small fish! Not worth it. I will go away, never come back! Please!"

"Well." Savage stood to his full height and sighed. "As the Albanian saying goes, I'm a great man. Peshku i madh ha të voglin. (Men are like fish; the great ones devour the small.)

BAM!

Savage stared at the semi-decapitated head, the thing split open like a pelican's mouth swallowing down a frog. The skull was fractured like a walnut, all the brain matter falling out. He stepped away from the bastard and stood in the middle of the room, the floor littered with dead blood relatives. He'd wiped them out so quickly, they probably never even felt it — their lifeforce sucked out before their brain and heart had a chance to catch up.

Blood on the wall…

Blood in the carpet…

Blood on the ceiling and furniture…

Blood sprayed on the television…

He checked each and every pulse. All gone.

He casually pulled out his phone and dialed Harlem.

"Wanna hear a bedtime story, Harlem?"

"Tuck me in…"

"Did I ever tell you the tale of a White trash Vagos MC murderous convict who fell in love with a beautiful, cold-hearted Albanian whore and bore a son of a bitch who dreamed of spilling blood, morning, noon, and night? They were Savages… This time, it has a happy ending…"

CHAPTER TWENTY-NINE

Big White Snake

S AVAGE SUCKED HIS teeth as he sat wide-legged in the living room, the San Francisco 49ers game in session on the tube at his parent's home. He played with a pair of Feng Shui silver and black balls that helped him pass the time. The metal spheres clicked and clacked together like chimes and tinkling wedding bells whistling in the wind. Mom sat across from him in a gray loveseat, her back straight, like a board. Her long legs crossed, hands clasped around her knees, her expression was ordinary, but there were tears in her eyes.

"And after today, to never speak of it again. Settled," she finally said in a somber whisper after several minutes had passed.

Savage nodded lazily and vaguely shifted his attention to the game. The balls in his hand kept rotating back and forth, back and forth, until he'd had enough and placed them beside him on the gray couch. Reaching for his dark sunglasses atop his head, he snatched them off and relocated them onto the coffee table. He was getting sleepy. The day had been rather mundane with the exception of his mother trying to keep herself together after being told of the fate some of her family members had faced.

As weariness took the reins, he heard his mother's breathing, so hard yet contained, as if she were trying to keep from hyperventilating. He shot her a glance from the corner of his eye, making certain she didn't suddenly go completely bat shit.

She made loud inhales and exhales, but then she calmed down, to the point he could no longer hear her breathing at all. For all he knew, the woman was fighting a now silent panic attack. It wouldn't have been the first time. Mom remained quiet for several minutes, then broke her silence with a bang.

"Сволочь! If he comes my way, I will shoot him between the eyes." She said it so casually, calling her brother a jerk, the sound of her voice like a feather fluttering in the air.

The man, she'd found out, had masterminded this entire fiasco. She'd never met him when she was still in Armenia. In fact, she'd never known he existed until her sister told her about him. He was a well-known criminal in their home country, a thief and swindler, and as his mother now knew, a double-crossing bastard. Savage would do anything to take away that pain, the sense of devastation she was experiencing that had little to do with money.

"So, did Dad tell you all who were involved?" She nodded. "It goes deeper than the ones that were in Miami. They'd been planning this for probably over a year."

"But there's more. Always more...They know what you do now, your work, Maximus." Her hands shook as she raked them through her hair. "They're afraid. They call me, ask me to not do anything. Say that I got what I wanted… They say, many of their sons dead, some first born. I tell them to fuck off… I tell them, what about *my* son?!" Mom's voice trembled as she pointed to herself. "Max, they say they're scared you will come again, after them."

"As they should be." He kept rotating those balls, back and forth, and a mean heat frothed from his cool core.

Mom withdrew into her shell again.

"I have the tickets for the pawn shop. T.V., jewelry… I get my things soon." She lifted her chin high as she stared absently at the television.

"I'll give you the money to get them out."

"No. I must do myself. My fault. All my fault." She hung her head for a brief spell. "Your father come to me in the night. He say, 'Karina… our son, our boy, go down to Miami just like he tell you. They wanted to kill our boy…' Your father take his two hands, he tear the house apart. Broken glass everywhere… anger, never seen him so angry. Not like this. He say to me, 'If they had killed our boy, I never forgive you, Karina. I love you, but I never forgive you if they did that…' And I know he meant it. You and he, so special." She smiled sadly. "Your father have a connection with you… different than with me. Your father laugh. He sing. He dance. He fight, and fight some more. He party and drink. He kill. Such passion. That's why I love him, my dear Maximus. He lives out loud. Like you." She turned to him and smiled ever so slightly.

Maximus nodded as he watched tears quietly fall down his mother's cheeks. He'd seldom seen her cry. It had to be a culmination of things bubbling forth within her. She'd already lost so much, and almost lost more than she'd bargained for.

"I look like you; I act like Dad. The best of both worlds." He grinned, making her laugh then. She swiped her knuckle against the side of her eye, mopping up the tears.

"Yes, true." She slowly got to her feet. "I have the food ready, and plenty of drinks, too. But, it's early."

"Yeah." Maximus glanced at his cellphone on the coffee table, noting the time. "I don't understand why you made all of that though for just the four of us. Anyway, Eva should be here, soon. She's excited to meet you both. When do you think Dad will back?" he asked as she walked away into the kitchen.

"Very soon."

Savage drifted off to slumber on the couch, only to be awakened by Zaire who'd made it to his parents' home. She had on a green jumpsuit with a white shirt beneath it. Her hair was pulled back in a taut ponytail, draped down her back, and she wore black Mary Jane high heels. She looked smart and sexy at the same time, like a librarian who was secretly sporting edible panties. He grinned at her, rubbed his eyes, and attempted to get to his feet to give her a hug and kiss. She pushed him back before he got a chance to move and kissed him on the lips. She shook a finger at him.

"Relax. You must be tired."

"How'd you get in here? I'm calling the police," he teased.

She laughed and playfully slapped his shoulder.

"Your mother let me in, silly. For the record, she and I

have been talking for a while. We let you sleep."

"You couldn't have talked long. I've only been asleep for like, five minutes, ten tops."

"You must've had been in a coma then, boy, because you've been asleep for over an hour! I have been here for a minute."

He looked around, amazed. He'd truly lost track of time. *Damn… I really was exhausted.*

"That's crazy. I need some real sleep tonight then."

"You were out like a light, snoring and all." She laughed, tickled so. "Your mother, oh my God, Max. She's beautiful!" Zaire added in a whisper, her expression serious. "You two favor, you know that? What a physically stunning woman. She seems nice, too."

"Yeah… to this day she makes a lot of guys half her age do double takes. My Dad always jokes she must've been drunk when she let him take her home. All right." He yawned, getting to his feet at last. "Moooom!" he called out. "Is Dad here yet? I don't hear him so he must not be." He yawned again and scratched his head then stretched.

"He's not here yet." His mother's voice was faint, as if she were at the back of the house.

"We need to call him then. He's late! Probably got arrested again for some bar fight. I swear he goes looking for guys to fuck with." He worked out a kink in his neck. "Get comfortable and have a seat, baby." He pointed to the couch. Several minutes later, they were cuddled up, sipping on wine coolers, when he heard the roar of a motorcycle, then another, and another.

"Did you hear that? Sounds like someone is outside,"

Zaire said.

"Yeah, I heard it." Before he could figure out what the hell was going on, the doorbell rang. His brows furrowed as he set his drink down on a motorcycle shaped coaster and got to his feet. "Mooom! Expectin' anyone?"

Dad wouldn't ring his own damn bell. Plus, the car was missing in his garage. He didn't take any of his bikes.

"No, I'm not expecting anyone." He heard the quick pitter patter of mom's bare feet as she made her way up the hall.

"Stay back," he said to the women when his mom arrived in the living room.

Gun drawn, he cautiously approached the front door. Muted voices drifted through and shadows moved about as he inched the thick curtains back from the front foyer area window. "It's my uncles! What the hell are they doing here?!" Savage laughed as he quickly unlocked the door and swung it open. On the front lawn stood about twelve Harleys and as many of dad's MC brethren. The men were rowdy as hell, some flicking joints into the lawn. In moments, they all trudged inside the house without invitation. Of course, they didn't really need it. They were *true* family. Abruptly snatched up like a piece of trash from the floor, he was drawn in multiple bear hugs while the smell of sweat, worn leather, and pure fuckery filled the place.

"Ahhhh! Max! My main man!" Chopper said as he took his turn and grabbed him, putting him in a loose, playful headlock. Chopper had a big, shiny bald head with a dragon tattoo on the side of it. The beast was about six foot seven and his voice was deep and gravelly. Many of the guys stood around high-fiving one another. Removing their sunglasses in a collective gesture, they stored them inside their jacket or pant pockets. Bandanas were tightened, belts loosened, and the atmosphere was bursting with instantaneous jubilation.

Soon, they were all sitting or standing in the living room, all of their damn eyes glued to Zaire, who seemed a bit nervous, averting eye contact. Mom passed out chilled bottles of beer as the guys made small talk, but it was clear that Zaire was the subject of their fascination.

"So." Chopper twirled his black handlebar mustache threaded with silver, pinching the ends between his fingers and rolling it to a fine point. "You and my nephew gettin' married, huh?"

"Yes. Yes, we are." Zaire answered proudly, her head held high now. Savage placed his arm around her and dragged her closer as they sat side by side on the couch.

"Mad Dog told us a while back that you were with her, Max."

"I know." Savage picked up the remote control and flipped channels.

"So, what's up? What do you two have in common?"

"Are you a dating specialist now? Some kind of marriage counselor? What is this? An intervention or some shit?" He smirked and shook his head. Chopper was used to people bowing down to him and feeling intimidated. Savage adored the man, but he was going to put a stop to this shit before it got started.

"Nah, your dad invited us over." Savage nodded in understanding. "And you don't have to worry about anything, I don't really have a problem with Blacks." The big man crossed his tattooed arms and stared at her.

"Chopper, cut the shit."

"Max, I'm talkin' to the little lady." The guy cleared his throat, and his gaze narrowed on her.

Zaire sat a bit taller and smiled.

"That's good that you don't *really* have a problem with Blacks. I would've spent every waking moment of the rest of my life tossing and turning, concerned about a man I don't even know by the name of Chopper taking issue with me." A few snickers filled the room. "You don't have to worry, either, Mr. Chopper. I don't *really* have a problem with big White guys with silly oversized mustaches that make them look like the Pringle's chip man, either. It's a damn good day to be unbothered."

Savage looked away, squelching a bout of laugher by catching his nose between his fingers and pressing his eyes shut, thrilled at her response. That was his baby, one of the many reasons why he was in love with her. A smattering of laughter filled the room, then grew louder. Chopper smirked and just glared at her for a moment or two, more than likely biting his tongue, then shook his head and burst out laughing, too.

"You've got a mouth on you, lady. That's good though." The man smiled, and it smelled genuine. "You can't be around us or with my nephew and not be able to hold your own. He's just like us. He's good as blood. Whatever happens to him, his mother, or his dad, we take seriously."

Just then, the front door swung open and Dad entered with two cases of beer and grocery bags draped over his arms.

"Fuck, man!" The old man chortled, his face red from the strain of lugging all that shit inside solo. Chopper got to his feet and a few of the other guys rushed to assist. "Get the chips 'nd shit outta my car, I've got ice cream in there, too. Hurry, it'll melt."

"Why'd you go get this shit, Mad Dog?" Acorn squawked. He was a newer guy, younger and small in stature. "I thought you said everything was already here?"

"It was, or I thought it was until I looked at what tha fuck she had out on the counter. I told Karina to just pick up some party shit, you know, the usual stuff, but instead she made some gotdamn wheat crackers with this pink fluffy cheese shit and black and green olive salad with corn on the cob in it. I say to her, 'What in the cream of corn hell is olive salad with fuckin' corn?!' It looked like a bunch of green titties on top of some lettuce!" Loud chuckles rippled throughout the room. "She had some bean dip, too, and it didn't look right, either. It was ass juice in a bowl.

"If I wanted to eat ass I would just spread 'er cheeks and go to town! Wouldn't have been the first time. I'm a proud ass eater, but don't lie to me and tell me it's bean dip… fuck outta here." Pockets of laughter burst in the room. "So, here I am, and that's where I've been." He huffed, looking exhausted. "I had to go out and get somethin' we could *really* chow down on, that's all," Dad said breathlessly.

He started to walk again, then suddenly stopped in his tracks. His lips curled in a big grin when his gaze settled on Zaire. She got to her feet.

"Hey, Dad. This is my baby… this is Zaire."

"Whew! That's what I'm talkin' 'bout! Pretty hair, too…

Is that all of your hair, baby? Because if my son tugs on it while he's givin' it to ya from the back, it would be a fucking shame if it slid off."

"What?! Excuse me?"

"You heard me, sexy chocolate thing, you." *I can't believe this shit... On second thought, yes I can.* "Can't play pony with a bitch that looks like Sinéad O'Connor... Gotta pretend to be an Indian 'cause ain't shit there but scalp. Whew! My son sure knows how to pick 'em!" Dad's smile was downright disturbing as he ogled her. "I bet you've got some sweet black pus—"

"Dad. Dad, no... no fuckin' way." Enough was enough. "Come on, now. Don't do this shit. She's not going to dig that sense of humor. Control yourself," Savage barked, putting a stop to the shit before the old man got going and ruined the whole damn day. He was a hypocrite, true, and he'd been no different in his style of talking to women when he was single, but that was beside the point. With a big, shit-eating grin, Dad quickly took Zaire in his arms, giving her a nice hug, as if he hadn't just been standing there acting like a senseless degenerate.

"Nice to finally meet cha, Zaire. Do you prefer Eva or Zaire?"

"Either one. I use Zaire for online, the podcast. It's my middle name. But either works for me," she stated in her professional sounding voice.

"Hmm, you talk like you're on air right now. Sound like a newscaster. The last time I was this close to a newscaster I was being led outta the courthouse on my way to jail in 2004 for stranglin' a pedo with a fuckin' teddy bear. I took the bear and wrapped it around his gotdamn neck! Put the squeeze on 'im! The fear of Gawd!"

Zaire's eyes grew large and she stepped back when Dad got all in her face. She forced a smile then nodded as he simmered down in an instant. *I warned her my old man is fucking crazy.*

"That… that's horrible. That the man would prey upon children, not the teddy bear, per se." She nervously cleared her throat and clasped her hands.

"But I'm the bad guy, right?!" Dad yelled, the veins in his neck straining. "He was in Target showin' his weenie to a little girl in the toy aisle so I made sure he got more than the bottom basement deal he bargained for. Bet he wished he'd been a Toys R Us kid that day! See, I saw how he was watchin' her, lookin' at her, so I followed him. Sure enough, he was up to no fucking good but I got arrested for assault! Can you believe that shit?! What about him tryna sell hotdogs to kids, huh?! Fuckin' sickos ruining the world! America is full of 'em, buncha pansy fuckity fuckheads doing weird ass shit! Line their asses up and get the firing squad! Who can look at a kid and get their rocks off?! Burn them all in Hell!"

"Pretend to be normal. You're going to scare Max's fiancée away. Horrible! No more talk like that," Mom snapped as she entered the room.

"*I'm* gonna scare Max's fiancée away?!" Dad pointed to himself as he glared at the woman. "Have you seen your son, Karina?! If *he* hasn't scared her away then nothin' I say or do could be much worse!" Dad ranted and raved, trying to defend himself as he followed behind her in the kitchen. The brethren walked to and fro, delivering bags of groceries to the kitchen. Scorpion, an older guy who had twin boys Maximus had grown up with, was a fair skinned guy with long platinum blond hair parted in two braids. His small muscles strained as he carted a big, heavy cake under a plastic dome in his hands, trying to watch his step. He slowed down, checked Zaire out, and winked.

"Nice to meet you. Don't be intimidated. You're safe with us, sweetheart." And then he went on his way.

Zaire crossed her arms. "You warned me they were some characters, but oh boy!" She laughed, shaking her head. "And you grew up around this your whole life, huh?"

"I sure did... proud I did, too. Most of these guys are amazing, Eva, loyal to a fault. Some have come and gone, some were killed – ones that I really looked up to. I still think about them. This is my family. There's nothing like a MC's funeral, Eva. It's wild. I hope you never have to attend one with me but that's impossible. You will. Some had drug overdoses, some moved away, some are incarcerated for life but the ones still here, I really value them and the ones that are alive but just going in another direction with their lives, I appreciate their influence in my life. When my dad was locked up, they were here, and vice versa. My dad was *that* motherfucker, Eva."

She put a hand on his arm, her eyes full of understanding.

"He takes care of people. It's just what he does. Half the time he was in jail or prison was for gun or assault charges. The other times? Trying to help another motherfucker out by any means necessary. If he had five dollars, he would give his brother four ninety-nine of it if he needed it. They all have a lot of respect for my dad, even some of the newer guys coming in because my dad doesn't take any shit, never backs down. He is a father figure to all the younger dudes and he's earned his stripes."

Just then, Dad came walking towards them, tilting a beer can to his mouth.

"All jokes aside, let me cut straight to the shit." He threw his head back and took a big swig. "If you hear anyone talk about you bein' Black in a negative way, come to me, all right, sugar?" He tapped on his barrel chest and winked at Eva.

She smiled and nodded. "Okay."

"I'll take care of it. It's just different for some of 'em is all. Some of 'em don't believe in race mixing, but will act respectful because they know if they don't, I will rearrange their fucking face. Some of 'em don't give a shit about any of that mess. As long as Max is happy, they're happy, just like me and his mother feel. Some of 'em don't see what the big deal is; they didn't even blink an eye but ya see, we live in a crazy world, Eva. I addressed this ahead of time so there would be less of a chance of something happening."

"We do live in a crazy world. Lots of things happening that shouldn't be."

"Oh, they should be." His brow arched as he took a hard gulp of his beer. "See, everything happening in this world was pre-written, meant to be. We set this wheel in motion. We can either fall in line, or we can fuck up and deal with the repercussions. We're animals, savages… My last name means a lot to me. It tells the truth." Dad's eyes grew steely. "If we, as people, regardless of our race or religious beliefs, put that shit aside and just realized we all want the same things in life, it would all be a hell of a lot easier but see, that's make-believe.

"That's not how *real* men move. Somebody has to be on top. People hate to be on the bottom. Been that way since the beginning of time. The only way we get do-overs is through our kids. My son here was my second chance." Dad grabbed him by the collar and pulled him close. Savage grinned, knowing his father was in the beginning stages of being drunk off his ass. "See, Eva, my father was a poor man. He was also a strict man, a tough man. Me and my brothers and sisters couldn't do shit right in his eyes. He felt like it was weakness to hug your kids, tell 'em you love them. Now, in fairness to my father, that was a different time period though, but I had vowed to never be that type of dad. Not to my daughter, Max's half-sister Shauna, or my son here.

"Max knows who his old man is. He knows I can get upset. He knows I would turn this entire fuckin' planet upside down for him, his mother and Shauna, too." Zaire's eyes welled with emotion and he sent her a silent message of love. "Now, here it is, all laid out on the table… Because my son is about to marry you, that'll make you my and Karina's daughter-in-law. The 'in-law' part is bullshit. It's just daughter. You're a member of this family starting today." Dad's expression turned dead serious. "Do you understand me, sweetheart?"

"Yes, I do." Zaire smiled.

"Good. 'Cause ain't shit going down for you or my son that's not kosher, without me knowin' about it. So, you're gonna bring your pretty ass in this kitchen and eat with all of us. I've got all sorts of shit, you name it. I bought fried chicken too, all right, but don't turn that into some racist shit because my White ass *loves* fried chicken!" Savage and Eva burst out laughing. The man was truly a piece of work. "I'm serious." Dad chuckled. "You're beautiful. Really."

"Thank you…"

"My son loves ya and he says you're smart 'nd funny. That's all I needed to hear." Dad took her by the hand, and the three walked into the kitchen. It was loud and boisterous in there, a party being had. "HEEEY! You nutsacks, listen the fuck up! In case you missed it, this is my son's surprise engagement party, all right?!"

"YEAH!!!"

"All right!" the guys cheered.

"Eva here is going to break bread with us. Her father is a firefighter and her mother a former beauty queen!" Eva giggled as several of the men clapped and whistled. "So, treat 'er right, get to know her, be nice 'nd shit. Let's eat!" One of the guys turned the radio up and Kansas' 'Carry On Wayward Son' was the first song to drift through. Zaire stood next to Mom, and they chatted while they fixed their plates… Savage took a moment to drink in that beautiful scene.

Eva, you're in. My Dad likes you, and he is a hard sell. Welcome to my crazy family. I love you, baby. This feels right. This is definitely where you're supposed to be. Right here, with all of us…

...Three months later

HE SURE WAS hungry.

"So, I think we can leave that over there," Eva said to one of the movers, who placed her vast collection of expensive perfumes near the vanity she'd just had delivered from the furniture store. The guy exited the bedroom while Savage sat on the edge of the bed, cutting into a green apple. He popped a slice into his mouth. "Thank you." She waved to another mover before he headed out. "I haven't moved in a while... Damn." She brought her shirt up to her face and wiped the sweat from her brow. "This shit is aggravating."

"If you would sit the fuck down and let them do their job, Eva, maybe it wouldn't be." He sliced once again into the juicy fruit. "Payin' all this money for what? For you to supervise their every move? You're in the way. Sit down. Take a load off."

"You know, you can jump up and help at any time. I like to be proactive about these things."

"Why in the hell should I lift a finger when I already had to go through extra measures to make sure you had everything you needed before you moved in here? You literally handed me a list of shit... 'Savage, have the walls painted this boring ass cream color. I want all axes and medieval styled décor removed. No black toilets. Get rid of the bearskin rug. Stock the refrigerator with sparkling water for my friends and me, and on and on… You're high fucking maintenance. I did all of that. It's done, so if I wanna sit here and eat this fuckin' apple and not lift one finger to help motherfuckers we already paid a shitload of money to so they can help you relocate, then I won't. Are you hungry?" He shook the apple at her.

"You're an asshole and no, I'm not hungry, so you can keep your little apple."

"I wasn't giving you any of my fuckin' apple. I had some sausage for you…" She sneered as he pointed below his waist. "Don't pretend to be a vegetarian now. It even comes with its own sauce. Been a few days since you had this dick in your mouth." He chuckled. "That's a three for one deal – you'd be finally silent and satisfied and I'd be happy, too. Win-win situation."

"I can't stand you right now, Savage." She chuckled. "And I hope you choke." Her eyes narrowed and then she winked. Showing him her middle finger, she turned to exit the room.

"I love you too, baby." He chortled.

A few hours later, things had finally quieted down. The movers were gone, their big truck vacated the premises and he was in the living room with Dorothy, his big albino snake. The snake was wrapped around his arm, her smooth scales gliding along the tattoos and muscles of his form. He kept a gun magazine open with one hand while he pet her with the other.

"Okay." He heard the shuffle of Eva's slippers as she drew near. "Looks like if we take that one light out of the closet and replace it with the one I showed you the other day, it should… Ahhh! Oh my God!" He smiled at her. "Savage! I told you to not have that damn snake around me!"

"She wasn't. We were in *here*… you were up *there*." He pointed to the staircase, a smirk on his face.

"I was fooled! I only learned two weeks ago you had a damn snake as a pet! I had no idea we had a roommate! She has to go, Savage! If she accidentally gets out of her cage while you are away for work, I am not going to be responsible for wrangling her up and putting her back."

"Dorothy isn't goin' any damn where. I've had her for four years and I told you if that happens again, just call that guy's number I gave ya and he'll come over and get 'er." He turned around and flipped another page of his magazine. "Besides, she's a harmless python. Aren't you, Dorothy?" he said in a baby voice as he brought her in for a kiss.

"Disgusting." The woman huffed and retreated to the kitchen.

After a while, he placed the gorgeous reptile back in her large cage he kept in a small spare room that was painted with a jungle mural. Yes, Dorothy was worthy of her own digs.

"I'll get you some more mice tonight. You've probably just finished digesting the last one," he said. He had some frozen ones in a special freezer that also housed fish bait and things of that nature.

When he walked back down the hall, he spotted Eva in the kitchen making a smoothie. She'd already sliced a couple of bananas and strawberries, and a bag of prewashed spinach sat on the counter near small containers of almond milk and cream. She wore a silky white robe, over panties and a bra, and she'd just taken a shower. Wet tendrils of hair cascaded down her shoulders and back.

She shook her ass to 'P.Y.T. – Pretty Young Thing' by Michael Jackson that played on the radio as she worked.

That shower she took was a waste of time. I'm getting some ass...

He began to rock to the beat and snap his fingers as he paraded towards her. She looked at him and burst out laughing.

"Turn that up, baby." She obliged and they started to dance and carry on together. "I think we might deserve the sexiest couple of the year award."

"Max, you are actually on beat!" she teased.

"I told you I know some moves! Not all White people have two left feet. I don't know why you keep being surprised... I can dance! I'm the one that taught you how to Salsa."

He grinned, moving his pelvis close to hers until he had her backed in a corner... The same corner she'd pushed him in when she'd torn his walls down, made him spill his guts. He wrapped his arms around her and brought her closer for a kiss. Her smile slowly faded, and his lust grew and growled... He picked her up in his arms and led her to the couch in a hurry, his dick saluting her through his damn jogging pants. In a flash, he was naked and had her on her back, legs wide open and her feet resting on his shoulders.

"Shiiit!" She bit into her lower lip when he sucked on her pussy, dispensing sluggish tongue prods in the warm, gushy hole between her soft thighs. Prince now crooned 'When Doves Cry' on the '80s R&B station. Rotating his tongue back and forth over her clit, he jolted when she quaked against him, coming undone.

"Eating your pussy like I eat my apples..." A stream of her nectar dripped from his lower lip. "One juicy nibble at a time..." Starting from the base of her nature, he raked his tongue all the way to the top, over and over, making her coo and shake once again as she held on tight to the pillow below her head. She rotated her hips, pushing herself against his mouth, wanting more. His lips and chin were glazed with her exquisite, sweet fluids. He reached up to massage her beautiful breasts over the lacy white bra that covered them. He squeezed and stimulated them as he devoured her, looking up at her every so often, getting off on the helpless expression etched across her face. He couldn't recall the last time he'd felt so free, so at ease...

She's here... She lives in my house officially now... No, this isn't my home any longer. It's OUR home...

I am eating out my future wife on our couch... Fuckin' beautiful. Welcome home, baby...

He groaned as these thoughts turned him on. His body needed her, and he had to have her right then. She screamed when he snatched her arm, flipped her on her stomach, and grabbed a fistful of her hair, situating her just so.

"Open your fucking legs, baby... Wide!"

She did what he said, then he drove his cock within her. He pulled her to him with a hard yank and brought her flush to his groin so he could have his way with her, slamming into her over and over with brute force. She clawed at the couch, moaning, calling him every name in the book, yelling and begging while the clapping of his groin against her ass reverberated in the room.

"Maaaax! God! Shit!" She reached around, trying to grab at his thigh and hold him back. He caught her hand and pinned it to her side. She cursed him out. "Too rough! Your dick is too big to be... ugh!!!"

"You're going to take this dick!" he roared. "Come on! Be a big girl!" He leaned down on her back, pressing all his weight onto her as he rocked his hips back and forth against her body. The woman's pussy became impossibly wetter with each nasty stroke of his cock.

"Ahhh! Too hard! You're killing my pussy!"

"This is how you like it! You want me to fuck you so hard you can barely walk! TAKE IT! TAKE THIS SHIT!"

"You big dick MOTHERFUCKER!!!" she screamed... then came, her nectar pouring from her pussy, coating his cock and running down her inner thighs.

He slowed down, but didn't stop. He kissed her shoulder, then the middle of her back. She came again, back-to-back orgasms wracking her as he lavished her beautiful body with sweet pecks. She looked helplessly over her shoulder at him.

"Max! Max...." Her eyes rolled as she sighed and cooed. "So.... so good... Oh, God..."

Giving her a moment, he slid his fingers within her pussy, using some of her natural juices to lubricate his cock. He turned her over onto her back, and she wrapped her arms lazily around his shoulders as they kissed and grinded against one another. He shoved one of the black throw pillows beneath her, then slid his cock into her asshole. Kissing one another, falling impossibly more in love, they lay in a locked embrace. He took his time rocking within her tight ass, delivering a bit more of himself until he was half way inside.

She winced and placed her hand against his chest.

"Need me to slow down?"

She nodded. He lovingly moved her hair out of her face, kissed her once again, and slowed his pace down. Much slower.

"Is that better, baby?" he whispered before bending down and kissing her tits over her bra.

"Yeah…"

He bided his time, caressing her, kissing her, loving her. He increased his pace every so often until finally, he was moving just fast enough to feel the friction he so desired. Never going past the half way mark of the length of his dick, he ensured she stayed as comfortable as possible while he fucked her in the ass. They sighed and she whimpered, both of them under each other's spell. He trembled and let himself go at last, wrapping his arms tight around her, flesh to flesh, and delivering fast, short thrusts.

"Fuck!" He spilled his seed within her tight hole, filling it with copious cum in fast spurts. Covered in sweat, he rose from his resting place and carefully pulled his dick out of her ass, some cream spilling out onto the pillow he'd used to prop her up.

After they got their bearings, they made it to the shower together where they washed each other, talked, and made plans for the day.

"So, everything is secure, and all of the deposits are paid. I have to go for another dress fitting tomorrow though," she said.

He adjusted the stream of water flowing over their bodies. She squealed when he lifted her up and placed them both directly under the spraying water. He lavished her with kisses, loving her more and more with each moment. At one point, he opened his eyes, but hers remained closed. He softly pressed his lips against hers for he could never get enough of her. Never wanted to put her down and let her go...

He was happy and crazy in love with the woman. *She's mine now. I don't have to leave her side. It feels so good to finally have someone to call my own...*

CHAPTER THIRTY

You Don't Want No Smoke...

T HE ALEXANDRIA BALLROOM was located in the heart of downtown Los Angeles. Eva had selected the King Edward ballroom in the venue, a most elegant site adorned with enormous teardrop crystal chandeliers, gold leaf ceilings, and tall ivory and gold walls with massive windows allowing just the right amount of natural light. There was even a lovely veranda that added that extra 'oomph.' She'd painstakingly picked out her ivory gown with layers of lace and had a myriad of alterations done to get it to fit just right. With a plunging neckline and traditional veil, it was stunning. Her sister moved her twelve-foot tulle and lace appliqué ivory train to the side to prevent tripping.

As she stood up front with the minister, a man she'd known from the church she attended on occasion, her guests appeared rather confused. She couldn't exactly blame them.

Typically, the groom was there first, waiting on his bride

to join his side. That tradition had been tossed out of the window. This time, it was the other way around. She'd made a deal with her husband-to-be. She was allowed to pick the place they wed, and spare no expense, but Savage wished to come through those doors in a way of his choosing. She had no idea what he had planned for he'd refused to disclose it, but as time ticked by, she became anxious with anticipation.

She gave a quick wink to her parents sitting in the front pew. They sat next to a man named Harlem and Austin, two of Savage's work colleagues and closest friends. Mom looked so beautiful and her father had walked her down the aisle, dressed impeccably in shades of blue. People began to murmur and talk amongst themselves as the revving of motorcycles grew closer and closer.

Oh, shit. It's him…

She lowered her gaze and smiled, soon feeling her sister, Allison and Kim's hands on her shoulders. Bracing herself, she was almost blinded by the light when the doors opened wide and in rode Harley after Harley down the aisle, the bikes blowing out smoke. The crowd cheered and screamed, some in shock no doubt as at least six bikers entered, Maximus' father leading the pack. They rode in real slow, one by one, dressed in black leather, blasting 'Magic Carpet Ride' by Steppenwolf. People jumped to their feet and shook their fists in the air, laughing, taking pictures.

Oh my God. Not in a million years would she have suspected such a thing to go down. Wait… yes she would; this arrival had Maximus Savage written all over it.

"Saaaavage! Yes, bitch! Now *that's* an entrance!" Kim screamed, getting into it, causing even more laughter to explode in the hall.

The music died down slow and easy; the motorcycles split in two equally divided rows and parked on the sides of the space. All six bikers, one at a time, approached Eva, giving her a kiss on the cheek and handing her a fistful of red rose petals until her hands were practically overflowing with them. Then, her father-in-law arrived, the last of the bunch, a light beauty dancing in his weary blue eyes.

Wearing a black bandana, leather jacket, and a t-shirt designed as a tuxedo, he pulled her close and kissed her softly on the cheek. She closed her eyes, blinking back tears. He smelled like bourbon, vanilla and cigarettes… simply perfect. Rather than place petals in her hands like the others, he reached into his pocket and pulled out a small silver ring adorned with an Indian chief head sporting an elaborate headdress. He slid it on her right finger, a coy smile on his face.

"Drop the petals at your feet." She did as she was asked, her palms now empty. "That's all of us, surrounding you, protecting you. We're all around you. You've got a huge tribe now." She sniffed and dabbed at the corner of her eye. "Lady, you've made my boy *very* happy. I've never seen him smile so much." He winked at her. "Karina and I love you already. You're one of us now, a true Savage."

He leaned in for another kiss but grabbed her chin and tricked her by stealing one from her lips!

"Oh, my God!" She laughed, in shock.

People cheered, while he pumped his fist in the air and thrust his tongue out before taking his seat by his wife in the front row.

The apple certainly doesn't fall too far from the tree...

Suddenly, the floor filled with smoke and Led Zeppelin's, 'Whole Lotta Love' blasted through the speakers.

Okay, it's cool. It's fine... She gave herself a pep talk as her nerves went overboard.

People began to bounce up and down out of their seats in excitement. Seven bikers, sporting black and white bandanas, walked in, each one wearing a blue handkerchief around their necks. One of the seven was her boo...

Savage stood in the middle like a rock. He wore a white leather biker jacket with black stripes about the shoulders with nothing underneath besides his tattoos and a couple of gold chains around his neck. Matching white and black leather biker pants and white and black biker boots that resembled the footwear of a Star Wars stormtrooper completed his cool ensemble. When he reached her side, he placed a kiss on her forehead, making her shiver from his touch.

"You look so damn beautiful." His voice rattled as the words, spoken softly, poured out.

This is it! I'm getting married!

The rest of the ceremony went, much to her surprise, in a typical fashion. They recited their traditional vows, exchanged rings, and when it was time to seal the deal, he gave her a kiss that swept her off her glass-slipper-covered feet.

Everyone jumped to their feet and cheered.

Savage began to walk forward, but she pulled him back.

"Wait a second, honey." Two adorable little boys, one Black and one White, approached wearing tiny white tuxedos and carrying a golden broom with a light blue bow on it.

They laid it down in front of them. Savage's expression brightened. The minster gave a countdown...

3...

2...

1!

They held hands and jumped over the broom. People applauded and clapped as white and blue streamers fell upon them. Wrapping her arm around his, she beamed, certain she was captured in a dream come true. No, things hadn't been easy. The journey had been long and hard some days, too. She'd fallen deeply in love with a complex man who made love to her mind, body, and soul. She couldn't imagine her life without him, unable to recall what it was like before they'd met. He looked death in the eye on a daily basis. He was truly a savage, but for her, he exposed his heart.

After shaking hands and hugging family and friends, they stepped out into the sunlight, the crowd following behind. There, in the front of the steps that led inside the venue, sat a white and gold special edition Harley Davidson. She gasped, never having seen such a thing in her life. He led her down the steps and they both got on it.

"I'm scared!" She giggled.

"Don't be. I've got you, baby." He turned it on and revved the engine. Allison approached her and removed her veil, then gave her a kiss on the cheek before waving goodbye.

Holding on for dear life, she rested her head on his back, unable to rid herself of the joy that would be with her for days, months, and years to come.

"I won't hold up the show too long. I know everyone is

hungry and wants their liquor and cake." Max was met with bursts of laughter. "We'll be back for the reception! Just want to take my baby for a little ride, Savage style! Whooooo Wheeee!"

He revved the engine a couple more times, the sound almost drowned in applause. She braced herself, smelling his cologne, the leather, and his masculine natural scent, overdosing on all that was her man. Without a single warning, the bike jerked forward, flying at warp speed down the road. She screamed in a mixture of fear and jubilation.

What did she expect? Her soulmate didn't live in the fast lane. He'd invented it...

...Two years later

"I DON'T GIVE a fuck. He can either wait for me or get someone else but I told him this is the last assignment for the next two months. There's a lot going on right now. My mother-in-law started new treatment with a doctor that specializes in paranoid schizophrenia, thanks to Longhorn, and the new experimental medicine she's on is working wonders but she has to be monitored for adverse reactions. Zaire has to be at the house a lot more often to watch her mom, take the load off of her dad so he can get a break and more importantly, I got a baby on the way, man." Savage tossed his gun into his bag and zipped it up. "This is fuckin' incredible. Shit, I'm not leavin' Eva until my child is born and if he thinks I'm going to Costa Rica, of all places, during that time frame, he's crazy. Her due date is in two weeks. My son could be here any day now."

"Yeah, I told him that. I know. They did the same shit to me too, back in the early 2000s. Look, don't take it personal, man. It means you're damn good at what you do and in high demand. They're afraid this guy is going to get away with it is all, Savage. We'll work it out, okay? I told you these things would happen. You have to be there with your family though for the important stuff. I get it. You don't want to miss the birth of your child. That comes first."

Savage walked out of the hotel room, dressed in clean, fresh clothing. It was a big change from the bloodied gray jumpsuit he'd had on hours before. Two brothers, Samuel and Paul Jones, had been on the FBI's Most Wanted List for thirteen years. Within ten hours, Savage had the pair bagged and put to rest in a Virginia morgue.

"All right, Harlem, thanks for the update. I'll call ya when I get back to L.A."

"No problem. Oh, I almost forgot."

"What?" He walked down the hotel hall, the carpet a burnt orange with cream and forest green spirals and swirls.

"I told you we were keeping tabs on your mother's family back in Albania."

"Yeah… and?" He slid out a cigar and lit it, not giving a fuck about the 'No Smoking' sign.

"Well, Saban, your uncle, had come up missing last month, just like I told you, and they found his body just this morning." Savage paused in his tracks. "He was murdered. One shot to the back of the head."

"Hmm, any word on who did it? I haven't been to Albania." He chuckled. "Can't pin it on me."

"They suspect it was a hired hit due to some text message they saw on his phone, but that's about it. They don't know who did it, and honestly, since he wasn't exactly popular among the locals, I don't think many care."

"All right, thanks for the info, man. I'll be in touch."

"Cool." Savage ended the call and made his way back to his hotel room. He sat on the bed for a spell, looking at his phone, gathering his thoughts. After taking a deep breath, he dialed Eva.

"Hey, baby," He smiled, trying to just get through the conversation.

"Heeey, Max." She yawned. "How are you, sweetie?"

"I'm good, baby. I'll be home in a few hours. About to head to the airport. I have to get my weapons clearance and all of that jazz, but hopefully it won't take too long. How are you doing?" He got up and tossed his cigar in the toilet, then sat down on the bed.

"I'm doing really well. I slept in a little this morning and recorded a few shows so they'll play during my maternity leave from the podcast."

"That's a good idea. That way you can concentrate on just me and the baby." He burst out laughing when he heard her sigh on the other end.

"I do not understand why you think my maternity leave means I will be catering to you, too." She chuckled. "You have a mother. This is about our child."

"Well, shit." He rubbed on his jaw. "You'll be stuck at home and the baby will have to eventually go to sleep, right?

I heard newborns sleep a lot. That's when it's Daddy time!"

"No!" She laughed. "That's not how this works. That's the time for me to take a damn nap. And remember, no sex for six weeks anyway, Max."

He rolled his eyes.

"Yeah... we'll see about that. Three weeks is probably long enough. I'm not waiting that long to get some pussy. Blow jobs only go so far."

"Six weeks is standard."

"Three is fine, just like I said."

"So you're a doctor now?"

"Nope. But I park my dick inside one practically every night." He was met with the dial tone and burst out laughing.

Soon, he drew serious and decided to get on with what he had to do. He called his mother.

"Mom..."

"Hello, Max. Nice to hear from you. Back home soon?"

"Yeah... Look, Mom... I, uh, got some information today." He braced himself. "I need to ask you a question."

"Yes?"

"Have you spoken to anyone in your family since the Miami situation went down?"

He was met with a brief silence.

"No."

"Dad had said you were very upset about how that all played out... That you were acting funny, havin' problems sleeping. He said that went on for a long time. Here's another question. You know that money you asked me for two months ago?"

"Yes..."

"Was it to, let's see, how can I word this, take care of some loose ends back home?"

"...Yes."

"Mmm hmm." He shook his head in disbelief. He had no idea his mother had it in her... His father wasn't a stranger to shooting a motherfucker square in the face, the nuts, anywhere, but his mom? No, she hadn't directly done it, but she might as well have... "How do you feel now?"

"Vindicated." She paused, then added, "They tried to kill my only child! THEY LIED TO ME!"

"Okay, okay, it's all right, Mom. I just... needed to be certain. I'll make sure no one can link this back to you... and don't tell anyone about this, ever." *There are plenty of ways to ensure that certain things come up missing, including cell phone records, money transfers, etc.* "So, I'm leaving Virginia. I'll be home soon, okay? I'll stop by."

"Okay. I... I love you, Maximus."

"I love you too, Mom. See you soon."

A wave of pure happiness... and closure... carried through with her words. He ended the call and got to his feet. Grabbing his bag and briefcase, he exited the hotel room. This time for good. He walked slowly down the hallway and approached the elevators. As he waited, he pulled out his earbuds from his jacket pocket and placed them on. When the silver doors opened, he pushed the lobby button. He rode down to the sounds of 'Roadhouse Blues', performed by the Doors.

Generation after generation, my family was made of nothing but savages...

My mother is a savage...
My father is a savage...
My son will be a savage...
It's a family affair...

People love to hate us, but without us in this world, there'd be nobody around to take out the fucking trash...

You're welcome, Beautiful.
Goodnight.

~The End~

Did you enjoy this story? Then please leave a review!
It's one of the coolest and most helpful things you can
do.

Thanks so much!

Please join Tiana Laveen's newsletter to get the latest and greatest updates, contest details and give-a-ways!

You can join her newsletter at:
www.tianalaveen.com/contact.html#newsletter

www.tianalaveen.com

MUSIC DIRECTORY

I have included a music directory to be used as an aid in the enjoyment of this novel. Sometimes, re-reading the scenes you appreciated with the songs that are mentioned, provides a whole new layer of satisfaction and understanding.

Please bear in mind that songs listed below may not be in the exact same order as they appear in the book. If you enjoy any of the songs listed, please purchase a legal copy of the tune and support the artist(s) whom created it. I am certain they'd appreciate it. ☺

SAVAGE Music Directory

1. Pink Floyd – 'Money'
2. Taylor Swift – 'Everything has Changed' featuring Ed Sheeran
3. Grandson – Bury Me Face Down
4. Cyndi Lauper – 'Girls Just Wanna Have Fun'
5. Jill Scott – 'The Way'
6. 50 Cents – 'In the Club'
7. Led Zeppelin – 'Kashmir'
8. Herb Alpert – 'Rise'
9. Cream – 'White Room'
10. Jefferson Airplane – 'Somebody to Love'

11. Strawberry Alarm Clock – 'Incense and Peppermints'

12. Deep Purple – 'Hush'

13. Vanilla Fudge – 'You Keep Me Hangin''

14. Ten Years After – 'I'd Love to Change the World'

15. Keith Sweat – (There You Go) Tellin' Me No

16. Keith Sweat – 'Something Just Ain't Right'

17. Rage Against The Machine – 'Calm Like A Bomb'

18. Herbie Hancock – 'Cantaloupe Island'

19. Prince – 'Uptown'

20. Prince – 'Why You Want to Treat Me So Bad?'

21. Danny Brown – 'Die Like a Rockstar'

22. Warrant – 'Cherry Pie'

23. Talking Heads – 'Psycho Killer'

24. Marky Mark and the Funky Bunch – 'Good Vibrations'

25. Outkast and UGK – 'International Players Anthem'

26. UGK – 'Diamonds and Wood'

27. Pimp C – 'Get Throwed' by Pimp C

28. Kansas – Carry On Wayward Son

29. Michael Jackson – 'P.Y.T. Pretty Young Thing'

30. Prince – 'When Doves Cry'

31. Steppenwolf – 'Magic Carpet Ride'

32. Led Zeppelin – 'Whole Lotta Love'

33. The Weeknd – 'What You Need'

34. Loco, Hwasa (MAMAMOO) – 'Don't'

35. Yuna – '(Not) The Love Of My Life'

About the Author

Tiana Laveen is a USA Today Best Selling author. She was born in Cincinnati, Ohio, though her soul resides in New York.

Tiana Laveen is a uniquely creative and innovative author whose fiction novels are geared towards those who not only want to temporarily escape from the daily routines of life, but also become pleasantly caught up in the well-developed journeys of her unique characters. As the author of over 50 novels, Tiana creates a painting with words as she guides her reader into the lives of each and every main character. Her dedication to detail and staying true to her characters is evident in each novel that she writes.

Tiana Laveen lives inside her mind, but her heart is occupied with her family and twisted imagination. She enjoys a fulfilling and enriching life that includes writing books, public speaking, drawing, painting, listening to music, cooking, and spending time with loved ones.

If you wish to communicate with Tiana Laveen, please contact her on Facebook or Instagram.